ten thousand
saints

Eleanor Henderson lives in Ithaca, where she is an assistant Professor at Ithaca college. She earned her MFA from the University of Virginia in 2005 and her writing has appeared in several American publications including *North American Review*, *Ninth Letter*, and *Columbia*, among others.

ten thousand saints eleanor henderson

Quercus

First published in the USA in 2011 by HarperCollins
This edition published in Great Britain in 2012 by

Quercus
55 Baker Street
7th Floor, South Block
London
W1U 8EW

A CIP catalogue record for this book is available
from the British Library.

ISBN 978 1 78087 217 9

10 9 8 7 6 5 4 3 2 1

Typeset by Ellipsis Books Limited, Glasgow
Printed and bound in Great Britain by Clays Ltd, St Ives plc

For Aaron

Behold, the Lord cometh with ten thousands of his saints,
To execute judgment upon all.

—THE BOOK OF JUDE

PART 1

Sad Song

ONE

I

s it *dreamed*?" Jude asked Teddy. "Or *dreamt*?"

Beneath the stadium seats of the football field, on the last
morning of 1987 and the last morning of Teddy's life, the
two boys lay side by side, a pair of snow angels bundled in
thrift-store parkas. If you were to spy them from above, between the
slats of the bleachers—or smoking behind the school gym, or sliding their skateboards down the stone wall by the lake—you might
confuse one for the other. But Teddy was the dark-haired one, Jude
the redhead. Teddy wore opalescent, fat-tongued Air Jordans, both
toes bandaged with duct tape, and dangling from a cord around his
neck, a New York City subway token, like a golden quarter. Jude
was the one in Converse high-tops, the stars Magic Markered into
pentagrams, and he wore his red hair in a devil lock—short in the
back and long in the front, in a fin that sliced between his eyes to
his chin. Unless you'd heard of the Misfits, not the Marilyn Monroe

movie but the horror-rock/glam-punk band, and if you were living in Lintonburg, Vermont, in 1987, you probably hadn't, you'd never seen anything like it.

"Either," said Teddy.

They were celebrating Jude's sixteenth birthday with the dregs of last night's bowl. Jude leaned over and tapped the crushed soda can against Teddy's elbow, and Teddy sat up to take his turn. His eyes were glassy, and a maple leaf, brittle and threadbare from its months spent under the snow, clung to his hair. Since Jude had known him Teddy had worn an immense pair of bronze frames with lenses as thick as windowpanes and, for good measure, a second bar across the top. But last week Teddy had spent all his savings on a pair of contact lenses, and now Jude thought he looked mole-eyed and barefaced, exposed, as Jude's father had the time he'd made the mistake of shaving his beard.

With one hand Teddy balanced the bud on the indentation of the can, over the perforations Jude had made with a paper clip, lit it with the other, and like a player of some barnyard instrument, he put his lips to the mouth of the can and inhaled. Across his face, across the shadowed expanse of snow-stubbled grass, bars of sunlight brightened and then paled. "It's done," he announced and tossed the can aside.

Bodies had begun to fill the grandstand above, galoshes and duck boots filing cautiously down the rows, families of anoraks eclipsing the meager sun. Jude could hear the patter of their voices, the faraway din of a sound system testing, testing, the players cleating through the grass, praying away the snow. Standing on his wobbly legs, Jude examined their cave. They were fenced in on all sides—the seats overhead, the football field in front, a concrete wall behind them. Above the wall, however, was a person-size perimeter of open space, through which Teddy and Jude had climbed not long before, first launching their skateboards in ahead of them, then scaling the scaffolding on the outside, then tumbling over the wall, catlike, ten feet into the dirt. They'd done it twenty times before, but never while people were in the stadium—they'd managed to abstain from their town's tepid faith in its Division III college football team; they abstained from all things football, and all things college. They hadn't expected there to be a game on New Year's Eve.

Now Jude paced under the seats and stopped five or six rows from the front. Above him, hanging from the edge of one of the seats, was a pair of blue-jeaned legs. A girl. Jude could see the dirty heels of her tennis shoes, but not much else. He reached up, the frozen fingers through his fingerless gloves inches away from her foot, but instead of enclosing them around the delicate bones of her ankle, he lifted the yellow umbrella at her feet. He slid it without a sound across the concrete and down into his arms.

"What are you doing?" whispered Teddy, suddenly at Jude's elbow. "Why are we stealing an umbrella?"

Jude sprung it open and looked it over. "It's not the umbrella we're stealing," he whispered back, closing it. Walking into the shadows a few rows back, he held it over his head, curved handle up, like a hook. In the bleachers above, there were purses between feet, saving seats, unguarded, alone, and inside, wallets fat with cash. Teddy and Jude had no money and no pot and, since this morning, nothing to smoke it out of but an empty can of Orange Slice.

Last night they'd shared a jug of Carlo Rossi and the pot they'd found in the glove box of Teddy's mom's car, while they listened to Metallica's first album, *Kill 'Em All,* which skipped, and to Teddy's mom, Queen Bea, who had her own stash of booze, getting sick in the bathroom, retch, flush, retch, flush. Around midnight, they'd taken what was left of the pot and skated to Jude's to get some sleep, but in their daze had left Jude's bong behind. When they returned to Teddy's in the morning (this was the rhythm of their days, three rights and a left to Teddy's, a right and three lefts to Jude's), the bong—the color-changing Pyrex bong Jude's mother had given Jude that morning as an early birthday gift—was gone. So were Queen Bea's clothes, her car, her toothbrush, her sheets. Jude and Teddy wandered the house, flipping switches. The lights didn't work; nothing hummed or blinked. The house was frozen with an unnatural stillness. Jude, shivering, found a candle and lit it. When Teddy opened the liquor cabinet, it was also empty—this was the final, irrefutable clue—except for a bottle of Liquid-Plumr and a film of dust, in which Teddy wrote with a finger, *fuck*.

Beatrice McNicholas had run away a few times before. She'd go out for a six-pack and come home a week later, with a new haircut and old promises. (She was no nester or nurturer; she was Queen Bea for her royal size.) But she'd never taken her liquor with her, or anything of Teddy and Jude's.

The boys had stolen enough from her over the years to call it even. Five-dollar bills, maybe tens, that Queen Bea would be too drunk to miss in the morning, liquor, cigarettes. She was the kind of unsystematic drunk whose hiding places changed routinely but remained routinely unimaginative—ten minutes of hunting through closets and drawers (she cleaned other people's houses, but her own was a sty) could almost always turn up something. Pot was more difficult to find at Jude's house—his mom's hippie habits were somewhat reformed, and though she condoned Jude's experimentation (an appreciation for a good bong was just about all Harriet and Jude had in common), occasional flashes of parental guilt drove her to hide her contraband in snug and impenetrable places that recalled Russian nesting dolls. In Harriet's studio, Jude had once found a Ziploc of pot inside a bag of Ricola cough drops inside a jumbo box of tampons inside a toolbox. While Queen Bea seemed only mildly aware that teenagers lived in her midst, sweeping them off her porch like stray cats, Harriet had a sharp eye, a peripheral third lens in her bifocals that was always ready to probe the threat of fast-fingered boys. So Jude and Teddy stole what was around: a roll of quarters from her dresser, the box of chocolates Jude's sister, Prudence, had given her for Mother's Day. They took more pleasure in what they stole out in the world: magazines and beer from Shop Smart (Shop Fart), video game cartridges from Sears (Queers), and cassettes from the Record Room, where Kram O'Connor and Clarence Delph worked. And half the items in Jude's possession—clothes, records, homework—were stolen, without discretion, from Teddy.

But this bold-faced thievery beneath the bleachers embarrassed Teddy. It was so obvious, so doomed to failure. Sometimes Teddy thought that was the prize Jude wanted—not the money or the beer or the cigarettes but the confrontation, the pleasure of testing the limits. Jude was standing on tiptoe, umbrella still raised like a torch, eyeing the spilled contents of a lady's bag. His tongue, molluscan and veined with blue, was wedged in concentration in the cleft under his nose.

"Hey," said someone.

Teddy tried to stand very still.

A pair of eyes, upside-down, was framed between the seats above them. It took Teddy a few seconds to grasp their orientation—the girl was leaning over, her head draped over the ledge. "What are you doing?" she said.

Jude smiled up at her. "You dropped your umbrella."

"No, I didn't." The girl had her hands cupped around her eyes now, staring down into the dark. No one else seemed to notice.

"It fell," Jude insisted, hoisting the umbrella up to the girl, his arm outstretched, letting it tickle one of her fingers.

"Just give it back," said Teddy. It was the way Jude always made him feel—tangled up in some stupid, trivial danger. Teddy closed his eyes. He didn't have time to mess around; his mother was gone. He needed money, more money than Jude could pickpocket with an umbrella. His body clenched with his last memory of her—the acrid, scotchy stink of her vomit through the bathroom door; the blathering hiccups of her sobs. Had she been crying because she was leaving, or just because she was wasted?

Then the umbrella, the pointy part, speared him in the gut.

"Ow, man." Teddy opened his eyes.

"You were supposed to catch it," said Jude.

Teddy looked up into the bleachers. The girl was gone. But a moment later, a pair of blue-jeaned legs appeared over the wall behind them.

They watched as the girl jumped from the ledge, her jacket parachuting as she plummeted. She landed feetfirst and fell forward to catch her balance, then strutted a slow-motion, runway strut in their direction. She stopped a car length away and stood with her hands on her hips, inspecting them. Her eyes were shining with disdain.

If you were a girl, Jude Keffy-Horn was a person you looked at, hard, and then didn't look at again. His blue eyes, set wide apart, watched the world from under hooded lids, weighed down by distrust, THC, and a deep, hormonal languor. A passing stranger would not have guessed them to be the eyes of a hyperactive teenager with attention deficit disorder, but his mouth, which rarely rested, betrayed him. He was thin in the lip, fairly broad in the forehead, tall and flat in the space between mouth and upturned nose, the whole plane of his face scattered with freckles usurped daily by a lavender brand of acne. He wore not one but two retainers. He wasn't tall, but he was built like a tall person, with skinny arms and legs and big knees and elbows that knocked around when he walked. He wasn't bad-looking. He was good-looking enough. He was the kid whose name you knew only because the teacher kept calling it. *Jude. Jude. Mr. Keffy-Horn, is that a cigarette you're rolling?*

Teddy shared Jude's uniform, his half-swallowed smirk, but due to the blood of his Indian father (Queen Bea was purebred white trash), his hair was the blue-black of comic book villains, his complexion as dark and smooth as a brown eggshell. By the population of Ira Allen High School he was rumored halfheartedly to be Jewish, Arab, Mexican, Greek, and most often, simply "Spanish." When Jude had asked, Teddy had told him "Indian," then quipped, nearly indiscernibly, for he was a mumbler, "Gandhi, not Geronimo." With everyone else, though, he preferred to allow his identity to flourish in the shadowed domain of myth. Teddy's eyelashes were long, like the bristles of a paintbrush; through his right eyebrow was an ashen scar from the time he'd spilled off his skateboard at age ten. Then his face had been cherubic; now, at fifteen, it had sloughed off the baby fat and gone angular as a paper airplane. He had a delicate frame; he had an Adam's apple like a brass knuckle; he had things up the sleeve of that too-big coat—a Chinese star, the wire of a Walkman, a cigarette for after class, which he was always more careful than Jude to conceal.

What's that kid up to?

That was the way the girl was looking at both of them now, under the bleachers. "What are you people doing down here?"

Jude stabbed the umbrella into the ground. "Hanging out."

"Are you smoking marijuana?"

"You can't smell it," Jude said. "We're out in the open."

"Can I have my umbrella, please?"

"Why? It's not raining."

"It's supposed to snow, for your information."

"Oh, for my information, okay. It's a snow umbrella." Now he was pretending that the umbrella was a gun. He held it cocked at his hip, the metal tip against his cheek, ready to shoot around a corner.

"Jude," Teddy said. "Over here."

He clapped his hands, and Jude obediently, joyfully tossed him the umbrella.

"Motherfucking monkey in the middle!" said Jude.

Teddy walked three paces toward the girl, head down, and returned it to her.

"Thanks," she said.

"Hey," Jude said.

"Brit?" In the bleachers above, two more girls were peering down at them. They never came alone, girls; they always came in packs. "What are you doing?"

"I'll be right there!" A moment later, she was gone.

"Brit the *shit,*" Jude said, but Teddy didn't say anything.

Jude Keffy-Horn, adopted by Lester Keffy and Harriet Horn of Lintonburg, Vermont, met Teddy McNicholas on the second day of seventh grade, in 1984. Teddy had moved there with his half brother, Johnny, and their mother from Plattsburgh, New York, across Lake Champlain. After school, Jude showed Teddy how to smoke a joint in a gas station parking lot, in the backseat of Teddy's mom's Plymouth Horizon, while she shopped for groceries inside. That Jude, not Johnny, or even Queen Bea herself, had managed to pioneer the first hallucinogenic experience of the person who would become his closest and really only friend made Jude happy. He didn't have much to be proud of, but he was good at sharing new and forgotten methods of getting high.

It was one of the few talents passed down from his father, who, before leaving for New York when Jude was nine, had grown several generations of *Cannabis sativa* in their greenhouse. Les had a year of college at Vermont State, one fewer than Harriet, followed by fifteen as a lab assistant in the botany department, a position that largely entailed mating strands of Holland's Hope with Skunk #1, which he offered at a deep discount to the department. Although Jude had been too young to apprentice, he'd observed the objects of his father's hydroponic ventures—Styrofoam, milk jugs, a fish tank pump—with reverence. He'd admired his father's self-reliance, and he'd learned early that, even in a nothing town like Lintonburg, Vermont, you could find fun with a little imagination and care.

With Teddy, he'd imbibed NyQuil and Listerine; tripped on dairy farm mushrooms; huffed gas, glue, and Jude's sister's nail polish remover; brewed beer in Queen Bea's bathtub; and during a period when they were watching a lot of *Mr. Wizard's World,* built a bong out of a garden hose and a coffee urn. Jude liked fucking Teddy up. He liked the dumb, happy look he got on his face, one eye roving, then the other, toward some distant, invisible moon.

Next year, Jude and Teddy were going to New York. Teddy's half brother, Johnny, lived there, too. They'd had $140 saved up in an empty pack of smokes until a couple of weeks ago, when they used it to buy some pot from Delph and the contact lenses for Teddy and two mail-order Misfits T-shirts. But when they saved some more money and when they were both old enough to drop out (Teddy would be sixteen in May), they were going to buy bus tickets to Port Authority and stay with Johnny until they could find a place of their own.

Johnny was eighteen now, and Jude's memories of him were obscured by the scrim of vodka he and Teddy would sneak from Johnny's He-Man thermos. Johnny would skip school on Ozzy Osbourne's birthday and grew his blond hair down to his ass. He'd keep notebooks full of drawings shelved in his closet, full of super-hero chicks and space-age cars and guys with thighs muscled like Rottweilers. He spent a lot of time chasing the boys out of the room he shared with Teddy, but he taught them both how to play guitar, and even let them play in his band, with Delph on bass and Kram on drums, Teddy and Jude sharing one untuned, spray-painted guitar, Johnny playing another, singing without a microphone. Everyone huddled on Queen Bea's front porch in their hooded sweatshirts and black jeans, bodies chattering in the cold. Jude's fourteen-year-old fingers stretched into cramps, frozen as wood, trying to follow Johnny's through Hendrix's "The Star-Spangled Banner." On Johnny's mismatched stereo, they'd play their stolen tapes—hard rock, heavy metal, hair metal, black metal, death metal, thrash metal, metalcore, hardcore, grindcore, punk—Black Sabbath and Whitesnake and Black Flag—and then methodically, with ears tilted to the speakers, they'd copy them. They dragged out the old orange extension cord and chugged away on Johnny's practice amp, decorated with Metallica stickers and glow-in-the-dark stars. They were Demon Semen, Baptism of Jism, the Deadbeats, the Posers, and finally the Bastards, which most of them were, more or less.

That was two years ago. Then Johnny turned sixteen, quit school, and left for New York with his pockets full of snow-shoveling money and two guitar cases, his guitar in one of them and his clothes in the other, to live with his father, who it turned out wasn't dead after all, and maybe Teddy's wasn't either. Turned out Queen Bea was maybe a big fat liar.

Teddy and Jude, on the other hand, were going to New York to start a band, and to get fucked, and to get the fuck out of Vermont, not to find their long-lost dads. Jude wasn't even going to tell his dad he was coming. He wasn't even going to look him up in the phone book. If he ran into him on the subway, he'd be like, Hey, how's it going, you fucking chump? Okay, see you around.

Lintonburg, Vermont, in 1987 was not a place of surprises. There was the second-run theater, the rec center, Wayne's Billiards. There was the Tap House, the jock bar, and Jacque's (Birkenjacque's), the hippie bar. There was the drive-thru creemee place, the pawnshop-music-store, and Champlain Park, where when you skipped school you could hide in the construction tunnels and smoke up, and there was decent skating at the university if you didn't get kicked off campus. There was enough to do so that you didn't necessarily want to put a hole in your head. It was the biggest city in Vermont, and this fact was reflected with smugness in the busy gait of its residents down Ash Street, the brick-paved pedestrian mall; in their efficient street plowing; in their towering thermoses of coffee; in the dexterous maneuvering of their four-wheel-drive station wagons and their one or two tasteful bumper stickers: BERNIE; GREEN UP; I L♥VERMONT. Lintonburg's relatively metropolitan status confused but did not ease the state of small-town disgruntlement that Teddy and Jude had perfected. There was, finally, the Ash Street Mall (the Ass Street Mall), where after leaving their post under the bleachers and skating down the hill through the bitter, lake-blown wind, they came across Jude's mother. She was sitting on a stool next to the entrance, smoking a cigarette and reading a paperback. Beside her was a table disguised by an Indian print tapestry and cluttered with glass ashtrays, vases, pitchers, bowls, in blues and sea greens and swirled, psychedelic pinks. Harriet's single professional fixture was a wooden sign, propped up against a set of mugs, that read HARRIET HORN HANDBLOWN GLASS.

No sign hung over the door of the greenhouse in their yard, where Harriet blew her glass and where she sold her bongs and pipes, the items that paid the bills, the items she couldn't sell on the street and had to hawk at summer music festivals on far-flung farms, Jude and his sister, Prudence, trailing behind her with baskets of pipes over their arms. Her studio didn't need a sign—people knew where to find her, just as they knew where to find the guy they called Hippie, who cruised town on his ten-speed bike and sold pot out of his fanny pack. They'd knock on the greenhouse door and she'd remove her safety glasses and happily make her exchange. Harriet Horn, the Glass Lady. "She can handblow me anytime," Delph had said more than once, not because Harriet was all that fetching but because she was, to other people—especially to Teddy—cool. Now the word fumbled in Jude's head—*handblow, glandbow, land ho!* He was vaguely dyslexic, messed up his letters even when he wasn't high.

"I don't have any money, birthday boy," Harriet said. She removed her glasses—enormous, tortoiseshell, spotted with fingerprints—and let them hang on their chain of plastic beads. With the tobacco-stained fingers of her wool gloves, she dog-eared her place in the book and placed it on her lap. Jude felt his buzz die a quick and common death.

"You haven't made any money today?" Teddy asked, sympathizing. He picked up a salad bowl and smoothed his palm over the inside of it. "This is really cold."

"Not enough money," Harriet said, gently taking the bowl back from Teddy. She was protective of her glass.

"Ma, not even like ten bucks?"

"And what do I get? A hug?"

When Jude refused, Teddy leaned cooperatively into Harriet's coat. For this, Harriet produced two wrinkled dollar bills from her apron pocket. Jude paddled his skateboard over to the table and covered up the *G* and *L* of the sign so it said HANDBLOWN ASS. "Look, Ted."

Teddy looked and nodded. He'd seen Jude do it before.

"You take your medicine, Jude?" Harriet asked.

"You mean pot? Yeah, but we need more."

"Jude. You didn't take it?"

"I did," Jude said, although he hadn't. For several weeks he'd been selling his Ritalin pills for a dollar a pop to a kid in his homeroom named Frederick Watt, who liked to take them before tests. A few times Jude and Teddy had taken a bunch at once and wigged out a little, but it was no fun doing drugs you were supposed to do. Jude was too old for Ritalin. He preferred mellower means of controlling his temperament, and his fingers itched for a joint. "Come on, Ma, I need more than two dollars."

"I believe you already got your birthday gift, fella."

"Yeah, well, something *happened* to it already."

Teddy shot Jude a look.

"What happened to it?" Harriet asked.

"Nothing," Teddy said. "He just lent it to someone."

"Who'd you lend it to?"

"We'll get it back," Teddy said. Quickly he and Jude exchanged a silent, reflexive pact. "It's just temporary."

"It better be," Harriet said, picking up her burning cigarette, which she'd propped in one of the ashtrays. "I spent a long time on that." She expelled a lungful of smoke and shook her cigarette at him, remembering something. "Your father called again. Eliza will be here at six-oh-five. She's taking a different train. Still staying till midnight, I think."

"Who's Eliza?" Teddy asked.

Jude thwacked him on the sleeve. "Eliza? The chick who's hanging out with us tonight?"

"His father's girlfriend's daughter," said Harriet, crossing her legs. *Eliza Urbanski.*

In the seven years since Les had left their family, Jude and Prudence hadn't laid eyes on him. His calls and cards came once or twice a year, cash less, although not because, as far as Jude knew, he didn't have it—he paid his child support on time, regular as rent. The last birthday gift Les had bestowed on Jude was for his thirteenth: subscriptions to *Playboy, Barely Legal,* and *Juggs*—the excess and range signifying both an uncertainty of the boy's tastes and what Jude considered a boastful display of financial prowess.

But on Christmas night, when he called to wish his children a happy holiday, he had announced that his girlfriend's daughter would be in town, skiing with her friends in Stowe for winter break—would Jude and Pru like to show her around? "She's about your guys's age," said Les.

"How old is that?" Prudence had asked him—she, even more than her brother, had moral objections to pleasing Les—and passed the phone to Jude.

It had been known for years that Les had a girlfriend, a ballerina from England. This brief characterization had so belabored Jude's imagination that he had been only abstractly aware that she came with a daughter. Standing with the phone in his hand, he had looked at his mother, who was scrubbing the empty sink with wanton cheerfulness, pretending not to eavesdrop, and understood that his father wanted to make her jealous. Skiing at Stowe—the girlfriend was probably loaded. Jude said okay, whatever.

Despite himself, he'd dreamt about the girl. Eliza. Dreamt, dreamed. It was a faceless, plotless, colorless dream—he knew only that she was there, the idea of her, and that, as with most dreams these days, he'd woken this morning in the viscid pool of his own anticipation.

The Ass Street Mall was long and dark, like a tunnel that went nowhere, and Jude had memorized every one of its uneven, roach-brown tiles. He and Teddy darted in and out of stores, up and down escalators, past the food court comprised of a Häagen-Douche and a Pizza Slut, searching for Jude's sister, who always had money, until they found her behind the glass wall of Waldenbooks. She was standing at the magazine rack with a pair of friends, reading *Tiger Beat,* and when she saw them, she looked up for a moment, then away.

Jude didn't see Prudence much, but when he did, he saw a girl in bloom. One recent morning, he'd walked into the bathroom and found her standing naked over the heating vent, pale and nippley and terrified. He thought immediately of their childhood pet, Mary Ann, a tabby cat who had nursed a litter of kittens on a set of pink, swollen mammaries the size and shape of his sister's. Since then, it had taken him a great deal of effort, when coming across the pastel bras hanging from the bathroom doorknob, to ward off that horrible, wet-haired vision. Teddy liked to point out that, not sharing the same DNA, Prudence was like any other girl in Lintonburg—in another life, if he hadn't been adopted by her parents, Jude could get a hard-on looking at her and not have to feel weird about it. There was no way his sister could give him a hard-on, but the possibility did make him feel lonely and sick. His sister was smart and pretty and she and Jude had nothing in common, and seeing her naked was seeing how irreconcilable they were.

"What do you want?" she mouthed now, flipping through her magazine. Her voice was far away, muffled through the glass.

"Forty bucks," Jude said, tucking his devil lock behind his ear.

Prudence's hair—ashy blond, the kind with a glint of gray in it, the kind Harriet used to have—swirled around the hood of her parka, and her braces, pink and purple, flashed like fangs. There was something sort of metallic about her, a silver, fishy glow under her skin. "Why?" she said.

"Because," Jude said, "I want to buy you a birthday present."

"It's *your* birthday. My birthday's in September."

"I know that," he said. He knew because Prudence was nine months younger than he was, and also because she still had the invitation from her party taped to her bedroom door, along with a Just Say No poster featuring Kirk Cameron. "I'll pay you back," Jude said. "You know what a fine brother I am."

Prudence stared at her magazine; her eyes didn't move. The two friends whispered something Jude couldn't hear, gold hoops swinging from one pair of ears, silver hoops from the other. Were they looking at Teddy? Teddy was looking at them.

"What happened to his glasses?" Prudence asked, nodding at Teddy.

Harriet Horn, after several years of sex with Les Keffy, her college sweetheart, had been declared infertile by a Lintonburg obstetrician. Her fallopian tubes were clogged like straws full of mud, but through this obstruction, right about the time Jude himself was being born (on the last night of 1971, in a New York City hospital), one of Les's relentless and ironic sperm prevailed. When Prudence was born, nine months after Jude was adopted, Harriet nursed them at the same time, one on each side, like two of Mary Ann's blind, slimy kittens. Jude, his mother told him, had liked to kick his suckling sister in the face. As a toddler, standing on a step stool, he tried to drown her in the basement sink, and when they were nine, she threw a pair of nail scissors at him, spearing the hollow under his right eye. He fingered this moon-shaped scar now, finding his pale image in the window. His forehead had left an oily streak on the glass, and he wiped it with his wrist.

"I'll pay you back, Pru."

"No, you won't. You're just going to spend it on you-know-what." With the nail-polished fingers of her right hand and the sign-language skills she'd learned the first semester of tenth grade, she spelled out something frantic.

"I don't know what that means!"

"Drugs!" she pronounced, cupping her hands against the glass.

Prudence's puritanical streak was a matter of mild embarrassment for their mother, but for Jude it was simply proof of their genetic divide. "It's my birthday!" he yelled. The itch in his fingers had spread to his hands, which he mashed into fists, pressing his knuckles to the window.

"I hate you, too!" Prudence shrieked, hands flying like fighting birds. Then she and her friends disappeared into Young Adult.

Jude scavenged. He probed a finger into the coin return slots of pay phones, vending machines, the children's carousel that had been broken for as long as Jude could remember. He found nothing but a lone gumball in a candy machine, which turned his tongue a defeated electric blue. To spend one's sixteenth birthday—and New Year's Eve!—in a shopping mall, with no pot, no beer, no prospects to offer a mysterious, loaded, out-of-town girl—it was too shameful to consider. He swallowed his pride and suggested they head for the Record Room. Maybe Delph would take an IOU.

Anthrax's "Soldiers of Metal" was playing over the store speakers. Behind the counter, Delph was preparing to thwack a pencil at the one Kram held pinched between his fingers.

"Boo!" Jude yelled, and Kram flinched.

"There will be no skateboarding in here," Delph called, shaking a finger at Teddy and Jude. "Out with those things, gentlemen, or I'll call mall security."

"No!" Jude said. "Not that fat guy on the golf cart."

"Don't start on fat guys," said Kram, who at eighteen had a full-blown beer gut. "I'll pin you right here, little boy." And he clambered over the counter and fell on Jude, digging his knees into his ribs.

Kram O'Connor and Clarence Delph III regularly put Teddy and Jude in headlocks, charged them outrageous rates for marijuana, and invented for them a seemingly tireless list of abusive nicknames. Teddy got the worst of it—Teddy Bear, Teddy Krueger, Teddy Roosevelt, Teddy Ruxpin, Teddy Graham, Teddy McDickless, McDick. Never mind that Delph refused to be called by his own first name, or that Kram got his nickname from accidentally tattooing his real name backward in a mirror. They had been friends of Johnny's, metalheads with muscle cars and big-haired girlfriends (Kram's car they called the Kramaro), and although they would be graduating, barely, in June, and although Johnny had left town two years ago, they still let Jude and Teddy follow them around, gave them rides, came over to Jude's every once in a while to jam and tell him how shitty his cheap guitar sounded. The purpose of their alliance they made clear: they required Teddy and Jude for news from Johnny, nothing more. Johnny was in a straight edge band. Johnny's straight edge band had played a show at CBGB. Johnny was tattooing full-time now, had traded an eight track for his own machine and some needles, and since tattooing was illegal in New York, as it was in Vermont, he had to do it from his apartment, a studio in Alphabet City that was literally underground. He'd stopped returning Kram's and Delph's calls months ago; his phone was turned off when he didn't pay the bill, he wrote Teddy, and he left it off. He could live without it.

Which meant Teddy was screwed. His mother had bolted, and his brother was the only person he could go to. But Teddy didn't have money for a bus ticket—he'd have to write Johnny and ask him to send some. It would be days before Johnny got the letter, and days before Johnny could send him the money. Teddy couldn't stay at home with the power gone out—he'd freeze his balls off—but he couldn't stay with Jude, either, not forever. He didn't want Harriet to know his mother had left. He wouldn't be able to stand her pity.

If only Teddy were sixteen—he would have been living with his brother already. Or maybe, if he was alive, with his dad. He didn't dare mention this to his mother, who had long ago forbidden the subject, or to Jude, who regarded curiosity about one's missing father as one of the telltale symptoms of being a fag, but he'd been thinking about his dad a lot lately. His whole life, his mother had been telling him he was dead, but then Johnny had found out that his own dad was alive. Didn't that mean Teddy's dad could be out there, too? But how did you find someone you knew nothing about, not even a name?

"You guys got any money I could borrow?" Teddy asked. He kept his voice down, though there were no customers in the store.

"What for?" Kram asked, climbing off of Jude.

"I want to visit Johnny," he said, keeping it simple and hoping Jude wouldn't decide to elaborate. But Delph and Kram didn't have any money, either. They'd gone broke buying Christmas gifts for their girlfriends.

"We'll settle for some pot," Jude broke in.

Delph snorted. "No more IOUs, Judy."

"Come on, man! We're dry."

"I don't need any pot," Teddy said. "I just need a bus ticket."

Delph leaned an elbow on the counter. "Listen to young Edward," he said. He had a dark, horsey mullet and a big moon of a face, craggy with craters, so white it was yellow. "He's gone straight edge, like his brother! Just Say No, right?"

"I still say he's lying," said Kram. "Michelob McNicholas? He'd go into cardiac arrest if he stopped drinking."

"Those straight edge kids don't fornicate," Delph said. "That's what I heard. Don't smoke, don't drink, don't *breathe* . . ."

"What, like Jehovah's Witnesses?" Kram said, rubbing his Buddha belly.

"The music's pretty wicked, though," Teddy said. "Johnny made me another tape. You guys heard that Youth of Today album yet?"

"Told you, Teddy Bear. We don't have that crazy rock-and-roll music in stock."

"Come on, Delph," Jude whined, impatient with the conversation. "Just a dime? It's my birthday."

Delph slapped the counter. "Jeezum Crow! I knew that, man."

"Aw, Delphy, you gotta hook him up. Man's sweet sixteen, right?"

"You finally going to turn in that V-card tonight, little man?"

Then they were talking about Eliza, the girl Jude would meet in a few hours at the train station. As if they didn't have girls in Lintonburg; they had to import them from New York. That was the sad thing about Jude and those guys, thought Teddy—they hadn't been anywhere. They hadn't seen shit. The other day Jude had insisted that Wichita was a state. He thought you got a girl to like you by stealing her umbrella.

Teddy made his way over to the *Y* section in Rock, scanning the cassettes, just in case. The Yardbirds, Yes, Neil Young, but no Youth of Today. Over the past few months, the negligible shelf of vinyl at the back of the store had been phased out by a growing bank of compact discs. Soon the Record Room would sell no more records. Teddy stood disheartened in front of the display, his hands crammed in his pockets. He was tired of Vermont, tired of the homemade drugs and the farm boy slang and the cold. He was tired of letting Jude cheat off his algebra tests. Just before winter break, the guidance counselor had called Teddy into her office and said, "Edward, have you given any thought to college?" The truth was, he had not, but the word chimed in his head for days afterward like the sleigh bells tinkling from the guidance counselor's earlobes. When Jude asked why he'd been pulled out of class, Teddy told him he'd been caught smoking in the boys' bathroom, then faked an afternoon of detention, studying alone under the stadium bleachers.

College he could not afford, but at least Teddy knew there was a world beyond Vermont. Before Lintonburg, he'd lived with his mother and brother in Plattsburgh; before that in Newport, Rhode Island; before that in Dover, Delaware; before that in Williamsburg, Virginia; before that somewhere in North Carolina; and before that in some places he didn't really remember, all the way down to Miami, where he was born. But he'd never been to Manhattan. In Manhattan, Johnny said, there were crates and crates of vinyl in every record store, a hardcore matinee every weekend at CBGB, endless concrete built for the wheels of a skateboard. And fathers. Jude's, Johnny's. That's where the fathers were. For a second Teddy could picture himself there, standing on the street in front of a building, a set of keys jingling in his hand.

Teddy had last spoken to his brother on Christmas. When Teddy handed the phone back to his mother and left the room, he could still hear her scolding Johnny about something in a desperate sort of whisper, as though she didn't want Teddy to hear. She was sitting on the couch, hunched over a beer, her bra strap slipped off her shoulder and out of her sleeve.

"All right, dude, just a dime," Delph was saying. If Jude met him at Tory Ventura's New Year's party at nine, Delph would gift him with some kind bud.

"Tory Ventura?" Teddy said, looking up from the cassettes. "Not that dickhead."

Tory was a senior, played football with Kram. He liked to grab Jude and Teddy by the scruff of their coats and slam them against their lockers. They all hated him, but his parents were out of town, and there would be three kegs. "It's supposed to be wicked," said Kram, doing push-ups against the counter, the armpits of his T-shirt dark with sweat.

"Bring your lady," said Delph.

"We'll be there," said Jude.

In the street, an inch or two of snow had accumulated, and it was still falling steadily. Jude and Teddy stepped soundlessly into it and carried their skateboards back to Jude's, where they made English muffin pizzas, splitting the third one in half. It was a big, bony house, first a warehouse and then a schoolhouse, and now Jude lived there with his mother and his sister. It was misleading to call it a house—it was a brick building in an alley, narrow as an ice cream truck, four stories tall if you counted the basement. Jude's father had bought it for $1,800 in 1969; he was in the middle of renovating it when Jude, and then Prudence, were born. When Les was finished (and he never really was, according to Harriet), the house was a monument of found object art. The shutters were made from leftover chalkboards; the steps were two separate spiral staircases joined together, one pine, one steel; the living room couch was a claw-foot tub with the front sawed off, lined with an orange mattress from an old chaise lounge and throw pillows Harriet had sewn with

her Singer. After the renovation project, Les devoted himself to the
less architecturally challenging greenhouse, and when he took its
profits to New York in the form of a Dodge camper van full of marijuana plants, he left the half-assed results of his ten-year enterprise.
They had no kitchen drawers: they kept their silverware in mugs.
They had no kitchen ceiling: just insulation and ducts and wires
like so many guts and veins.

The basement still held the scent of antique allergens—sawdust,
chalk, the fertilizer that had been stored here half a century ago.
In one corner was the Bastards' equipment, still occasionally
revisited—Jude's third-hand guitar, Kram's beat-up drum kit, Johnny's old amp. The rest of the room was scattered with cardboard
boxes, sawhorses, an old door leaning against the wall, a bicycle
with a plastic baby seat, and an assortment of wooden school chairs.
Some of them, stacked yin-yang style, were turned into makeshift
easels from the years when Harriet taught life drawing, slabs of plywood wedged in their upturned legs, yellowed drawings held up
by clothespins. A single bare bulb hung from the low ceiling. Jude
turned it on, then went straight for the bottle of turpentine over the
sink. "Just to tide us over," he said. His cold fingertips fumbled. His
heart, though, was warming up like an eager, rattling engine.

"What are we doing?" Teddy asked, sitting down on the basement couch. It wasn't really a couch. It was the row of seats Jude's
father had removed from his van sometime in the seventies.

"Give me that underwear."

From his pocket, Teddy presented the underwear he'd stolen
from Victoria's Secret. Jude soaked the panties with the turpentine.
They were silky and pink, with a pink tag still dangling. "Remember this?" He plunged his face into the panties as if drying it on
a towel. It had been a long time since he'd inhaled this particular
elixir, but the sensation was recognizable right away. It smelled like
being twelve, being with Teddy, being a redheaded boy in pajamas,

and before long Jude's nostrils were flaming nicely, and warm, acid tears were burning his eyes.

Jude passed the panties to Teddy, and Teddy pressed them to his face; they made a little hollow boat in his open mouth. It was a moment of weakness—he wanted to smother the thought of his mother, of their dark, empty house. He breathed in vigorously, then broke into laughter. Teddy's laugh was sloppy, muffled, embarrassed, and usually accompanied by closed eyes. He sat like a blind man, mouth agape, waiting. That was how trusting Teddy was.

"This is wicked," Teddy said.

Jude sat down beside him and took another huff, choking on a noseful of fumes. "Is it *panties*," he asked, "or *panty*?"

"There's only one," said Teddy.

A dish towel or a paper bag would have worked just as well, but it was wonderful, getting high off of a panty. Jude put his head between his knees. For a moment he felt as though he were floating on or in the ocean, he felt as though he were made out of water. Then he panicked, drowning, and grabbed Teddy's ankle and held on.

He sat up. "Dude, you know you're staying here, right?"

Teddy reached for the panty and breathed. Snowflakes beat against the two ground-level windows. "Maybe for a little while."

"For good, man. For bad, whatever. Richer or poorer."

Jude redampened the panty. Teddy was quiet. Jude said, "All right, you fag?"

TWO

The train car was empty. She liked the long, silent chain of seats, the domed ceiling above, dark as a theater's. She sat listening to her headphones, socked feet resting on the seat ahead while she looked through her reflection to the black screen of snow. She always felt at sea when she was outside New York—giddy but lost, disbelieving how abysmal the world was. Cocooned here on the train, she could be anywhere. She could step outside and find herself in heaven, or Alaska.

But it was better here than in the bright white terrain of the last week, the fake snow on the slopes, the fluorescent lights of the room at the resort, where she did coke and shots with Nadia and Cissy and Cissy's older sister and rolled her hair in curlers so tight they burned her scalp. It was better than being at home, where she watched videotaped episodes of *Santa Barbara* with her mother, smoked on the fire escape, taught herself David Bowie songs on the piano, and practiced makeup on Neena, the live-in house-keeper, whom she bribed with coke—the poor woman really had a problem—to cover for her when she snuck out. And it was better than being at school, whatever school she'd find herself in when the semester began. She had been kicked out of two boarding schools in a year and a half—both times for drugs, the second while skinny-dipping in the school's Olympic-size pool.

She'd thought finally she'd have the chance to go to public school, but her mom had pulled some strings at some desperate place in New Jersey that agreed to consider her application for the spring semester (no doubt for an increased fee). To the first question in the essay section—*What are your personal goals for the future?*—she had responded with 250 words about her ambition to become a makeup artist, written in eyeliner and beginning with "My personal goals for the future, as opposed to my personal goals for the past . . ."

While Les had applauded her creativity, her mother had tossed the essay in the trash compactor and sat down at the Macintosh computer that looked like an object from a spaceship in the ancient opulence of their apartment, the Oriental rugs and pewter ashtrays and crystal chandeliers, and proceeded to respond to the second prompt: *Describe a person who has had a dramatic impact on your life.* "The person who has made me what I am today," she read aloud, her manicured nails typing clickety-clack, "is my mother."

If Eliza had been forced to respond to the question herself, she would have written about Les. Her dad, an in-house counsel at a downtown brokerage, had died of a cerebral aneurysm when she was three, but by the time she was ten her mom had had the good sense to meet Les and keep him around. Les was the best thing about her mom. He was moody and lazy and seriously stubborn and he went days sometimes without showering, but from time to time he got her mom high, which was what she really needed, and he had this you're-on-my-team respect for Eliza that continually surprised her. He'd let her paint his toenails. He'd let her crash on his futon in the East Village when she fought with her mom. He knew all the vegetables she didn't like, and he'd tweeze them out of her stir-fry with a pair of chopsticks.

It was strange, then, wasn't it, that he paid his own children so little attention. In the only picture Les had of them, they were toddlers in a bathtub, their hair sculpted into soapy Mohawks. These were the babies *he had deserted,* orphans, really. And one of them a *true* orphan, adopted at birth, from her own New York. "What are their names again?" she occasionally asked him, even though she knew, just to hear him say them. Now he would say "Dick and Jane" or "Simon and Garfunkel." She wondered, as the Amtrak sighed to a halt in Lintonburg, what they knew of her.

Out on the cold platform, the world was white, even in the heavy dark. The snow had stopped. On the other side of the tracks, a wilderness of cars, frozen in the lot over the winter holiday, lay buried under it. No one was around except for two boys, lurking a few cars down—that darkly dressed, alley-dwelling species of boy you could depend on for directions if you dared ask. She was about to do so— she was a city girl, not easily afraid—when one of them called her name. She must have nodded, or waved. Here they came, trotting over, cigarette smoke trailing behind. "Hey." They stopped at a safe distance, nodded their heads. "Are you Eliza?"

Two boys: she had not expected this. There was a black-haired one and a red-haired one, whom she deemed to be Jude. She had composed a picture in her head, an accelerated version of the children in the tub, but now, in front of these real-life faces, it dissolved. She snapped off her Walkman, slipped her headphones from her ears, and let them fall around her neck. "That's my friend Teddy," said the redhead. "I'm Jude."

"Jude," said Eliza. His eyelids were heavy. Was he high? Then, raising her voice over the roar of the train roaring away, "Hi, but I thought I was meeting a girl, too? Prudence?"

"She had plans," said Jude, who was smiling painfully. "Plus, she's sort of young for her age. How old are you?"

"Fifteen."

"So's Prudence. I'm sixteen."

"It's his birthday."

"On New Year's Eve?" Eliza asked doubtfully.

"I didn't ask to be born then. I just was."

"Are you getting your license?"

"No. My mom doesn't have a car."

"Oh." Eliza adjusted her backpack. "Well, happy birthday."

"You don't have any stuff?" Teddy, the dark-haired one, asked.

"Just this." The rest of the bags she'd taken to Stowe had gone home on the plane with her friends, who were spending New Year's Eve in Times Square, she explained. "Fucking last place on earth I'd want to be tonight."

"You haven't seen Lintonburg yet," mumbled Teddy.

"We're going to a party," Jude said. "But it doesn't start for a while."

"You don't have another cigarette, do you?" Eliza asked. "I smoked my last one in the bathroom on the train."

Jude unveiled the pack of American Spirits he'd taken from Harriet's carton.

"Thanks," Eliza said, taking out a lighter. They all stood in a circle on the platform, staring at the red eyes of their cigarettes, trying to keep warm, no obvious place to go. It was not hard to fend off the disappointment that she wouldn't be meeting Prudence. She had been curious to know what Prudence looked like, to observe her from afar, but it was Jude, she realized now, that she had wanted to meet. Girls irritated her, intimidated her, and finally bored her; around girls she became territorial, sniffing their asses, showing her teeth. It was not a part of herself she liked. Around boys she was herself, she could relax; she had nothing to win but them.

Still, she'd expected . . . something different. The novelty of a foreign exchange student. Provincial fashions. Elaborately laced snow boots. These boys looked like they'd just stood up from Les's stoop on St. Mark's Place.

"You guys get into a fight or something? You look sort of bloody."

Under the streetlight, she could see that Teddy's mouth was ringed with red bumps. At first she thought it was acne, but Jude had it, too, a raw, rosy stubble, like a beard of hives.

"No, it's huffer's rash," said Jude. "It happens sometimes."

"From turpentine," said Teddy.

"Turpentine," she mused. Maybe they did have their tricks in the country. Maybe they wouldn't be impressed by the cocaine in her makeup bag. "Are you fucked up right now?"

"Unfortunately, no," Jude said.

"It wears off pretty quick," said Teddy.

"I thought it was part of the Dracula punk thing." She tipped her cigarette toward Jude's devil lock. "You into the Misfits?"

Jude and Teddy exchanged glances.

"They're not bad," said Jude.

"I saw them at Irving Plaza when I was ten. It was my first show. With the Necros and the Beastie Boys."

"No shit?"

"It was some show," she said, looking up at the Vermont sky, remembering. So this is where Les used to live, in this snowcapped village, with his other family.

Jude said, "Your mom let you go to a show when you were ten?"

"Not by myself."

"Who took you, then?"

She watched her smoke rise white in the air, and then her breath, fainter. "Your dad," she said. "I sat on his shoulders."

*

Jude's desire for girls was indiscriminate, feverish, and complete; he wanted them all equally, and he wanted them not at all. Blondes or brunettes, big ones or small ones—they were cold, fragile, impenetrable creatures, all desirable as they were undesirable, all perfumed and pretty. To get one, he would have to get near one. He'd attempted this at a barn party in Hinesburg, kissing the girl unkindly and without asking, kind of pressing her up against a wall, and the whole drunk drive home in the backseat of the Kramaro, he'd felt so bad that he hadn't said a word about it to anyone, not even Teddy.

Eliza was different and not different. She was a girl, a painted doll. Her hair, bobbed to her elfin ears, was thick and black, her heavy bangs straight as a blade. Her eyes, too, were black, Egyptian, or was it an effect of the makeup shadowing her lids, the stiletto lashes, the feline inflection of the black, what was it called, eyeliner? Her lips were red, her skin translucent as wax paper. Her coat was white and puffy and slick, with cinched cuffs and a hood that looked like it was made of feathers, and she wore tights and a kilt. She could not have been much more than five feet; he could have opened up his own coat and smuggled her inside.

The fact that she possessed knowledge about his father, for instance that he still sold pot and that he still owned his 1968 Dodge camper van, was what was disconcerting. It was as thrilling and as freakish as if she had revealed to him that she was his flesh-and-blood sister, come all the way from Manhattan to find him.

"Here's the thing," she said, getting down to business. In an effort to offer her the Vermont experience, they'd taken her to Ben & Jerry's, the only place on Ash Street that was open on New Year's Eve. Her treat—Jude and Teddy were still broke. It occurred to Jude to be embarrassed, but she insisted on paying, peeled a starched twenty out of a wallet that looked like lizard skin. They sat in a booth, Eliza on one side, Jude and Teddy on the other. She said, "I think your dad wants to be part of your lives."

Jude licked his cone. New York Super Fudge Chunk.

"Lives?" Teddy said.

"Jude's and Prudence's. Sorry."

"He said that?" Teddy asked.

"Not like, those exact words. But I *sense* it."

"My dad's a prick," said Jude. "He doesn't want anything to do with me."

"How do you know, though?" Eliza asked. There was a gap between her two front teeth, just wide enough to slide his napkin through.

"Because I haven't seen him in seven years?"

But that was the thing, Eliza said. Les felt that Jude and Prudence wouldn't want anything to do with *him*. He'd been gone so long that he felt he was better off leaving them alone. "I think he feels bad about everything. I can tell he does."

"What's 'everything'?"

"You know, deserting you. Not being there for you."

"Where's 'there'?"

"Jude, okay, listen." Eliza stabbed her spoon into her cup of Cherry Garcia. Jude did not want to listen. Whatever she had to say wouldn't be true, not because he knew his father better than she did but because his father no longer existed. He was a voice on the phone, that was all.

"You should have seen him at Christmas. He got drunk—which I've never seen him that drunk—and he was *crying*, Jude. It was after he talked to you on the phone. He was standing out on the balcony, and he was alone, just *crying*."

"You were there? When I talked to my dad?"

"Isn't it sad?"

Jude said it was sad that he'd sent her to be his messenger.

"Oh, he didn't. He wouldn't do that. He just thinks I'm here to, you know, meet you guys."

"Why *are* you here?"

Eliza deposited a lump of ice cream on her tongue and swallowed. "I was in the neighborhood."

"Stowe's not really in the neighborhood," Teddy pointed out.

She shrugged. "I feel bad, I guess. I'm hogging Les all to myself."

Jude laughed. "Really, that's okay. You can keep him." Then, having lost his appetite, he turned his ice cream cone over onto the table. "No offense, but it's not really your business." The cone settled, and then began to melt.

Teddy was working on his own cone. Jude looked at him and Teddy looked back. Teddy's rash looked like a birthmark, a twin scar that bound them together. They were parentless; they were orphans, fiercely so. Eliza, Misfits or no, could not get to them. Her red mouth was pouting. Jude wanted to lean over the table and glide his tongue against the groove between her teeth: that would shut her up.

"Maybe you should go see him," Teddy said to Jude.

"What?"

"Maybe you should give him a chance."

Jude looked at him. "Don't mind Teddy. His mom left this morning. He's feeling homesick."

Teddy fired a look at Jude. It was the same look he'd given Jude in front of Harriet earlier, drained of all its pleading warmth. Their silent pact had been broken.

"She left?" Eliza asked. "Where'd she go?"

"We don't know," Jude said. "We just woke up and she was gone."

"Just—gone?"

"Just gone."

Eliza put her small white hand on top of Teddy's brown one. "Oh, *shit*. What should we do?" Her nails were painted with red polish, now chipped. Jude wanted to put his hand on top of theirs, as if they were making a promise or cheering before a game, but he didn't know what they would be cheering for.

On Christmas, Les had asked her, "Do you know what your problem is?"

"I don't appreciate my mother."

"That's true."

"Or my trust fund."

"That, too."

They were sharing a bottle of wine on his fire escape overlooking St. Mark's Place.

"You're young," Les said. He got like this when he was tipsy— enigmatic, flirtatious—but now he was full-on drunk. "You're naive, girl. You're a drama queen. You're a sad-story addict. You're drawn to them like a moth to a flame. You believe you can save the world by saying so."

"Whatever," Eliza said.

"Fine," said Les. "Go up there. Scatter your pixie dust."

Salvatore "Tory" Ventura lived on Lake Champlain in a colossal stone house, bearded with ivy, that Jude and Teddy had passed a thousand times. Up and down the street, cars were double-parked, jammed in snowbanked driveways and scattered across the white lawn. A guy who was not Tory was manning the door, and with an indifference that Jude took as a sure sign of their triumphs to come, he waved the three of them in, through the foyer, past the piles of coats and shoes, through the marble kitchen smelling of microwaved food. In the cavernous, wood-paneled living room, "Pour Some Sugar on Me" was drowning out Dick Clark. People were crowded around the coffee table, playing poker in the low light, and Jude recognized them as he recognized semifamous people on television.

Wasn't she from that one show? Wasn't she in his homeroom? It was nine o'clock, but he didn't see Delph or Kram.

Twenty-odd years ago, when Les and Harriet had been in college here, they'd met at a party. Les once told Jude it had really been an *orgy,* that he had found Jude's mother's body in a pile of other bodies (a mass like a writhing octopus), and that she'd been wearing nothing but a string of love beads, purple and pink. He'd taken her hand and pulled her out, Les to the rescue.

Since then, the health of Lintonburg's hippie movement had followed a series of dips and inclines, the same undulating route of the Dow Jones, for which most of the New England Boomers, by the end of Vietnam, had abandoned their peace pipes. By the time Les was fired from his lab position at Vermont State in 1980, the town's marijuana market had dried up. His customers got promoted, got pregnant, got older.

But then there were their kids. By the end of 1987, at Ira Allen High School, the hippie thrived again, enjoying with the jock a marriage of tolerance, if only for their sheer numbers. Metalheads and punks, though, were few and far between, and they knew how to watch their backs. At Tory Ventura's house, no orgy greeted Jude with outstretched hands. He and Teddy and Eliza entered the room just as someone was snapping a picture: they would be forever captured in a photo they didn't belong in, blinking against the flash. Escaping from the room, they took cover on the landing of the staircase, in the shadows of the wide window seat. Eliza went in search of beer while Teddy and Jude stayed put, keeping an eye out for Kram and Delph.

"She knows her way around a party," Teddy observed.

"She's not shy," Jude agreed.

"You like her?"

Jude looked out the window. "She's awful damn nosy."

"She's just trying to be nice."

In the backyard below, a bonfire was blazing. The light caught a flash of glass—a beer bottle soaring into the lake.

Teddy said, "She's pretty, though, right?"

"She's pretty," said Jude.

Here came another girl now, slithering down the stairs, and up her denim skirt went Jude's eyes. Whether Tory Ventura, escorting her, caught Jude's glance, Jude didn't have time to decide. Tory grabbed Jude's devil lock and gave it a jerk, as if milking a cow. "I like your pigtail, Maybelline."

Tory had given Jude the name in Spanish II on the day Jude had made the mistake of borrowing his sister's acne concealer, a tube of what looked like flesh-colored lipstick. He gave Jude and Teddy a hard time in the halls, for Teddy's glasses, Jude's retainers, their band T-shirts. It didn't help that the members of the Christian Fellowship Club had started wearing T-shirts that reconceived the logos of these bands—*Prayer* instead of Slayer, *Megalife* instead of Megadeth— implicating Teddy and Jude in the same substratum of hallway prey.

"You and your boyfriend been making out?" Tory asked Jude. He was staring with disgust at the rash around their mouths. "Looks like you got a giant hickey."

"It's from huffing," Jude said. "Turpentine? To get *high*?"

Tory was wearing a hot pink T-shirt with the sleeves rolled up, a pair of pleated khakis with a braided leather belt, and boat shoes with no socks. From his pocket, he withdrew a tube of ChapStick and circled it lazily over his lips, concealing the whole tube in his hand like a kid would hold a crayon. "Hell you doing here, anyway?" he asked Jude, his lips shining.

"Hell *you* doing?" Jude asked, feeling bold.

Tory laughed. The girl, still standing at his side, combed her fingers through the dark hair at the nape of his neck. "It's my house, dipshit. Who invited you? Fitzhugh?"

Jude hopped down from the window seat, and Teddy followed.

The fact that Tory Ventura suspected Jude might have been invited to his party, by a person named Fitzhugh, whom Jude didn't know; that a girl who had taken a train to see him was fetching him a beer; that Lintonburg might in fact be bigger, more generous than he'd believed, gave him courage. He ran a slow finger around the bruised contour of his lips.

"Fitzhugh?" he said. "You mean the guy who gave me this?"

Jude grabbed Teddy's elbow, and they took off running. A group of people had gathered on the steps below, trying to move past, and they dove through them, taking the stairs two at a time.

Outside, the night was so cold it hurt to move through it. It was 9:35, and Delph and his pot weren't anywhere. They found an unlocked LeBaron and slipped inside, Jude in the driver's seat, Teddy in the passenger's. They scrunched down low, even though they didn't seem to have been followed. "Why do you always have to piss people off?" Teddy said.

He was breathing heavily from the sprint out the door. He could feel the snow in his shoes and the sweat cooling in his armpits. The car reeked of beer.

"He pissed *me* off."

"You always want to get in a fight."

"So?"

"So you'll never win."

Teddy opened up the glove box. Inside were a manual, a flashlight, and a box of condoms.

"Let me see those." Jude grabbed the box, opened it, and let the package unfurl. The condoms they'd stolen from Shop Fart when they were thirteen were hidden, still unopened, in an empty Mötley Crüe cassette case in Teddy's dresser drawer. Now Jude tore one off the pack, tossed the rest back into the glove box, and turned on the overhead light, which Teddy snapped off.

"You want everyone to see us in here?"

Jude pocketed the condom. "I was *reading* it."

"You think Eliza's going to do you just because it's your birthday?"

"Shut up, Ted."

"You're so sad."

"Shut *up,* Ted!" Jude jumped at him, mashing Teddy's face in his hands. Teddy found Jude's mouth and sank his frozen thumbs in deep, and Jude bit down. They'd done the blood brothers thing when they were twelve, cut open their fingertips with a paring knife and made them kiss, the hands of God and Adam, E.T. phone home, almost as faggy as last night, in Teddy's still-bright bedroom at Queen Bea's house, when they'd shared a mouthful of pot smoke—a *shotgun* was what it was called, a word Jude had taught him—one breathing it into the other's mouth like a secret. Now their fluids slipped under each other's hands again, spit, snot, sweat, the tears from Teddy's eyeballs as Jude bored his knuckles into his sockets, Teddy trying to blink with his eyes closed, Jude snorting and gagging and elbowing the steering wheel, hitting the horn, which turned his gag into a cackle, which made Teddy laugh, too. Teddy pried Jude's fingers off his face. Jude bent Teddy's fingers back. Teddy screamed, "Uncle! Uncle, my contact!" Jude let go, and a cool wind flew into Teddy's right eye.

"Don't move," Teddy said. "I lost my contact." He scanned his lap, the seats, the floor, but the car was thick with darkness, and he could see out of only one eye. He took the flashlight out of the glove box. "Help me," he said. Panting, he passed the light over the dashboard, the gearshift, their bodies. Maybe it was still in his eye. His glasses were at home, tucked safely in the drawer with the condoms, and the thought of them there, useless to him, just out of reach, made him start to cry, so that both eyes, the seeing and the unseeing, now spilled hot tears.

"It's all right, man," Jude said. "We'll find it."

And he did, plucked it off of Teddy's own cheek, where it had affixed itself to his moist skin. Teddy took it from him, fragile as a jewel, and looked at the soggy dome on his fingertip, too tired to put it back on. He would wait until his eyes dried out. He would sit here and wait. Maybe Johnny knew where their mother was. Maybe they could find her and bring her home. Or maybe Johnny could help him find his father. He'd asked him as much in his last letter, a question he wouldn't admit to Jude. It was as if, by asking about his father, he'd made his mother disappear.

"Jude, I got to get to New York," he said.

Jude gripped the steering wheel. "All right," he said to the dashboard. "If you're going, I'm going, too. I'll go see my dad. You know how to hotwire a car?"

"Now? What about Eliza? You don't even know how to drive." Delph kept saying he was going to teach them. Delph was always saying shit.

"We'll take her with us, man. We'll steal some keys."

Teddy turned off the flashlight and put it back in the glove box. He looked at Jude, who had his seat belt buckled. Jude believed they were in their getaway car, their Batmobile, the DeLorean that would transport them, with a rocket-fart of fire, back to the future.

"You ready?"

Teddy's eyes were closed now. He said he was.

"All right," Jude said. "Let's haul ass."

"Let's go."

"All right. Let's do it."

But neither of them moved.

She'd told him her name was Annabel Lee. She didn't remember his. That was many minutes ago, and still she stood in the bathroom doorway, trapped by his large arm, bumming cigarette after cigarette, letting him refill her plastic cup from the keg in the tub. She supposed she could have walked away. Why didn't she walk away? He lifted the silver necklace out of the collar of her coat, bounced the charms dumbly in his hand. It was hot in here—did she want to take off her backpack? Her coat? She did not.

It was her punishment for making this trip. Instead of spending her New Year's Eve talking to some drunk prick in New York, she would spend it talking to some drunk prick in Vermont. He could have been any of the guys from home she'd let lift her necklace out of her coat. The weekend after her bat mitzvah she'd lost her virginity to a lacrosse player named Bridge Fowler, her friend Nadia's stepbrother, at his dad's place in the Catskills. She'd met him there when she went over with Nadia to ride a horse named Athens, and when Eliza went back with Bridge they snorted coke—another first—off of a silver serving platter, then did it in the barn. Afterward Bridge put on his loafers, lit up a cigar, and set off on a walk to visit the horses. He never touched her again. He passed her along to his friends, one weekend after another, weekends singed with the chemical smell of cocaine and latex and new cars, the smell of having achieved something she'd had little doubt of achieving.

Now Teddy and Jude had left her to fend for herself, and she was fending. She was a girl who knew how to fend.

Well, she came, she saw. Sipping beer from her cup, the remains of her red lipstick staining the rim, she felt lost and tired, but serene. She had wanted to lay eyes on Les's children, to be known to them, and one out of two wasn't bad. Strange, how she felt that she knew Jude already, how she already missed him, wished it were he standing in front of her, breathing into her ear. She had known him and Teddy only a few hours longer than this guy, but they were her companions for the evening, her guardians. She imagined Jude appearing and whisking her efficiently into one of the quaint, New England bedrooms—there would be exposed beams, a quilt. There would be kissing. He'd make stupid jokes. He was eager, young. He was sort of dangerously adorable, like one of those wide-eyed donkeys that would either kick you or eat out of your hand.

Then what if he came back with her to New York. What if he moved in with his dad. Would Les laugh at her then?

And then there was Teddy—not Jude, but Teddy—saying, "There you are!"

His rash had faded a little, but his eyes were swollen, and his cheeks were flushed.

"I've been here the whole time." She slipped her hand around Teddy's back and kissed his cheek. "Missed you, baby."

Teddy looked petrified only for a moment, then hooked an arm over her shoulder. He nodded. "Me, too. You, too."

"This your boyfriend or something?"

"His name's Teddy," said Eliza.

The guy laughed bitterly and emptied the rest of his beer. "You kids have fun," he said and made his way past them to the keg.

"Thanks, *baby*," she whispered. "That guy was ready to maul me." The line for the keg nudged them farther into the brightly lit bathroom. "Are you okay?"

"I'm fine. Let's just go."

"You look sort of ruffled. What happened to you?"

A girl, drunk and laughing, sat on the toilet with her underwear around her knees. Behind her, three or four people bent purposefully over the bathtub, trying to extract the last frothy drops from the keg. The guy who'd been talking to Eliza announced that it was dry. The crowd, disappointed, muscled back out into the hall, pushing Eliza up against the sink. She slipped off her backpack and hopped onto the counter, Teddy jammed against her knees, until everyone slowly filed out of the room, leaving the two of them alone. On the way out, the guy turned off the light and pulled the door shut.

"We should go," Teddy said, but he didn't move to turn the light back on.

She said, "My train doesn't leave till midnight," although she wasn't sure what time it was now. She took a swig from her cup. She was drunk, she knew, but not beyond reason. Someone tried the handle, but the door didn't budge.

"I guess it's locked?" she whispered.

"I can't see, anyway," Teddy said. "My contact fell out and I can't get it back in."

"Where is it?"

"Right here, in my hand."

Eliza put down her cup. "You're going to lose it. Let me see it." She was still sitting on the rim of the sink, her knees grazing his hips. She felt him find her elbow through her coat and then her hand. He placed the lens in the middle of her palm. It felt like a wet breath. She popped it in her mouth as though she were swallowing a pill, and let it soak on her tongue.

"What are you doing?"

"I put it in my mouth." Her voice slurred around the lens. "It keeps it moist."

"Oh. I just got them. I'm still getting used to them."

"Come here. Which eye is it?"

He led her hand to his right eyelid. His lashes were stiff with cold. Holding him by the ears, she eased his head back, then spit the salty lens onto her fingertip. She had saline solution in her backpack, but she didn't want to turn on the light. She liked the idea of her saliva lubricating this kid's eyeball. Gingerly she drew back his lid and fit it over his eye.

"Quit squirming."

"Sorry."

"Is it in?"

After a moment, Teddy said, "I think so."

On the other side of the door, someone else jiggled the knob, then gave up. The floor was vibrating with music and a few feet away people were laughing. She was afraid Teddy was about to turn on the light. Instead he said, "You live in New York, right?"

He told her the story. He was moving there. He had a half brother named Johnny in Alphabet City. Teddy had no money; Johnny had no phone. Could she take a message to him?

Eliza was the one to turn on the light. For several seconds they blinked at each other, as though surprised that the other was made of pigment and flesh. From her backpack she withdrew a pen and a sheet of the stationery she'd taken from the inn, and he wrote down his brother's address and Jude's number. He told her to tell Johnny to call him there. She liked the idea of carrying a message, riding through the snowy night to deliver urgent news to a stranger. She wrote down her own phone number and tore it off, and Teddy put it in his pocket. "You're not going to lose that, are you?" It was suddenly something that was important to her, not being lost to him. If she held on to Teddy, she could hold on to Jude. "Why don't you just come back with me tonight? I'll cover your ticket."

"What about Jude?"

"We'll bring him with us. He can live with his dad. It would be perfect!"

Teddy turned his eyes toward the empty red cups littering the bathtub. Here it was—a free ticket, dropped into his lap. He allowed himself to imagine the prospect of a solution, an adventure.

"I don't know if Jude can come tonight," he said. Eliza could hear him swallow. "And I don't know if I could just take off with you. I feel bad enough we're doing this."

She gave his shin a gentle kick. "What are we doing?"

He laughed nervously. "Standing around like retards."

Eliza reached for her backpack again and began rummaging around in it.

"What are you doing?"

She fished out her makeup bag and unzipped it. "I have a little something in here." After fumbling for a moment, she produced a razor and a small plastic bag. She was glad she'd saved some.

"Jeezum Crow," Teddy said.

Eliza laughed. "You're so country. Haven't you done this before?"

"Uh-uh. Only thing I ever snorted was ground-up chalk."

She tipped the powder onto the counter and gathered it neatly with the razor's edge. Then she took a bill out of her wallet and rolled it up. She did the first line, and then Teddy copied, expertly. After a few seconds, he staggered back and leaned against the wall. He nodded rapidly, eyes closed. Then he looked at her and grinned. He had very, very white teeth. They each did one more line, then finished Eliza's beer.

"Let me see this," Teddy said. She felt his cold fingers on her clavicle, the weight of the chain snaking against her skin. He cupped the charms in his palm, jiggled them like a pair of dice. He inspected the locket, the Star of David, the keys, then tucked them back inside her coat. "Neat."

"I like yours, too," she said. She tapped a finger on the cool disk around his neck.

"It's for the subway. My brother sent it to me, for when I go to New York." He looked down at it, holding it just under his nose. "It's missing the silver circle in the middle, so my brother says it's lucky."

"It must be," Eliza said. "I've never seen one like that." Teddy let the token hang. "How do you feel?" she asked him.

"Now? Wicked. How come you didn't tell us you had this before?"

"I was saving it." She crammed the plastic bag into her makeup bag and the makeup bag into her backpack. "We should turn the lights off again."

"We should do that."

They were little kids, playing a game. She turned the light off, found Teddy's cold face in the dark, aimed her mouth at his, and kissed him. It was so dark she was asleep, dreaming. It was a dreamy kiss.

"So are you Indian?" It seemed safe to ask, now that they were in the dark. He was shaking a little. It was probably, she realized, his first time. This made her want to pull him close and pat him on the back, which she did.

"Yeah. Gandhi, not Geronimo. But my mom's white."

They kissed again, leaning forcefully into each other. "Don't worry. We'll find her." They kissed until a knock sounded at the door. Eliza and Teddy held their breaths, trying not to laugh. The doorknob rattled, and the visitor disappeared.

Teddy whispered, "He's looking for us."

"Who?"

Teddy didn't answer.

"I don't think he'd mind," Eliza said, but maybe she wanted him to. Maybe she wanted Teddy to tell Jude. Maybe she wanted Teddy to pass her on like Bridge Fowler had, like an expensive new drug. *Try it, you'll like it.*

She peeled off her coat, and the coat, electrified with static, zapped the air. A shock of blue sparks sputtered between them. "Whoa," they said together. She found her way up onto the sink again. His cold hand found her knee, and then her hip, and then the long, goose-bumped length of her arm, and then the sleeve of her T-shirt, and then darting through this opening, the hand swallowed a breast whole.

Les was wrong. She wasn't young. She didn't want to save anyone; she wasn't in love with other people's suffering. She wanted to be consumed by it, eaten alive.

*

Jude roamed. They had split up—Teddy upstairs, Jude downstairs—but Jude searched upstairs, too, wandering the hall, trying doorknobs, looking not only for Eliza but now for Teddy, Delph, Kram, anyone but Tory, for beer, for the bathrooms, all of which seemed to be locked. He drank a watery centimeter of beer from an abandoned cup, but it only made him thirstier. He found the kitchen phone and called Delph, not caring how late it was, and left a message after his father's nerdy voice: "This is Jude. Where are you?"

Days seemed to have passed, whole, eventless weeks, since the girl had knocked on the driver's-side window. She had a wall of blond hair and a low-cut top that Jude stared down as she leaned over, cleavage that went and went. Could they move their car, please? They were blocking her way. And hey, actually, was this their car? Um, not really. It was their friend's. They'd go get him.

On a wicker love seat on the back porch, Hippie was passed out in a Santa hat, his glasses knocked askance. He'd graduated the year before, but he still hung out with the high school set, cruised his bike around the school parking lot each afternoon. The story was that in exchange for pot, Hippie was under Tory's protection, which meant that instead of being robbed by Tory, Hippie chose to supply him. Leaning over, Jude nudged his shoulder, and Hippie sat straight up, palming the leather fanny pack at his waist.

Jude said, "Hey, you got anything left?"

Hippie squinted at him. An icy wind blew through the porch screen. "Who are you again?"

"Jude. Jude Keffy-Horn."

Hippie adjusted his glasses. "Your mom's the Glass Lady?"

"How do you know my mom?" It wasn't until Jude had asked the question that the answer became obvious. He'd never wondered where his mom got her pot since his dad left town.

Hippie said, "We've traded services a few times."

Jude did not like the sound of that. He tried to banish the image of his mother engaged in a business exchange with Hippie. "How about a dime for some of my mom's glass? That's a good deal."

"Hippie's not doing any trading tonight," said Hippie.

"Or how about this?" Jude reached into the inside pocket of his coat and revealed two round, white pills, fuzzy with lint. "A little vitamin R. I'll toss them in."

"Hippie takes cash."

"Come on, man. Be a friend."

"Sorry, brother. Can't help you out." Hippie leaned his head back against the love seat. From the pool table behind him, Jude took a pool stick and thrust it like a javelin through the porch screen, startling himself and Hippie, who leapt up from the couch. The wind whistled through the hole in the screen.

"Screw you," Jude said. "You're lucky I don't steal that fag bag off you."

He kicked open the screen door, trundled through the snow, and pissed into a dark corner of the backyard, leaning a hand on the cold, slickly painted fence, drilling a steaming hole in the snow. As a kid he had done this with his father many times, stood beside him in the outdoors and pissed with pleasure into snow or gravel or grass, the sun or the moon on their faces.

It was just after his ninth birthday that his dad had left. This day was always the same. The false jubilation, the snow.

"You making pee pee, Maybelline?"

Jude zipped up. When he turned around, Tory Ventura was a black silhouette against the distant floodlight on the porch. Behind him were five or six more silhouettes. What remained of Jude's earlier bravado quickly sank.

"That's him," said Hippie's voice.

"That's him," said a girl, the girl who had discovered Jude and Teddy in the car.

Tory stepped closer. Jude could see only his outline, his moon-limned shoulders and knuckles. "You been vandalizing my house, Maybelline? You been messing with my car?"

The bonfire shivered at the far end of the yard, crackling with the smoky voices of the figures standing around it.

"It was unlocked," Jude said, ignoring the first question. "We were just trying to stay warm." How the fuck hadn't he known that Tory Ventura drove a LeBaron?

Tory stepped to Jude's left, and Jude stepped to the right, doing a little do-si-do. The light now fell flat on Tory, revealing his face to Jude, all but his deep-set eyes, darkened with circles below, as though with permanent paint, and Jude whiffed a swift air-gun shot of the beer on Tory's breath. "You come to my party without an invitation," Tory said, "and then you destroy my property?"

"I didn't mean to," Jude said. "I was supposed to meet some-one."

"You're going to have to pay for that," Tory said, and for a moment Jude thought he meant money.

Then Tory took a step forward and shoved Jude back into the snow. It wasn't a particularly brutal shove, but he didn't try to get up. The snow had stopped falling and the sky was clearing, a gauzy cloud traveling over a spray of 3-D stars. Down the waist of his jeans, the packed snow numbed his back.

"You think you and your little friend can just walk in here, you little freak?"

"We didn't—"

Tory kicked at the snow, his boot stopping just short of Jude's face. Snow pelted the molars in Jude's open mouth, the inside cor-ners of his blinking eyes. He had never been jumped before, and he braced himself for the boots. More than any other moment in that endless and disappointing day, he wanted to be blacked out, knocked out, out cold, gone. But when the boots came, they kicked him over, flipping him onto his belly like a fish in a pan. Coming down on his chin, he bit his tongue. Warm blood filled his mouth. He heard the zip of a belt through belt loops and then he felt the belt, not on his back but around it. The others held him down while Tory threaded the belt around Jude's trunk, clamping his hands behind his back and cinching it over his crossed wrists. They grunted wordlessly, as though lassoing a calf. Jude closed his eyes. Then, through the ear pressed to the ground, the ear listening for his tribe to come stampeding to his rescue, he heard the gentle trickle of liquid, a tributary making its slow way through the crystals of snow, and he opened his eyes to see the golden pool forming before him. Beer. He opened his jaw for it as Tory shoveled in the handful of soaked snow—he struggled to bite down on his knuckles, but already his mouth was too full—and just as he heard the woodpecker reel of laughter above, and the halfhearted protest of one of the girls, he discerned the true contents on his throbbing tongue, and tasting the ammonia through the aluminum of his own blood, his mouth stuffed open with snow as with a pair of balled socks, he gagged, and then vomited, his mouth now filling with vomit as well.

When Teddy and Eliza found him alone in the snow, perhaps ten minutes, perhaps an hour later, they were standing elbow to elbow, as though hiding something between their bodies. They unbuckled the belt and helped him to his feet. "Oh, shit," Eliza kept saying, her hand over her mouth, but Teddy was dusting the snow off Jude's jeans, saying, "You're fine! You're fine, right? You're fine, man, right?"

Jude tried to spit into the snow. He couldn't feel his tongue or his face.

Teddy was sort of panting. Teddy was messed up. Jude did his best to cock his head. *Are you messed up?* he asked with his eyes, and Teddy's black eyes blinked back, with painstaking slowness, with remorse, *Yes*.

*

They practically had to force Eliza onto the train. She wanted to stay until they were home safely, but Jude wouldn't let her, and Teddy pressed his hand to the small of her back as she climbed the stairs of the car. She didn't have to ask Teddy if he was coming with her. She knew he couldn't leave Jude now. Teddy watched the train disappear without him.

Now he let the force of the snow, falling again, carry his body down the hill, past his own street and his empty house, toward Jude's. The antiseptic flakes burned his skin. His heart was skidding on ice.

"You okay?" he asked Jude for the fourth time.

Jude nodded, hobbling stiffly beside him. He was holding something. Out of the pocket of his jacket snaked the end of the braided belt, wet with snow. "Where were you guys?"

Teddy had hoped to find something heroic about Jude's defeat, something that could be salvaged and spun into a story for Johnny or Delph or Kram. But now it felt unusable, a black stain, and entirely tangled with the bright memory of what he'd done in the dark while Jude lay outside in the snow. That was a story for another time, too. "Looking for you," Teddy said.

Up ahead, the frozen lake was lit like the ocean, like there was nothing on the other side. Now that Teddy was leaving this place, he had a biting fondness for it, a feeling that was unfamiliar to him; he'd left the other cities of his childhood without regret. He kicked the snow as he walked, spraying arcs of white mixed with the pebbly dirt beneath. She'd tried to kiss him again as they dressed in the dark—he could feel her raising up on tiptoe—but he'd swooped out of the way to feel for his jacket on the floor. He'd meant to punish himself, withhold one last indulgence, but he knew by her stunned silence that he'd punished her instead. "He's probably worried," he'd explained, zipping up the jacket. The cold teeth of the zipper bit his hand.

"Dude," he said now as they entered the alley behind Jude's house, "when we go to New York, we'll get away from that asshole. Everything will be different."

The streetlight shone on the patch of dirt where, in the spring, Harriet planted her garden. "Yeah, for sure." Jude stepped into the light and then through it, past the greenhouse, toward the office building next door. Teddy followed.

In front of the building's air conditioner, Jude knelt in the snow. He put his hands on the pipes that curled at the side of the machine. Fumbling, he pinched and pulled in the dark until he found the right valve.

The last thing Teddy wanted was another experiment. His heart was still shuffling frantically, and he wanted to still it, to burrow under the warm covers on Jude's top bunk and fall asleep. But Jude was on a mission, and he needed a partner, and after what had happened, Teddy could not refuse him. He had expected a glowing green light, something that might simmer wickedly in a test tube, but in the end the freon was a lot like the turpentine—invisible fumes, cheap and fickle, that turned you into your own ghost. They knelt, knees frozen, and sucked the valve like a straw, Jude blowing Teddy a mouthful, Teddy tonguing the night air until they were sky high, kite-light, whites-of-your-eyes fucked-up. There was a fire in the sky. There were fireworks. It was a new year. Bursts of red and gold flowered above them, petals of color fading and falling with the snow, and Teddy went up there. He felt himself float up into the alley, up over the lake, evaporating.

In the morning, it was Harriet who found them. Jude heard her before he saw her—the crunch of her boots over the snow. When he opened his eyes, the sky was twilight gray, and she was standing above him with a snow shovel hanging from her hand like a claw. He couldn't feel his body. The world had tipped sideways.

"What on earth are you boys doing?"

Teddy was curled up on the ground beside him with his hands between his knees. His face was a mask of ice. Jude tried to answer, but he couldn't speak.

The shovel fell. She threw down her gloves. His mother's hand was like a hot iron on his face. She had a hand on Jude's face and a hand on Teddy's; she was the warm current between them. "Jude, be still," he heard her say. "Teddy, wake up." When Teddy didn't open his eyes, she lifted his elbow, then dropped it. "Teddy, honey, wake up!" She clapped her hands, as though to scare a flock of crows from her garden, and the three beats echoed in Jude's waiting ears, taking flight through the valley and up into the morning.

THREE

The Atari comes on Jude's ninth birthday. It's three Christmases after everybody already has one, but when his father brings the package downstairs after dinner—the whole thing wrapped in that morning's *Lintonburg Free Press,* the cords coiled around it and the joystick balanced on top, as if somebody had packed up the cat—Jude's so excited he doesn't care that his father bought it at the Ferrisburg Flea Market.

"Look at that," his mother marvels, coming into the kitchen. She's wearing her silky rouge-pink dress and smoking a cigarette and smelling like patchouli. She puts her hand in Jude's curls.

"It's got Frogger in it!" Jude says, pulling out the cartridge still wedged inside. On the wood paneling of the game system, the numbers 44.99 are written in Magic Marker, but the first 4 is in a different color than the second, and in his dad's handwriting.

"You shouldn't have spent so much money," says his mother dryly to his father, who is flossing his teeth at the table.

"Nothing's too good for my birthday boy."

It's the night of his parents' New Year's Eve party, and for once Jude doesn't mind sharing his birthday with his parents' friends. The house is full of eggnog and balloons, which that afternoon Jude helped to blow up. His dad rubs a stray one on Jude's head, letting it hang above him like a cartoon thought bubble. Then he sends him upstairs, promising he'll wake him at midnight.

In the bean bag chair in his room, on the black-and-white TV with the rabbit ears, he plays Frogger, winning again and again. He's played it at Frederick Watt's house, and each time he's kicked Frederick Watt's ass. There is no greater exhilaration than the mad dash of the frog against heavier and heavier traffic, the leap from log to log across the croc-infested waters, the perfect dance of plunking oneself safely in one of the boxes at the top of the screen, unless it's watching one's little sister being squashed repeatedly by a truck, two leaps into the street. No matter what those boxes at the top of the screen are or why a frog would want to be in them—each time the circus music begins again, death has been evaded, shelter has been found.

But after Prudence, crying, tired of dying, goes to bed, Frogger ceases to jump. The screen is a storm of grays, the street, the river, a jumble of shapes just out of reach. Jude removes the cartridge, blows mightily into it as he's seen Frederick Watt do, but the thing's broken. His heart beats with disappointment. Downstairs, Paul Simon is singing "50 Ways to Leave Your Lover," to which Jude and Prudence know all the verses. There's laughing, and that high-pitched delight in women's voices. *Just slip out the back, Jack.* He puts on his bathrobe and his boots and climbs out the window, down the rusty fire escape from the third floor to the first.

Through the thin yellow curtains, he can see the party taking shape in the living room, just below eye level. There are the Hausers and the Mayhews, and the lady who poses for the life drawing class Harriet teaches (she's wearing clothes), and the Donahoes, and the rest of the botany professors and their pretty wives. The glasses in their hands are filled with liquid the color of fluoride rinse, except for Mrs. Donahoe's, which looks like it's filled with ginger ale. She's wearing a sheer white dress with a slit up to her thigh. Jude kneels to find the part in the curtains. He can see Mrs. Donahoe's nipples, and her outie belly button, which looks like a SpaghettiO. She's examining the ice in her glass. She looks, Jude thinks, sad.

He sits up straight. He's on the bottom rung of the fire escape, his legs dangling over the edge, and when he turns around, he can just see the roof of the greenhouse. He can see the Christmas lights blinking in the window of the office building next door—red, green, red—and the wreath of mistletoe his father has hung on the front of the camper van parked in the alley below. He can hear the front door of the house opening and closing, and he can see Mr. Donahoe, the department chair, come around the corner in his overcoat. He's big and tall, with a shock of white-blond hair and a nose with a cleft in the middle, like one of those monster strawberries. He leans up against the side of the van, in its shadow. Jude sits very still, thinking that if he can make himself invisible, something will happen. What seems like many minutes later, his mother comes out of the house, her camel-colored coat draped around her shoulders, a martini glass in her hand. In her unlaced snow boots, she walks to the van and, unsurprised to find Mr. Donahoe there, lights a cigarette beside him. The two of them are talking close, so close Jude can't hear them, their lips moving just a few inches apart. The van is called the Purple People Eater, because Jude's dad painted it lavender and once fit twenty-four friends inside it.

The Donahoes have been coming over to play poker for years, dancing in the living room and smoking the Donahoes' hookah after sending Jude and Prudence to bed. One night that summer, when his parents went to the Donahoes' house for dinner, they left Jude and Prudence in the van parked in the Donahoes' driveway, too cheap to hire a sitter, with their comic books and Cracker Jacks. A slumber party, Les said. Jude told Prudence ghost stories, swallowing the orange glow of the flashlight in his mouth, until she cried herself to sleep in her sleeping bag.

And one morning not long ago, when Jude asked his mother where his father was, she looked at Jude as though trying to think of a good lie, and then, changing her mind, said, "He's on the Donahoes' boat with Mrs. Donahoe." She was emptying a glass ashtray in the garbage can, and she banged it so hard it split down the middle and sliced her finger open. Jude has been on the Donahoes' sailboat before. It's named *Feelin' Groovy*, and below deck there's a bed.

But the way Mr. Donahoe is leaning into Jude's mother's hair is more businesslike than romantic, conspiratorial in the way Jude and Prudence occasionally are. They look worried, Jude thinks. He can't hear their whispers, only the music inside, and the early fireworks bursting here and there over Tamarack Street, and over the lake, where other people are having parties. Jude's mother pours the green liquid from her glass into the snow, drops her cigarette in the puddle, and goes inside. After she leaves, Mr. Donahoe, who once for no reason gave Jude a very valuable collector's copy of *Captain America 100*, takes a piss beside the van, then follows her. The snow has started again, white flakes floating down like feathers in a pillow fight.

It's snowing still, maybe several hours later, when Jude wakes up to more sounds in the alley—the slamming of the van door. Crawling from his bed, still in his bathrobe and boots, he opens the window and hangs his head outside. The bottom half of his father is disappearing into the Purple People Eater, a flashlight bobbing inside. Jude thinks he must be sleeping in the camper, as he has been known, in warmer weather, to do. Instead he emerges with the sleeping bag in his arms. He's now wearing a pair of snow boots, a parka, and the dashiki he wore to Woodstock. He's halfway to the greenhouse, waddling through the snow, when he stops, panting heavily, then looks up at Jude's window.

"What?" he says.

Jude doesn't say anything. The cold air is burning his ears and his nose.

"Come on, then," says his father, shuffling along again.

By the time Jude reaches the greenhouse, his father has turned on all the lights—twelve overhead lamps, plugged into a network of extension cords—and the warm room is getting warmer. The light is bright and orange, and the air smells sweet and spicy at the same time. It's been a while since Jude was allowed in here.

There is no glass, no hothouse plastic, no natural light. But it's green, and it's a house of sorts: an aluminum shed painted the color of a tennis court. All around—on shelves, beneath tables, in a kiddie pool that neither Jude nor his sister has ever played in—are his plants. They're the greenest green Jude has seen all winter, and some of them, the ones wrapped in chicken wire, the ones sprouting purple flowers, are taller than he is. Jude's father takes out his army knife. From one of the dried branches hanging upside down from the clothesline, he carefully cuts away the outer leaves, removes a thimbleful of hairy bud, and then, sitting down in the old rocking chair, packs his brown glass pipe with it. The greenhouse is the size of Jude's bedroom—big, the whole third floor of the warehouse— and as he burrows into the sleeping bag at his father's feet, he wishes he could sleep in here instead.

"I thought the lights weren't supposed to be on at night," Jude says. In the orange light his father's left cheek is an angry red. "What happened to your face?"

His father puts two fingers to his cheek. He has a soft, pale, leathery face, with splotches of pink age spots along the roots of his hair, which he parts down the middle. Since he was a teenager he's worn it long and stringy, to his shoulders. His overgrown beard is the same copper color, the rim of his mustache stained tobacco brown. In the summer he wears cutoff jeans and flip-flops and no shirt, walking around the house scratching the copper curls on his chest. Now he pulls the hood of his parka over his head. "Born that way, champ," he says.

Jude puts his hands behind his head, gathering his shoulders into the depths of the sleeping bag, which smells like gasoline and his mother. She used to take it camping at Camel's Hump with Jude's father, who now has a piece of pot caught in his beard like a crumb. Jude asks if he can try some, but his father shakes his head.

"You let me try the eggnog with rum in it."

"Reefer is for grown-ups. But some grown-ups are too grown-up for it. Some grown-ups think it's unfashionable now." His father takes a smooth hit. "I'm afraid I'm not needed here anymore, champ." When Jude says nothing, his father asks, "You know why people smoke reefer? It's a comfort, champ. It restores you, like sleep. It makes you like a baby again, a sleeping baby. Know what I mean?"

"No. You won't let me try."

"You're already a baby. You don't need to become one again. When you're older, you'll know."

"I'm not a baby. I'm nine today."

His father rocks slowly in his chair. "You're right. You're not a baby anymore."

"Do you know what Mom and Mr. Donahoe were talking about outside?"

He stops rocking. His gray eyes, which have been rolling around the greenhouse with a liquid dreaminess, fall on Jude's face, as though he's just spotted him there, lying at his feet. He looks almost pleased.

"As a matter of fact, I believe they were talking about *moi*."

"How come?"

A sheet of snow tumbles off the warming roof.

"I'm going to tell you something, champ, because I need another man's opinion. Okay?"

"Okay."

"Mrs. Donahoe, she's pregnant. You know, she's going to have a baby."

Jude absorbs this information. As cold as it is outside, he's hot in his sleeping bag, his forehead sweating under the lights. "Then why were they talking about you?"

"Well, because I'm the one who made her pregnant. You know how that happens and everything?"

Jude nods slowly. He knows, more or less. When he asked his mother where babies came from, she drew him a diagram in colored pencils.

"And what do you think about that?"

"Is Mom pissed?"

"Yes, she is. She's very pissed and doesn't want to be married to me anymore. And she'll probably be even more pissed that I told you all this, but you should know the truth. You're a big guy. You can handle it, right?"

Jude is lying perfectly still, even though he wants to crawl into his father's lap and touch the red spot on his cheek. He wonders if it was Mr. Donahoe who hit him, or Jude's mom.

"What will happen to the baby?"

"We find ourselves in a strange position. Do we keep the baby? What happens to the baby?"

"Where will it go? Does—will it be Mr. and Mrs. Donahoe's?"

"It's a possibility."

"But where will the baby go if they don't?"

His father takes a quick hit of his pipe, then puts it down on the workbench beside him. Reluctantly he exhales the smoke.

Then something occurs to Jude. "The baby's going to be my brother or sister, isn't it?" He was just a baby when Prudence was born. He doesn't remember his mother being pregnant.

"Would you like a baby brother or sister? Would you like that?"

"I guess," Jude says, because his father sounds as though he needs cheering up. His eyes are glassy and wet, like they are when he tells scary stories about Vietnam, stories he's stolen from friends who were there. Jude remembers one about an arm in a tree, waving.

"Here's the thing." Jude's father rubs his beard. "There are lots of things that can happen to babies. Sometimes—sometimes babies aren't born at all. Sometimes when they do get born, they get raised by their parents, and sometimes they get raised by other people. For example, what's the name of that program you and your sister watch, with the black kids?"

"*Good Times*?" Jude is so glad to have a question he can answer he lets out a breath.

"No, the one with the two boys and the white father."

"Oh, *Diff'rent Strokes*."

"*Diff'rent Strokes*. So, for example, those children are being raised by someone other than their real parents. They're adopted, right?"

Jude nods.

"So, as a matter of fact, we planned to wait, your mother and I, to tell you together, but your mother would wait forever if she could, and I don't have that long, champ. I think you're old enough to know." He leans forward on his elbows, so Jude can see up into the dark spheres of his nostrils, and tells Jude that he's adopted, too.

Jude doesn't make a sound. He presses the sleeping bag over his nose, breathing in his mother. He smells Cracker Jacks, midnight in the Donahoes' driveway. For a moment he thinks, *Mr. Donahoe's my dad,* but that doesn't make any sense, but nothing else makes any sense, either.

Where did he get this red hair? asked a friend of his mother's once, pawing through it as though she'd never seen red hair before.

Jude's father places a palm on top of Jude's head. His touch, neither hot nor cold, shouldn't feel like anything, but it does. His dad isn't his dad; he's just a man. He tells Jude that his real mother was just a teenager, and that he was adopted from a hospital in New York City when he was ten days old. "You were as little as a rabbit. You could fit right here." He puts one finger on his thigh and one finger on his knee. "It's quite common, really. Aristotle was adopted. Lee Majors was adopted. Lots of people are, and you wouldn't even know it."

Jude squints up into the bright lights. He thinks of Mrs. Donahoe's belly button and the little lump of a person inside her. Inside his sleeping bag, he dips his finger into the warm hollow of his own navel. Later, at a less finite moment, he'll come to imagine his nine months in utero with not only curiosity but nostalgia. He'll understand what his father meant about marijuana—its deep, peaceful sleep; its small, fragile gift of forgetting. He'll imagine that being high is something like being unborn, alive but not present, and when he's savoring a mouthful of smoke, he'll sometimes find himself swimming toward that drowsy, padded place—brainless, blind, curled in the pink womb of a stranger.

Then the room goes black. The lamps blink once, then are gone. When Jude's eyes adjust, they find the soft light in the doorway, nine candles that illuminate his mother's stunned face. She is wearing her coat over her dress, and her unlaced snow boots, which have tripped over the extension cord. The cake looks homemade.

In the house, the party is counting backward to one. Then it bursts into a roar.

"How could you tell him?"

Jude looks at his father sideways. He's not sure which part she's talking about. He wishes he could unknow all of it, just tilt his head and shake it out of his ear, like bathwater.

After the last guest has gone home, Jude's mother comes to his room and sings to him. This is what he remembers most of all, years after his father is gone—pretending to be asleep while his mother sings at the foot of his bunk bed. Her face is lit by the slice of light through the bedroom door, and her breath smells like peppermint and liquor. She's too drunk to remember all the words, but it doesn't matter—he already knows them. It's his song, the one he was named for, and she's sung it since he was a baby. He knows all about carrying the world on your shoulders, all about letting her into your heart, all about making the sad song better.

FOUR

It was two-thirty in the afternoon when Eliza woke up. She couldn't sleep on the train, too amped from the coke and Teddy and what had happened to Jude, but by the time she'd gotten home, the sun rising orange above the Manhattan skyline, she was tired enough to crash. Now she threw off the covers and looked down at her body. She was not hungover. She was not enrolled in school. And her mother was not home. She sat up and reached for her backpack on the floor, found the slip of paper on which Teddy had scrawled his brother's address. East Sixth Street.

In the shower she reviewed the details of last night, trying to recall if Teddy had touched the parts she washed: her wrist, her belly button, her earlobe. He had not touched her excessively. He'd been quiet and polite. The only thing new was her surprise: she'd expected this time to be different. And perhaps worse, she had the feeling that Teddy would not tell Jude what had happened. The night would be lost, a secret between the two of them, as though they'd done something wrong. Only now did it occur to her that they might have. She had done it on a bathroom sink with some guy she didn't know, in some state she'd never set foot in again. When she did it with guys who knew her, her reputation, her money, her address, at least she was not entirely alone. She would wash off the shame of one weekend with the next.

But she did not want to wash off what had happened last night, and it was because, she decided, she liked Teddy. She had not liked Jeffrey Dougherty or Hamish Macaulay or Bridge. She had only wanted them to like her. With Teddy, though, she didn't stop when he produced no protection. "Not on me," he apologized, and she locked her ankles around the fragile length of his torso, as though climbing an unsteady tree, and whispered, "It's okay." She'd come so far, the train and all, and Teddy was sweet. He was almost certainly a virgin, disease-free.

Was that it? Did she like Teddy? Perhaps it wasn't him she'd wanted; she only wanted something to happen. She wanted access into the life Les had left behind, a tunnel out of New York, and now she had it—a mission. Teddy needed her help. When she was dressed, contacts in, teeth brushed, makeup done, she pocketed the address, donned her headphones, and rode the 1 train to the 7 to the 6. Traveling from the Upper West to the Lower East Side could take nearly an hour, but she enjoyed the busy anonymity of the subway. She wondered what Teddy was doing, if he was thinking about her at all, if he'd stayed the night at Jude's, if Jude was okay. It had been a cold kind of shock to find him facedown in the snow. For a moment, she'd thought he was dead. The evening had been momentous enough already, awkward but complete, and then it had ended on such an unpleasant note. They hadn't parted on clear terms. She'd wanted to stay with them, make sure that Jude got home all right, but they'd made her get on the train, and with Jude there she and Teddy couldn't say much but good-bye. What would they have said, if Jude hadn't been there? And if Teddy hadn't been there, what would she have said to Jude?

The neighborhood east of Tompkins Square Park was unknown to Eliza. Her mother was the kind of New Yorker who lamented the gentrification of the Lower East Side but, when passing a junkie on Les's comparatively safe St. Mark's Place, would grab Eliza's hand and hurry her by. Eliza burned through two cigarettes while she walked from the Astor Place station, past Les's building, across Avenues A, B, C (A: you're Asking for it, B: watch your Back, C: you're Crazy) and approached D (you're Dead), watching the addresses, walking purposefully, trying to blend. She turned off her Walkman, kept her ears open. "Wassup, baby girl?" a man called from the top of his steps. But most of Alphabet City was sleeping, bums dozing peacefully in snow-padded alleys and doorways. A spiral of smoke rose out of a metal garbage can, but its effect was more reassuring than spooky. On a clear afternoon like this one she could almost believe the windows had been shot out by stray baseballs. Up ahead, the East River glistened as bluely as Lake Champlain.

On the south side of the street, the buildings were numbered haphazardly. There was no answer at apartment A in the first building she buzzed, and there was no apartment A in the second. The next building was hollowed out—no doors, no windows. She could hear the faint throttle of music, but she couldn't tell where it was coming from. In the basement of the second building was a narrow storefront. The awning and the shuttered door were both painted the same ochre as the building, and no sign hung above it. At the bottom of the staircase that led to it, the landing was carpeted with trash, but as Eliza moved down the steps, the music became louder, and then very clear. Hardcore. She stood outside for a moment, listening to it.

I'm as straight as the line that you sniff up your nose
I'm as hard as the booze that you swill down your throat
I'm as bad as the shit you breathe into your lungs
And I'll fuck you up as fast as the pill on your tongue!

Before she could change her mind, she knocked insistently on the metal door. No answer. She knocked again. A few seconds later, the music stopped, and a voice called, "Who is it?"

"I'm looking for Johnny?" she said.

The person on the other side struggled with the door, kicking it several times. Then slowly it squeaked open. Eliza's eyes alighted on a guitar, a drum set, a card table, a couch, and an orange cat sitting in what looked like a dentist's chair before landing on the blue-eyed boy of eighteen or twenty who stood in the doorway. His head was stubbled, all but bald, muscular as an apple, but the hair he did have, on scalp and cheek, was as yellow as a toddler's. His face was heart-shaped: broad forehead, severe cheekbones, chin like a spade. He wore a small gold loop through each earlobe, a strand of wooden beads wound three times around his neck, and although it was nearly as cold inside the apartment as it was out, only a pair of camouflage shorts. From his waistband, the dark, serpentine shapes of tattoos climbed up the downy path to his navel, across the ladder of his ribs, circling the pale sinew of his arms, feathers and scales and flames and gods, sea green and devil red.

Across his chest were the words TRUE TILL DEATH.

"I'm sorry," she stammered, trying not to stare. "I thought you were someone's brother."

He tugged at one of his earrings. The nest of hair in his armpit was golden and sparkling with sweat. "What makes you think I'm not?"

Absently, she introduced herself. She must have looked like a runaway, shivering in her coat, standing on broken beer bottles in a neighborhood she didn't belong in. Maybe that was why he was so quick to extend his hand—each tattooed from wrist to knuckle with a fat, black *X*—and smiling, as though any friend of his brother's was a friend of his, say, "Johnny McNicholas."

On the way to the pay phone at Tompkins Square Park, walking back across the four avenues, they talked about everything but the boys' mother. Eliza was brief on that point, because it was difficult, she realized, to relay bad news to a stranger, and because she didn't really remember what Teddy wanted her to say. She said, "I guess your mom's missing? He wants to know if you know where she is," but she didn't think that was quite right.

She almost said, "He wants to move in with you," but how could Teddy live with him there? In the glimpse she'd gotten of his apartment, it was surprisingly—even hauntingly—neat, but the couch seemed to be the only place to sleep, and the whole room was warmed by an ancient space heater. She counted three cats. He was paying next to nothing in rent, he'd said, and the place was buried enough to serve as a tattoo studio and big enough to serve as a practice space for his band. "Prewar," he'd joked. "Private entrance." While he'd looked for a quarter, she'd explained her tenuous link to his brother—through her mother, Les, and Jude. Acquaintances, four times removed.

They passed two clusters of pay phones with the phones missing entirely, the arterial wires flowing to nothing. Eliza offered him a cigarette, but he declined. He was straight edge—didn't smoke, didn't drink.

"I heard the song," she said, exhaling. "It's funny, you having a brother that's, like, the opposite of you."

"We're more alike than we look," he said, and Eliza worried that she'd offended him. She hadn't wanted to get Teddy in trouble. She hadn't told Johnny anything about last night.

"I don't know Teddy that well, actually."

In the phone booth at the corner of Tompkins, a man was sleeping. Johnny knocked gently on the glass to wake him and, address-
ing him by name, asked if he could use the phone.

"You got to call your old lady, Mr. Clean?" The man stumbled
out of the booth, the smell of urine following him out into the cold.

"You know it, Jack." One of the man's eyes coasted luridly over
Eliza, staring through her, before he wandered into the park. The
tents across the park were blue and yellow and army green, made
out of cardboard and bedsheets and tarps, drooping with snow, and
she might have thought she was in a third world country, or on a
battlefield, or at some abandoned circus, if she hadn't known she
was standing in her own hometown. The park was full of tents, and
this was why it was called Tent City, and seeing it she felt a dull stab
of shame and distaste. Not long ago she had heard on the news that
a man had frozen to death in this park. Or maybe it was another one.

"Is that guy blind?"

Johnny looked up from the number he was dialing. "He's just
a faker. Hang around a sec, would you? Make sure I have the right
number?"

She'd been hoping to, of course. She wondered if there was a
gracious way to insert herself into Johnny's conversation. She would
linger at a distance, pretending not to eavesdrop, and then tell him
not to hang up. She'd ask Teddy how Jude was feeling, if he'd had
any word from his mom, what his plans were.

"Prudence, hey, it's Johnny McNicholas. Teddy's brother.
Remember me?"

The snow that had fallen the week of Christmas had hardened
into slick, icy mounds, stretching across the park like the tentacular
roots of trees. She missed the cold purity of New England.

"Who did?" Johnny asked.

Eliza thought of the snow that had fallen over them last night, the
flakes like small, wet mouths, whispering.

"Where is he?"

Johnny was standing up straight in the booth, gripping the phone cord. Eliza pulled the collar of her coat tight around her ears. She had been too young when her father died to remember her mother's face when she got the call, but she'd imagined it. She had not known until now that she'd imagined it, but she had, a thousand times; she knew this grim dream as well as she knew her mother's voice.

Johnny's eyes froze, and then darted for a place to land, and then pinned her where she stood.

Prudence hadn't gone with them to the hospital. The vehicle into which Jude's stretcher was fed had room only for their mother. The sirens had woken her, and by the time she'd found her bathrobe and slippers and dashed down the stairs, the paramedics were already loading the boys into the twin ambulances, their bodies draped in blue blankets, and from the look of them there was no reason to believe that one was alive and one was dead. The same substances were discovered in their systems—THC, alcohol, petroleum distillate, and chlorofluorocarbons—except in Teddy's there was also cocaine. Whether this distinction was of significance the doctors could not say. Her brother had fallen into a severe state of hypothermia, but Teddy had died of heart failure before he'd had the chance to freeze, had been dead all night behind their house, not far from the bed where Prudence had been sleeping.

She spent two nights at her friend Rachael's. Rachael's mother, who was a student at the New England Culinary Institute, practiced her foie gras on them both nights, and each time it tasted marvelous. Rachael's father kept talking about his frat brother Rusty who'd OD'd in college, and they all went to church on Sunday morning and prayed that Teddy's soul would be accepted into heaven. Afterward Rachael's sister took them to the mall to buy black dresses to wear to the funeral, which was held at the same church the day after Jude was released from the hospital.

Beatrice McNicholas wasn't there. She'd disappeared. Her housekeeping clients were questioned, but nobody had a clue where she'd gone, and as far as anybody knew, she didn't know her son was dead. After two days, when it was determined that neither of Teddy's parents could be found, that Teddy's father couldn't even be identified, Johnny, Teddy's closest living relative, barely eighteen (who had borrowed Les's camper van to make the drive from New York, after Eliza enlisted his help), signed the papers giving permission for his brother to be cremated.

The service was attended by Jude, Johnny, Harriet, Prudence, Kram and Delph and their parents, Rachael and her parents, the guidance counselor and two teachers from Ira Allen High School, and six or eight dutiful, well-dressed students, mostly girls, whose names Prudence knew but Teddy probably hadn't. They had received permission to miss half of their second day back at school, and arrived on a school bus, the driver of which, a large black woman with pink curlers in her hair, also attended. The minister read a passage about shepherds and lambs. Delph played "Stairway to Heaven" on Jude's guitar, but it wasn't tuned. Jude wore a white button-down shirt, navy blue Dockers, a pair of Vans, and a clip-on tie borrowed from Delph.

Before Johnny returned to New York, he went through Teddy's room in Queen Bea's abandoned house, taking with him Teddy's posters and clothes and record collection and the cardboard box of ashes. The rest of the family's furnishings were sold in a yard sale organized by Kram's mother, the proceeds from which she later sent to Johnny, folded in a cream-colored note she signed *Joan,* which he studied for some time before placing the name.

*

In the ICU, Jude had breathed warm air that tasted like the beach, listening to the Darth Vader rasp of his lungs. Salt water flowed in his veins, sugar and saline, thawing his limbs. His temperature when the ambulance arrived had been eighty-seven degrees. He had been shivering violently—his mother believed he was having a seizure— and if he'd been any colder, they said, his body would have shut down, and soon his heart would have stopped beating.

On the third morning in the hospital, the young doctor who had overseen Jude's MRI, the one who wore a ballpoint pen speared through her elaborate French twist, led Harriet into her office. When she drew a folder from a stack on her cluttered desk, Harriet knew what was coming: the bill. She had signed three or four consent forms already, on clipboards balanced on her knee beside Jude's bed, but no one had mentioned money, and she hadn't mentioned that she didn't have any. Before the divorce and for brief periods afterward, she had invested in family health care plans of the discount variety, but her children were rarely sick. It was cheaper to pay for Jude's Ritalin out of pocket than to cover the monthly premiums. For the big things, like the children's braces, she called Les.

She would, of course, have to call him again. She had called him the day it happened (strangely, he already knew the story—his girlfriend's daughter and Teddy's poor brother, who had somehow become associated, had just burst through the door with the news), but she'd been too panicked at that point to discuss finances with her ex-husband—or, for that matter, to talk to the daughter, whom she'd hoped could fill in the details of the previous evening. The detective assigned to Teddy's case soon took care of that, questioning the girl and Teddy's brother and Jude's friends Kram and Delph. Jude, when the oxygen mask had been removed, volunteered that the huffing, both times, had been his idea, and that the marijuana had been Teddy's mother's (how easily it could have been her own!), but nobody seemed to know anything about how the boy had gotten his hands on cocaine in Lintonburg. In the end, Harriet wasn't certain it mattered. Thankfully, the police officer was discreet, and kind; he did not wish to badger a boy in a hospital bed. No foul play had taken place, just an accumulation of poor choices.

"Mrs. Horn," began the doctor, extracting the pen from her hair.

"*Ms.* I'm divorced. In fact, I never took my husband's name. Always just Ms. Horn."

"*Ms.* Horn—"

"I hope you have some more papers for me to sign," Harriet said lightly, putting on her glasses.

The doctor produced an exasperated smile. "Actually, I was just reviewing your son's records. Tell me—this might come as a shock, but—has he ever been assessed for fetal alcohol effects?"

Harriet, who had been sitting, she realized, in a rather unlady-like position—knees apart, back slumped, pocketbook in her lap, wearing the same sack of a dress she wore yesterday—now sat up straight. She removed her glasses, let them bob on their chain. A trivial amount of alcohol had been found in Jude's system, but it was the freon that had caused him to pass out. And he was okay now: scheduled to go home that afternoon. She said, "Jude's sixteen."

"Yes, I know. Most children are diagnosed at a younger age, but not always. And I see that he's adopted. Was he tested for birth defects as an infant?"

"I'm—I don't know. I don't think so."

"Is anything known about the pregnancy?"

Harriet shook her head. The doctor scribbled. She knew almost nothing about Jude's biological parents. That was the way most New York State adoptions had worked then.

"And he's on methylphenidate. Kids with FAE or FAS are often diagnosed with ADHD, often have trouble in school, even trouble with the law, which is why it's so important to take precautionary measures. Now, the hyperactivity and dyslexia, combined with the adoption and the telling facial features, lead me to suspect—"

"Hold on, facial features? What—you have to spell things out. FAE?"

"Fetal alcohol effects, which includes fetal alcohol syndrome." The doctor, who appeared to be all of twenty-one years old, went on to describe Jude's cranial symptoms with a precision—as though she, not Harriet, had kissed the boy good night every day for sixteen years—that pierced Harriet's very brittle sense of reality. She felt dazed, dizzy, listening to the list that reduced her son's face to a series of tribal malformations. Short, upturned nose; flat space between nose and mouth; thin upper lip; small chin; short eye openings—

"His *eye openings*—are just fine. Are perfect. I—"

"Perhaps it's a mild case," the doctor said, not unkindly.

Harriet said nothing. She was suddenly exhausted. She had slept about ten minutes in two days.

"Think about it awhile. When Jude has had time to recuperate, bring him in." He would just need to undergo a few tests—motor functions, language skills. The doctor recommended a birth defects specialist whose name Harriet promptly forgot. "A firm diagnosis could be helpful to you. You could consider other medications. It could help answer questions about the source of your son's behavior."

"The source," said Harriet dreamily. She looked down into the gaping pocketbook on her lap. In it was the detritus of her slipshod motherhood—keys, Kleenex, aspirin, cigarettes, checks decorated with the Grateful Dead dancing bears, a Snickers wrapper, an old shopping list, and a dime bag inside an Altoids tin inside a glove, which she decided then and there to flush the next time she had the chance. She closed her eyes. She could fall asleep right here, disappear. How wonderful it would be to find the source of all this, to blame it on some other mother.

*

At home, she was a shadow, a voice. She flitted in and out of his dreams, in and out of his room, opening the curtains, picking up the clothes from the floor, leaving a mug of warm milk on the night-stand. Sometimes she sat at the edge of his bunk bed, humming his song but not singing the words, running a hand over his arm or ankle, still trying to return heat to his body. Most of the day and most of the night he lay curled on his side with his back to the room, his Walkman turned up, his nose pressed to the cold wall.

Delph and Kram visited every day after school, always together. One sat in the bean bag chair, one in the wooden school chair with the butt cheeks scooped out. Again and again they apologized for not showing up on New Year's Eve—their girlfriends had dragged them to another party. If only they'd gone to Tory's instead! Maybe things would be different.

But mostly they didn't talk about Teddy. They talked about school, what new albums were coming out, how Kram had hid-den a sensor chip in the sole of Delph's shoe to set off the Record Room's new security alarm. They brought things in paper bags—tapes, porn, cigarettes, candy bars, pot. They'd crack the window and smoke some together. When they climbed down the fire escape, fat Kram would pretend to get stuck in the window, trying to make Jude laugh. Then the Kramaro would roar away, fast as it could go.

She allowed him time. She didn't want to push. She left breakfast on his desk in the morning, toast and eggs he ate at some point, leaving the crusts behind as evidence, then walked to Ash Street, where she sat in front of her table from eight in the morning to eight at night, chain-smoking, reading the same page in her library book over and over again. The bookmark was a pamphlet on FAS. On the front was a picture of a pigtailed girl on a carousel. Jude had been a happy child, exuberantly, senselessly happy, but also gloomy, and unpredictably hostile, and strange. He bit, and he kicked, and he threw. At five or six, he'd brought to her in a shoe box a collection of gifts: a button, a toy truck, some coupons she'd clipped, the husk of a beetle. When she'd responded with inadequate awe, he'd given her a black eye. His fists were still pummeling when she lifted him by the armpits, his little legs wheeling, his face sopping with sweat. Where did this person come from? she'd thought. One of her drawing students, suspecting Les, had called in the domestic violence agency from Montpelier, and she'd had to swear up and down that her abuser was in kindergarten.

A week after he came home from the hospital, she sat on his bed and said, "Jude, honey? You're going to have to get back to school soon." She was rubbing his calf rapidly through the blanket, as though trying to start a fire. When she saw what she was doing, she put her hands in her lap. "You don't want to get too far behind."

Jude said nothing. He was wearing his headphones, she realized. He was lying on his side, facing the wall, his body entwined in the sour-smelling sheet. The only times she'd heard him leave the room all week were when he crossed the hall to the bathroom, and evidently it hadn't been to take a shower.

The next morning she came into his room before the sun rose. "Come on, babe, I started the shower." She made the mistake of sitting on his bed, sighing loudly, and slapping him—tap, tap—on the bottom.

Into the pillow, he said, "I'm not fucking going. Ever."

"Jude," she warned, reaching to slip his earphones from his ears.

He spun around at her so fast she flinched. His eyes were distant and glazed, but they burned right through her. It was seven o'clock in the morning.

"You're stoned," she said, more to herself than to him. Of course he was. Why wouldn't he be? What else were Delph and Kram bringing him in those paper bags?

That afternoon she listened for the jangle of the fire escape as they left his room, and then leaned into the passenger side window of Kram's car as it was about to drive away.

"I know you think you're helping, boys. I appreciate it, I do. But if you help him anymore, I don't think he's ever going to get out of bed."

They hung their heads, nodded at the dashboard. Nobody felt compelled to look anybody else in the eye, and she was glad.

And then there was Prudence, crawling onto and across Harriet's bed, skulking in her nightgown like that clingy old cat of theirs, depositing her sullen head on her mother's breast. Harriet spread her open book across her lap, removed her glasses, ashed her cigarette, and kissed the part in Prudence's hair. "What is it, babe?"

"When's Jude going back to school?"

Every day that Jude missed school, the attendance office called with a recorded message. Two of his teachers had called. The principal, whom Harriet had had the pleasure of meeting several times before the funeral, had sent a letter, asking Harriet to come in for a conference, which she did, not bothering to take off her coat. She could feel the disapproval steaming off of him, just as it always had, dressed up in courtesies. She thanked him for his patience. Her son just needed a little more time.

"He just needs a little more time," she told Prudence.

"How much time?"

"Pru, stop it with the baby voice. Talk to me normal."

"How—much—time?" Prudence sassed, propping her head up on her hand.

"Your brother's sixteen now. If he wants to drop out, there's not much we can do about it."

With her finger Prudence traced one of the diamonds on the faded patchwork quilt. "People are saying he dropped out, and *I* don't even know if it's true."

Harriet ashed her cigarette again in the ashtray on the night-stand. "People will say all sorts of things."

"Someone said Teddy killed himself. He didn't, did he?"

"Of course not."

"And Rachael said someone said *Jude* killed him, that the drugs were all his idea."

Harriet put her cigarette to her lips, then removed it. "How can that be true," she asked, "if Teddy killed himself? Which is it?"

Prudence sighed. "You shouldn't smoke in bed."

"You shouldn't tell your mother what to do."

It irritated Harriet and comforted her, the persistent morality of her secondborn. She, too, had been named for a Beatles song, a fanciful name given by fanciful parents (but it was a good song!) who couldn't have known how apt it would grow to be.

She had a funny thought: if she had a spouse, it was Prudence. Prudence was the one who shared the worry about their Jude. But now Prudence had surprised her. She would have expected her daughter to be the one to intervene with Jude, to try to speak some sense into him, but Pru was as apprehensive around Jude as Harriet was, hovering at his door but never daring to knock. As far as Harriet knew, she had not laid eyes on her brother since he'd returned home.

What were they so afraid of? He was just a teenage boy.

The next evening, the first evening his friends didn't come, Harriet brought dinner to his room—macaroni and cheese with sliced hot dogs—and took her seat on the bunk bed. He was lying on his stomach, facing her. No headphones, but his eyes were closed. "Jude, hi," she said, as though she'd just been passing through the hall and decided to drop in. "Look, I'm not going to bug you about going back to school. I know you'll go back when you're ready." His eyes remained closed. "I just want to tell you that, if you need medicine, we can get it for you. If you need to talk to someone, someone professional, you can do that, too. If you're not taking your Ritalin, we can—"

Jude emitted a long, painstaking groan, intended to obscure her voice.

"Jude, they've got drugs for depression now. All kinds of things."

A louder groan, flat, dispassionate.

"Jude, *Jesus*." She tapped him on the bottom again, as if to turn him off, and oddly, it worked. "I spoke to one of your doctors when we were at the hospital." She was looking at the pamphlet in her lap, speaking quickly. "She said your birth mother might have drank alcohol, drunk alcohol, while she was pregnant, and it could be the reason you've been having so many problems, and apparently it's fairly common. She said there are drugs for this kind of thing, you just have to get tested, and apparently the drugs are just *phenomenal.* . . ." She trailed off. She placed the pamphlet on the bed beside her and gave it a pat. The fact that she had a history of communicating to her son through pamphlets with titles such as *What Are Nocturnal Emissions?* did not make her cowardice any more bearable. Still staring into her lap, she didn't see her son's eye, the one not pressed to the pillow, peel open, slow as a budding flower, fix itself to the side of her face, and then close.

FIVE

Delph and Kram began to come separately, or not at all, and when Jude's stash ran out and the minutes were stinging and clear, the afternoons they didn't come were like open wounds. When they did come, they didn't bring pot. "That fruit will kill you, dude. You should keep the brain cells you have left." Delph said he'd run dry. He was actually thinking about giving the stuff up.

"I got money," Jude said, staring at the slats of the bunk above him, where Teddy had drawn a marijuana leaf with a pencil. Jude's father had built this bed.

"No you don't."

"I'll pay you later."

"You get your ass out of bed," Delph said, "and I'll think about it."

But the longer he stayed in bed, the harder getting his ass out of it was. Every point of his body that touched the mattress burned, no matter how much he tossed and turned. The tissue that made up his body no longer seemed to be muscle. His limbs felt like dead branches. He looked at the pale legs lying in front of him and wondered how they could be his, how his organs powered on, oblivious.

But that night, after Delph left, while his mother and sister were eating dinner downstairs, Jude swung his legs over the side of the bed. He walked past the bathroom and down the stairs, farther than he'd walked in a month. He took all twenty-eight dollars from the leather purse hanging on Prudence's doorknob. Then he got dressed, grabbed his Walkman, and descended the fire escape. It was easy to be quiet—his body was so feeble it could barely produce a sound. Being outside was like being on Mars. The dark itself felt bright. He could smell everything: the sweet and sour Panda Palace, the methane of Dairy Road dung. A styrofoam cup whispered across the slushy street, following him.

It took him nearly two hours to find Hippie. He was smoking a cigarette in front of Birkenjacque's, his dog hanging off a leash.

"Weren't you the guy who threw a pool stick at me on New Year's Eve?" Hippie didn't entirely remember. He just remembered seeing Tory whip that belt out—*whoa*. "I had no part of that, by the way. Hippie's a lover, not a fighter."

"No hard feelings," Jude said, showing Hippie his money.

"Is it your friend that OD'd?" Hippie asked.

It was his curiosity on this point, Jude suspected, that softened him. Hippie gave him a cigarette, and they walked to his apartment on Sunset Court, a room over a garage on the lake, the moon shining oily white on the water. Jude bought a bag and Hippie threw in some papers and they shared a joint, sitting side by side on the couch, under a windshield-size silkscreen of Bob Marley, watching *Remington Steele*.

Sometime around one in the morning, as he climbed through his bedroom window from the fire escape, every muscle of his body aching, Jude heard a door open and restless footsteps cross the floor below. He knew it was the sound of relief—Jude had gone out into the world, and he had come back.

Still, there was no more money after that night. They kept it where he couldn't find it. That night, long after he heard the last door close, he tiptoed downstairs to Harriet's room. His mother and sister were asleep in her bed, Harriet flat on her back, Prudence curled on her side. Only their hair touched, the bronze ends lost in each other on their pillows. On the dresser was his mother's wallet, and in it was a single, soundless dime.

His thoughts had lingered on Eliza Urbanski, tripped across her, dragged their feet, and he had hurried them past, out of her reach, out of an unconscious respect for Teddy: she didn't belong in the mourning of his friend. But now, sober, his head as clear as an empty fishbowl—he had finished off Hippie's bag in two days—Jude couldn't keep her out. He saw her red mouth, the spiderweb tear in the knee of her tights. He saw her standing over him with Teddy, elbow to elbow, silent as repentant children. Fucked up on something, fucked up in a way neither Teddy nor Jude had been before. Cocaine, someone told him later. (His mother? A cop?) No one knew whether it was the cocaine that killed him, if the huffing alone would have been enough to stop his heart. No one knew anything.

Looking for you, Teddy had said when Jude had asked where he'd been that night. Teddy was doing cocaine, and maybe he was with Eliza, or maybe Eliza knew where he'd gotten it, or maybe she didn't. If she was lying, she wasn't the only one. *Looking for you,* he'd said.

He was too sober to sleep. He played Duck Hunt on his Nintendo, leaning on his elbows at the foot of the top bunk, Teddy's bunk, the dark room silver in the light of the black-and-white screen. By the time he finally drifted off, his brain was full of arcade dreams, the gray shapes still playing behind his eyes. He counted the raining ducks like sheep.

Two days after the pot ran out, Jude woke up to an empty house, put on his headphones and his hooded sweatshirt, and skated unsteadily back to Hippie's apartment. No one answered his knock. He looked around for something to open the door with, found a plastic ice scraper stabbed in the snow, and for several minutes rattled its edge in the keyhole uselessly before giving up and hunting for a spare key—under the mat, in the mailbox, on the window ledge, and finally in the wooden birdhouse, where it was entombed in snow.

Inside, the place was dead still. He opened cupboards, closets, drawers, rattled around the contents of the kitchen trash. In the bedroom, a mangy dog lounged across the bed, eyeing Jude with a restless boredom. When Jude approached, the dog didn't move. Jude whispered, "You're not a very good guard dog, are you?" The dog—was it a girl dog?—raised her eyebrows. Were they eyebrows? "Or are you a good dog?" he asked her, his voice strangely high. "You know I'm good?" He placed a tentative hand on her head. He could feel the grit of dirt in her fur, the bony shape of her skull. He worked his hand into the mass of her neck, her long, tight belly, smooth as the curve of a guitar. For a few minutes he lay down on the bed beside her, his arm looped around her warm body, feeling her breathe, feeling his own body tingle and pulse.

In the closet were overalls and lumberjack flannels, Birkenstocks and boots. Under the bed he found sleeping bags, a hiking pack; on the dresser was an envelope of photographs. "Where does he keep it, girl? Huh?" Most of the pictures were of Hippie and his family at Christmas, Hippie in his Santa hat, people pulling ribbons off of gifts, but the last few in the roll were of a different party—a group of stoners raising peace signs. It was Tory Ventura's house. With a start Jude recognized an overexposed sliver of Teddy—eyes closed, midstride, his mouth forming a silent, careless word.

Jude folded the picture and put it in his wallet. Turning to go, as though it was what he had come for, he almost missed the bathroom. He ducked back in, opened the medicine cabinet, the shower curtain, and in a sealed bucket under the bathroom sink, found four gallon-size freezer bags, each packed full of pot. Jude pressed the cool plastic of one of them to his face. It smelled like a miracle. It was as big as a loaf of bread, probably half a pound. Hippie wouldn't miss one of them. He would miss it, but it was better than taking all of them. Jude skated home with the bag tucked in the pocket of his sweatshirt. He looked pregnant.

He was halfway inside his room, one leg on each side of the open window, the skateboard tossed in on the floor, when he saw that his mother was sitting on the bottom bunk of his bed. She had an issue of *Thrasher* open on her lap.

"Where were you?"

Jude sat straddling the windowsill, looking down into the alley, three stories below. His room had begun to secrete its own body odor. He closed his eyes, exhausted and weak. For a moment he thought he might throw up.

He felt himself sway, slip. When he opened his eyes, his mother had caught him by the hood. She helped him swing his leg over the sill and slide down to the floor.

"What happened to you? Where'd you go?" She closed the window against the cold. "I'm glad you're getting out." She gathered her skirt and squatted down beside him. The handkerchief in her hair and the moccasins on her feet made her look as though she were foraging for food in the wilderness, or coaxing an animal out of hiding. "But you're not strong enough to climb up and down that fire escape. What *is* that?" She came closer, knelt in front of him, and raised a hand toward Jude's belly. With a force that surprised them both, he smacked her hand away. She fell back on her heels and sat staring at him for a few seconds, wide-eyed with shock. Then she stood up and hurried out of the room.

He hid the stash as Harriet would, nesting it inside a jacket, then inside his backpack, then under the bed. Then he went to the bathroom and stepped into the shower, but the water hurt his skin too much to stand under it. He sat on the floor of the shower, leaning his head against the tile, half sleeping in the steam.

When he returned to his bedroom, he found that his bed— both bunks—had been made. Lying atop the fresh sheets of the bottom one was the plastic bag. Except for a glaze of fine, green dust, it was empty.

Delph came over the next evening. He did not bring pot. "Guess who came into the store today." He sat leaning forward in the desk chair, his elbows on his knees, rubbing his palms together. "Hippie." He'd been looking for Jude, Delph said—did he know where he was? "I'll hand it to you, dude—you have some balls."

"What'd you tell him?"

"That there was no way a trustworthy guy like Jude Keffy-Horn would have swiped his weed."

"Thanks," Jude said.

"No sweat. But you know what this means. Tory won't be far behind." Delph looked at his hands. "You know better than anyone that you don't want to piss off Salvatore Ventura." Jude could see he was struggling. Delph didn't want to get involved in Jude's problems, but because he'd left Jude and Teddy hanging at Tory's party, he already was. "I'd lay low for a while. That's all I'm saying."

Delph left it at that, climbed out the window and down the fire escape, and when Jude woke up the next morning, his mother was outside the window, standing on the same landing. She was fastening to the railing of the fire escape what seemed to be a padlock, which was looped through what seemed to be a chain, which was looped, tight as a fishing line, through the handle at the bottom of the window. Jude watched her through the glass. "It's for your own good," she called, her voice nearly swallowed up by the wind outside. "And don't you dare try to break the glass! You'll bleed to death."

Jude suspected his mother wanted not only to lock him in but also to lock others out, and through the teeth of his anger, he was grateful. Should Hippie or Tory or one of their comrades pay him a visit, Jude would be bolted safely inside.

He stared at the belly of the top bunk. He was so sober he could feel every particle of his fear, as distinct as the hair on his arms.

So when a man appeared at the same window several days later, Jude thought he might be hallucinating, a trick of a mind gone unstimulated for too long. He was listening to *Wasted . . . Again* on the stereo and playing Mario, the cord stretched up to the top bunk. A sound like a key in a door fluttered in his ear, then a series of minor crashes across the fire escape. Jude turned drowsily around, and as he watched a person climb through the window, the game control slipped out of his hands and off the bunk, then clattered to the floor. It was snowing outside, a soft, steady snow, and when the man emerged fully in the bedroom, there were snowflakes in his beard, crystalline, whole. He was wearing a pair of Carhartt's, a white linen shirt, a lined denim jacket, and a New York Yankees cap. Only when Jude saw the shadowed eyes beneath its brim did he recognize the man as his father.

"Sorry," said Les, blinking away the snow. "Didn't mean to alarm you." He held up a key in one hand and the wet padlock in the other. "Your mother sent it to me."

Jude sat straight up in bed, his head almost grazing the ceiling. "What are you doing here?" His heart was slowing, relieved—he'd been certain that the person at the window had been sent by Hippie.

"Kidnapping you," Les answered, dancing his fingers in the

air. "I've come to take you away from this suicide trap they call a town." He took off his hat and shook the snow from it, revealing a crown of matted hair, cut short now, and a glossy bald spot. He smelled of cigarette smoke. "Don't tell the girls I'm here yet, okay? I want a few minutes with you first, man-to-man. Man-to-crazed-teenager." He looked around the big, unlit room, at the wool rug, the yellow bean bag chair, the unmade bunks with their pillows kicked to the floor. He approached the poster hanging over the desk—H.R. of the Bad Brains, life-size, dreadlocked— and sized him up. Months ago Teddy had stabbed a cigarette in H.R.'s mouth, but last week, in a moment of desperation, Jude had reclaimed it, and now there was a hole there. The cigarette had tasted like sawdust. On the desk Les set down the lock and key, and turned on the metal desk lamp, illuminating the tapes and records scattered across the floor. The unspooled tape from one of the cassettes lay tangled on the rug. "Turn this stuff off, can we?"

Jude said nothing. In addition to Black Flag, the Nintendo music was still playing. Mario had fallen off a cliff and the black GAME OVER screen was flashing.

"I'm sorry," Les said. "Do I have the right bedroom?" He lowered the volume on the stereo himself, then walked over to the TV— he knew right where the button was—and snapped it off. "She said you weren't talking, but Christ. You dropped your thing," he said, picking up the game controller and handing it up to Jude.

"You look different," Jude said. He didn't extend his hand. Les put the controller on the bed. "You're bald."

"Yeah, well, you look a little different, too. What's with the hair?"

Jude put a hand to his mangled locks. He'd forgotten he had hair.

Les was shrugging out of his wet clothes, his head bent to his waist, tossing them on the rug in a soggy pile. "You got some dry clothes your old man could borrow?"

Naked to his underwear, Jude's father was goose-bumped and hairy. He had wide, square shoulders and a long torso, kidney-shaped love handles hanging over the waist of a pair of red briefs. His arms were white and meaty, his legs football-coach stout. Jude recognized the lightning-shaped scar on his ankle, the one he'd had since he nicked himself with a chain saw, barefoot, while slicing their bathtub couch in half. Grudgingly, Jude eased down from the top bunk and went to his dresser. He found his navy blue sweatshirt, the one with the pocket he'd hidden the pot in, and a matching pair of sweatpants. He held them out to his father.

"So, I hear you've been stealing large amounts of illegal drugs." Les stepped into the pants, almost losing his balance, and after sniffing the sweatshirt, pulled it over his head. "You making a habit out of that?" His hair was sticking up like Jude's now.

"Not really," Jude said, climbing back up to the top bunk.

"That's good." Les sank into the bean bag chair in the corner. It made a sound like a ball deflating, swallowing him up. "Smoking pot is one thing. Stealing it is another. I'm very sorry about your friend Teddy."

Jude crawled back under the covers and pulled them tight to his chin. "Why?" he said to the ceiling. "You didn't know him."

"I've met his brother," Les said, and Jude remembered with reluctance that it was Les who had paid for the funeral, who had lent Johnny his van.

They were both quiet for a while. On the record player, the last song ended, and the arm crossed back to its resting pose. When Jude looked down at his father, his knees were spread wide and the crook of his elbow was covering his eyes. Was he sleeping?

"Why didn't you just come in the front door? Why'd Mom send you the key?"

Les let his arm drop to his lap. His gray eyes were small and glazed. He was exhausted, or high, or both. "For safekeeping," he answered. "She was afraid she'd break down and unlock you."

It was February. Black History Month, the Winter Olympics, Valentine's Day carnations sold in the cafeteria for a dollar apiece. Prudence had no valentine, but she had long entertained the notion, as far-fetched as she knew it was, that her father might return, and that he'd bring her flowers—an offering, an apology.

But when he appeared in the kitchen one day, he was carrying only a pair of shoes, as though he were curious what was in the fridge. Her mother had warned her he was coming—her parents had agreed it was best that Jude live with his dad for a while—but still it stung that Les had come to see her brother, not her. Jude, the adopted one, had always found a way to hijack the attention of his parents and the sympathy of strangers. No one seemed to remember that Les had abandoned her, too.

"How's it going, Lester?" she asked, with the theatrical boredom she'd practiced.

Les, unruffled, said, "Asi, asi," seesawing his hand. "How you doing, kid?"

Prudence put her hands out in front of her, as if doing push-ups against a wall, and pumped her arms twice.

"What's that, sign language? What's it mean?"

"Awesome."

She let him plant a scratchy kiss on her forehead. Then he put on his shoes and said he was going to round up some dinner.

"He's here," Prudence told her mother, opening her bedroom door without knocking. Her mother, who already knew, who also had been listening all day for the sound of the van, nodded but didn't look up from her book. "Why does Jude get to go to New York?"

"Do you want to go, too?"

"With Dad? No."

Prudence stood, studying her mother, whose socked feet were propped up on a pillow. Her cigarette hung over the ashtray, smoldering. This was the bed her parents had slept in. This is where they'd made Prudence. Prudence, visited by nightmares, had climbed into this bed a thousand times, pressed between her parents' warm bodies.

"Are you wearing my blue eye shadow?"

"No," said her mother.

"He's pretty bald," Prudence pointed out.

At this, Harriet raised both eyebrows, but still her eyes hung on the page.

When Les returned from his errand, he brought with him a cardboard carton of milk shakes and a bag of Al's French Frys that smelled strongly of cheeseburgers. He dragged the bean bag chair to the middle of Jude's room and turned on the Nintendo. With the fingers of one hand he played the buttons of the control pad like a keyboard, the other hand retrieving fries from the bag.

"Make yourself at home," Jude said, taking a seat beside him on the rug. He took the controller out of his father's hand and started playing, sending Mario leaping across the screen.

"Do you know there's a Kmart on Garden Boulevard? And all these gas stations. I barely recognize this town. It looks like Disney World."

In the reflection of the TV, Jude could see the two of them, the shiny blocks of their distorted foreheads.

"So that's how you do it," Les said, his mouth full. "Very nice. How do you make him jump?"

"A," Jude couldn't help answering. "The red button."

"And B?"

"Makes you go fast."

Les nodded. "Want a cheeseburger?"

Jude said no, even though he did.

"I got one for your sister. Her favorite."

"She doesn't like them anymore," Jude said. "She mostly eats salads and stuff."

"What for? Is she a vegetarian?"

"I don't know."

"She's not having sex, is she?"

Jude fumbled with the controls, tripping over a turtle. "Definitely not," he said.

"I need your help with this one," Les said, sucking a sticky finger. "Do I try to talk to her, or do I give her some space?"

"Who? Prudence or Mom?"

"Prudence," Les said, waving his hand.

Jude thought about it, zipping through the clouds, through strings of musical coins. "You could ask her to come with us to New York," he said. He hadn't agreed to anything himself. He was considering his options. If he lived with his father, he would have to avoid Teddy's brother. At the funeral, Jude had been too chicken-shit to approach Johnny. He had only stared at the back of his bald head, a numb sort of amazement strangling his guilt (how much the back of his head looked like Teddy's!).

But New York was a big city. If he stayed with his mother, Hippie and Tory would surely find him. Stealing pot wasn't a crime that could be reported to the police, but he did not want to find out what other punishments were in store. He did not want to end up in the hospital again. Plus, who was Jude going to get his pot from now? His father had pot. His father wanted Jude to live with him. So what if his mother had put him up to it? If he stayed here, his body would shrink and atrophy, like a limb in a cast.

"I don't know if there's anything for Prudence in New York," Les said. "She's sort of a small-town girl, isn't she?"

"Yeah," Jude admitted.

"She'd get swallowed up by New York. Besides—where would she sleep?"

"Where would *I* sleep?" Jude asked.

"In the loft," Les said. "Kind of like a bunk bed, with a ladder and everything. Only below you is the living room."

"Do you have cable?"

"Check," Les said. "No video games, though. You'll have to bring yours."

"Do I have to go to school?"

"'Fraid so, champ."

Champ. After Champlain's Loch Ness monster. He'd forgotten his dad called him that.

"Forget it, then," he said. "I'm not going to school."

Les blew his nose in a napkin, then tossed it across the room at the trash can. He missed. "All right, fine. New York public schools are dreadful, anyway. You'd be safer on the street. But you'll have to find some kind of gainful employment. And you have to promise not to tell your mother."

Jude pressed the pause button. "When are we leaving?"

"First thing in the morning. We've got to get out of this house. Can you feel the negative vibes in this place? That's what happens when you get more than one female under one roof. They all start bleeding on the same schedule." With effort, he stood up from the bean bag chair and stretched. "Get your stuff together. And get a shower and a shave, will you? You look really awful."

In the bathroom, Jude acquainted himself with the things he'd need on his trip, all of the essential items that belonged to him. His retainer case, Noxzema, deodorant. He stepped all the way into the shower this time, letting the warm water pelt his skin until the burning became uniform, sufferable. He shampooed with Prudence's pink, perfumey bottle, but it did nothing for his hair but work it into a tangled, fragrant nest. Standing in front of the steamy mirror, bath towel wrapped around his waist, he combed at it, knot by knot. Then, with the inside of his wrist, he cleared the steam from the mirror and put his face close to the glass.

He looked, of course, nothing like his father. He had never looked like anyone. That was why it had been such a shock to open the pamphlet his mother had left him—days later, bored out of his mind—and see the faces that looked like his. He had felt as though he were looking at a family photo album, brothers and sisters he didn't know he had. It had given him a chill. And yet he'd opened it again and again, waking up in the morning, in the middle of the night, brushing a finger over the wide path between his nose and mouth. He did so now, stroking each hair. He looked hard in the mirror. There were a lot of them. Thick, bristly, rust red hairs.

Teddy had started shaving not long before he died, had made a show of walking around with little kernels of bloody toilet paper stuck to his neck. Jude hadn't had anything to shave. But while he'd been sleeping away the last six weeks, his peach fuzz had gotten fuzzier. He ran a finger over his chin, across his cheeks, between his nipples, under his arms, untucked the towel from his waist— he was hairy as hell. From under the sink, he took one of his sis- ter's pink plastic razors, and from the shower, he took her shaving cream. This time he didn't fear the image that came, uninvited, to mind—Prudence standing naked, right here where he stood. Maybe it was because he'd finally caught up with her, or because he already sort of missed her, or because for once, luck had come to him, and not her. He slathered on the cream, uncapped the razor, and went slowly, sensibly about it. When he was done, his face was bleeding in three places, but he liked the burn of the hot water on his skin. His cheeks were as smooth as his sister's.

And then there was the hair on his head. When he combed at the knots again, tears came to his eyes. Another hunt under the sink and he found the rusty nail scissors, the ones that Prudence had hurled at his face, and with them he snipped away at the most hopeless of the kinks. Before long a heap of hair the size of a small red rodent had amassed in the bottom of the sink. One devil-lock-size clump fell heavily to the bath mat. What was left he lathered with shaving cream, the gel foaming white, his head flowery and cool. He circled the razor around his head in a ring, from his ears to the tip of his quite nicely shaped skull, until there was nothing left but scalp.

Then he stuck his head under the faucet, letting the warm water wash the hair down the drain. He looked in the mirror. He was round and pink, like a baby. A blue vein swam up his neck from his collarbone to his temple. He was tired and sweaty from the steam.

He took another shower, scouring himself with the fresh bar his mother had stocked in the soap dish. He remembered all the ways she'd looked after him—bringing him meals, folding his laundry, the pairs of socks curled up like snails. His father had never done those things for him. That was what was so strange about imagining Les with Johnny McNicholas, comforting him after Teddy died. Until now, clean and clearheaded, Jude hadn't thought that someone else might have needed taking care of.

SIX

The classrooms were cold, the buildings square, the grounds skirted by leafless bushes as stiff as coral. The teachers were overdressed. The kids were gloomy and skittish, with poor posture, aggrieved by their low PSAT scores. Eliza decided if she heard one more person say "I'm just not good at taking tests," she would hang herself. Every weekend she could, she took the train from Jersey an hour back to her mom's place in New York.

Perhaps because the curators of the school were accustomed to this breed of luckless, moneyed offspring—those plagued by attention deficit disorders and indiscreet drug habits—they were as surprised as Eliza herself that she was, *when she applied herself,* good at taking tests. She was good at reports and papers and presentations, a diorama of the Globe Theatre, with a square of tissue paper for each window, canary yellow. To say that she had lost herself in her studies would imply a surrender, an accident; she was lost, but she had lost herself willfully, as one does when being chased. Into each fluorescent classroom she leapt sharpened pencil first, into Western Civ and British Lit and Algebra II and Attic Greek, into the labyrinth of protasis and apodosis and second aorist subjunctive active and her favorite, the optative of wish:

May we be killing / kill the goat.
If only we may be killing / kill the goat.
I wish that we may be killing / kill the goat.

Cocaine had been until then purely recreational; only now did she understand its functional power. She stayed up late, long after lights-out, listening to the Buzzcocks on her headphones and studying flashcards by flashlight until her contacts burned her eyes; she woke early, read *The Canterbury Tales* in the dining hall over breakfast: a cinnamon-raisin bagel, dry. It was all she could get down. For her intramural, she swam lap after lap. That she had no friends was of help. She didn't bother making any. She was glad enough to be rid of the old ones. She sniffed around only enough to find some Izod who sold coke, which she cut in her dorm room on a Bakelite hand mirror while her roommate Shelby Divine was at squash practice or in the bathroom, or behind the sheet Shelby had hung on a clothesline between their beds, for privacy. The most skin Eliza had seen on Shelby was her wrists. "I'm not a lezzy, you know," Eliza said, the first time Shelby had disappeared behind the sheet in her bathrobe. "Oh, I know," Shelby had apologized. Shelby was from Charleston. She had a voice like sweet tea.

One evening late in January, as the two of them lay belly-down on their beds, the curtain drawn back, textbooks spread before them, Shelby asked, "Who's T.M.?"

On the front of her chem folder, Eliza had drawn a pulpy heart, stabbed with an arrow, Teddy's initials bleeding fatly inside. She slipped off her headphones. "Teddy," she said, surprising herself. "Teddy McNicholas." She hadn't spoken his name aloud before, and the peal it produced was more solid than the hollow sound that had tolled and tolled in her head.

"Is he your boyfriend?"

Shelby was wearing an ankle-length nightgown of virginal white and a spotless pair of socks. Eliza pressed her pencil into the seam of her open book. "Not exactly."

"Was he your first love?"

"Not exactly."

Shelby turned on her side. The bedsprings creaked. "Well, who is he?"

Eliza wished she had a cigarette to take a drag from now. She would send a cloud of smoke out into the black-and-white night, dense and full of meaning, interpretable.

"He's a boy who died," she said flatly, picking up her pencil, but there were real tears in her eyes, for she wasn't selfish, she wasn't unfeeling, she wasn't. But were the tears for Teddy, or for her? Were they for what she'd lost, or what she'd done?

She hadn't given a thought to the cocaine. She'd nearly forgotten about it—barely two lines apiece!—until the look Johnny had given her there at the edge of the park, the phone hanging limply in his hand, her nostrils burning in the cold.

Teddy was a big boy, she told herself. He could have said no.

If only he'd gotten on that train with her!

She had wanted to make something happen; she had asked for heartbreak and she'd gotten it. And it was bigger than anything in her life. She wanted to forget Teddy, and she wanted something to remember him by.

She was aware of this paradox in a subliminal way, and of Johnny's and Jude's part in it. She wanted to know them, too; she wanted to forget them. She tried hard to drown them out. She ignored the blank page of her underwear, didn't count the days, thought past and around and through them. If she occupied her brain—*If only we may be killing / kill the goat!*—she could think herself out of it. Because she couldn't be. There was no fucking way.

The thing was, no one in New York knew Teddy was dead, because no one in New York had known Teddy existed. New York was its own solar system. Maybe once Sid or Kevin had seen a letter hanging around, had said, "Hey, who's this from?" and Johnny'd said, "My kid brother." Maybe not. Maybe someone had said, "Hey, Johnny, you got any family?" And maybe Johnny, keeping it simple, had said, "Not really." He'd left Teddy with his mom so he could live with his dad, and after his dad went to jail, Johnny didn't go home. He was doing his own thing. He'd send Teddy a mix tape now and then, a subway token with the center cut out. Now the subway token was gone, who knew where.

Through January, into February, in Chuck Taylors and undershirt, over cracked sidewalks, under claws of elms, Johnny skated. He tried to get lost, make a maze of the city, turned north, then left, then right, then west, chased a bumper sticker, a blue jay, turned up the volume on his Walkman. Through both sides of Minor Threat's *Out of Step* and through both sides again, through paradise and slum, past falafel cart and flower shop and carriage ride, over cobblestone and manhole, past brownstone and mirrored steel, past Les Keffy's lavender Dodge van, on a different block each week, the parking tickets on the windshield faded and dried like autumn leaves, past the vacant, piss-stinking newsstand, past one building that had burned down, past another, past the dealers and the crackheads and the squeegee men, past every bum who knew his name, past every thug who'd stared him down, *Go ahead, asshole, kill me,* but no one did, and always when he stopped, lungs packed full, expelling white breath into the air, there would be the city, inexorable and vast, and a subway station that threatened to lead him home.

He skated to the river, to the bodega, to Venus or Sounds or Some Records or Bleecker Bob's, or Angelica Kitchen, or across the Williamsburg Bridge to the Hare Krishna temple in Brooklyn, to shows at CBGB, the Ritz, the Pyramid, the Limelight, Irving Plaza, ABC No Rio, Wetlands, Tramps, skating home in the dark bruised and frosty with sweat, standing under the showerhead until the water went cold. He did push-ups and sit-ups and chin-ups—up! up! up!—cleaned the minifridge, fed the cats, made the bed, made a pot of chamomile tea, teapot whistling on the hot plate, the space heater and the stereo and the tattoo machine, the mouth of the guy he was tattooing, staring down the needle for hours, at hair follicle and inky vein, busy busy busy, and the mouths of all the guys in his band, and all their amplifiers, as much noise as electronically possible without blowing the circuits, that was the trick.

Sometimes his skateboard would take him to the southern point of Manhattan, and he'd look out over the bay past the dollar-green Lady Liberty to the distant biscuit of Staten Island. Somewhere over there was the Arthur Kill Correctional Facility, where his father and uncle lived. Now that his mother had disappeared and his brother was dead, they were the only family he had left, but his father was dead to him, too, as dead as his mother had told him he was in the first place.

For his antiseptic lifestyle, plus the white T-shirt, bald head, and gold hoops, Johnny had been dubbed by his friends Mr. Clean. He hadn't had a drink or eaten meat or smoked a cigarette in almost two years. There was no reason to start now. The sannyasis at the Hare Krishna temple promised that renunciation of desires brought peace.

She chose a New Jersey town she'd never set foot in before, whose name she'd heard uttered only by the train conductor. Cissy's older sister had had one, and Eliza's own mother had had two. You called; you made an appointment. Eliza made the call from the hall phone in the dorm, cut swimming that afternoon, and walked from the station to a clinic in the corner lot of a Grand Union shopping center, next door to a travel agency. One of the clinic's store windows was shuttered with plywood; the miniblinds in the other were shut tight.

Inside the door, behind a chest-high counter, stood a security officer dressed in a blue shirt and tie, like a person who worked in a museum or airport. His mustache was tobacco stained like Les's, and his name tag said BILL T. He gave her a brisk nod, not quite looking at her, and made a motion with his hand—*C'mere*—that implied he wanted her to hand something over. A form of some sort? Her fake ID, also from her coke dealer, which put her at twenty-two?

"Your handbag, miss."

Eliza took off her headphones and tapped the bottom of the book bag hanging on her back. "I just have this."

"Let's see it, please."

To her left, framing the entrance into the office, stood what appeared to be a metal detector. Beyond it, the waiting room was nearly full. A dozen girls, black, white, Hispanic, all of them looking exactly fifteen, sat staring into magazines and clipboards, beside mothers or boyfriends or sisters, silent. She said, "It's just a backpack."

"You'll get it back directly, miss. Just need to take a look."

One of the girls, wearing a pinafore dress and Keds, was very pregnant. About three inches from her face she held a book with a plain red cover, titled in gold letters *You Can Live Forever in Paradise on Earth*. Eliza had been trying to keep Teddy out of her head, but now she couldn't help picturing him in heaven, a place she was pretty sure she didn't believe in, sending down a quizzical, disappointed look.

"I'm not—comfortable," she said, looking from the man to the girl, back to the man, "giving you, since I have some private things in here. Can I—"

"It's policy, miss."

"Okay." The girl flipped a page and rested an absent hand on her belly. "I'll leave it in the car." Before he could say anything, she turned around and pushed herself out the door, the chime ringing blandly behind her.

When she walked in the door of her mother's apartment on Riverside Drive, a cone of incense was burning on the coffee table beside a glass of blood-colored wine. Eliza's mother was perched on the divan, pumping a ThighMaster between her knees and talking on the cordless telephone. It was Friday evening. Neena's night off.

"All right, darling, she's here," she said and hung up. To Eliza, she said, "I thought you might be the delivery boy. I ordered from the Brazilian place." She glanced at the watch face on the inside of her wrist. "You're a little late."

Eliza slipped her keys into her backpack. "I missed the first train."

"Did you?" Her mother put the ThighMaster aside, picked up the wineglass, and padded across the wood floor in her ballet slippers to kiss Eliza between the eyes. "I just ordered some *feijoada,* with hearts of palm. I wasn't sure."

Eliza plucked the glass from her hand. "Can I have a sip?"

"You don't normally *ask*. How was your week?" Taking Eliza by the shoulders, she kissed her repeatedly on the forehead, pecking like a bird, while Eliza looked deeply into the pool of wine. When the kissing was over, Eliza put her lips tentatively to the glass and drank. "That was Les. Guess what. He's gone to Vermont, to fetch his son."

Eliza swallowed. "To *fetch* him?"

"Yes, to bring him here, to live with him for a while. I'm *so*—"

"Why?" said Eliza.

"Well, he's been having a difficult time. Of course he has. I think it'll be good for Les, don't you? And the son, I hope."

"When will he be here?"

"Tomorrow, I guess. If that vehicle will make it back."

"I'm going to start on some homework real quick."

"Oh, you had calls. Nadia and Cissy both called the other night—they said they've been trying to reach you at school."

"Okay. I'm going to real quick just start some algebra, while it's fresh."

"Darling?" Diane Urbanski had a pert, compact face, her eyes dark and round, eyebrows full, skin white as cream; she wore her black hair, always, in a French braid. Her grandparents had been Russian Jews. Together they had sailed to England from Murmansk, her grandmother pregnant with their only child, her grandfather fleeing the Great War. On the passage over, he died of the 1918 flu, and their daughter, Eliza's Babushka, never met him. "I'm happy you're making a fresh start," Diane said and smiled.

In her room, Eliza locked the door, took off her coat, turned on the stereo, and emptied her backpack on the bed—sweater, wallet, keys, books, makeup bag, which she also emptied, hands shaking as she dug through it, the lipstick and mascara and contacts case clicking as they fell, and the itty-bitty plastic bag dusted pink on the outside with a bit of stray rouge. She enclosed it in her hand and held it to her heart, which was racing. The security guard wouldn't have looked through her makeup bag. He wouldn't have found it. And what if he did? It wouldn't have been the first time she was caught with drugs. Why had she let him scare her away?

She dumped the cocaine on the glass nightstand, cut it into four pretty lines, and then, kneeling on the carpet, staring at it with such concentration she felt she might have an aneurysm like her father, that her brain might burst from uncertainty, she swept the powder onto the floor and collapsed crying across it, a soundless crying that hurt.

Something to remember him by. She wondered if this was how her great-grandmother had felt, sailing across the Arctic to a strange country, suddenly alone. Eliza was pregnant by a dead boy, and whatever was growing inside her felt dead, too.

As a brother, Johnny had been unreliable, usually in and out of the house, like their mother, usually high on something. Perhaps because of this, his memories of Teddy were disturbingly few, and without pattern. Traveling with their mother from motel to motel. Climbing the yellow tree behind their trailer in Delaware, where someone else's father had left a tree house. Locking him in the trunk of Delph's car. Walking him to the emergency room when Queen Bea was off somewhere, Johnny's T-shirt pressed to Teddy's bloody forehead, when he fell off the porch banister trying to do a rail slide. Johnny had slept in Teddy's bed with him that night, Teddy spooked and pretending not to miss their mom, the stitches through his brow bone as clumsy as shoelaces.

Most of his memories of Vermont did not have Teddy in them. Filling notebooks with band logos, supermen, marijuana leaves. Getting stoned before school in the Kramaro. Waking up hungover in the parking lot behind Birkenjacque's. He had always been careful to exclude Teddy from his fun, even after Teddy was running around with Jude, stealing their mothers' cigarettes—"Not yet, little man, get out of here"—but he, too, had huffed, he and Delph and Kram, from a gas can in Kram's garage. He had once been stopped by a cop north of town, high on ludes, driving along the lake in Queen Bea's Horizon without his lights on. "I'm practicing," was all he could think to say, and the cop had let him off with a warning. That was how lucky Johnny was.

That was what he thought of, what had kept him on the morning of the funeral from strangling Jude Keffy-Horn. *He's just a kid.* How many mornings, when Johnny was his age, could he have been the one to wake up dead?

A true sannyasi, he told himself, neither hates nor desires.

Johnny prided himself on his forbearance, his adaptability, on his skill in coexisting with all walks of life. In his neighborhood, it was a matter of survival. Before he had laid claim to it, or it to him, he had wandered into Tompkins Square Park one evening to get some sleep after his falling-down-drunk con of a father, whose couch he'd been sleeping on in Staten Island, had stolen all his money. That night in the park, his guitar case was stolen with all his clothes inside. The next day, he found the guy around the corner— the case still had the Bad Brains sticker on it—and Johnny picked it up and used it to break the guy's jaw. Turned out the guy was blind. Robbed by a blind guy. After that, Johnny watched his back. But rather than making him enemies, the incident had made him allies. He'd broken Blind Jack's jaw! Dude didn't mess around. They were all scraping by together.

But there had been other rituals of neighborhood hazing. He'd been robbed again, chased, roughed up to the point of need-ing stitches, which he didn't get, wearing the scars like tattoos. Compared to some, he was lucky. One night in Tompkins, he saw Rafael, one of the kids who turned tricks in the park, stumble out of the bathroom they called the comfort station soaked to the waist. Johnny kept walking, didn't offer his help. You didn't go in there, not if you weren't looking for something. He'd thought that some guys had just dunked him in a toilet, but Blind Jack told him later that Rafael had been raped, that some ladies from St. Mark's Church had taken him to the hospital to get stitched up. Johnny didn't see him again.

Then one night Johnny ended up at a straight edge show at CBGB, alone and falling-down drunk, and met a hardcore drummer named Rooster DeLuca, the first straight edge kid he'd ever known. That was the beginning of the end for him. In no time, Johnny was staying at Rooster's place, and Rooster had him hooked on the drug that was no drugs. Fuck the dealers, Rooster said, fuck the drunk drivers, fuck the frail-ass gutter punks with marks up their arms, fuck Robert Chambers and the prep school jocks with coke up their noses and their dicks in some crying girl.

At twenty-two, Rooster was hardly a kid. He lived on Avenue B, across the street from the park. He was built like a lumberjack— big, hammy shoulders, muscular legs—and he had a Brooklyn accent like a mouth full of chew. If he'd grown up in Lintonburg, he might have played football with Kram. But he'd grown up in Bensonhurst, and his only sport, other than skateboarding and stage diving, was running deliveries for his uncle's deli, driving around salami sandwiches on his BMX. To the milk crate bungee-corded to the handlebars he'd attached a cardboard sign that spelled out, in black electrician's tape, GO VEGAN. He'd gotten his name from the red Manic Panic Mohawk he'd sported back when CB's was barely open. Now he was as bald as Johnny—it helped in their neighborhood to look like a skinhead, and the tattoos helped, too. Johnny's earrings and Krishna beads did not, nor his new straight edge status. Dealers tried to bully him into buying and selling. "You too good for us, Mr. Clean?" Johnny winked and negotiated. When he got his own apartment, and then started tattooing, he offered them free work. When he and Rooster and a couple of other guys started a straight edge band called Army of One, and started getting good, and put out a record, people from the neighborhood came to their shows. Seeing those bums and drunks in the audience, wearing his band T-shirt, filled Johnny with a backward sort of pride.

Now when Johnny and Rooster walked the streets together, they got nods, they got waves. Johnny knew their names. Jerry the Peddler, Mary, Froggy. Jones, who was always jonesing. Blind Jack's friend Vinnie, who was going to die of AIDS any day. Soon enough Johnny's own nickname was spoken with as much affection as ridicule, and Johnny liked it. He liked the goulash of his neighborhood, the alphabet soup, the insults spoken in foreign tongues. He liked the steady comfort of the Missing Foundation—anarchists, guerrilla musicians, graffiti artists—and the territorial badges they sprayed across the Lower East Side, warning off the encroaching slumlords of the East Village. *$1500 Rent, your home is mine, 1988=1933.* It was said that the toppled martini glass meant *The party's over,* but Johnny liked to think of it as a symbol of sobriety, like the brave anomaly of the Temperance Fountain in the middle of Tent City. Faith, Hope, Charity, Temperance—like the lyrics to some straight edge song. He liked to think of his own role in the neighborhood as a force of benevolence. Not a missionary but a monk. He led by example.

So Jude Keffy-Horn? Johnny didn't know if he could forgive him, but he could tolerate him.

Jude was on his mind a lot as he walked these streets. His brother's best friend, the person who'd been with Teddy when he died. One February afternoon, Johnny hallucinated him. He was on his way to Astor Place to play laser tag on the subway when he spotted him, entranced by an arcade game in front of Gem Spa. Johnny stopped. Was it him? His head was shaved. He was taller. A frosty breeze shuttled down the block. A carousel of Oakley knockoffs spun. Across the street, a cigarette hanging from his mouth, yes, Jude was on a skateboard, but he was standing still.

SEVEN

They'd arrived just after dark, the Manhattan skyline a shadow through the van's windshield. They might have made better time had Les not insisted on pulling over to the side of I-87, upon learning that Jude had never driven a car, to give him a lesson. For nearly an hour Jude had maneuvered the Purple People Eater ineptly down the emergency lane, the vehicle flying out in front of him, then jerking to a stop, a sequence for which Les had an odd patience, as though they had all the time in the world here in this dimly lit pod, until finally Jude got the van into gear and stayed in the driver's seat until they had to stop for gas. It was a long drive, and both of them, exhausted, had gone to bed as soon as they were home.

Now, waking up from a deep sleep, Jude blinked his eyes at the ceiling, uncertain for several seconds where he was. He sat up and hung his legs over the ledge of the loft. From his point of view he could see the closet-size kitchen, the open door to the bathroom, and the living room, which consisted of a television on top of a barrel, a chest serving as a coffee table, and a futon, on which his father sat, packing the bowl of a glass bong. The place wasn't big enough to turn a skateboard around in. Through the tall window was a row of storefronts across the street—one sign said simply EAT—against a bright winter sky.

"This place is a shoe box," said Jude.

Les looked up. "It is indeed, but it's a rent-controlled shoe box. Got it years ago from a lady friend who went back to her husband. Left me the apartment and a cat. It died."

"Was it the lady friend you got pregnant and left your family for?"

Les took a deep hit—he used a barbecue lighter to light the bowl—and savored the smoke for a moment. He was wearing a long, twill nightshirt, steel blue with white piping at the collar and sleeves, and a pair of ancient leather slippers. Also his Yankees cap. So long ago had his father confided in him, so silent was his family on the subject of Les's betrayal, that Jude was no longer sure he hadn't made it up. At some point he had learned, perhaps through osmosis, that Ingrid Donahoe, who had salvaged her own marriage, had ended up having an abortion.

"It was not. It was another lady friend, after. Before I met the lady friend I have now. Come down and join me."

Jude climbed down from the loft, every muscle still sore. He took a seat beside his father on top of a knit blanket and pillow. "You slept here last night?" Gratefully he took the bong and, with the barbecue lighter, fired it up. It had been a few days. It hit him hard.

"You can see why Eliza's mother doesn't spend much time here. It's my master plan. If you're going to bring a woman home, make it *her* home. That's a good rule in general, but especially considering the size of this place. You okay?"

Jude was coughing like an amateur.

"Am I making you nervous with the girl talk? Listen, you're going to see a lot more girls with that new haircut of yours."

"You like it?" Jude rubbed his head, then his chin, a habit he'd picked up in the last thirty-six hours. He'd sprouted some bristle.

"No, I mean you'll actually be able to *see* them, without all that hair in your eyes. Do you see the positive influence I'm having on you already? I thought your mother was going to kiss my feet when she saw you."

"It wasn't you. My hair was all"—he coughed again—"knotty."

"Take it easy, champ." Les gave Jude's back a few slaps. "You haven't tried reefer till you've tried Uncle Lester's reefer. Do you know what today is?"

Jude took another hit. "Saturday?"

"Monday. The fifteenth. Distribution day." He looked at the clock on the wall. "In exactly five minutes, my first guy will be here for a pickup. They come one by one. Six guys in six hours, twice a month, in and out, clean as can be. Don't even have to leave the apartment." He lit a cigarette. "This business is a science, like anything else. You have to have a schedule. You have to have rules. So, like us."

"What?"

"This new arrangement. There's some other matters to discuss."

"Like what?"

"Like I snore. I move my bowels from six-fifteen to six-thirty-five every morning. And I own a handgun."

"Does it shoot?"

"That's what they do, champ. It's in a case under the kitchen sink. A thirty-eight special. I call it McQueen. Don't touch it unless I tell you to, in which case it's loaded, so watch out."

"Why would you tell me to?"

Les gave an I-know-nothing shrug. "Also, there's the matter of a curfew."

"Great," said Jude, but when he thought about it, his brain stretching the word, softening it—was his dad's shit that good?— it seemed a shiny fragment of adult vocabulary, somehow allur- ing. He'd never had a curfew before. Delph and Kram did. "When is it?"

Outside the window, a bird flickered on a tree branch. A bird in New York. All his life Jude had seen the same birds, and this one— he'd never seen it before. It was an amazement. When he thought about walking downstairs and outside into the daylight it was diffi- cult to control his nerves. "Well," Les said, "if you can demonstrate that you're in possession of your faculties, if you return eventually from wherever it is you're going, which proves you can remember where you live, if you're wearing the same clothes you went out in, if you can continue to convince me, *Hey, Dad, I'm just a kid having fun, I drank a beer at the Centre Pub, or what have you, but I don't have a knife sticking out of my stomach*—then I'm willing to forgo a curfew."

"Did Mom say that was okay?"

Les stood, put out his cigarette, picked up the blanket, and began sloppily to fold it. "It doesn't matter what your mother thinks. Look, I know she has serious concerns about you staying here. I can't blame her. Would you help me with this thing?" Jude stood up and took two corners of the blanket. "Put it this way. If you don't get into trouble, your mother doesn't have to know about it. Now, we happen to have different definitions of trouble. Your mom wants me to be a rehab clinic for you, man, but come on, you've got a liking for this stuff I can dig." Jude matched one of his corners to the other. "But I happen to have a classy operation here that could get screwed up overnight if, you know, Officer Friendly started sniff- ing around. Which means if I catch you stealing a candy bar, you're going straight back to the Green Mountain State. Understand?" Like dancers, they stepped toward each other, the blanket dipping between them. Les took it, folded it in half, and stuffed it and the pillow inside the coffee table/chest.

Then he led Jude through the closet under the loft—through coats and dry-cleaning bags, his old dashiki—to a padlocked door. Jude never would have known it was there. "Voilà," Les said, spinning the combination, and opened it onto another closet, walk-in size. The smell hit Jude like whiplash. He hadn't smelled marijuana like this since his father's greenhouse, and the memory of that place, mixed with the heavenly bouquet of free-flowing drugs, produced in him a strange quickening. The walls of the closet were lined with shelves, which were lined with plants, which were green and farmy and rich, their leaves crawling with flowers like lavender caterpillars, the sodium bulbs beaming lovingly upon them.

From behind them, muffled through the closet, the buzzer rang. "What'd I tell you?" Les said. He picked up one of the five-gallon buckets, then closed the door and locked it, and they shoved through the hanging clothes back out into the apartment. Les pressed the intercom button by the front door, and a voice said, "Trick or treat. It's Davis." Les buzzed him in, and a moment later, someone could be heard clunking up the stairs and then panting into the apartment, in a ski cap and a red leather jacket, trailing frosty air. He called Jude's father *my man* and flashed a gold tooth when Les introduced him. Jude could count the number of black people he'd had a conversation with on one hand. There were two black kids at his high school in Vermont, and both of their parents were professors.

"I didn't know you had a kid, man. He's a little man himself." Davis asked Jude what was hanging and said he looked like his dad. Les winked at Jude and said thanks. He said that Jude had come to stay with him to experience some of his world-famous Purple Haze.

"I was just going to tell Jude that this is the only stuff on the market worth smoking." Les sat down on a kitchen stool. "Would you agree, Davis?"

Davis nodded heartily, resting a foot on the bucket of pot. "Premium stuff."

"Jude got in a little trouble up north. Too much of a good thing, if you know what I mean."

"I hear you."

"What my thinking is, is the key to enjoying reefer is moderation. You know what I'm saying, Davis—you're a moderate fellow, aren't you?"

"You know I am, man."

"You're a smart guy," Les said, crossing his legs, ankle to knee. "You've got a day job. Have I ever seen you on the steps next door with a needle in your arm?"

Davis said he hadn't been over there in years.

"Let's be realistic," said Les. "A fifteen-year-old kid in New York—"

"Sixteen."

"—he's going to find some fruit if he wants it, no matter how much Mommy and Daddy say no. And when he does, you don't want him getting shwag from some Joe in Tompkins."

Davis admitted he used to buy from one of those guys. A guy who carried a grenade in the pocket of his trench coat.

"So I can't tell my kid not to smoke reefer," Les said. "But I can tell him not to smoke *other people's* reefer." One of his slippers was dangling from a white, veiny foot. "My stuff's safe. It's robust. It's cut with nothing but love. And it won't get you arrested or dead."

"Is it free?" Jude asked, rubbing his head.

Davis laughed and started counting out his cash. "A smart-ass," he said. "Like his pop."

Before, when Jude had allowed himself to imagine the city of his birth, he'd pictured it the way he'd pictured faraway capitals like London or Berlin—wide gray sidewalks choked with adults in long coats, with leather briefcases and good haircuts, no children in sight. They might as well have spoken a foreign language. It was the New York he'd seen in the pages of a social studies textbook—a woman with a mild-mannered Afro waiting for a bus, smiling at her newspaper. In the caption was the word *commute*.

In the stories that had been passed from Johnny to Teddy to Jude, fun in New York came in pockets—an underground tattoo parlor, a bar fight with nunchucks. The hardware of Jude's and Teddy's fantasies all surrounded a shadowy, borderless colony called the Lower East Side, the graffitied place where kids zipped by on their skateboards, too fast to see. Jude had known he wanted to find that place.

So when he got there and found out that *there* was practically on his doorstep, that his father's apartment on St. Mark's Place was a Chinese-star throw from the Lower East Side, he was both elated and wary. He wasn't used to this kind of luck. A day didn't pass when Jude didn't see a Mohawk. Mostly the Mohawks hung out in front of Sounds, the record store with the neon sign humming in the window. Jude knew this because, the first week he lived in New York, that was mostly where he hung out, too, burning through packs of cigarettes. When he wasn't there, he was in front of Enz or Manic Panic, looking at all the leather in the windows. Once he saw Keith Richards or someone who looked very much like him walk his dog out of Trash and Vaudeville. Otherwise, he was at Gem Spa, buying lottery tickets or cigarettes or beer (all of which, to his astonishment, he could buy if he said they were for his dad), or playing one of their sidewalk arcade games (Paper Boy was his favorite—when you rode your bike too slow, you got attacked by bees) or drinking a delicious beverage called an egg cream. There were also games at the Greek place at the Third Avenue end of the street—they had Tetris, as well as hot, dripping gyros served so fast they smoked while you ate them. And the video games at the Smoke Shop, which

Jude thought of as the Smoke Sho, since the *p* no longer lit up, were inside, which was good when it snowed. The Pakistani couple that owned the place gave him change for a dollar, smiling crookedly and calling him *my friend*.

You couldn't say it wasn't a friendly street.

There was the woman standing outside the St. Marks Hotel. Dark-lashed, peroxide blond, in an acid-washed jean jacket, she placed one of her leg-warmered ankles in Jude's path. "You need a smoke, honey?" He'd finished the first cigarette and had started the second, chatting amiably with her about Vermont, a place she'd never been—"It's quiet," he said, struggling for the right word, "and cold"—when she took a step toward him, so that the zippers of their jackets kissed. While studying her face from this proximity (his brain was slowed by pot, he couldn't be blamed), he began to suspect that a woman like this did not talk to a boy like Jude for free. He thanked her for the cigarettes, called her "ma'am," tripped on a shoelace as he turned to walk away.

There was the guy in the Coca-Cola sweatshirt, walking up and down the block, singing, "Whatchyou need? Whatchyou need?" He wore another sweatshirt underneath, hood up, and he took big, loping steps, as though about to bounce into a run at any time. He bounced directly into Jude, clapped him on the shoulder. "Whatchyou need, my man?"

"Nothing. I was just—"

The guy spun away, had a place to be. He walked backward down the street, pointing at Jude. "You know me, man. I'm here."

After a few days, Jude learned to keep his head down. He bought a cone at the Korean ice cream shop downstairs, trying a new flavor each time, and then he walked back and forth, up one sidewalk and down the other, listening to the melody of Spanish and something like Russian floating on the cold air, over car horns and boom boxes and backing-up trucks. (Two or three times, at night in the loft, Jude thought he heard gunshots. "A truck backing up," his father would say. "Go back to sleep.") Jude walked past the punks, the bums, the Hare Krishnas, past the Italian restaurant where a body had been discovered in the Dumpster out back, past the rehab center next door, a beaten-up warehouse where people attended AA and NA meetings on the first floor and then spent the rest of the day shooting up on the stairs in front of the building. On each of the orange steps was a verse of the black stenciled warning NO DRINKING, NO SMOKING, NO POT SMOKING. He'd never seen anyone shoot up before. Often they fell asleep, their bare, mottled arms flung across the steps.

There were days when he thought this street might be his future. Getting high with his dad in the morning, chain-smoking, giggling at the news—the Supreme Court ruling against Jerry Falwell, Mayor Koch calling Reagan a wimp in the War on Drugs. A wimp! "You wimp!" they called each other for the rest of the day. Besides his father (and his mother, who had called to make sure he hadn't run away), he talked only to strangers. When he had the energy, he did a few push-ups, trying to gain back his strength.

Some weekend, Les said, when Eliza was home from boarding school, they'd go up to Di's for dinner. Les didn't ask Jude about Teddy or Eliza or Johnny, or what had happened that night; he didn't talk about school or a job; he didn't ask Jude to do anything he didn't want to do. Whether this was out of respect for Jude's fragile state or because it didn't occur to him to do so, Jude could not be sure.

Whatchyou need, my man? For days afterward, the question turned over in Jude's baked brain. He imagined the hooker's red mouth, the silk of her baby-doll hair, the sublime dilapidation of a room inside the St. Marks Hotel. He imagined the uncharted highs of some powder or serum or plant, the crinkle and weight of a plastic bag in the hand. Why the fuck had he said no? From his father, he already had a generous supply of marijuana, and money to buy whatever other vices he desired. He had only to decide what.

After a week in New York, bored and stoned and brave, he ventured eastward, toward the place he understood to be Alphabet City. Somewhere over here lived Johnny McNicholas. Wind whistled through empty windows. Bums lay mummified in doorways. When he paused to admire the two stone-faced buildings from the album cover of *Physical Graffiti,* two men across the street watched him from a set of steps. Jude kept walking, trying to keep his eyes down, noting the artifacts of the gutter. Cigarette butts. An island of snow impaled by a syringe. When he reached Tompkins Square Park, a square of land so unparklike, so like a cemetery of living dead, he turned immediately around. His dad's block was scary enough.

"Where you going, amigo?"

The two men he'd passed before crossed the street toward him. One had his hands deep in the pockets of his coat, a posture that Jude was learning to fear. The other was sipping from a bottle in a brown bag and staring at Jude with a single, yellowy eye. The lid of the other was sealed like an envelope. Jude couldn't help staring back. Before he could move, the first guy stepped up to him and patted him down. He dipped his hand into Jude's jacket pocket, withdrew his Walkman, and, tugging at the wire, whipped the headphones off Jude's head. From one of the back pockets of Jude's jeans, he removed his wallet; from the other, a pack of cigarettes. The Misfits' *Walk Among Us* was still playing distantly. The guy ejected the tape, glanced at it, and handed it back to Jude. "You can keep this," he said and winked.

This little tango, from beginning to end, took no more than ten seconds, and the swift, shrewd incursion of another person's body recalled the beery breath of Tory Ventura. But Tory wouldn't have bothered to pat Jude down. Only later did it occur to him that the guy had been checking for a weapon.

He'd had the foresight to remove the picture of Teddy from his wallet, to hide it among his father's books. Forty or fifty of his father's dollars—money he would have blown on the temptations of St. Mark's—was all that was stolen from him. Who did he have to tell about girls and drugs, anyway? Whatever Teddy could reply, from Les's dusty shelf, would come with the narrow-eyed disapproval of the dead.

And Jude was glad for a reason to stay away from Alphabet City. What he wanted he couldn't buy on the street, and even more than hookers and dealers and bad-ass, one-eyed Puerto Ricans, he feared Johnny McNicholas.

"Keffy-Horn, you son of a bitch."

Jude looked up from the screen, where he was pedaling diligently away from a swarm of bees. Johnny was standing at the edge of the sidewalk. A woman in a headscarf steered a shopping cart between them. When she passed, Jude's mouth was hanging open, as though he should be the one surprised to find Johnny here, living and breathing on a street corner in New York. His cigarette fell to the street. He was high as the moon.

"Hey, Johnny, hey."

Jude stepped off his skateboard and shielded his body with it. Johnny could see him taking in the tattoos through his thin white T-shirt. "What the fuck you doing here?" He put his hand on Jude's shoulder and gave him an ambiguous little shake.

"I'm here. I'm here, I'm living with my dad now, yeah."

"Here?"

"Across the street, yeah." He pointed.

"I been there." Johnny crossed his arms. "He was real good to me, your pop. He helped out." Johnny was about to say Teddy's name, but he stopped. Instead he said, "Did I say you could wear that jacket?"

Jude looked down at his body. The parka was reversible, army green on the outside, bright orange on the inside, fat and shiny as a sleeping bag. "It's not . . . it's mine. It's not yours."

Johnny had once bought an identical one at the Salvation Army in Lintonburg. The thought of that store, with the ceramic bowl of freebies at the counter—broaches and buttons and little bottles of half-used nail polish and eight tracks no one wanted—and the terrified look on the poor kid's face, this kid from Teddy's life who now wore Johnny's uniform—made Johnny want to give him a bear hug. He did, slapping him several times on the back.

"I'm just fucking with you, man! Shit, you live in the *Village*. We're practically neighbors."

When Johnny released Jude, Jude was smiling a large, uneasy smile. "I tried to find you yesterday, but I didn't know where you lived."

"I live, like, four blocks that way."

"Yeah?"

"You doing anything right now?"

"Just, no, just nothing."

"Can you drop your board at home? I'm meeting some guys at the subway, going to play some tag."

Jude said he had not yet been on the subway.

"What color shirt you got on?"

Obediently, Jude unzipped his jacket. Under it was a Black Flag shirt, white.

At the cube sculpture on Astor Place, a dozen guys were selecting laser guns from a duffel bag, strapping targets to their chests. Half were in black T-shirts, half in white. Some wore sweatshirts underneath. Some had *X*s drawn on their hands. Two had *X*s shaved in the back of their heads.

"Mr. Clean!" one of them said.

"You got an extra?" Johnny asked. "I found this guy on St. Mark's. Name of Jude."

"Hey," Jude said, tying his jacket around his waist. They chorused back.

"Gentlemen," Johnny began. "Astor Place to Union Square. Use only number six trains. Anyone who gets arrested is on their own this time." Over the St. Marks Hotel, the early moon was pale as a cloud in the ice blue sky. Jude took a gun and a target. "Stay off the third rail. And no pulling the emergency stop. Elliot." They all glared at a kid in black, his laser gun resting sheepishly on his shoulder. "Black shirts first." The black team filed down the uptown subway stairs, and a few minutes later, when the sound of a departing train rumbled beneath them, the white team, Jude and Johnny among them, descended behind them.

In the cold, dank dungeon of the station, the smell of urine took Jude's breath away. Graffiti, as thick and indecipherable as the tattoos on Johnny's arms, covered the walls. Garbage, decomposed beyond recognition, littered the floor, and it took Jude a moment to distinguish a body among the wreckage, bundled under a dust-coated blanket, alive, he hoped. Without a glance at the sleeping man or the attendant in the glass booth, each of Johnny's crew jumped over the turnstiles. Jude did the same. When the next train arrived, a sluggish, green-eyed 6, they all stepped into different cars, except Johnny and Jude, who got in together. Then, when the train got going, Johnny led Jude to the back of the car. He yanked open the door, and they watched the black walls of the tunnel fly past. Jude's legs felt as though they were made out of sand. He held tight to an overhead bar while Johnny dashed across the platform to the other car. "Come on!" He stood in the doorway, waiting.

Jude could feel his lungs heaving. It was freezing down here. He braced himself against the door frame to keep it open, clutching the stitch in his side.

"What's wrong?" The door was still open, the train clacking.

Jude glanced over his shoulder. A few people were sprawled across the orange plastic seats, listening to headphones, sleeping, none of them aware of the plastic machine gun Jude held at his side. Three kids near the opposite end of the car were tagging one of the doors, two of them standing guard while the third sprayed. Jude closed his eyes. He kept them that way for a long time, or what seemed on his father's pot to be a long time. His high had diminished only faintly, and Jude was aware of the flux of his thoughts, rocking roughly along with the engine, the open door roaring. The metallic rattle of a can of spray paint. The fumes, overwhelming. Even across the train car, they were as strong as if Jude were huffing them himself.

They'd played laser tag before, Jude and Teddy and Johnny and Delph and Delph's cousin, who owned the set. Running barefoot on the pavement, in summer grass. Jude and Teddy hiding behind a parked car: *shhh*.

How to say how shitty he felt at that deafening threshold, how unworthy, nearly sick, so cowardly he couldn't open his eyes, the guy whose brother he'd killed waiting for him on the other side? He shivered at the thought of Johnny finding out how low he'd sunk, stealing drugs for a free high, while all this time Johnny, sober and upright, had been hopping train cars. "Just don't look down!" Johnny called helpfully, and it was suddenly so ridiculous, this fear of the *subway*—he'd huffed freon!—"You wimp!" said his father, "you wimp!"—that Jude opened his eyes and, laser gun cradled across his chest, crossed the platform in one dexterous leap—Mario sailing from cliff to floating bridge, Pitfall Harry traversing tar pit—and when the train screeched to a halt ("Fourteenth Street, Union Square"), Jude kept going for one slow-mo second, hooking an arm around a pole to catch himself, laser gun *ch-ch-ch*-ing to a stop.

Here he was. The noise was gone and he was inside again, in another, identical, freezing cold car.

"C'mon," Johnny said, unfazed. He dragged Jude out through the doors just before they slid closed again. They raced down the platform, their laughter echoing against the Lego-yellow tiles, the aroma of wet garbage and hot exhaust and the cool iron earth, a man pissing in a corner, a woman shaking a can of change, Johnny winning by a good ten yards, until, halfway up a flight of stairs, he was shot. Jude heard the sound—*keo, keo, keo,* the fighter planes of Space Invaders—and saw the red light exploding from Johnny's chest. Staggering backward two steps, Johnny clutched the target over his heart with one hand, grabbed the railing with the other, and groaned, "Go, man! Go on without me!" Jude did, but not before firing up at the top of the steps, illuminating the target of Johnny's dark-shirted killer, who fell quickly, without ado, out of sight.

Jude turned around and ran in the other direction, up another set of stairs. He ran past a homeless mariachi band, a troupe of break-dancers, endless stretches of graffiti. He ran past a white-shirt and returned his salute as they crossed paths. He ran past a black-shirt and fired at him from the waist, but it was just a regular guy smoking a cigarette, his eyes filled with confusion and fright. At the end of the corridor, Jude followed the signs to the down-town platform and the sound of the arriving train, and slipped into the last car just as the doors sighed closed. He kept running, car to car, his legs throbbing, his breath inflating his smile. People looked at him, people looked away, some gasped or screamed, he could be arrested or chased or shot at for real, but he was too fast. Jude had not yet been told about Bernie Goetz, the Subway Vigilante, had not heard the Agnostic Front song "Shoot His Load"; he did not comprehend fully the fear of the woman he sent shrinking into her husband's overcoat. In one car, he shot and killed an unsuspecting black-shirt who'd made the mistake of putting down his gun to tie a shoe. In another, he shot poor Elliot, whose gun, apparently broken, fired soundlessly back at Jude. At Astor Place, he ran off the train, outside, down the uptown stairs again, under the turnstile, and back on the 6. And back and forth, uptown, downtown, until he couldn't find anyone anymore, until it seemed he was the only man left alive.

When he finally surfaced, it was dark. Aboveground, the air smelled as clean as New England, and the sky was like a deep blue sheet unfurled above him, like the sheet his mother would put on his bed, letting it hang in the air for a moment before it dropped. The stars were coming out above the newsstand on the corner, the magazines and candy bars lit up like prizes. For the first time in many weeks, he felt awake. He thought about lighting a cigarette but instead inhaled the evening tonic of the street as he walked up and down his block for a while, then home.

EIGHT

Johnny gave him a key, said "*Mi casa es su casa*." Played him No
for an Answer, Straight Ahead, Wide Awake, Project X. Took
him to his friend's half-pipe on Houston, to the Cyclone at
Coney Island, the elm tree in Tompkins where the first Hare
Krishna ceremony had taken place, with Swami Prabhupada and
Allen Ginsberg, to all the places he would have taken Teddy if he'd
been the one alive and living in New York. He showed him how to
empty the coins from a pay phone, where to find lead slugs for video
games, how to suck subway tokens. (First you slipped a matchbook
into the slot. Then you waited for someone to get his token jammed.
Then when he left you put your mouth to the slot and sucked it out.
One of the few useful lessons Johnny's father had shared with him
during their brief association.) Jude ate up everything. "What are
these?" he asked, stabbing a chickpea from his chana masala at one

of the many Indian restaurants down Johnny's street. "They look like little asses."

Now that the scene was exploding in New York, everyone had started to look the same—kids from Westchester and Connecticut loitering on the sidewalk in front of CB's, sporting the band T-shirts they'd bought the previous weekend, looking for drunk kids to beat up. Johnny had tattooed every inch of their bodies—*SXE* on the inside of their lips, *X*s on their hands—and he was running dry. Even his own band, Army of One, which was as central to the scene as any other, which sported legions of fans who knew his lyrics by heart, who spit them back at him onstage, had begun to disenchant him. Not long ago, one of his customers, no older than Teddy, had asked him to tattoo ARMY OF ONE across his chest. Johnny had declined. "You're going to regret that one, kid," he said, and he realized then how fleeting the scene was. He believed ardently in all the virtues his own body was tatted up with, but his brother was dead, and one day Johnny would be, too. Permanent ink only lasted so long.

But now, here was Jude, wide-eyed and green and full of gratitude, and every word that came out of Johnny's mouth was a marvel. The kid was an empty canvas. So he lived with a drug dealer. That couldn't be helped. "When you going to take me to the temple?" he'd ask. "When you going to take me to a show?"

Johnny gave straight edge a soft sell, combining good-natured ridicule with a casual dose of guilt tripping.

"How you like living with your dad, Jude?"

"It's all right."

"I hear his weed is out of this world."

"It's pretty good."

"So, how long you plan on walking around like a zombie? Like, indefinitely?"

"I guess."

"Good plan, kid. Sounds like you got it all figured out."

The band was practicing at Johnny's place, waiting raptly in their positions. Nothing got them off more than watching the exhortation of a new kid, and they knew it had to be handled with care. They hadn't objected when Jude had shown up smoking a cigarette; they'd even invited him to jam with them and agreed he wasn't bad. "Taught him everything he knows," Johnny said. He'd introduced Jude as an old friend, leaving out any mention of a brother. After they covered Minor Threat's "Straight Edge," the song that spawned the phrase, Johnny told Jude that Ian MacKaye had written it for a friend who died of an overdose, and that was the closest they got to talking about what happened to Teddy. Johnny could see it sinking in, though, the dots connecting before Jude's frozen eyes, the straight edge constellation. Any day now, he'd be taking the plunge.

"You seen any of that girl Eliza?" he asked Jude after the band had left. "Your dad's girlfriend's . . . ?" Johnny's cat Tarzan purred obscenely against Jude's chest. Johnny reached over, picked up the cat, and placed him in his own lap.

"Just that once," Jude said.

Ever since Johnny's own father had ripped him off, he had been wary of anyone whose intentions appeared too pure. Eliza was no exception. She'd been with Teddy the night he died—surely she had been present for the cocaine, surely she could have done something to save him—but she'd sworn that they'd hardly spent any time together, that they had been split up at the party. The closest she'd been to him was when she'd helped him put in his contact lens. The idea of Teddy stumbling blindly through his last night on earth, and the intimacy, however brief, with which this girl had known him, had filled him with a loneliness that dispelled his suspicion.

The restaurant where Diane Urbanski had made a lunch reservation for four was a Japanese place on Amsterdam that Les called "schmancy." Aside from the red floor pillows and the menu, the place had no pretense of authenticity—its single waitress was a blond woman dressed head to toe in black, and Prince streamed from the speakers. The building had an airy, industrial feel, with silver air ducts hanging from the high ceiling and walls cushioned with black leather, as if to protect diners from injuring themselves. Besides Jude and Les, however, the place was empty, a fact that didn't prevent their waitress from seating them at the bar while they waited for the rest of their party. Diane and Eliza were late. They were always late, Les said. He took the opportunity to order another decanter of saki. It was a stormy March afternoon, and through the window, they watched the sky open up. They drank the saki from miniature cups that had the name of the restaurant printed in red on the side—*Rapture*. It looked as though it had been written in lipstick. "Crapture," said Jude bitterly, which made Les chuckle.

By the time the woman entered the restaurant—shaking off her umbrella, high-heeled boots clicking on the tiles—Jude was full of a warm, heady fuel. Despite the umbrella, Di was soaked—her jeans dark at the thighs, black hair spilling from her braid—but her dark eyes were giant with relief, a nearly sensual pleasure from getting out of the rain. She was a petite, boyish woman, the size of Eliza, who was not there. Jude felt his own relief steam off of him. Di shook Jude's hand vigorously and gave him a noisy kiss on each cheek. "I'm all wet," she said, her British accent thick and throaty as she slipped out of her coat. "I'm so sorry." Her perfume smelled like some sultry jungle flower.

They were seated at one of the low glass tables in the front window, Les and Di on one side, Jude on the other. Les made a show of getting down on the ground, exaggerating his drunkenness, saying his bones were too old to sit on the floor. "No Eliza today?" he asked.

Di shook her head somberly. "She's not been feeling well. I fear it's the flu. The flu frightens me *so*."

Jude spread open his menu. Maybe Eliza *was* avoiding him. Maybe she was faking. Les recounted for Jude Di's résumé, beginning with the flu that killed her grandfather. She was born in London, had moved to the States at eighteen to be a part of the New York City Ballet. Now she taught ballet to little girls at Lincoln Center. Les went on nervously, Di deflecting his praise.

"I don't know why we couldn't meet at Dojo," Les said, frowning at the menu. "They have Oriental crap there." It was becoming clear to Jude that, despite Les's apparently bottomless pockets, his tastes were still those of a Lintonburg boy.

"They have better Oriental crap here," said Di. She inserted her hand into the pocket of Les's jeans, gemmed rings sparkling on her fingers, retrieved his cigarette lighter, and lit the two tea candles on the table. When the waitress came over, Di ordered without looking at the menu, then poured tea for all of them when it came.

"I've been dying to meet you, Jude, but you have to practically clobber this guy over the head to get your way." With her black hair and powder white skin, Di looked almost Japanese herself. "Tell me how you like New York."

"I like it," Jude said. The tea tasted like dirt, but after the pissy aftertaste of the wine, he welcomed the warmth. Johnny drank tea. Herbal, no caffeine. "It's a lot cooler than Vermont. There's a lot more things to do. I like that there's so much music everywhere."

Di nodded appreciatively. "What sort of music do you enjoy, Jude?"

Jude put down his cup. "Lots of kinds, but mostly hardcore?"

"What does that sound like?"

"You know what punk is?"

"Darling, I'm from England. The Clash? The Sex Pistols?"

"Yeah, it's like that," Jude said, becoming excited, "but faster."

"Faster?" Di said skeptically.

"Why does it have to be so fast?" Les wondered. "What's wrong with slow?"

"Darling, there's such a thing as being too slow."

"I know what I'm talking about here. I recall escorting your daughter to five or six hundred punk concerts. I don't understand the hurry."

"Your father's a tough critic. If it's not Creedence Clearwater Revival . . ."

"And in New York," Jude went on, "lots of the hardcore scene's straight edge, which means no one does drugs."

"Really? Is it religious or something?"

"Well, sort of. Like, my friend Johnny said Gandhi once took a vow to abstain from eating meat, and drinking, and, you know, being promiscuous. It's kind of like that."

"Fascinating."

Les gave a dismissive chuckle. "Straight edge? That's what they're called now? In my day, we called them squares." He took out his cigarettes, lit one up, and scooted the pack across the table.

"It's not like they're too lame to do drugs," Jude said, ignoring the cigarettes, suddenly defensive of Johnny and his friends. "Some of them are recovering addicts," he said, using Johnny's phrase. "Some just have parents who are addicts."

"Well, I think that sounds like a wonderful organization," said Di, waving away Les's smoke and Jude's remark as the waitress set down their food. Everything was cold and pink. Jude slipped out his retainers when Di wasn't looking and hid them in a napkin under the table. "I wish Eliza would get involved in something like that. She never took to ballet. She's not normally one for self-discipline." She took a bite of something slippery-looking. "Salmon. It's good. Try it."

Jude captured a jiggly piece with his chopsticks.

"But, do you know, I believe she's turned a corner? Knock on wood." She knocked lightly on Les's bald head. "She's been positively *sober*. Doesn't take wine with dinner. And quite *studious*. She barely even comes home anymore, stays at school all weekend to study." She spewed a few grains of the rice she was chewing. "I wonder if she's finally growing up," she said. "Is it possible?"

Jude looked to his father, who was putting out his cigarette. Which of them was she asking? "Sure," Jude finally said, with false enthusiasm. How did he know? He barely knew the girl.

"Or perhaps," Di began. She stared dreamily into her plate, fiddling with her chopsticks.

"What?" said Les.

"Perhaps . . ." She looked directly at Jude. "I know she didn't know your friend terribly well. But I do believe she was quite shaken by what happened to him. Having to speak to that detective. And having spent the evening with the two of you, just before it happened. That sort of brush with death can cause one to reexamine lifestyle choices. Don't you think?"

Jude looked out the window at the rain-soaked street. Suddenly he was sure that Eliza had been with Teddy while Jude had searched the house for them, and there was nothing he could do about it then, and there was nothing he could do about it now.

"I'm sorry, darling. I certainly didn't mean to upset you."

"No, it's okay," Jude said.

"We're so glad you're here with us." She gave Les a sideways smile and stole a roll of sushi from Jude's barely touched plate. "Don't you like your food?"

After lunch, they all took a taxi downtown. It was Jude's first cab ride, and he studied the map of dick-shaped New York posted on the back of the driver's seat. Here they were—Di showed him with a wine red pinky nail, leaning across his father's lap—and here was where they were going. They were full of food and tea and wine, sleepy and dry. Out one window, Central Park sped past, and on the other side, blocks and blocks of gray. It was the sterile, efficient, adult New York Jude had figured didn't exist, but somehow it was reassuring to him, the boundless span of this island. So many blocks between Upper and Lower—it made his stomach lurch with plea-sure. They flew through the yellow traffic lights, rain blurring the bare trees, taxis kicking up puddles.

When the cab dropped them off in front of Les's apartment, an ambulance was parked at the curb. One of the guys shooting up on the steps of the rehab center had OD'd, and the paramedics were sliding his stretcher into the back like a sheet of cookies into an oven.

Later, months later, when Jude thought back to the way it all went down—how did a burnout like him end up straight edge?—he'd remember that ambulance, just like the one he'd been uncon-scious inside. Its red cross, when viewed from the right angle, was an *X* on its side.

He didn't follow his father into the apartment. Instead, he got on his skateboard and flew to Johnny.

"Don't get too attached to these," Johnny told Jude. "It's just so you don't get your ass kicked in the pit." When he was finished with one hand, he started on the other, two Sharpie-black *X*s, each leg an inch wide.

"Where's the *X* come from?" Jude wanted to know. The smell of the marker was making him dizzy.

Johnny told him. When Ian MacKaye's first band, the Teen Idles, wanted to play all-ages shows in D.C., they proposed that the 9:30 Club mark kids' hands with an *X*, the way they did on the West Coast, to show that they were underage. Before long, the straight edge scene had co-opted the symbol. "You don't want us to drink? Fuck you, we don't want to drink anyway!"

"How long's this going to last?" Jude asked. He held up his hands, making two fists.

"Long as you want it to," Johnny said.

In the fall, CBGB & OMFUG had banned Youth of Today, Gorilla Biscuits, and Side By Side for stage diving, a legendary show according to Johnny, but Army of One was still allowed to play. The place was dark and small and packed with bodies and Johnny strolled onto the stage as though he were not a person who appeared in fanzines pasted up by fourteen-year-olds in their tighty whities in Albany, Cleveland, and L.A. He strolled out with Rooster and the rest of the guys and, midstride, without a word of introduction, began convulsing. There seemed to be a malfunction with the sound system, a tape in fast-forward, a ribbon of feedback. Then the guitar started up, and the nuclear explosion of drums, and Jude realized that the sound he'd heard was Johnny's voice. He was not having a seizure but singing. Not singing but vomiting a ceaseless torrent of small, sharp objects—nails, needles, gears, batteries, Hot Wheels, pennies—which came clanking out as though they'd been swallowed.

The shrooms had been a bad idea.

They used to hunt for them, Teddy and Jude, on the farms along Dairy Road, leaving their bikes in the ditch and crawling on hands and knees through the dark. Maybe a cow pie would be flung, maybe a cow would be tipped. Maybe they'd eat a handful right there in the grass, like hunter-gatherers, and trip on the stars, and go or not go to class the next morning.

So when the guy approached Jude at the edge of Tompkins that afternoon, selling not some sidewalk-cooked chemical compound but Mother Earth's gold-flecked mushrooms, Jude had bought a bag and eaten two right there, popping them like Twinkies. It was his exception to his father's rule—an exercise in reminiscence. Still, Johnny had promised to take him to his show today, and then to the temple in Brooklyn. If he knew he was on something, he'd leave his ass at home. As they walked together to CB's, Jude had tried hard to straighten the bending buildings, to calm the breathing trees. He was good at nothing if not faking sobriety.

But now, safe inside the club, there was no reason to fight the trip anymore. No one was looking at anyone but Johnny. The stage wasn't a stage but a knee-high platform, and Jude was drawn to it, as if tied to a rope. Was it fame? The band was glowing. It was the yellow lights, the vibration of the speakers through the concrete floor, but it was also just the band, it was Johnny, the loops in his ears shining like real gold. It wasn't fame. Famous people were untouchable, unknowable. Jude could see the pores glistening on Johnny's scalp. It was unfame, the opposite of fame—he was touchable and entirely knowable, he was memorizable, like a sister or a dog. Jude fought through the field of bouncing bodies. A dance had started up in front of the stage, a boisterous, good-natured ritual that involved hurling one's body, like a sack of flour, at other bodies. Arms windmilled, shoes flew. Everything within an inch of stage diving. Jude was close enough to the band to feel the radiance of their sweat, their spit.

He found himself in the middle of things. Or he put himself there. He jumped, and his body remained in the air for several hours before he landed on somebody's shoulder. He was half helped up, half shoved away. He spun sideways into another wall of people, his chin smashing against someone's tattooed head, his sweat-soaked T-shirt sealed to someone else's back. Not one of them was a girl. One girl, or two. Some dude, passed above their heads, fell on him. The rubber heel of a sneaker came first. For a second, he stood on Jude's arm, climbing down him like a ladder. Then there was Johnny—was the show over, or just his set?—helping them both to their feet.

"Steady!" Johnny called. Or had Jude only read his lips? He couldn't hear him. Johnny mouthed something else, smiling sadly, and then was sucked back into the crowd. The words formed a silent space in Jude's empty head.

Steady!

Teddy!

He felt suddenly that he was in hell. It was wonderful. The room was black and close and singed with the forbidden, it felt miles underground, the perfect expression of testosterone and the structures of sound stimuli. The set wasn't over; Johnny was still singing. He'd stepped down from the stage. Johnny drifted back toward him, his face appearing and disappearing like a strobe. Jude shoved him, without malice, only because that was physics, only because Johnny had a body and so did Jude. Between them, a pit opened, the size of a body that could have dropped from Earth but didn't.

Then the train rocketed beneath the river, transporting him from one room to another. But the room he landed in was the same one he'd left: bodies, music, stage. Only here they left their sneakers at the door, and this room was bigger, big as a ballroom, and filled with an apricot light and incense so sweet Jude had the urge to wet himself. From each corner of the room, a voice wailed

Hare Krishna, Hare Krishna, Krishna Krishna, Hare Hare
Hare Rama, Hare Rama, Rama Rama, Hare Hare.

It was the walls. It was God. God was singing. Then he saw the man sitting in the middle of the room. He was an ancient Indian man in a white robe, playing an organ and singing into a mike. Around him, men and women sat chanting with him, some on mats, some on the lacquered wooden floor. In front of him, gold curtains hid the stage; behind him was another man, also old, also Indian, propped in a throne, draped in orange, topped with what looked like an orange bathing cap. He sat very still. Men and women and children approached him with candles and incense and flowers, sprinkling the petals at his feet. They bowed down to him, kneeling and pressing their foreheads to the floor. Jude watched from the sidelines as Johnny did this, as naturally as if he were putting on a kettle for tea. It was only when Johnny returned to him that Jude saw that the man was a statue.

"That's Krishna?" he whispered.

Johnny shook his head. "His Divine Grace Srila Prabhupada. Before we worship Krishna, we worship his devotees."

A drum circle was forming around the organ player, boys and men joining him one by one. They wore robes or jeans, sherbet orange sweatshirt over sherbet orange skirt. Some wore beads like Johnny's around their necks; some wore a smudge of white paint on their foreheads; some had bald heads with a tuft of hair at the back. The drums were grenade-shaped, two-headed; someone was playing hand cymbals; then someone else was, too. Jude had a rubbery memory of the gymnastics class he'd taken with Prudence as a kid, the two of them tumbling across the slippery floor in their socks.

Then the music stopped. Slowly, the gold curtains drew back. Bodies scattered, found an empty space, bowed to the floor. On the stage, nestled in an elaborate, canopied throne, adorned with a jeweled crown and a brightly colored lei, was Krishna. Krishna was smiling a beatific smile. Krishna's face was milky blue. He was rosy-cheeked, bare-chested, no bigger than a fifteen-year-old boy. Krishna looked like a mannequin in the window of Macy's, a queenless king riding a float in the homecoming parade.

The organ started up again, then the drums. People sprang up from prayer, started dancing. They sang, *Hare Krishna, Hare Krishna, Krishna Krishna, Hare Hare*. They sang to the stage, swaying, as though watching Krishna perform. Jude would not have been surprised if they had raised their lighters. Bodies pressed in. Painted women danced by, raising carnations to his nose; he breathed them in. He closed his eyes for some time, floating, and when he opened them, Johnny was gone. Jude turned, blinded by the golden stage—there *were* lighters, darting around the room like fireflies—and stumbled into a log. It was a soft log, damp and mossy. The log was Johnny! Johnny was still lying facedown on the floor, his arms spread out in front of him like Superman.

Heavily, Jude fell to his knees and cat-stretched out beside him. The floor was cold and smooth and smelled of a piney wax. Here were the parts of his body that touched the ground: his forehead, his armpits, his chest, his belly, his hips, his knees, his toes. His hands, each scored with an *X*. He had never lain like this before. A socked heel stepped apologetically on his pinky; a gauzy skirt tickled the nape of his neck. His eyelashes fluttered against the floor. He felt long, emptied, flattened.

A tide ripped through him, first a ripple, then a roar.

The subway.

The train sped under him, rattling his ribs. Head still down, Jude slipped the bag of mushrooms from the pocket of his jacket and gobbled the rest of them up. Maybe because he feared his trip would wear thin, because he wanted, why not, for the night to go out with a bang. Maybe because he knew already it was the last night he'd be high. He felt himself peel away from the past, saw the hollow corpse of his former self, lying like a log, as he stood.

The room was on fire. Krishna was aglow on the stage, smiling at Jude through the flames. Arms windmilled, shoes flew. Bodies passed, hand over hand, above the crowd. They levitated above him. The wax dummy smiled his Mona Lisa smile at Jude. Half-boy, half-god. Half-Indian, half-white. Jude danced for the god boy, and the god boy let him dance.

The flames came up to greet him. Jude passed one of his *X*'d hands through them, felt the white heat melt his fingertips, then his wrist, then catch his sleeve. Then he fell to the ground.

*

Les Keffy had just sat down on his futon, to the Yankees' opening game, to a cold can of Pabst Blue Ribbon and three hot dogs
bedecked with mustard and relish, when the phone rang. It was
April already, and the breeze floating through the open door to the
fire escape carried the promise of reasonable temperatures, and the
smell of fried food from the restaurants downstairs, and the voices of
the fifty thousand fans 150 blocks north, his own not among them.
He had scored two MVP tickets from a guy he knew who sold faux
Rolexes in Chinatown, but Jude had turned him down to attend a
show at the Ritz. Di was at a dance conference in Chicago, but he
wouldn't have asked her to go with him anyway, had stopped asking her years ago, and Eliza, who was usually reliable for that sort of
thing, he hadn't seen in weeks. He had sold the tickets to one of his
distributors, lost twenty bucks.

With reluctance he stood and moved away from the TV, where
Mattingly was walloping a double. Picking up the phone on its fifth
or sixth ring, Les muttered, "Good boy."

"What?" It was Eliza.

"I'm watching the game. Yanks and the Twins." He stretched the
cord as far as it would go, craning to see. Only when he was on the
phone did his apartment seem large. Standing at the kitchen counter, he might as well have been watching the TV across the street.
"How lovely to hear from you. I thought you were MIA. Were you
sick or something?"

"I was. I'm better. Now I'm better."

"I wish you'd called earlier. I could have used a date for this
game."

"Is . . . air?"

Di's cordless phone, for which she had paid six hundred dollars,
produced an irksome static; it sometimes captured the voices of her

neighbors, or the line of her live-in housekeeper, who wandered in and out of the conversation, oblivious. Les called them the voices in his head.

"Stand still and say it again, honey."

"IS JUDE THERE?"

Strikeout for Ward. A cordless phone would come in handy now. "He's not. He bailed on me. It's too much to ask that my one and only son show an interest in baseball. Or meat eating, or any other, you know, institution of male bonding. He's not even smoking reefer with me anymore."

"Really?"

"You think he's maybe a queer?"

"I don't *know*." Eliza sighed. "I don't even know him. I met him *once*! Where is he?"

"He's at a *show*. With his pal Johnny."

"Johnny?"

"They're thick as thieves. He's brainwashing my boy. He quit smoking, quit drinking, quit eating *meat*. You want to come over and eat some wieners? Smoke some happy stuff?"

"*Jude* quit all those things?"

"He saw the light. He had a conversion experience. An eight-hundred-dollar conversion experience. Stuck his hand in a plate of candles at the Krishna temple and got second-degree burns up his arm. Landed in the ER."

"Oh, shit. A plate of *candles*? Is he okay?"

"Aside from having his arm all wrapped up. Johnny tackled him before the burn got too deep. It's his left one, so he can still wipe his ass."

"Do you know when he'll be back?"

Who was at bat? He couldn't see, couldn't hear. "What do you want with Jude, anyway?"

"I need to talk to both of them. I really want to talk to them."

"You whine about meeting my kids, and then when one of them finally materializes, you disappear."

"I've just been busy. You *told* me to apply myself. I've had a lot going on!"

"Wait, what are you doing home on a weekday?"

"Who . . . home?"

"What? Say it again."

"ALL RIGHT, FINE. I'm on my mom's phone. I wasn't feeling well, so I took the train home."

"Aren't you not supposed to do that?"

"You wrote a note, saying you were taking me on a trip."

"That was nice of me."

"Les," said Eliza through a burst of static, " . . . tell you anything, right?"

"Sure, honey."

Then a kid's voice, not Eliza's, said, " . . . not fair, it's totally not fair."

"Quit your whining, man," said Les, eyeing the hot dogs across the room, surely gone cold, as the Twins performed a double play that was truly not fair, and Eliza's voice danced inextricably with the ghost of a stranger's, their words sometimes nearly making a sort of sense.

"JUST TELL HIM TO CALL ME," said Eliza, and Les hung up.

The doorman was expecting them. They rose in the mirrored elevator, Jude's stomach dropping through the floor. Inside the apartment, a vacuum cleaner was running, and they had to ring the bell several times before a small, dusky-skinned woman answered the door. She was wearing a sports bra and leggings, between which, bisecting a lumpy stomach, ran a scar the same purple as the polish on her fingers and toes. A red spot hovered just above her eyes. "Thank goodness," she said. "She been cry and cry." Through a living room that looked like a wing of the White House, down a hallway hung with the frowning visages of Eastern Europeans, the woman led them to Eliza's room, opening the door without knocking. "Two boys in your room okay?" she said, but then left, closing the door behind her. A moment later the vacuum cleaner started up again.

Jude had never been in any girl's room but his sister's, but Eliza's looked just as he would have expected one to. A Beastie Boys poster hung on the rose-papered wall, and a pair of ballet slippers was slung over the back of a rocking chair, in which sat a family of stuffed bears, one wearing a Yankees cap. On the dresser was a cluster of photographs: a man who was not Les with a dark-haired baby swathed in his arms; a long-locked Eliza aloft in a bat mitzvah chair. In the wicker wastebasket beside the bed were clouds of Kleenex and four or five empty Yoo-hoo bottles, and in the double bed, which was pink and ruffled and plump with pillows, Eliza lay with the covers pulled up to her chin. It was two o'clock in the afternoon.

He had known, as soon as his father had relayed the message, that it was about Teddy. There was no other reason for Eliza to summon them to her mother's apartment. "Just come over," she'd said, "and you'll see." On the silent train uptown, Jude felt a calm settle over him. Not because he looked forward to whatever revelation Eliza had in store, but because he welcomed the relief of pressure. It was as though Johnny and Jude had been engaged in a staring contest, each daring the other to speak Teddy's name first, and even though it meant he would lose, Jude was desperate to blink.

"What happened to your hair?" Her voice was hoarse, her eyes and nose red.

Jude and Johnny both put a hand to their heads. "I cut it," Jude said.

"Nice sling." It wasn't a cast, but Jude had never broken a bone before, so he had people sign it. Johnny, Les, Rooster, a nurse named LaCarol, the couple who owned the Smoke Sho. "There should be a marker in my desk drawer." Johnny retrieved the marker and Jude sat on the edge of the bed while she found a blank space to print her name in capital letters. "Does it hurt?"

"Not really. When I change the bandages. Mostly it itches. This guy saved my life," he said, slapping Johnny hard on the back.

"Stop, drop, and roll," Johnny explained.

"What happened, exactly?"

Jude could sense she was stalling, but he didn't mind stalling with her. "These women carry around these plates of candles. You're supposed to wave your hands through the fire and over your head"—he imitated with his free hand, as though washing his hair—"but I held my hand in there too long and it got my sleeve. I was tripping on shrooms."

He had confessed this to Johnny, who had not been surprised, as well as to the receptionist, the doctor, and LaCarol, who had swaddled him in ointment and bandages. No one arrested him, no one blinked. But it had felt good to come clean under those penetrating hospital lights. *Last time I do that,* he'd told the nurse, loud enough for Johnny to hear.

On a white television with a built-in VCR, a soap opera was unfolding. Jude and Johnny watched it for a moment. They looked at each other, then at Eliza.

"What'd you want to tell us?" Johnny finally asked.

Eliza muted the television, but she kept her eyes on the screen. "Well, two things. And the first is very bad. You'll want to kill me, probably."

Jude and Johnny did not dispute this. Johnny stood in the middle of the room; Jude sat on the bed.

"Damn, I'm *starving*," she said. "I don't know when's the last time I ate."

When they said nothing, made no move to cajole her, she sighed. She looked as though she had been in this bed for a long time. Jude smelled the familiar sour-milk smell of body and bedsheet.

He said, "You're the one who gave Teddy the coke."

In the other room, something expensive collided with the floor. The vacuum cleaner squealed, purred, and died. Slowly, nearly undetectably, Eliza nodded. Jude looked at Johnny: his face registered nothing.

"I've stopped using it, though. Not right away, but I've stopped. As soon as I knew for sure. You don't even have to say anything, because I *know*. I'm already being punished." She was sniffling repeatedly. "I didn't want to stop but I stopped! That must mean something, right?"

She reached for her bottle of Yoo-hoo and took a ravenous gulp, spilling the milk down her chin, down her throat, following the silver chain into her cleavage. It was a little girl's nightgown, white, cotton; at the neckline was a bow with a pearl in the center. Maybe it was that pearl, maybe it was just seeing her again, maybe it was the consolation of having an accomplice, but even before she started to cry, Jude felt an empathetic loosening in his own chest. Johnny sat down beside Jude, and they dabbed her gingerly with tissues, mopping up chocolate milk and tears. She covered her face with her hands, talking into them as she cried.

"What are you saying?" Johnny said. "What's she saying?" he asked Jude.

"All I want is Yoo-hoo!" she yelled, removing her hands. "Why does it have to be Yoo-hoo? Why can't I crave something that won't make me fat? And I don't have any *friends*!"

"I don't think it'll make you *fat*, necessarily," said Jude helplessly, inspecting the label.

"I feel enormous. I'm enormous."

"You're not enormous," Jude said.

"I've been *studying*. I got a ninety-nine on my British Lit midterm!"

"Eliza, is there something else?" said Johnny. "Just tell us."

"I didn't think it would show this quickly," she whispered, very still now, her eyes very wet. "It was practically overnight." She pushed back the covers and lifted her nightgown enough to reveal her belly. She stared down at it, her hair veiling her face. It looked like his sister's belly, only plumper. Eliza's belly button was stretched wide.

"You can't tell?" Eliza asked.

Jude and Johnny both began to stand. Then they lowered themselves again. Jude thought of Ingrid Donahoe. He thought of his birth mother.

"You're not . . . ?" Johnny said.

Eliza covered her belly.

"Jeezum Crow," Jude whispered.

Later, Jude and Johnny would admit that they'd thought the same thing. Jude had looked at Johnny, and Johnny had looked at Jude, and for a moment each was certain that the other was the father. And then as quickly as this thought had appeared, before Eliza could withdraw from her nightgown the subway token, dangling from her necklace among the other charms like a hypnotist's watch, another thought, awful, miraculous, displaced it.

NINE

The furnace ticked, then hammered, then moaned, then ticked. From the street, the metallic thud of a Dumpster lid, a distant horn. Les, on the futon below, snored through it. Jude was so distracted by his thoughts that the sounds seemed to visit from someone else's dream.

One-armed, he climbed down from the loft, wrestled on jeans and shoes and sling, gathered skateboard and watch and keys in the dark. By the glow of his father's barbecue lighter, he found the slim black case under the kitchen sink. In it, blank-faced as a power drill, sleeping on its side on a bed of eggshell foam, lay McQueen. Jude slipped it into the pocket of his jacket and left his father alone with the furnace.

In the park, a boom box was blasting Warzone:

Don't forget the struggle
Don't forget the streets

He did not intend or wish to put the pistol to use as he coasted across St. Mark's, along the lightless Avenues A, B, C, but he was glad for its leaden company. The shadowed figures he passed did not disturb him. No light showed at the bottom of Johnny's door. Jude knocked anyway. No answer. He unlocked the padlock with the key Johnny had given him, hauled the door open, and turned on the light.

Blinking at the brightness, the three cats—Montezuma, Genghis, Tarzan—inspected him from their various perches. Jude smelled curry and the carbon whiff of cat litter. On a dish towel on the kitchenette counter, a single bowl and spoon lay drying. On the card table was a plastic laundry basket, and inside it, a block of bleached white T-shirts, crisp as a stack of paper.

Johnny's skateboard was not by the door. He had told Jude he was going to bed early, that he had a headache, but Jude should not have been surprised that Johnny, too, had been unable to sleep. He was probably skating the city, trying to exhaust himself. "Well, that's interesting," he'd said on the train on the way downtown that afternoon.

Jude had said nothing.

"You didn't know? About the two of them?"

Jude sat down on the couch. He propped a foot on each of the upturned record crates. Beside him, on top of a sketch pad, lay a well-thumbed paperback. *The Laws of Manu.* On the cover was a painting of a bejeweled god, not Krishna, four-armed, two-faced, like a conjoined pair of one-eyed jacks. Jude opened it to the place where a blank envelope marked a page.

79. A twice-born man who (daily) repeats those three one thousand times outside (the village), will be freed after a month even from great guilt, as a snake from its slough.

"Those three what?" Jude asked Tarzan, who was polishing his whiskered cheek on Jude's knee. He would like to find those three things so he could repeat them. He flipped through the book. In another chapter, several passages were underlined in blue ink:

> 59. . . . let him restrain his senses, if they are attracted by sensual objects.
>
> 60. By the restraint of his senses . . . by the abstention from injuring the creatures, he becomes fit for immortality. . . .
>
> 62. On the separation from their dear ones, on their union with hated men. . . .
>
> 63. On the departure of the individual soul from this body and its new birth in (another) womb, and on its wanderings through ten thousand millions of existences . . .

Jude closed the book and closed his eyes. It was the longest string of words he had read in a while, and their shapes swam behind his eyelids. When he opened his eyes, he looked down at his mummied arm, the mitt of his hand, the blue sling busy with signatures. ELIZA. He slipped off the sling and unwound the bandage. It had been a nightly ritual for the last three weeks, and he decided he was finished. Healed. A sickle-shaped scab sliced across his forearm, and his palm was rough with scar tissue. He held up his hand, wiggled his fingers. He was supposed to see an occupational therapist twice a week, but fuck it: the doctor said he'd play the guitar again.

Johnny had been surprised the following Sunday when Jude wanted to return to the temple, but they had accepted him back without question; most of the devotees hadn't even noticed the fire that night. During the Vedic lecture, he believed he saw the priest nod at him. Devotion to Krishna—renouncing worldly possessions, abstaining from alcohol and drugs and meat, chanting the names of god, working only for him—was the way to end the cycle of death and birth, to cast off the guilt (this, like *The Laws of Manu,* was the word he'd used) of the material world. Jude wanted to be devoted. He had never been this clean before, and he only wanted to be cleaner.

Teddy's body had been cremated; Jude didn't even know where Johnny had scattered the ashes. But there was still something left of him. Eliza was pregnant, and Teddy was being reincarnated in this life.

He picked up Tarzan and settled him into his lap. Tarzan's family jewels were the size of meatballs, but still, as Jude massaged the doughy, nippled Braille of his belly, he could not banish the word *womb* from his mind. Generally, even when his coked-up best friend was not the seed bearer (had it been in a bedroom, another parked car?), Jude was uncomfortable with the idea of babies, of sex and pregnancy and bodies and birth. He'd been sprung from another woman's womb. He'd drunk from her umbilical cord. Babies were like girls: they were breakable and entirely mysterious; they had nothing at all to do with him.

But look: Eliza, too, had once seemed unknowable, and now he and Johnny knew something about her that no one else did.

"I wouldn't have gotten him fucked up," she'd said, "if I knew you were going to."

Jude had countered: "Well, neither would I."

The full weight of the news descended upon them slowly, over moments and weeks, a package from a heaven-sent stork circling lazily down to earth. In the window of a stationery store near Union Square, alongside wedding invitations and business cards, Jude saw a birth announcement tied with baby blue ribbon: *We welcome with love our gift from above!*

Their secret had disarmed them; it had safely placed them all on Teddy's team. They spoke of it with giddiness and gravity, or with panic, or with a sense of duty, but always with breathless disbelief at their unexpected fortune. (Science was so messed up! The friction of two bodies could make something that wasn't there before. You could rub together two sticks and start a fire.) The conversations took place at Johnny's, or walking down the street, or across the table at Dojo's, or on the phone; it was one conversation, without beginning or end; it adopted its own code; it repeated itself; it spun around them, binding them like the silky threads of a web or a cocoon, an amniotic sac.

JUDE: Shouldn't we tell your mom?

ELIZA: She'll just make me get an abortion.

JUDE: Why would she make you get an abortion?

ELIZA: Because. She told me, "If you ever get pregnant, you're getting an abortion."

JUDE: What about my dad?

ELIZA: He'd just tell my mom.

JOHNNY: It's better if no one else knows. This way we can control it.

ELIZA: Well, I can't keep it a secret forever. People at school will start to notice. Someday the baby's going to, you know, get born.

JOHNNY: People will find out when they find out. But at least we can keep it under wraps for now. After a certain point, you can't get an abortion.

JUDE: But where will the baby live? Are you going to raise it with your mom? Are you going to go to school?

JOHNNY: We'll cross that bridge when we come to it.

(Johnny was always saying, "We'll cross that bridge when we come to it.")

JUDE: What about going to the doctor? Have you been to the doctor yet?

ELIZA: I don't know where to *go*. All I have is Dr. Betsy. She's a *pediatrician*.

JOHNNY: What are they going to tell her? "Yes, you're pregnant"?

ELIZA: And don't I have to go with an adult? My ID sucks.

JUDE: Johnny's an adult. He could say he's your boyfriend.

ELIZA: Yeah, but he's not my guardian. You need a guardian to
            sign forms.

JUDE: There are *tests* and things. You can find out if the baby's
            okay. She did *coke* while she was pregnant. Isn't that
            bad?

JOHNNY: Yes, it's bad. It's very, very bad. But what's done is
            done. They put mothers in jail for that in some states.
            You want her to have the kid in jail?

JUDE: No.

ELIZA: No.

JOHNNY: We don't need a doctor yet. We can live without a doctor.

You could live without most things most people depended on,
according to Johnny: a family, a phone, a furnace, a taxable income,
a high school diploma. And he was sort of right. Here they were,
three teenagers, planning for a baby, and the sky was still high above
them, winter blue; it hadn't fallen.

Jude's mother called every Sunday.

"Do you mean *completely*?"

"Completely." He and Les had agreed not to tell her about the
fire incident. There was no need to worry her.

"Even marijuana?"

"Completely."

"Alcohol? Cigarettes?"

There was no sound for a few seconds. Then Harriet said evenly,
"Good for you."

He could picture her standing in the kitchen with the bone-
colored phone to her ear, the kinky, too-long cord wrapped around
her, dragging on the floor. Jude's heart, which had been sort of holding its breath, deflated.

"Whatever. Don't believe me."

"Honey, I believe you. I'm surprised, is all. I hardly know what to expect anymore. One day you're the one getting into trouble, and now that you're gone it's your sister, and you're the one—"

"What's wrong with Pru?"

"Nothing. She'll be fine. Of course I've been hoping this would happen for you, this was my distinct hope, but it just seems too good to be true. Living with your dad . . . I didn't expect . . ."

"I gotta go, Mom. I'm going somewhere."

"Wait. How's school?"

"Fine." He had generated a setting and cast of characters for this lie—East Side Community High School on Twelfth Street, where he had seen some sketchy-looking kids shooting hoops behind a chain-link fence; teachers named Mr. Prabhupada and Mr. Omfug. "I got a ninety-nine on my British Lit midterm."

Harriet paused. He'd gone too far, he realized. "Jude. You telling me the truth?"

The fact that she didn't believe him—that his recovery was so implausible, his soul so unsaveable—made him want to hang up. She was the fucking Glass Lady.

"True till death," he said.

"What's that supposed to mean?"

"Nothing. It means you don't have to worry about me anymore."

"Don't be so hard on your mom," Les said after Jude hung up. "She's got reason to be worried." One thing Jude knew about his father, had known about him since he turned nine years old, was that he couldn't keep a secret. Still, he was caught off guard when Les spilled the beans. Some weeks back, Harriet's studio had been vandalized. Smashed to shit. All the fish tanks full of all her glass pieces. Vases, bowls, bongs, pipes. A baseball bat, probably, but the only evidence left behind was a beer bottle, scattered among the broken glass.

"What? Who was it?"

Jude had been sitting on the floor in the kitchen, slumped against the refrigerator while he talked to his mother, his back still sticky with sweat from the matinee at CB's. Now he sat up straight.

"She doesn't know for sure. But she says the kid you ripped off came looking for you the day before with some other dude."

Jude ran a frantic hand over his head. Hippie. Tory. He'd just spent hours slamming his body against a roomful of shirtless New York hardcore boys. The boys of Vermont seemed very far away.

He saw his mother standing over the shards of her studio, the glass twinkling around her. He saw her sweeping it into the dustpan, heard the heavy thud of the glass sliding into the trash.

"I'm going to kill those drunk fucks," he said. "I'll kill them."

"Slow down now, champ." Les was packing the bowl of Gertrude, his second favorite bong. "For one thing, your mom doesn't want you to get upset. She thinks you're not strong enough. But you got to know who you're dealing with here."

"Why didn't they just steal everything? Why'd they go and smash it all?"

Les shrugged. "Maybe they just wanted to scare you. Sounds like the damage has been done."

"My ass. It's a threat!" Jude got to his feet, opened the refrigerator, and emptied a bottle of chartreuse Gatorade down his throat.

"They're just hicks, these kids," Les said. "Still, you don't really want them using their baseball bats on you. It's a good idea for you to stay here a while, don't you think?"

"Fuck that," Jude said, tossing his empty bottle in the sink. "We have to go back. You can bring McQueen."

Les lowered his lips to Gertrude and, with his barbecue lighter, took an experimental hit. He liked to believe he was the kind of father who would teach his son to fight back, but his son's extremes made him want to offer him the peace pipe instead. The kid had come to him in a coma, and now he was raging for combat. When Harriet had called him to Jude's rescue, he had felt a startling kinship with the boy, a sense of molecular fulfillment that, despite Les's absence in his life, Jude had become the idle, brooding pothead that Les had been as a teenager. Now he recognized none of himself in his son. Surely this turbulent little reverend with the military haircut was not Les's flesh and blood. And then he remembered, with a slow, dismal shame—he was always forgetting—that he wasn't.

"Jude," said Les. "I know you feel guilty about dragging your mom into this mess. But I hardly think firearms are necessary."

"So you're just going to leave her alone up there? Like you did before?"

Les let the accusation hang in the air with his smoke. As exaggerated as his son's logic was, he could not suppress the clammy grip of his own guilt.

"Forget it," Jude said. "We're going out again."

"We are?"

"Me and Johnny and Eliza. They're meeting over here."

"Don't tell me. You're going to church."

"It's not a church." Jude scrounged around in the kitchen drawer, through matchbooks, rolling papers, subway tokens, the collection of MoMA magnets that Di had once stuffed into Les's Christmas stocking—*The Starry Night,* the Campbell's soup can—until he found a couple of crumpled dollar bills. "It's a temple."

"I thought temple was Jewish."

"It is. Or synagogue."

Les shook his head sadly. "My son the saint. St. Jude. You know how you got that name, champ?"

" 'Cause of that stupid song," said Jude.

Les waved his hand. "Your mother liked the song. I liked the saint. He's my favorite. Kind of overlooked, but a fellow to be reckoned with. Loyal, brutal, with that club of his, his head on fire. But you know what? They killed that son of a bitch with an ax."

"Because he was a traitor?"

Johnny buzzed, and Jude buzzed back. He cracked open the door.

"That was Judah," said Les, whose religious training was the sum of one semester of biblical literature and thirty years of cross-word puzzles. "Jude was the loyal apostle, like yourself. But too much loyalty is dangerous, too. Your mom's a tough cookie. She can take care of herself."

Les remembered her as he'd last seen her, when he'd come to retrieve Jude—older, sharper, her face more deeply lined. But she was the same Harriet, the only woman who'd accepted him for the dreamer and schemer that he was. She was an artist, but she had never bought him a collection of MoMA magnets.

Just then, in compelling imitation of a tea leaf reader he'd once had a fling with in Lintonburg—all sequins and gold and spookiness—Di burst through the door. At her heels were Eliza and Johnny. As often as he saw the boy, he could not get used to the ear-rings, which reminded him, now that he thought about it, also of the tea leaf reader. (His fortune: you will leave your wife. Had she been baiting him, or had even the gods pegged him for a bastard?) Eliza was wearing her father's extra-large Harvard sweatshirt, which always broke Les's heart a little.

"I finally got to meet this Johnny," said Di. "He held the door for us."

"Hey there, John Boy," said Les. He couldn't help having a soft spot for him, too, ever since the day he'd learned about his brother and showed up at Les's door looking like the walking dead. He, too, was an underground businessman, and in a neighborhood that made St. Mark's look like Fifth Avenue. For that he'd earned Les's respect. But behind the competent, tattooed facade was a kid who needed a swift kick in the ass.

"How you doing, Mr. Keffy," Johnny said. The kitchen was as crammed as an elevator.

"How about a little sundress, honey?" said Les. "It's spring." These days Eliza was as hard as Jude to keep up with. Now she was back in the city on weekends, running around with Jude and Johnny, no longer Bookworm Betty. "I don't get it. The boys are dressing like girls and the girls are dressing like boys."

"See?" Di rapped Eliza on the elbow. "I say that and she takes my head off."

"You ready to go?" said Jude, distracted, glum.

"Wait." Di made a gun of her hands and aimed it at Jude. "We're having a birthday dinner for Eliza. Not this Saturday but the next. You're coming?" She swung the gun around at Johnny. "You come, too, Johnny."

"I told you I don't want a party."

"Can't you just get her some magnets?" Les suggested.

With excruciating slowness, Di lowered her hands. The look on her face could have cracked ice.

"I like the magnets," he said gently.

"We're going," Eliza said and kissed her mother's cheek.

"Now, where is this temple?"

"In Brooklyn," said Eliza. This seemed to satisfy her mother.

"How come Eliza doesn't go to the matinees with you?" Les wondered.

The three of them exchanged a distinct look.

"It's a little rough for girls," said Johnny, just as Eliza said, "I had to study."

Les picked up the bong and held it under Jude's nose. "A little Gertrude before you go? Offer it to Krishna. It's godly stuff."

Jude said nothing as he followed Johnny and Eliza out the door.

"It was great meeting you," Johnny called to Di. "Thanks for the invite."

"Not this Saturday," said Di, "but the next!"

The door slammed shut, the children's voices disappearing down the chamber of the stairwell. Di sighed. "We might as well go, Lester," she said, clapping her hands soundlessly together.

According to the book Jude had given her, the fetus at eighteen weeks was the size of a bell pepper. Eliza couldn't decide if that was incredibly big or incredibly small. She was still nowhere near certain she had made the right decision, but it was too late now, and that, at least, was some kind of relief. Too late. Oh, well. No turning back. The fetus, whom she'd named Annabel Lee, had fingerprints, eyelids, and nipples.

Eliza's own nipples had gone tender with goose bumps, expanded and purpled; her breasts, scrawled with blue veins, were full. She had been fairly certain, before getting pregnant, that they had reached their full dimensions—she had not set her hopes above an A cup—and this sort of monstrous growth was not the final spurt of puberty. She wished she had someone to show them to. Wives had husbands to marvel with. Other women had boyfriends or doctors or sisters. Teddy had handled them in the dark, more timidly than the other boys, but just as vacantly. No one had studied them, like a painting or a car or a song. They were hers alone.

Night after night she'd climbed into the narrow bed across from Shelby Divine, listening to Shelby's peaceful snores in the dark, more awake than she'd ever been on any drug, her body riveted with her secret. And morning after morning she'd woken up sicker than she'd been with any hangover, so sick she'd felt she was full of a poison. She threw up only once. Mostly her sickness just simmered inside her, suffocating her from the inside out.

Thankfully, the nausea had subsided, and in its place, just as persistent, were Johnny and Jude, bringing her prenatal vitamins, bringing her an IT'S OK NOT TO DRINK button from a Pyramid show, calling her on the hall phone to remind her to eat breakfast (*"Nei-ther* of them's your boyfriend?" asked Shelby), waiting for her at Penn Station on Friday afternoon to fight over carrying her back-pack, bearing Yoo-hoos and bags of sugared peanuts they'd bought from the street vendor outside. Throughout the week she craved those peanuts, the sweet, salty beginning of the weekend, Jude and Johnny standing at the end of the corridor like two dopey grooms.

On the following Friday afternoon, Johnny surprised Eliza by meet-ing her at the train station in Jersey instead of picking her up in New York. He wanted to hang out, he said, just the two of them; he wanted to see the town where she went to school, and she was so pleased to see him that she didn't object to being away from the city for a few more hours. They walked from the train station to the movie theater, down the sidewalk lined with patches of gray ice, and saw *Friday the 13th Part VII,* sharing a bag of Twizzlers. When they emerged from the theater, it was dark outside. Two guys skat-ing down the middle of the street cut over to the curb when they saw Johnny, calling, "Mr. Clean!" Turned out they'd met in the city, at a show at the Ritz. They talked for a few minutes, comparing tattoos, while Eliza watched the traffic pass by. One of them wanted DRUG FREE across his knuckles. Or maybe STR8 EDGE? Johnny told him to stop by.

"Must be nice," Eliza said after they'd ordered at the Italian res-taurant next door, "to be known by everyone."

Anyone who needed a tattoo, or a double tape deck, or space to practice, went to Johnny. He would have made a fine drug dealer. Last fall he had organized a benefit show in Tompkins Square Park, with eleven bands and food donated by the Krishna temple. And last weekend, some band from California he'd met through the mail—the *mail*—had crashed at his apartment, four guys and another four roadies. Eliza had knocked on the door early the next morning to find them sprawled out over every surface, tangled in and out of blankets, in boxers of every imaginable pattern and color. She had never felt so full of desire and so undesirable, pregnant in a gray Harvard T-shirt big enough to be a dress, standing before ten half-naked boys.

"I might as well have been invisible to those guys out there," she said. "Do I really look pregnant?"

Johnny unwrapped his silverware and pressed his paper napkin neatly to his lap. "Don't take it personally. They're probably not into girls."

Eliza studied the tablecloth. She aligned her fingers in the red and white squares, as though she were playing piano. "What about you, though?" she asked.

"What about me?"

She looked up. He was leaning on the edge of the table, his chin cupped in his hand, scoring her with his watery blue eyes. She was staring back so hard, hunting for a fragment of Teddy, that she had to drop her eyes again. "I mean, we know how *I* got here." She patted her stomach.

"I don't need to know the details."

"Well, *I* do. Come on, Johnny. We're friends?"

Johnny cleared his throat. "We are."

She leaned across the table. Dean Martin was singing "That's Amore." A white-haired couple was seated two tables down, each poring over a paperback. "So are you really going to wait till you're married," she whispered, "or what?"

"Eliza—"

"Not that there's anything wrong with that. I mean, I'm a walking advertisement for abstinence. I just mean—"

"What makes you think I haven't . . . ?" Johnny showed his empty palms, then turned them over on the table. Through the ink on his bony hands grew the finest blades of gold hair.

"Oh."

"Just because . . ."

"Oh. Wow, Mr. Clean. You're full of surprises. I just figured, you know . . ."

"I mean, I'm not a freak," Johnny said, avoiding her eyes. "I'm, you know, as red-blooded as the next guy."

"Sorry. It's none of my business."

"It's okay," he said. "I mean, Teddy—I can see why he liked you." He managed a smile, and now it was Eliza who couldn't look him in the eye. "You shouldn't be so hard on yourself, okay? You look great."

They were walking back to the train station to catch the nine-forty-five to New York when he said, as though he'd just remembered to mention it, "So when your mom finds out you're pregnant, I think we should tell her I'm the father."

He was carrying her backpack over one shoulder, like a school-boy walking her home. She stopped, and he turned to face her. She was about to spout something smart-ass, but she stopped herself.

"You do?"

Johnny shoved his hands in his pockets. "People are going to notice soon. They'll want to know who the father is. There's no way your mom is going to let you keep the baby if she knows the situation." Eliza said nothing. She nodded. "So this is the best way. This way we'll be twice as strong. We'll tell her we *both* want to keep the baby." His voice was soft, apologetic, but he was sure of himself.

"But will we?"

The old couple from the restaurant tottered slowly down the sidewalk, propping each other up. Eliza and Johnny stepped aside until they passed by.

"What we'll do is we'll say"—he put his hands on her shoulders—"we'll say we're together. A couple."

"We'll *say* we are?"

"Well, maybe we should be." Johnny shrugged, glancing out at the traffic, as if suggesting maybe they should get dessert. "I want to help raise this kid. Why not do it together?"

Eliza stared into the blank screen of his white T-shirt. When she didn't answer, he placed his finger under her chin and tilted her head slowly, slowly up until her eyes met his, the way a parent will prepare a child for a reprimand, or the way a man will prepare a woman for a kiss. It had been a long time since anyone had touched her so intently, and a hot little hummingbird quivered in her chest.

"Okay," she whispered. But he didn't kiss her.

By the time they took their seats on the train, she was so exhausted, so thoroughly confused, that she fell asleep against Johnny's shoulder, and although Jude had been in and out of her thoughts all evening, it wasn't until the next morning, when he called her at her mom's, more than a note of panic in his voice, that it occurred to her he might have been waiting for her the day before, at Penn Station, a bag of sugared peanuts in his hand.

"Johnny didn't tell you? He picked me up in Jersey."

"He didn't tell me anything. I went to his place and he wasn't there. I went to the station and you weren't there."

Eliza sat up in bed. She slipped her hand under her nightgown and over her stomach. She said she was sorry. She said she didn't know. She told him about Johnny's idea, relating the details as they came back to her, aware of the stony silence accruing on the other end of the line. "It's the best thing," she said, "don't you think?"

Jude skipped temple the next day. He told Johnny he had a headache. Instead he went to Johnny's, sat down on the couch, and picked up *The Laws of Manu*. A new set of passages was marked by the envelope and underlined in blue ink.

59. On failure of issue (by her husband) a woman who has been authorised, may obtain, (in the) proper (manner prescribed), the desired offspring by (cohabitation with) a brother-in-law or (with some other) Sapinda (of the husband).

60. He (who is) appointed to (cohabit with) the widow shall (approach her) at night anointed with clarified butter and silent, (and) beget one son, by no means a second. . . .

63. If those two (being thus) appointed deviate from the rule and act from carnal desire, they will both become outcasts, (as men) who defile the bed of a daughter-in-law or of a Guru.

"What's with this voodoo shit?" he asked when Johnny came home, a full three hours after the ceremony had ended. Jude had been dozing on the couch, and now he did have a headache. He held up the book. "Fucking clarified butter?"

Johnny dropped his tattoo case and placed a styrofoam container of leftovers on the record crate in front of Jude. "It's all that was left."

"You got it for me?"

Johnny crossed to the kitchen and brought back a fork. "You can have it."

Jude, in fact, had not had dinner. He removed his retainers, opened the box, and began efficiently to eat, unhappy with himself for being hungry. Johnny returned to the kitchen sink, the single sink in the apartment, and dispensed a caterpillar of toothpaste on a toothbrush.

"Did Eliza go with you?" Jude asked, his mouth full of naan.

"She did. She likes that voodoo shit." Johnny jammed the toothbrush in his mouth. "She's a spiritual person." He cleaned his teeth with a ritual fervor that involved both arms, his eyebrows, and his hips. A yeasty lather of Colgate drooled down his chin.

"Where have you been, though? It's like midnight."

Johnny turned to the sink, spat, and rinsed his mouth. When he faced Jude again, a spot of toothpaste had blossomed over the heart of his T-shirt, white on white. Jude pointed it out.

"I had a house call." Johnny peeled off the shirt and tossed it into the empty laundry basket. Across the rather pale, rather hairless plain between his nipples, Krishna was playing his flute. This among rubies and sapphires, ocean and fire, sinuous Sanskrit dictums the meaning of which Jude did not know, Xs and more Xs, TRUE TILL DEATH hanging from his clavicle like the iron plates of a necklace, none of which Jude had glimpsed but through the tissue of Johnny's T-shirt, though he wondered now if Eliza had.

"You just did a tattoo?"

"I can't even see straight. I'm taking a shower, and then I'm going to bed."

"When you going to tattoo me, man? You said."

"You don't want to start, man. I'm telling you. You won't stop. Good night. Or stay if you want, since you've made yourself so comfortable."

"What if I pay you?"

"Maybe," he said, pausing in the doorway to the bathroom. "Any more questions?"

Jude stared at the inside of the wax container, the oily, electric orange residue of his meal. When he'd told Johnny about what Hippie and Tory had done to his mother's studio, Johnny had been sympathetic, then suspicious. Why had those guys targeted her? Jude finally told him the truth—he might have stolen a little pot from Hippie—and Johnny just shook his head, disappointed.

Still, Johnny had seen no reason for Jude to dive back into trouble in Vermont. "Don't we have enough on our hands?"

He had a point. Sitting in Johnny's apartment, Jude felt the mass of that responsibility. He was tired. But maybe Johnny was taking it into his own hands now. "Eliza told me you're going to pretend you're the father."

Johnny was tugging at his bottom lip. The tattoo on the inside, below his gums, said, simply, NO. "It's the only way, man."

"But are you guys just friends, or . . . ?"

Blood beat in Jude's ears. He wasn't sure which answer he wanted to hear.

"*Just* friends?" Johnny said. "None of us are just friends anymore."

Les was on the toilet four mornings later, hitting Gertrude and doing the *Times* crossword, when the phone bleated in the insistent, lonely way it does at sunrise, when the news is rarely good. Les allowed it to ring. Just as the sound became insufferable he heard his son's descent from his bed, the gargle of his voice, and after several more moments, an ambivalent knock on the door.

"Dad?"

Leaning his head back and closing his eyes, Les released a billow of smoke to the ceiling. "Son."

"We got a problem. Can you hear me?"

Les wondered if the "we" referred to Jude and himself, or to Jude and the person on the phone.

"Can it wait a sec? I'm only about one-third done here."

"Can you just hurry up?"

"Go on and tell me. I can hear you."

Nothing for a few seconds but the wobbling of the mirror on the back of the door.

"Eliza's on the phone. She's at school. You won't get mad, right?"

Les balanced the crossword on the edge of the sink and the bong on the crossword. The prospect of helping Eliza—the prospect of helping Eliza without getting mad, as Di would—gave him satisfying pause. "I won't get mad."

"And you won't tell her mom?"

"Unless she's dying. Or she's killed someone."

On the doorjamb, painted over but still legible, were the pocket-knife scars that recorded the stature of some other tenant's children. Les had penciled in Eliza when she was little enough for that sort of thing—Di wouldn't allow it at her place—but the graphite had long ago been smudged away.

"She's bleeding."

"What sort of bleeding?"

"You know, woman bleeding."

Les scratched at his beard with his pencil. "Uh-huh?"

"The thing is, she's pregnant, though."

The pencil slipped from his grasp. As he bent to retrieve it, his forehead collided with the bong, which clattered into the sink, spilling its contents onto the newspaper.

Les put his hand to his forehead. He pressed hard, thinking.

"What should we do?" his son asked.

From the sink, Les retrieved Gertrude's glass slide, which had snapped off at the base. It lay helplessly in Les's palm, an amputated finger, dainty as an icicle, dumb as a dick.

"For God's sake, kid, haven't you heard of a rubber?"

The waiting room at the Mount Sinai Emergency Room, where Eliza had met them with her backpack and a look of being lost and not lost, as though she had a standing appointment for lunch there each week and was scanning the room for her date, was upholstered in a maroon a little too much like the color of blood. There were the usual amenities: issues of *Prevention* and *Reader's Digest* that looked as though they'd survived a flood, the floor toy that involved sliding colored beads on shoots of wire, the *Today* show murmuring on the television in the corner, broadcasting from several sunnier blocks away news of the presidential race. It was early for emergencies, 8:20 according to the clock on the wall. The only other patients to make an entrance were a febrile toddler over her mother's shoulder, and a construction worker, who on the site of the hospital addition had nailed his hand to a two-by-four.

"Maybe it's for the best," said Les when they were alone, feeding himself a jelly doughnut he'd had the foresight to purchase, with a twenty-ounce cup of coffee, between the subway station and the hospital. "She's young. She's not ready to be a mom. It's nature's way of taking care of things."

Jude sat with his elbows on his knees, speaking to the hemoglobin-colored carpet. "How does it happen, exactly? Is it . . . is it just blood?"

Eliza had insisted on going into the examination room alone, had remained around long enough only for Les to whisper, "You keeping anything else from me? Are you a Mets fan, too?"

"I don't know, champ," he said to Jude. "You know who should be here is Johnny. If he's the father, he'd want to know. Why don't you call him."

"He doesn't have a phone. He's going to be mad," Jude let out.

"Why?"

"Not mad. Just—sad."

"Sad," Les agreed. He slurped his coffee. "But it's a relief you're not the father. You get tied up in it, the lady's grieving, distraught, she's guilty, you're guilty, everyone's feeling lousy. Be glad you're not involved. Babies," he said. He nudged Jude's arm and indicated the walls around them. "You know you were born here?"

Jude looked at his father and shook his head.

"It's true." Les leaned back and crossed one hairy leg over the other. He was wearing his gray suede Birkenstocks with the broken clasp, one of the straps flapping like a tongue. His calves were the size of cantaloupes; they bore no resemblance to Jude's. "You were tiny as a rabbit. And you had this shock of red, red hair." He hovered his hand over his Yankees cap, indicating. "Your mom and I were sitting in the nursery in rocking chairs, in scrubs, with these shower caps on our heads, like they were afraid we were going to give you the plague. Just waiting for you." He wasn't watching the television now but the empty space in the room. "We waited there forever, just rocking back and forth. Your mom was terrified they'd changed their minds, that there was a problem. She wanted a cigarette so bad and all she had was this king-size bag of M&M'S. She ate the entire bag of M&M'S, waiting for you."

Jude had not heard this story before, and it was only after hearing it that he realized he'd had a picture of his first meeting with his parents, and this was not it. He now understood why his father had chosen this inconveniently located emergency room, ninety blocks away: it belonged, in his mind, to a baby hospital. Second-degree burn: Beth Israel. Miscarriage: Mount Sinai. If Jude's heart were not already preoccupied, it might have been warmed by his father's lumbering logic.

"She prefers Snickers now," Jude answered, not looking at him. Then, "Did she tell you I might have FAS?"

Les nodded. "Yes, she did."

"Retard disease," said Jude after a moment, because his father was cruelly silent.

"Not retard disease. It's a disability."

"It's why I'm always in trouble and fuck my numbers up so bad."

"Fuck your numbers up how?"

"Mix them up. Turn them around. Letters, too. You didn't know that?"

"I guess not," Les said. "Look, who cares? It's just a fancy name for your birth mom indulged a little too much. So did half my generation, okay? We didn't know any better. Your mom smoked like a chimney when she was knocked up with your sister. Not to mention a little wacky tobacky now and then."

"She did? While she was pregnant?"

"She said it helped with morning sickness," Les said, shrugging dubiously. This piece of trivia made Jude feel better and worse at the same time, but Les looked pleased with himself, as though he'd wrapped up a nice father-son conversation. The fact that his father had tossed off the story of his birth in a waiting room while watching the *Today* show, might just have easily not shared it with him (as his mother surely would not have shared it with him), was enjoying the memory like he was enjoying his jelly doughnut and the prospect of pulling one over on his girlfriend, left Jude with nothing else to say.

The sliding doors to the street blew open then. Through them came three young black men, two propping up the third, whose jacket pocket was soaked with blood. The boy's head was rolled back on his neck, and the yellow whites of his eyes were still. He made a sound as though he were choking on his tongue. A bubble of blood came up and sat poised on his open mouth for a moment before breaking.

It wasn't until nearly an hour later, when Eliza returned to the waiting room, pale and smiling and still pregnant, that Jude could drain that blood from his mind. She was spotting—it wasn't a miscarriage, but an infection—and Jude was so relieved that he clutched her arm and whispered, "Bacterial vaginosis!" as though they were the loveliest words on earth.

"I saw her on the monitor," Eliza told them on the subway ride home. "They did an ultrasound. She's jumping around like a jumping bean! Do beans jump?"

"She?" said Les.

"Annabel Lee," Jude explained. The doctors said they could determine the sex of the baby, but Eliza didn't want to know.

They begged Les not to tell Di, and Les, after enjoying their pleas for a while, agreed. "A baby," he said, looking worried for the first time in his life. Jude told Eliza about the man who'd come in bleeding. Had he been shot? they wondered. Stabbed? Had he lived or died? Jude wanted to put his hand on Eliza's belly, but he didn't. He hadn't known, before that morning, how badly he wanted Teddy's baby to be born.

Johnny was not pleased that Eliza and Jude had confided in Les, but he did not complain that they hadn't consulted him first, because, as it happened, Johnny had been indisposed at the time. The morning Eliza was admitted to the ER, he wasn't in his apartment but in Rooster DeLuca's, a scrappy little studio near Charlie Parker's old building, making a house call for an eight-headed dragon he'd been working on for months. The first several appointments had taken place at Johnny's, but lately he'd insisted on a new arrangement. It was risky to sneak his equipment through the street, but it was riskier to have customers visit his apartment at all hours. Most of Johnny's tattoos were done by his friend Gomez, whose whole studio not long ago had been raided and fined by the Health Department. And last week the artist they called Picasso had quit after one of his customers fell over and died of AIDS. The city had banned tattooing in the sixties because of hepatitis B, and AIDS made hepatitis look like a cold sore. "Too dicey these days," said Picasso, but now Johnny had a new crop of customers. He was terrified of the virus—he sterilized every needle—but he was too broke to be picky. He would tattoo anyone.

It was the most extensive single tattoo Johnny had performed: the entire expanse of Rooster's broad back, armpit to armpit, skull to ass. It was the one empty canvas left on his generously inked body. He had a hairy fucking back, Rooster, each black hair as long as the time since their last session, since the tattoo had healed enough to allow more work. On the Murphy bed that took up most of the room, Rooster lay on his stomach. On the nightstand, Johnny's kit, plastered with band stickers, splattered with ink, lay openmouthed. Johnny sat on a stool, spreading a sheet of shaving cream on Rooster's back. He worked the razor down the slope of his spine, rinsing it after each stroke in a cloudy mug of water. When he was done, he mopped up the cream with his cloth, took the Vaseline Rooster kept in the nightstand, and applied a dollop to the right shoulder blade.

"How's it lookin'?"

"I thought you fell asleep." They spoke loudly now over the sound of the needle.

"I did for a minute," Rooster said. "I was dreamin' about pancakes. I'm hungry."

"You're always hungry."

"You work up my appetite, baby."

Johnny worked the foot pedal, filling in the seventh head. He was getting close to the end. "One more visit," he said, "and I think I'll be done."

"Then I'll have to come up with somethin' else for you to do."

The needle was riding the dune of Rooster's back, veining the thirteenth eyeball of the dragon, and Johnny found himself picturing what Eliza's narrow back would look like.

"Rooster?"

"Yeah?"

"You've been with girls, right?"

"It's been a long time."

Johnny wondered if he could bring himself to do it. It couldn't be so different. A body was a body. "What was it like?" He'd tattooed a few girls before, and had felt a kind of awe at the smoothness of their skin under his hands.

"Where's this comin' from?"

"Just curious."

"You thinkin' about that girl?"

Johnny didn't say anything. The needle throbbed in his hand.

"Well, you wouldn't have to worry about knockin' her up." Rooster laughed, bumping the needle.

"Don't laugh, man!" Johnny let up on the pedal and withdrew the needle. "You fucked up the eyeball!" He wiped at it with his cloth. The needle had scratched the dragon's cornea, tracing a red tail through it. "It looks like he's crying blood!"

"Can you fix it?"

"Fucking A."

"Fuckin' right."

Johnny snapped off his gloves. Rooster sat up. His chest was dark with the same stubborn, wiry hairs, and imprinted with the texture of the tousled sheets. He wasn't laughing anymore. For months, before Johnny had gotten his own apartment, this was the bed he'd slept in. He'd never quite been able to bring himself to leave it.

"Why don't you sleep in my bed?" Rooster had asked him that first night he'd rescued him from Tompkins, almost two years ago.

"No, man," Johnny had said. "It's your bed. You take it."

Rooster had looked at him, placing the big, calloused palm of his hand on Johnny's neck, and said, "That's not what I meant."

Rooster did the same thing now, stroking Johnny's Adam's apple with his thumb. He was gentle, always gentle, but Johnny felt his breath stop, choked with indecision.

"You want to know what it feels like? Bein' with a girl?" Rooster dropped his hand. "It feels like bein' a fuckin' coward."

TEN

In the kitchen, Neena was butterflying a leg of lamb, an indelicate procedure that recalled neither lamb nor butterfly, but a bloody approximation of log splitting, diapering, and liposuction. She had learned the method from her grandmother, a billy goat of a woman four and a half feet tall, in the kitchen of the hotel where she worked in Chandigarh. Until she came to America, it was the biggest kitchen Neena had ever seen. This kitchen, on the Upper West Side of Manhattan, thirteen stories in the air (it had taken some time to explain to her family back home why the address was the fourteenth floor), had a six-burner gas range, a refrigerator that dispensed ice crushed or cubed, and a wine rack so full that taking a bottle home now and then was like taking a pin from a pincushion. The boyfriend (he was not a boy, but he was dressed like one, in sandals and cutoff jeans and an untucked Hawaiian shirt) was opening the second bottle of the evening. He refilled his glass and then Neena's, spilling a puddle of wine on the counter. "Looking good, girl," he said with a whistle, at either Neena or the lamb, and, taking the bottle, drunkenly exited the room.

Stepping into the air-conditioned parlor, away from the aromatic, ovened kitchen, Les saw that the guests had arrived and were arranging themselves on various pieces of furniture. Eliza sat on the ottoman beside a pyramid of gifts, Johnny and Jude in the pair of wingback chairs. "Wow," said Johnny, who was wearing, of all things, a linen sport coat, "your home is really beautiful, Ms. Urbanski." He took in the claw-foot coffee table, the baby grand posed like an open-jawed shark. He was eyeing the painting hanging over the piano, the backside of a reclining male nude.

"That's Pierre," Les explained.

"Thank you, Johnny." Di draped herself over the divan. She was wearing jeans and ballet slippers and an indigo-colored leotard, which swept low on her very fine back, and she was balancing a wineglass in her many-ringed fingers. This left Les standing at the margin of the room, but he was glad to keep his distance. Di hadn't looked at him since earlier that afternoon, when she'd sent him out to pick up her order at the bakery.

He was content being her errand boy: that was how he atoned, how he returned to her good graces. He had done his best this afternoon, and now the living room was festooned with the pink wishes of the Upper East Side's finest merchants—bouquets of balloons; crimped streamers; sixteen frosted cupcakes from Payard, plated in wedding cake tiers and bedecked with silver bullets. *It looks like a baby shower,* Di had remarked to Eliza. *Doesn't it?*

Eliza was shaking one of the gift boxes now. For her birthday dinner, she had belatedly taken Les's advice and chosen a dress, a strapless, coral-colored dress with a ruffled skirt and pumps to match. Full, but not full enough. She looked as though she'd swallowed one of those big, curvaceous autumn squashes. "Gucci," she guessed.

"Nope. Go ahead and open it," said Di. Eliza did, not taking her time. Inside was a silver watch, slender as a bracelet.

"Ooh, Tiffany's!"

Eliza was a thrift store hound; she was not one to exclaim over costly gifts. Di wasn't really one to give them, either. They were putting on a sick sort of show, bending over backward to please each other. Eliza leaned over and placed her wrist on Johnny's knee, and Johnny fastened the watch for her. Then she trotted over to kiss her mother's cheek. It was unbearable, watching a person who was in the dark, especially when it was you who had put her there.

"Going to check on that lamb," Les said, mostly to himself, and returned to the kitchen.

Eliza balled up the wrapping paper, tossed it at Jude, and tied the ribbon around Johnny's thigh. "Thanks," he said.

"It's a garter," she explained.

"Would you boys care for wine?" Di asked, picking up the open bottle that Les had left on the table.

Jude and Johnny declined. "They're *straight edge*," said Eliza in a mock whisper.

"Of course. I forgot. Eliza?" She lifted the bottle. Eliza shook her head, crossed her legs, and stared at her shoes.

"I'm feeling kind of yucky," she said and patted her belly heartily. At this, Jude could not help but direct a desperate glance at Johnny. What was that about? And what was with the getup? She was nearly five months pregnant.

Di stood up, walked over to her daughter, and held the back of her hand to her forehead. "You don't have a fever, darling."

"Something smells good," Jude said loudly.

"It really does," Johnny agreed.

"Neena's doing a lamb," Di said.

"Mother, you know they're vegetarian. They don't eat lamb."

"Of course. *Vegan,* isn't it?"

"*Vee*-gan," said Jude helpfully. "*Vay*-gans are from the planet Vega."

Di returned to the divan, turned sideways so she could stare into the picture window behind her. The sun was sinking over New Jersey. "Listen to you three, with your secret codes." She sipped her wine. "You're all very busy together, aren't you?"

"We've been going to the temple a lot," said Jude.

"When I was sixteen, I was dancing seven days a week. I didn't have time to run around the city with a couple of boys."

"Johnny's eighteen," Eliza pointed out.

"Oh?" She raised her eyebrows, impressed. "An adult. What do you do, Johnny?"

"I'm a musician."

"And a tattoo artist," Eliza added. Jude looked at her with concern, but she waved her hand. "What's she going to do—call the police? She's practically married to a drug dealer."

"We are *not* married, practically or even remotely," said Di. "Do you make a decent living with tattoos, Johnny?"

"Getting there," Johnny said. He was sitting comfortably, legs crossed, nibbling macadamia nuts from a glass bowl he cupped in his hand. "I save money by working out of my apartment."

"And where is this apartment?"

"Mother, what does it matter?"

"What about college? You don't live with anyone? Your family?"

"*Mother*, don't be rude!"

"I don't have any family, ma'am." Every pair of eyes in the room dropped to the floor. Johnny shifted his to the painting above the piano. The man's back was as smooth and as rippled as a conch.

Di sipped her wine thoughtfully. "I'm awfully sorry about that."

"I bet this one's Burberry," said Eliza, ripping the paper from one of the larger gifts. This time she was right. Inside was a checked wool scarf, feathered at the ends and wide as a shawl. "Oh, I love it!" She whipped it extravagantly around her neck and crossed the room again to Di. This time, she sat down square on her mother's lap, startling the wine from her glass. "I love it, I love it, I love it!" she said, kissing her mother's cheek each time. Di went with it, kissing her back. They cuddled; they cooed. Eliza wrapped them both in the scarf. Di buried a hand in Eliza's side, tickling her. Eliza shrieked, leaning back luxuriously, her shoe balanced precariously on her foot.

At this point, Les returned from the kitchen, balancing three glasses of soda water. In the pocket of his shorts were the two letters, now freckled with red wine: the bill from Mount Sinai Hospital for the balance of services rendered (he'd thought he'd paid the whole thing), and the notice of expulsion from Eliza's school (*We regret to inform you . . . unanswered phone calls . . . take truancy very seriously . . . out-of-town permissions . . . disregard for disciplinary probation . . .*). Both had arrived in Di's mailbox that afternoon, and by the time Les arrived to help with the party, Di had burned through half a pack of cigarettes. For once he'd managed to keep a secret, but after Di confronted him with those letters, he broke down, spilled all the details—the ER, the baby, the father.

"Jeezum Crow," he said now, clanging the glasses down on the table. "Just tell her."

Di stopped tickling. Eliza stopped giggling. No one seemed sure which one he was talking to. Les withdrew a pack of cigarettes from his pocket and lit one, then tossed the pack and lighter on the table. Jude sat frozen. Johnny worked a macadamia nut in his cheek.

"You give me hell about keeping it from you, but now you're just torturing the girl! And *she's* so desperate to tell you, to get an ounce of support from you, she's got it written on her dress! I didn't tell her, Eliza, but she found out. And by the way, you're kicked out of school."

"I know," Eliza mumbled, sliding off her mother's lap.

"You girls are two of a kind." He looked at Di. "Why do you

think she doesn't tell you anything? Because you control the shit out of any situation you get your hands on! And why do you think she does that, Eliza? Because you're so goddamn out of control! *Three* schools you've been kicked out of? It's a good thing your mother's sending you to one of those Florence Crittenton homes, because at this point no other school would take you."

Les stopped for a breath. His hands shook as he held the cigarette to his lips. He had never felt entirely at home here, in this apartment bought with Wall Street money. Les was everything Daniel Urbanski was not. He was all the long-haired men Di had given up for marriage. Her downtown man. Mother Nature's Son. Her joker, her smoker, her midnight toker. "Blessed are the pot sellers, illusion dwellers!" So many nights they'd spent adrift on her waterbed, smoking joints with the windows open, Simon and Garfunkel anointing their unlikely union. But it seemed that the illusion had been his.

"Florence who?" Eliza asked.

"*I'm* sorry, Lester," said Di coolly, leaning over to snatch up the cigarettes. "I didn't know you were so concerned about education. *I'm* the irresponsible parent. *I* didn't notice that my fifteen-year-old daughter is pregnant because she was *enrolled in school*. I suppose I could have kept better tabs on her if I let her drop out and smoke *reefer* all day. Maybe I could build a special room for her to have sex in, with a heart-shaped bed and a big mirror on the ceiling." She lit a cigarette and drew on it forcefully.

"Mom, you don't smoke anymore." Eliza crossed her arms over her stomach, gripping her elbows.

"I don't smoke pot anymore," pointed out Jude.

"She's not fifteen anymore," pointed out Johnny.

"I'm sorry—*sixteen*." Di spoke slowly, without anger, clipping each word. "Fully prepared to raise a child."

"You don't have to talk about me like I'm not here! I've got resources. I've got money, a lot more money than a lot of mothers have. When I turn eighteen, I'll have enough money—"

"Enough money for what, Eliza? What will you do until then? I've already got a room set up for you at a facility upstate. I called this afternoon."

"I'm not going to any fucking facility!"

"They take your baby," Jude said, pitching forward. "That's what a 'facility' is."

"They don't *take* it," Di said. "They don't sell it into slave labor. They give it to parents that can take care of it properly."

"Like my dad?" Jude said.

Through the picture window, Manhattan was now curdled a pale twilight blue. No one had moved to turn on a light, and Jude could feel the darkness sifting through the room. He was glad his father's face was shadowed by his Yankees cap.

"You're angry that Di found out, but I didn't tell her," Les said. "I chose to cover for *you*."

"Of *course* you chose him. Anything to make *Jude* like you. Anything to be a *pal*. Leave the fathering to someone who has the time."

"Oh, Christ."

"Has it occurred to you," said Di, "that Eliza might not be in this situation if she weren't desperate for a little attention from a father figure?" Raising his wineglass to his lips, Les momentarily lost his grip. He fumbled it like a football, a red tide rising to find the lapel of his shirt, before he caught it again. No one moved to get a cloth from the kitchen; no one offered the soda water that sat, untouched, on the table.

"You can blame me for fucking up my own kids," said Les. "But don't blame me for fucking up yours." He put down his glass, gouged out his cigarette in the ashtray, plucked up a cupcake, and kissed the crown of Eliza's head. "You're not fucked up. I'm just saying." Eliza sat with her elbows on her knees, hands covering her face. "Happy birthday, sweetheart. I tie-dyed you a Yankees shirt—it's around here somewhere. You can call me." His sandals slapped the marble floor as he crossed the room. The door closed noisily behind him.

From behind her hands, Eliza smelled ginger and garlic and cooking meat. She kicked off her shoes. In her bare feet, she stood up and wandered in the direction of the window. She said, "I'm sorry I've disappointed you, Mother, but I—"

"Darling, no." Di put down her glass. "I'm not *disappointed* that you're pregnant. I'm disappointed that you didn't *tell* me. If you'd come to me, we could have *done* something about it."

Eliza rested her hands over her belly. "Well, that's why I didn't tell you." Typical of her mother, she thought—who cared whether the problem was school or drugs or boys or a baby, as long as she got to choose the solution?

But Les was right: they were two of a kind. Eliza was as stubborn as her mother. She was halfway through this solution of hers, and yet standing there she was not at all sure whether she'd chosen it because it was what she wanted or because it was what her mother wouldn't.

Or because it was what Jude and Johnny wanted. She looked at them, two pairs of blue eyes watching her as though she were an afterschool special.

"What are you looking at?" she demanded of them. "Don't just sit there. I'm doing this for *you*."

"What do you mean?" asked Di.

"She means," said Johnny, standing up, "that I want this baby as much as she does." He crossed the room, sneakers squeaking against the floor, and pressed a palm to Eliza's belly. "Right?"

Her stomach fluttered. She could feel each of his fingertips through the layers of taffeta. No one but the ER doctor had touched her pregnant belly, and now, as if the baby had been awoken, she felt a tiny quiver again, like a goldfish swimming against the fishbowl of her belly.

But Johnny didn't feel it. He was digging in his pocket for something, dropping to his knee, saying, "I've got a present for you, too."

"Oh, mercy," said her mother.

Annabel Lee was telling her something, but she didn't know what it was.

"You can't marry her. She's sixteen years old! Not without parental consent."

A tail-stroke, a wing-beat, a slither through the grass.

"I can in New Jersey," said Johnny, opening the box.

The boyfriend's boxer shorts were gone, his toothbrush, the glass pipe he kept cinched in a chamois sack at the bottom of the hamper, where he thought no one would look. His crossword puzzles were not in the basket in the master bath; his bottles of beer did not roll in the crisper. Whether these things had been fetched or discarded Neena did not know. She was not particularly sorry to see them go.

The morning after her birthday party, zipping an enormous cowhide suitcase on her bed, Eliza announced that she was leaving. "Don't let her out of your sight," her mother had instructed Neena before leaving the apartment herself an hour earlier, but when Eliza threw her arms, quite abruptly, around Neena's neck, the woman did not feel she could hold her captive. Neena was not confident she could construct a sentence in English adequate to express her confusion, embarrassment, worry, and joy. With gratitude she had several times accepted the girl's cocaine, which her son had traded a friend for a VCR, an interview suit, and a 1972 Dodge Coronet, but she did not know how to accept a good-bye hug.

Downtown Les was chasing a fly with a flyswatter when the buzzer buzzed. When he opened the door in his undershirt, Eliza was sitting on her suitcase, breathing heavily. "What are you doing, crazy woman? You carry that up the stairs?" Les dragged it through the kitchen and into the living room, where Eliza collapsed on the futon. Then he brought her a glass of water.

"Where's Jude?" She gulped from her glass.

Les, standing, swatted at the drone that swept by his ear, his hangover indistinguishable from the insect that orbited his head. "Gone somewhere on his skateboard." With his flyswatter, he indicated the suitcase. "What, are you moving in?"

"Not with you. I'm on my way to Johnny's. I don't think he's home yet." She placed her glass on the coffee table, lifted her necklace out of her collar, and gently bounced the charms in her hand. "I had to get out of there before my mom came back."

Les turned the flyswatter on Eliza, fanning her. "Just so you know, it's a terrible idea."

"Moving in with Johnny?"

"Marrying him. Jude told me."

A sticky strand of Eliza's hair batted in the draft of the fan. "Papa, don't preach," she said. "You have any better ideas?"

"You can stay here with me. Sleep in the loft. Jude can sleep in the bathtub. When the baby's born, we'll sell it on the black market. I know a guy in Jersey City who can get ten thousand bucks for a white kid."

"What if it's not white?"

"Five," said Les.

Eliza unzipped one side of the suitcase, slipped her hand in, and withdrew a chamois bag, which she tossed to Les. Les caught it against his chest. "She must have junked everything else last night. When I woke up this morning, she was gone."

Les opened the drawstring and slid out the glass pipe. It was baby-shit brown marbled with streaks of green, squat as a mushroom and smooth as a stone. Not the prettiest thing, but she was reliable. Inside the bowl was an ancient bud, which he dug out like a booger and dropped on the carpet. "Harriet!" he said. "This old girl must be twenty-five years old. My ex's earliest work. You meet my old lady when you were in Vermont?"

"I didn't have the pleasure."

"She's a piece of work."

He thought about her while he stroked her namesake, the curve of the woman's thickened hips not unlike those of the pipe. He thought about the way, back in February, he'd approached her bedroom door—*their* bedroom door—the five musical knocks he'd played on it. He had intended only to say good night. Instead he'd found himself smelling the patchouli and cigarettes in her hair, the warm mama scent in the crook of her neck, like borax and breast milk and the sawdust of their bygone household, and as he walked her backward to their bed, she had smelled him back.

Now he went instinctively for the cookie jar on the kitchen counter, took out a thimbleful of pot, and packed it in the pipe. They'd been like a couple of teenagers, pawing at each other, up all night, like the teenagers they'd actually been when they'd first smelled the crooks of each other's necks. He was back on the couch by the time their children, now teenagers, had woken the next morning. And now Eliza was pregnant and her suitcase was packed and out of it snaked the black lace of some undergarment he preferred not to identify.

"What do I call you now? My ex-almost-stepdaughter?"

"Don't get sappy on me, Lester."

"Will you still come visit me?"

"I'll be down the street."

Les sat down beside her and took a hit on the pipe. It settled him, loosened his bones. It tasted, somehow, like Vermont. "When's the wedding?"

"Sunday, I hope. Johnny's out taking care of the details now. It's going to be at the temple."

"I'm guessing you don't mean Emanu-El."

"Are you coming?"

Les took her hand in his and examined the ring. The stone was no bigger than a lentil, and almost certainly not a diamond; he knew a guy who sold these on Fourteenth Street. "You really love this kid? This Hare Rama with all the jewelry?"

Eliza withdrew her hand sharply. She took up her necklace again, jogged the charms.

"He appears to be noble," Les went on. "A stand-up guy. But why marry him? You're already knocked up. Why not cohabit for a while, play it by ear?"

"That's what you'd do, isn't it. Play it by ear."

"I find it's the best organ to play by." He swatted at the fly. "Although I've been accused of playing by others."

Eliza was scrunched down on the futon, her body practically horizontal, her hand absently rubbing the T-shirt stretched over her belly. "What if it was Jude's kid? Would you and my mom still want me to give it away?"

"If it was Jude's kid, well, we'd all get married and live in one big incestuous duplex."

"It would have been better, wouldn't it," said Eliza, gazing into space.

Les tried to picture it: a new age sitcom family, the four of them taking turns with the nighttime feedings. A grandfather at the age of forty-three. It was no more outrageous than the idea he'd had, in the early hours of St. Valentine's Day, his ex-wife catching her breath beside him, of returning to his old life. Not taking any vows—just staying there in that bed. Just playing it by ear. But in the morning Harriet had wordlessly deposited a plate of scrambled eggs in front of him, and then he'd whisked his son away. And now neither of these options was available to him, his old family or his new. The phone rang, and Les got up and went eagerly to it. He found himself hoping it was Jude, the thread that now held his families together.

Instead, he heard the familiar static of a cordless phone.

Les listened to the voice crack through the noise, to the voice and the static and the fly and the door-buzzer peal of his headache. The voices in his head. Had he seen Eliza? He had better tell her if he'd seen Eliza, he had better tell her where that punk lived, if he didn't want the cops involved, if he didn't want a drug-sniffing dog at his door, if he knew what was good for him.

Les was not entirely sure that he did.

"I'm sorry," he said. "I can't hear you very well." And he placed the phone in its cradle.

"Oh, God. Is she coming over?"

"Hold on."

"She's coming to find me, isn't she?"

"Hold *on,* girl. I'm thinking." It was over, he was thinking. It was not the first time he had hung up on Di, or she on him. There had been other fights, accusations, betrayals, the obvious incompatibilities, but now he had crossed a line. He had stepped between Di and her child.

"I wish there was a place we could *go.* Someplace safe where she won't find me." Eliza was sitting up now, leaning over her belly, her face in her hands. "We can't stay at Johnny's! He doesn't even have AC!"

Les picked up the phone and dialed the number that, the dozen or so times he'd dialed it in the last seven years, he was always surprised to remember.

"What are you doing?"

He listened to the dial tone, fanning himself with the flyswatter now, fanning himself as though putting out a fire. He had a wild idea as he waited: that his ex-wife was pregnant with his child, that this child would be the one he wouldn't screw up, that he could have his old family and his new one under one roof. *Honey,* he'd say, *I'm coming home.*

"Is Jude okay?" Harriet asked when they'd said their hellos. She sounded impatient, or maybe just anxious, out of breath, the way she had when he'd admitted to her that yes, he'd told Jude about the kids who'd broken into her studio. She had just run inside from the garden, or upstairs from the basement, where she was doing a load of laundry. She was not a woman longing for her husband to come home. Their children were the players in a business arrangement, and what had happened in their marriage bed was an olfactory fluke. *What did you do to him now?* said her voice, which might as well have been the voice of the woman he'd just hung up on, the other woman he'd deceived and failed, whose faith he'd neglected to earn.

"He's fine," Les said. "More than fine. He's clean, he's cured. His rehabilitation is complete."

What was he saying, Harriet wanted to know.

A dark shape spun in the corner of Les's eye, and he slammed the flyswatter on the counter. When he lifted it, the fly was stamped to the back, its papery wing still fluttering. He had done it without a thought, and now it seemed a horrible accident. It broke his heart.

"Remember," he said, "when you asked me for a favor?"

Three and a half blocks east, in the building Jude was passing on his skateboard, Johnny was eating a green apple in Rooster's apartment. The previous phase of the eight-headed dragon had not had time to heal; Johnny had not brought his equipment with him. From the pillow where his head lay, he could see the edge of the dark, drawn curtains, into the bright morning. This sheltered calm reminded him of the motels he'd frequented during his nomadic childhood, moving from city to city with his brother and his mother, all their possessions in the hatch of their sun-roasted car. He remembered playing Marco Polo in a motel pool, a scrape on his cheek from grazing the fiberglass floor. He remembered jumping on the motel beds with Teddy. He remembered Teddy, when he was still a baby, sleeping in an open suitcase Queen Bea had lined with a towel on the floor, and now Johnny imagined carrying Teddy around in that suitcase, safe inside in the dark. He felt its handle in his palm. Now Teddy really could fit in that suitcase again. He was a few pounds of ashes in a kitchen canister he kept on his closet floor.

He did not share these things with Rooster. Rooster, unlike the rest of New York, knew Teddy had existed, and knew he was the one who had knocked up the girl Johnny would marry on Sunday. But today Johnny didn't feel like talking about the past. "You ever been to California?" He took a crisp bite of his apple.

"I wish," Rooster said.

"You think it's a good place to raise a kid?"

"You ain't movin' to California. Not without me."

Johnny didn't say anything.

"I see. That's why you gotta leave. Because I tempt you to the dark side."

"I told you. I can't do it anymore."

Rooster raised his head from his pillow. His jaw, still bruised a mealy blue from a rough day in the pit, tightened. "This ain't Vermont, baby. This is New York. Fags don't jump off tall buildings here. They don't have to meet in dark rooms. Here we have parades."

Johnny chewed the tart meat of his apple. Of course they still met in dark rooms. Down in the park, a few hundred feet away, they were meeting right now. Rafael, the kid who'd been gangbanged in the comfort station, was not appearing in any parades.

A truck hit a pothole in the street outside. Johnny's clothes were folded on the stool beside the bed, the Chuck Taylors posed on top emanating the subtlest locker-room stench. "When I finish this apple, I'm going to take a shower, and then I'm going to get dressed, and then I'm going home."

"And what about the band? You're sure you're not quittin' 'cause a me?"

"Don't get a big head, Rooster. I'm getting married."

"You're sure you're not gettin' married 'cause a me?"

"You can pick up your drums whenever. You don't need me."

Rooster, lying on his stomach, tapped a single, solemn drumstick against the floor. "So you're gonna shack up together, you and Yoko Ono and this baby."

"Look, lots of cultures do it, okay? The Jews, the Mongols. I've been reading about it. When a man dies, his brother steps in to marry his wife. It's in the Bible. It's called levirate marriage. In Africa, they call it widow inheritance."

"That's goddamn romantic."

"There's even something like it in *The Laws of Manu*. If a guy can't procreate, his wife takes up with his brother so they can have a kid."

"There's a word for that, baby, but it ain't *widow inheritance*. It's called livin' in the closet. Fags have been doin' that for thousands of years, too."

Johnny had finished his apple. The core was browning in his hand. "*The Laws of Manu* says after the baby is born the woman and the brother can go back to being how they were. Platonic."

"So you're gonna be happily married to your platonic widow wife. You'll still be kissin' her every morning and every night, in fifty, sixty years."

Johnny didn't know what would happen after the baby was born. Maybe he'd love the baby so much he'd figure out how to love Eliza, too. Maybe they'd all move to California and live in a tent on an ocean cliff, and he'd walk Teddy's baby on the beach.

Rooster added, "Unless we're both dead of AIDS."

Johnny looked up. Rooster had his back to him, the defeated mass of his body still collapsed facedown. They'd never said it aloud, not to each other. They talked about the people they knew who were wasting away, the bums and junkies and squatters, people whose own families refused to visit them in the hospital, and in their obituaries—if they even got obituaries, let alone funerals—were listing the cause of death as pneumonia, cancer. Cancer! Together Johnny and Rooster shook their heads at the injustice.

But wasn't Johnny as cowardly as everyone else? In the hushed alleys of their neighborhood, where the virus glinted like the silver needles left on the sidewalk, it was easy for him to pretend that it was a junkie disease. He never talked about the possibility that one day it might catch him, too. He and Rooster were careful, always scrupulously careful, and yet it was Johnny's unvoiced fear that this was how he'd be found out: one day he'd get sick, and even though no one would say it everyone would know why.

"Silence=Death," the new AIDS posters went. The triangle symbol was as ominous as the Missing Foundation's toppled martini glass.

Maybe, if things were different, Johnny could say the word back to Rooster now. AIDS. He could tell Rooster how scared he was. They'd go get tests, and put it behind them, and together they could sail down Fifth Avenue on a parade float, throwing confetti into the wind.

But now? If he was found out, no one would let him raise Teddy's baby. And if he got sick, he wouldn't be *around* long enough to raise the baby. Before long, he'd be wherever Teddy was. Gone. And he wanted to be alive.

Johnny sat up, but Rooster didn't move. He didn't show Johnny his face. Rooster was a big man, but for the first time, his body now looked like a brittle thing, each knuckle of his spine visible. What Johnny would remember was that ink-ruined plane of his back in the dim room, Johnny's imperfect work branded forever in his pores.

"Just take your fuckin' shower," Rooster said.

To the wedding of his best friends, the first wedding he had ever attended, Jude wore the same clothes he'd worn to Teddy's funeral. Johnny had wanted him to wear a robe, maybe in yellow or gold (Johnny's was white), but Jude had grown tired of the details Johnny had planned—the vermilion powder he would dab on the part of Eliza's hair, the firmness of the eggplants for the fire sacrifice. He had sent Jude out to buy six bouquets of roses, which Jude had then disassembled, petal by petal, for the guests to toss at the bride and groom—the householders, Hindus called them—while Johnny and Eliza had taken the PATH to Hoboken to apply for a marriage license. So Jude stood firm on his choice of attire, the one act of disobedience he could muster. Les, for his part, wore the suit he had worn to his own wedding in 1969, chocolate brown, with a vest that could not be buttoned.

The rest of his clothes, along with the handful of possessions with which he preferred not to part, Les had packed into his trunk. After arranging with Harriet the details of the children's arrival, he'd placed a call to a friend in Chinatown, and thirty minutes later two guys had arrived with a truck and a dolly and four empty refrigerator boxes, which they filled with his plants, wrapped in cellophane, and carted out of Les's apartment into the bright of day. The cash would cover a ticket to anywhere in the world, but he hadn't bought one yet. He'd go to the airport and pick a city he couldn't pronounce. He gave the keys to his camper van to Jude, along with McQueen, who would not pass through airport security. The keys to his apartment he left to his friend Davis, who was in need of a sublet, having been evicted from his own studio for failure to pay the rent. Jude had witnessed all of this with the dejected respect one had for people with destructive talents, like winning hamburger-eating contests. He should have known his father was exceptionally good at leaving, at transforming a crisis into an efficient and practiced good-bye. Finally, his father gave him five hundred-dollar bills, for the "reimbursement" of Jude's dealer. "Be nice to he who keeps you in weed." It was the one lesson he left Jude with, and Harriet's one condition for allowing Jude to return to Vermont with his friends. She could not keep him padlocked in his room forever, and she couldn't afford to lose any more glass. Hippie would have to be paid.

For the week preceding the wedding, to protect her from her mother, Les had established Eliza in a room at the St. Marks Hotel. To protect her from the St. Marks Hotel, he'd established Johnny there with her, in a single room with a double bed, because it was the cheapest. He said to Jude, "They can't get into any more trouble than they already have." They didn't see her until Sunday evening, when she appeared at the temple in her sari, her palms and bare feet covered with henna tattoos.

At the wedding, while the priest chanted and waved his incense and spoke of sacrifice, while Johnny and Eliza exchanged flower garlands instead of rings and tied their shawls in a knot to symbol- ize their union, while the fire pit raged so hot that Jude's eyes stung with the sweat from his brow, he kept his eyes on Eliza's feet, on her ankles, her heels, the space between her toes, on each spike and whorl of ink, and imagined them in Johnny's hands while he applied the ink to her skin.

After the vegetarian feast, Jude drove his father's van around to the front of the building (already packed with their bags, equipment, record crates, and the three cats—Johnny's single caveat) and held open the door while Johnny, carrying a laughing Eliza, piled into the back. The sun had set over Brooklyn, and Jude fumbled a moment to find the headlights. In the darkness of the van the rearview mirror reflected only the dimmest of shapes—the happy members of the temple waving from the curb, Jude's father already hailing a taxi, and the profiles of the newlyweds it was his duty to chauffeur home, one indistinguishable from the other.

PART II

The Householders

ELEVEN

At the Texaco station on Grammer Street, the only gas station in Lintonburg open in the middle of the night, two cars sat in the parking lot, and one of them was a shit-colored Camaro with a Black Flag bumper sticker and a Pizza Hut dome on the roof. Inside the gas station, Kram had one arm lost deep in the beer case. He was wearing a Pizza Hut shirt and a Pizza Hut hat and khaki pants that matched his khaki hair. When he saw Jude and Johnny file in, he whistled. "Jeezum Crow! What are you guys doing here?"

He furnished them both with quick, back-pounding hugs, wrestling Jude in half and sawing his knuckles over his skull. "I didn't recognize this little shit without the hair! What'd you do with your devil lock?"

"The demon has been exorcised," Johnny said. "He's an angel now."

"Yeah, right!" Kram let Jude go and grabbed a fistful of Johnny's white wedding robe. "You're the angel! Look at this. What is this, Halloween?"

"*You* look the same," Johnny said. "Still got your gut."

"That's all muscle, McDickless. The ladies love it."

"Pizza Slut, huh?" Jude asked.

Kram stood up straight, hitching up his khakis. "Yeah, well, I wasn't getting any hours at the Record Room. You know Delph made assistant manager over there?"

"Oh yeah?"

"*I'm* the one got him the job there. And I've got a hell of a lot better taste in music."

"That's debatable," said Johnny.

"Shit, you grew up, Judy. You're taller than me."

Jude did feel older, but maybe that was just because Lintonburg felt the same. Following route 7 north past the twinkling vistas of Middlebury and Vergennes and Charlotte, past the shuttered flea market grounds and the round sheep barn and the shore of the thawing lake, past the snake's tongue where route 7 forked into Grammer and Champlain, and then two rise-and-falls until they reached the Day-Glo torch of the gas station, Jude had felt that he could drive that road with his eyes closed, even if it was his first time actually driving it.

Nothing had changed.

"Fucking bullshit is what it is." Kram was telling them about the P.E. credit that would keep him from graduating next month. A starting linebacker for four years, and they were talking about a P.E. credit. He didn't want to go to college anyway; he wanted to get back into music. "This is perfect. You still got my old drum kit in your basement, Judy? You guys still got guitars? We could revive the Bastards! The Bastards live!"

Johnny put his hands on Kram's shoulders. "You high, man?"

"No, man, I haven't done that shit in weeks. Delph doesn't sell no more."

"Really?"

"He's a working man now. More money, more hours, more responsibilities, blah blah."

Johnny now offered Jude a look. Jude knew he was wondering the same thing he was—whether, during the time Jude had spent in New York, despite Kram's late-night beer run, he and Delph had taken their own steps, however blind, toward sobriety. Whether they might not be so hard to recruit to their team.

"We got to let Delph know you're in town. What are you lesbians doing back here, anyway?"

A bell jingled, and Eliza entered the store. Pregnant, barefoot, in her sari. Her cheek was impressed with the handle of the suitcase she'd slept against. "Hey," she said, "do you think they have any Yoo-hoo?"

Harriet had been dreaming of her ex-husband, the two of them trying to catch fish in nets on a boat very much like Jerry and Ingrid Donahoe's—had she ever been on another boat in her life, in forty-three years of living on a lake?—when the wheels of his ancient van turned over the gravel behind her house. It took her a moment to remember that he was not the one driving. She leapt out of bed, pulled on her robe, and ran a toothbrush across her teeth before stalking downstairs, where her son was filling a bowl at the sink. He'd packed some muscle on his frame, and she watched from the bottom step of the spiral staircase as he placed the water on the floor and a tiger-striped cat, purring at his ankles, drank gratefully from the bowl. Through the kitchen door, two more teenagers appeared, each of them holding another cat, and while the scene should have terrified her—six new bodies in the house, seven if you counted the baby—the way the kids carried themselves, tiptoeing, whispering, stroking the animals' ears, reassured her.

She did not wish to be in the middle of Les's girlfriend's business—or ex-girlfriend, as the case may have been—but she found herself without much choice. If she'd refused Eliza and Johnny, she'd be refusing Jude, too, and the fact was she'd missed him. So she wouldn't think about the pregnant girl, about what would happen to her when she was no longer pregnant. It was not her business. She was merely providing temporary shelter to two kids who needed help. Every summer her favorite aunt and uncle had taken in foreign exchange students, and the homeless at Thanksgiving, and in more than one winter storm along route 7, she and Les had let hitchhikers climb into the back of their van. More than once, they'd been the hitchhikers.

She was thinking of Les as she dropped off the final step of the stairs, recalling the February morning she'd woken up to find him on her couch. If the children were to find out! Seven years had passed since she'd seen her ex, since she'd been with any man at all. Could she be blamed? Did she say yes to him when he called because she'd said yes to him in her bed? The only thing she could do that morning was keep busy, keep him quiet, make scrambled eggs. She'd do the same thing now—eggs and toast and bacon, a pot of strong coffee for her guests, at four-thirty in the morning.

But none of them drank coffee, and the boys didn't eat bacon and eggs. Johnny made buckwheat pancakes instead, and Eliza praised the Vermont maple syrup. They told her about the trip, and the wedding, and the way Les had come through for them, and Jude showed off the gruesome scar on his arm, which had healed to a raisiny, hairless glaze. After breakfast, while Jude napped, Johnny washed the dirty clothes they'd brought. "No more quarters! I could do laundry all day." He had grown up quite a bit since Harriet had last seen him skulking down Ash Street, a cigarette tucked over his ear. She was not sure Jude knew how to operate a washing machine. That was the consequence of her indulgence, the apologetic spoiling of an adopted child. Prudence cleaned without being asked, but now Harriet wondered if she had ruined any hope of self-reliance for Jude, if she had poisoned him against helping himself. Even Eliza, who had grown up with silver spoons, who apparently knew nothing about birth control, who had *Les* for a role model, sprang up from the table to help with the dishes.

It was not until Harriet made her way back upstairs to shower and change that it occurred to her it might be nice to have a full house. Prudence had become secretive, eating her meals in her room, stretching the phone cord as far as it would reach up the stairs. One night Harriet had caught her sneaking down the fire escape. It was as though, in deference to her absent brother, Pru were impersonating him.

She passed her room on the second floor, climbed the next flight of stairs to the third, and, after tapping lightly on her son's bedroom door, eased it open. He was lying on his side with his bare back to her, and she stood there for several moments watching him sleep. After Teddy's death, it was a sight that used to send her stomach up into her throat, but it didn't worry her now. She understood that she had Johnny to thank for that.

So he didn't know how to do laundry. She'd do his laundry a million times.

The householders settled in. They learned how to use the remote control, to jiggle the handle of the second-floor toilet. Harriet pored over an old vegetarian cookbook, her glasses dusted with flour. "Can you eat egg whites, Johnny? What about fish?" And one rainy day, Johnny and Harriet spent the whole afternoon in the basement, Johnny admiring her old drawings, Harriet admiring his.

"So your new friends are a hit," Prudence observed one morning. "Mom practically Frenched them both at dinner last night." Waking up to an otherwise empty house, Jude had wandered into his sister's bedroom, where she was getting ready for school. Harriet was in the greenhouse, and Prudence didn't know where Johnny and Eliza were.

He stood in the doorway, examining the fixtures of the room. The trundle bed where Eliza had slept the last several nights was closed, a pillow and folded blanket piled neatly on the floor. On the door, Kirk Cameron had been replaced by a calendar of male swimsuit models. The word *Frenched* was licking uncomfortably at Jude's ear, and he wondered suddenly about the question his father had asked about Prudence, whether she was having sex. He studied her smoky eyes, the medley of bracelets—safety pins, braided strings, glittery bangles. Was this the kind of girl who had sex? Who Frenched and had sex?

"You got your braces off," he said.

Prudence grinned, revealing two rows of aligned teeth. "Tada!" she said, and in this single word, Jude swore he smelled American Spirits.

"Have you been smoking?" He came close and sniffed her. "Do you smoke now?"

With the heel of one of her boots, she shoved him away.

"What are you smoking for? It's like seven in the morning."

"Give me a break. You used to smoke more than cigarettes."

"You're not smoking pot, are you?"

"What is this? Because you're straight edge now, you get to harass me?"

"That's what straight edge is all about."

Prudence shot him a look of distrust. "What did you do with my brother? The guy who used to sniff Sharpies while we watched cartoons? That was like two weeks ago."

"Well, you were Citizen of the Week like two weeks ago. What happened to you?"

She went to her dresser and spritzed on some perfume. "I liked you better before."

"You like Johnny, and he's straight edge."

Prudence shrugged. "Johnny's cute." In the dresser mirror, she rolled up each sleeve of her T-shirt. "So I don't get it. They're married, but they sleep in separate beds?"

"Prudence."

"It's sort of weird, isn't it?"

Jude sat down on the bed, picked up the teddy bear, and put it down.

"I guess it would be weird, too," Prudence considered, "if they slept in the same bed."

"Where would they sleep, anyway?"

"Mom has that big mattress in her studio. She doesn't give a shit. They're married. But Eliza said Johnny said Mom wouldn't let them."

"Eliza said that?"

"I'm just saying. *I* don't care."

"You don't have any idea where they are?" He was staring blankly at the calendar, at Mr. May, and now his eyes went to the thirteenth. "What's today, Friday?"

"Yeah, Friday the thirteenth. Boo!"

Jude had known the day had been coming, but he had managed until now to push it from his mind. He wanted to smoke something, a cigarette, a joint.

"Look," Prudence said, "she can sleep in here, whatever."

"Thank you, okay?"

"But what is it, like a marriage of convenience?"

"Prudence! Where did you get that?"

"Well, they don't seem . . ."

"What?" Jude asked. He wanted to know. He wasn't sure what sort of marriage it was. They hadn't kissed at the wedding, and their first night home, when Eliza realized she'd left her toothbrush at the hotel in New York, Johnny had gone out and bought her a new one. At eleven o'clock at night, instead of just letting her use his.

"Like, in *love*. Like a husband and wife." Prudence zipped up her backpack and slung it over her shoulder. "Like Mom and Dad used to be."

The first night Eliza stayed at the St. Marks Hotel, her mother had shown up at Les's apartment and bullied him through the intercom until the super chased her away. Les assured her that Eliza was safe, and Eliza hadn't heard from her since. She wondered if her mother thought she was staying at Les's, or somewhere else in New York, if she were checking hotels by now, or calling the people she thought were still Eliza's friends. Sometimes Eliza assumed she'd get the police involved, and sometimes she thought it was the last thing she'd do. She knew Di was as ashamed of Eliza's running away as she was of her pregnancy—she simply wouldn't want anyone to know. Her purpose had been served, anyway—Eliza was out of sight in a place where she couldn't embarrass her mother. No doubt she told people Eliza was still away at school.

That first night in the hotel, Johnny had stripped to his boxers, folded his clothes neatly on the chair, stretched out on the bed beside her, and said good night. She was wearing her gray toile pajamas and she'd just washed her hair. He lay there, eyes closed, arms folded across his waist. He'd turned off his bedside lamp, but by the light of hers she admired the curve of the Krishna beads across his throat, each bead as tiny as a baby tooth, and the artwork across his belly and chest, winding around his arms. She'd never seen so much skin so darkly tattooed, the ink so heavy it looked three-dimensional, and she couldn't help it: she placed her fingertips on the green wing of his shoulder.

He flinched, eyes bolting open. He sat up, then lay back down. She apologized, her face was burning. "We're going to be married in a few days," she reminded him. "Isn't this what you meant? When you said we were going to be a couple?"

Johnny tried out a nervous laugh. "Of course," he said, sweeping his knuckles over her cheek. But could they wait? It was old-fashioned, but wasn't that the best way? Les had asked him to protect her here. It was just a few more days.

She thought it was sweet, how respectful he was. He reminded her of Teddy. He ended up sleeping on the floor, and they joked about it, the pregnant bride-to-be saving herself for marriage.

Then, when they'd arrived at Jude's house, Johnny told Eliza that Harriet wanted them to sleep in separate beds. Eliza would sleep in Prudence's room, and Johnny would bunk with Jude. "Sorry," Johnny had whispered the morning after their first night there, handing her a dish to dry. "I didn't know it would be this way." It was just temporary, he said, until they found a place of their own. The arrangement was acceptable enough. Prudence mostly stayed out of Eliza's way, offered her the first shower, cleared her a corner of the closet.

A few mornings in, while Prudence was in the shower, Johnny woke Eliza and asked her to take a walk with him. It was early, not even seven, but every boy who'd ever asked her to take a walk only meant one thing. She put on lipstick, sprayed a shot of Prudence's perfume down the collar of her sweater. The morning was chilly, the glittering lake appearing now and then between blocks. The root-split sidewalks were stamped with children's handprints, the telephone poles with staples from long-gone flyers. A row of close-set bungalows lined each side of the street, in white and putty and gray, with cement porches and torn screens, AC units hanging out of the windows. The one Johnny stopped in front of was on the side that backed up to the woods. It was slate blue, set up on cinder blocks, a child's red wagon capsized in the long grass. A FOR SALE sign stood beside it. For a moment, Eliza thought he was going to knock on the door, or pull out a key. Maybe it was an old friend's place that would be empty for a few hours. "Landlord must have put it up for sale," Johnny said.

He'd been here to gather Teddy's things after the funeral. He just wanted her to see it, too. They sat on the bus stop bench across the street and a few doors down, watching the tall pines behind the house bend and sway.

"It's his birthday," Johnny said.

"Friday the thirteenth?"

"He'd be sixteen."

They sat in silence for a moment longer. It didn't feel like a moment they were sharing. The breeze spun the rusty wheels of the wagon in the yard. Maybe it was a neighbor's. She found herself wondering if it belonged to a boy or a girl. What was left of her buoyant mood was carried away in the wind, the hope of kissing her husband on a bench in the morning sun. She could only picture Teddy coming in and out of the door across the street. She supposed that's what Johnny had intended.

The last time Johnny saw his mother, he was the age Teddy would be now. She was drunk, and he was packing his things. "He's a snake," she warned him. "A snake charmer. Don't let him charm you."

She was speaking about his father, a man named Marshall Cheshire. For most of his life, Johnny had known nothing about him. As far as he and Teddy knew, their fathers were dead, both killed in car accidents before they were born, and when they would ask their mother about them, she refused to elaborate, her silence the face of both a cold, hardened grief—*two* lovers killed! *two* tragic

accidents!—and a disappointment in her sons' frailty: big boys did
not cry over their dead fathers. So when kids asked Johnny about
his dad, he said he didn't have one, because he didn't. This was a
lonely fact but, for Johnny and Teddy, not a strange one. They had
no other family. Their mother's parents had also died before the
boys were born, and they had no aunts or uncles, no godparents, no
cousins. They had their mother, more or less.

Until one late-winter afternoon shortly before Johnny's sixteenth birthday, when he and Teddy were pushing the Horizon up
Grammer Street to the gas station, their mother coasting in neutral,
her fat arm hanging out the window. It was not the first time they
had run out of gas on the side of the road, but this hill was steep
and slick, and their mother had to lose some goddamn weight. The
man who pulled over to help them was not a neighborly Vermonter
but, Johnny guessed from the accent, a New Yorker. It wasn't until
the car was safely steered into the station and Queen Bea lumbered
out of it that the man recognized her. In her youth, she had been a
slimmer woman.

"Bonnie?" he said, and then: "Bonnie! Bonnie Michaels!"

Queen Bea actually jumped. She jumped backward. Then she
lowered her fat ass back into the car and slammed the door. The
guy had to knock on her window for a good minute. "It's me," he
said, laughing, pressing his face to the glass. "It's not him! It's Max,
Bonnie! It's not Marshall!"

Johnny later gave considerable thought to what she might have
been thinking about in that car. Was she considering denying it?
Saying no, mister, you got the wrong lady? I'm Beatrice, Beatrice
McNicholas? When she finally stepped out, she appeared to have
collected herself. She began fiddling with the pump, dribbling gasoline over her boots.

"What the hell are you doing up here?" she demanded. "This
is Vermont."

The man was on his way to a hockey tournament in Montreal. He was meeting some old friends from the joint. He had just stopped to get gas! And Marshall had almost come with him! But Marshall's probation officer had told him it was a bad idea to leave town. He and Marshall had moved from Miami back to Staten Island. Wait until Marshall heard who he saw in fucking Vermont.

Then he seemed to remember the two boys standing on either side of him. A shadow fell over his face. He had steel gray eyes and a three-day beard and sunken cheeks carved with acne scars. He wore a navy knit cap. He looked from Johnny to Teddy back to Johnny again. "I guess that's him?" he said, nodding to Johnny, and the instant Johnny saw the man's sheepish, scarecrow smile, he knew his mother was a liar.

"I'm your Uncle Max," he told Johnny. "Marshall's brother."

"His *twin*," Queen Bea spat.

And Teddy standing there with a shadow fallen over his face, too, trying to figure out where that left him. He cupped a hand over his eyes, trying to see the man more clearly. Then his eyes slid over to Johnny.

"You think my dad's alive, too?" he asked Johnny that night. Queen Bea had gone off to get drunk somewhere.

Of course he was alive. They were all alive! Who knew how many people their mother had killed off? Two tragic accidents!

Johnny thought about Teddy's question. He remembered a man with a dark mustache, an accent, breath like curdled milk. Ravi. He remembered hiding in bushes of sea grape while Ravi pruned them, and Ravi scolding him for touching the marble statue on his shelf, as smooth as the inside of a conch shell. For years the memory of Ravi had lived among the memories of Queen Bea's many ex-boyfriends. It hadn't occurred to Johnny until now that he could be Teddy's dad.

But Johnny, feeling guilty over his newfound father, had said, "I doubt it, Ted."

Before long he left Vermont and moved into his father's apartment in Staten Island. Johnny's own brother, until then his only male family, looked nothing like him, and now here were not one but two men with Johnny's face. All this time, Marshall said, Bonnie had been keeping Johnny from him—so much lost time they had to make up! Marshall took him to the Hard Rock Cafe, to Coney Island. Twice he took him to Madison Square Garden—first to a Rangers game, then to a Bob Seger show. After the concert the two of them got high in Max's parked Chevy Blazer, Marshall's usual faraway look even more faraway, his steel gray eyes drifting over the windshield, and Marshall said, "Your mom was a piece of work," and that phrase seemed right, seemed to explain everything—she was a liar, yes, but also the kind of woman men wrote songs about and regretted loving and were helpless over, and for that night, Johnny felt like a son, as though he had a mother and a father, parents who were screwed up in a legendary, acceptable way, their romance so terrific and terrible she had written him off as dead, and so maybe his dad was as much of a drunk as his mom and so maybe he'd known he'd knocked her up, but he'd rambled on, that's what the rockers did, Robert Plant and maybe even Bob Seger and those silly hippies, didn't they all have love children scattered all over the map? And then the next morning, seventeen days after Johnny had moved in with his dad, the blackened husk of the Chevy was found in a parking lot off the Long Island Expressway, the Blazer blazed, a witticism at least one local paper picked up on in its back-page crime log, and not long after, Max and Marshall Cheshire were arrested for insurance fraud, shipped off to Arthur Kill—shipped *back* to Arthur Kill—but not before Marshall had managed to cosign a checking account in Johnny's name and make off with all the $469 Johnny had earned shoveling Lintonburg driveways. Brothers went down together, they went down in flames, but your kids, they were expendable. That was when Johnny moved into Tompkins. He didn't have bus fare back to Vermont, and even if he did, he wouldn't have gone home. He would not return with his tail between his legs for his mother to say "I told you so."

So he left his brother at home to go down in flames alone.

On Teddy's birthday, watching his old house from across the street, Johnny had pictured Queen Bea packing up her car in the middle of the night. He'd come close to telling Eliza then that his mother had left because of him, because he'd done something stupid: he'd called her. From the same phone booth where he'd received the news of Teddy's death, he had spoken to her on Christmas. In his last letter, Teddy had affixed a surprising PS: *I want to find out if my dad is alive. Ha-ha, I know you said not to bother, but will you help?*

When Johnny had finally started talking to his mother again after his father went to jail, she'd said she'd been trying to protect him from Marshall. "I was trying to save you the trouble," she said, and Johnny had almost felt sorry for her. Who knew how far you could trust her (you certainly couldn't throw her very far), but she said Marshall had also ripped her off, and slapped her around, and when she was pregnant, too. That was why she'd changed her name, she said. That was why she'd told Johnny he was dead. They'd shared accounts. He knew how to find her. She didn't want him tracking her down.

But what about Teddy's dad?

"He's dead," she'd said quickly. "Dead, dead. Don't go looking for him, John."

He didn't believe her. But he believed she was scared. He believed that Teddy's father must be a monster, too, a monster worse than Marshall Cheshire. He told his brother to forget his dad. "It's not worth the trouble, Ted."

After he got Teddy's letter, though, Johnny stewed over it for days, the letter propped up over his sink. He remembered the white moons of Ravi's fingernails, the black hairs on the back of Ravi's hands. He had to be Teddy's dad. What if he was a good guy? What if he wouldn't break Teddy's heart?

Finally, on Christmas morning, he called Queen Bea. He wanted to give her the chance to tell Teddy herself. "He's asking about his dad," he said. "I know it's Ravi. I know he's alive. He deserves to know him." If she didn't tell them where he was, he told her, Johnny would find him on his own.

And on New Year's Eve, she was gone. What had spooked her so powerfully Johnny didn't know, but it was enough to send her away for good. Queen Bea was the one who'd left Teddy alone for Eliza and Jude to pump full of drugs. But Johnny might as well have packed up her car and driven her away.

TWELVE

What was there to do, back in Lintonburg, but start a band? "We'll bring straight edge to the people," Jude told Johnny. "It'll be a sight to behold." Kram and Delph were on board. They'd both been dumped by their girlfriends. They had no college plans. The grassy summer stretched before them.

And so one Saturday morning in May, the former members of the Bastards gathered in Jude's basement for their first practice in two and a half years. They dusted off their equipment; they plugged in; they tuned. Johnny, the only one of them who'd been in a serious band, ran them through the hardcore standards, Delph thrashing over his bass, Kram trying to keep up on the drums, and Johnny and Jude each on a guitar, like the metal gods they'd once dreamed of being. Jude's guitar was in bad shape, but by the end of the day, they'd even pieced together one and a half songs of their own.

"Shit's fast," Kram said, sweat dripping from his chin.

But the Bastards was no longer a sufficiently menacing moniker. After practice, Jude armed himself with chalk, leading the band name brainstorm on the basement chalkboard:

The Ass-Kickers
The Righteous Ninjas
Salvation Army
Just Say Hell No
The Underground
The Law
X-Ray
X-Men
X-ecute
X-emplify
Against All Odds
Origin of Trust
What Peril Falls
When Truth Hurts
Friend or Foe (???)

It was very likely the greatest number of words Jude had voluntarily composed, and he felt a frenzied sense of accomplishment.

"They all sound like the title of a *60 Minutes* story," said Delph, who had cut off his mullet and was now sporting a crew cut. Kram chuckled, and Delph said, "Shut up, moron, you've never seen *60 Minutes*."

"Why don't you just call yourselves the Get-Along Gang?"

Everyone had forgotten Eliza, who was sitting at the top of the stairs. She had been drifting in and out of their practice all day. She didn't look up from the toenails she was painting.

"Ha-ha," Jude said. "Hilarious."

"Maybe you shouldn't make fun of things you don't know any-thing about," Johnny told her.

"How could I know about it?" she asked. "You wouldn't take me to any shows."

"That was for your own safety," Johnny reminded her.

"Whatever," she said, blowing on her nails. "I don't really care what you call yourselves."

"I don't like any of the names either," Kram admitted.

"There are a lot of *X*s up there," said Delph.

Kram and Delph had adapted quickly to the presence of John-ny's new wife, treating her with a distant awe. Jude had told them that the baby was Teddy's. It had been a relief to tell someone, and he hadn't thought twice about it. Wouldn't Teddy want them to know? But Johnny had gone ape. What if it got out? Jude didn't see why it mattered. It wasn't like he'd told his parents. And Johnny and Eliza were married now.

Jude doubted it was a coincidence that Delph and Kram had jumped back into the band with such little resistance. Kram, he was a pushover—he would have joined an a cappella group if Johnny had asked him to—but two months ago Delph was selling pot, and now he had joined a band that was, at present count, 50 percent straight edge. It was the baby they were in awe of, Jude thought, the little punk Eliza carried in utero, the embryonic offspring of drug-ruined Teddy. As they'd inventoried their ancient equipment this morning, lifting the sheet off the rusty drum kit, the heady, homesick feeling of being together again sparkled with the slow-falling dust, and Jude recognized what was holding them together. It was the unspoken absence of the missing band member.

But it appeared Jude still had some convincing to do. He did care about this band. He hadn't cared about much before. He didn't care about school, or girls, or his family; he'd cared only about get-ting fucked up, about getting Teddy fucked up, about getting Teddy to laugh that fucked-up laugh, and now that laugh tormented him. He wanted to wipe that laugh off the face of the earth. He wanted to wipe the smile off the face of every hippie he met.

"This isn't boarding school," Jude said. "This is not the talent show, this is not your mom's church bake sale, Kram." Now he had his place at the front of the classroom, stabbing the air with his chalk, and Johnny took a seat in one of the schoolhouse chairs, as though to say, *Let's see what you've got, grasshopper*. Now Jude was the one who had something to sell Delph and Kram, even if they'd already been sold. Pictures of the insides of clubs they'd never even heard of. A record label, distribution, tour dates. In Delph's expression, Jude could see the familiar battling forces of excitement and suspicion. But no. It's true. Go to New York. Go to D.C., L.A., Boston, even Connecticut. You'll see. This was not MTV. This was not Ticketmaster. This was not get-discovered-in-a-shopping-mall. Start-a-record-label-in-your-dorm-room-and-turn-into-millionaires. Make-your-dad-your-manager-so-he-can-sell-your-rights-and-fuck-you-over. Fuck millionaires, fuck managers. This was 100 percent grassroots—of the people, by the people, for the people. This was jump off a stage and know ten guys will catch you. This was fuck your dreams and make your destiny.

Jude let his chalk rest at last. He was sweating. Johnny, legs crossed, gave him a nod of approval. When Jude looked up at the top of the stairs, Eliza was gone, and he couldn't say when she'd left.

Delph and Kram, though, they were still there.

"Well, hell, man," Kram said, picking up Johnny's tattoo machine and pointing it, like a gun, at some undetermined target, "let's play a show."

Unless you counted the bruises and Indian burns he'd exchanged with Teddy and his sister, or the routine wedgies and noogies he'd endured from Delph and Johnny and Kram, Jude had never been in a fight, had bullied his way haltingly toward fights with kids several years younger than he was, had talked on various playgrounds about kicking so-and-so's ass, but his efforts had proved unheeded. The incident on New Year's hardly qualified as a fight, fights requiring mutual advancements of opposing sides. But New York and the pit and rehab had pumped Jude full of a giddy courage. In his bedroom in Vermont, he listened to Project X's "Straight Edge Revenge" again and again, dragging the needle back to the beginning when it was over. He wanted to go after Hippie and Tory. He wanted revenge—for New Year's Eve, for Teddy, for the final insult of involving his mother. The beer bottle they had left behind, as carelessly as Tory had left his belt, was all the authorization he needed. They were asking for it.

Jude had learned in New York that bands weren't just bands. They were troops. They were tribes. And now he was no longer an army of one. The Bastards were back.

But Johnny wasn't about to be drafted into a stone-throwing youth crew—he'd survived that scene in New York, and he wanted to leave it behind. "Let's play music," Johnny said. "No rough stuff, Jude. Okay?"

Jude said, "You don't know what an asshole Tory is." He told Johnny what he'd done to him on New Year's Eve. "It could have been Teddy," he said. "And now he did this shit to my mom?"

"We don't know it was Tory," Johnny reminded him. Ever since they'd found out about the baby, Johnny had gone all civil disobedience. It was like he'd found religion, and his religion was Teddy's kid. He went on about nonviolence, the Upanishads, the five moral virtues. Sure, in Alphabet City, they were hard to follow, Johnny said, but he didn't pick fights; he only finished them. "I've got a kid on the way," Johnny said. "I'm not landing in jail just to settle the score with some dickhead jock and his dealer."

"Fine," Jude said. "Stay out of it, then."

After the band's second practice, during which Jude became increasingly less devoted to his third-hand Ibanez, he went with Kram and Delph to the pawnshop on University, where Jude and Teddy used to play Metallica songs until they got kicked out. This time, though, Jude's wallet was full of his father's cash. Over his shoulder, he hung a Les Paul Classic in Bullion Gold. Gently used, but it gleamed.

"Aren't you supposed to use that money to pay for the pot you took?" Delph asked.

Every morning since Jude's return, his mother told him that, before things got worse—before God forbid those boys came back and broke into the house—he'd better pay back Hippie. A peace offering. Jude promised her that he would.

"Never liked that guy," Kram said. "Got a stick up his ass. *Oh, my weed is so divine.*"

"Stuff's weak," Delph agreed.

"Fuck him," Jude said. "He waged war on my mom's greenhouse. He's not getting a penny from me."

"I'm telling you," Delph said, "it had to be Tory. No way Hippie has the balls to carry that out by himself."

"Hate that guy, too," said Kram, though this was news to no one. Over four seasons of football, they'd heard plenty about Kram's poignant attempts to coexist with the guys who tea-bagged him and headbanged him and once cut off a lock of his hair. Kram was a big guy, but on the team, he was alone. He even claimed they'd tried to bully him into their locker room circle jerks—"Don't be a pussy, O'Connor." Jude did not believe that Tory Ventura fagged around, but Kram's hatred for Tory was pure. Jude would have quit after the first practice, but Kram just really loved playing football.

"It's not like he knows I have the money." Jude plucked a liquid gold C from the guitar.

"I don't know," Delph said. "Five hundred bucks is a lot of

dough. Even if it wasn't Hippie who did it, he'll still be coming after you for that money."

"Then we'll find him before he can find us," said Jude.

Neither Delph nor Kram stopped him from handing over the five crisp hundred-dollar bills, along with his old guitar, and leaving with the Les Paul. They walked through the dazzling sunshine to the Kramaro, Jude's guitar case heavy as a cannon. He was out of hiding.

The next morning, when Harriet again made her plea, Jude fed his toast into the toaster and said, "Taken care of."

This is what Harriet knew about the girl who had given birth to her son: she was Caucasian, and in 1971, she was unmarried and she was sixteen. With these stark facts Harriet had sculpted a number of identities over the years, characters who would visit but not quite haunt her dreams. Most often she appeared as a flower child, a freckled Village nymph with miles of long red hair. She was a girl who liked boys and Dusty Springfield and getting stoned, and one night had had too much fun in the back of a car; she was the girl Harriet would have been if she were ten years younger and hadn't spent her adolescence in a sweater set and a Maidenform bra it would take years for her to burn. For the young city girl who Did the Right Thing, Harriet felt a dangerous sense of gratitude, as though Harriet owed her, as though one day the girl would come to collect, would materialize to reclaim Jude and see what a mess Harriet had made of the boy.

It was not until last January, when the young doctor had offered her brisk diagnosis, that Harriet's image of Jude's birth mother had changed. Now she was a drunk. A sixteen-year-old drunk, a ghetto dweller, a street urchin, with questionable hygiene and poorly fitting clothes and the same alcohol-melted facial features, as though they were a family trait. Or she was a prostitute. Or she was a junkie.

It pained Harriet, the distaste she now felt for the mother of her own child. The only silver lining in this dim picture was that the girl (she was a woman now, of course, but she would always be a girl to Harriet) would be too drunk, too uncaring, or too dumb to look for Jude, and even if she did—this was perhaps an even greater relief— too incompetent to recognize Harriet's own incompetence.

Still, she'd had an irrational fear that he would run into his birth mother in New York—the place of his birth—that one day he would see his own face looking back at him on the subway.

Or worse: that he'd seek her out.

But he had come home to her instead. And he'd brought with him a pregnant sixteen-year-old girl. One morning while the boys were out and Prudence was at school, Harriet fed Eliza a tablespoon of apple cider vinegar to soothe the heartburn she'd woken up with. "It sounds backward, but it works," she assured her. They stood at the butcher-block kitchen counter, both of them still in their pajamas. Eliza cringed as it went down, but after a few seconds, her face softened. "It *does,*" she said in wonder.

"When I was pregnant, I drank this stuff like water." Automatically, Harriet was careful not to say *When I was pregnant with Prudence,* to exclude Jude unnecessarily. "They don't tell you about the heartburn, do they? Or the hemorrhoids? The varicose veins?"

"Hemorrhoids?"

"You still have those to look forward to. They should include *those* in the sex ed video, right? That would solve the teen pregnancy crisis."

Eliza's eyes closed, and her hand went to her chest. She was either absorbing the molecules of her relief or fighting off tears. Harriet had meant her comment as a joke, but of course it hadn't been received as one. She put her hand to her own chest. Maybe she *hadn't* meant to joke. Maybe she was trying, in her sarcastic way, to parent *someone* in this house. Jude had admitted, before she could bring it up, that he'd lied about going to school in New York. This she had suspected, and it was an affirmation to know that of all the dark and mercurial sentiments that commanded her parental life, the one she could still count on was distrust. She had known it was too good to be true! Strangely, Jude's disclosure of this fact made the rest of his conversion more plausible. Of course, he didn't plan on returning to school in Vermont, either. He was working on his music. He was no *good* at school, he whined; music he was good at. They had started a band again, he and his friends. He was up early, he was eating breakfast, he was practicing with a diligence she had never known him capable of. This very moment he and Johnny were downtown at a *meeting* with the chair of the rec center board, trying to get her to let them use the space for their "shows." Could she be blamed for enjoying the peace for a while, for letting his truancy go? The spring term was almost over, anyway. He could go back, start fresh, in the fall.

But poor Eliza: Jude did what he pleased, and Eliza got heartburn. "Christ," Harriet began, "I'm sorry." She waited for several seconds for Eliza to begin to cry, and when she didn't, Harriet finally thought to put her arms around the girl anyway. Eliza accepted the hug more mightily than Harriet was prepared for. They stood on the tattered rug in the middle of the kitchen, Eliza's clammy forehead on Harriet's collarbone. She was small, smaller than Prudence, and even with the firm mound of her belly between them, she had the brittle bones of a child. "I miss my *mom*," she said, almost inaudibly. This remark, combined with the inability to remember the last time she'd held her own daughter this way (who was she to think Prudence wouldn't come home knocked up?), nearly brought Harriet to tears herself.

"Of course you do." Harriet cupped the back of the girl's head, giving it a little massage.

"*She's* supposed to be telling me this stuff."

"I know, honey."

"She's not even *looking* for me."

Gently, Harriet shifted the girl out of her arms. At first she had worried distantly about the mother locating Eliza. Wasn't harboring a runaway a crime? In truth, she'd felt that Eliza's return to New York would be the inevitable and appropriate conclusion. She had not wanted this girl's water breaking in her home.

But then Les had called late one night shortly after the children's arrival, Harriet tripping downstairs to the phone. "Sorry," he'd said. "I'm on mountain time."

"Which mountain?" Harriet had asked, half-asleep.

"Eliza's mom is looking for her. I just thought you should know."

The private investigator Di had hired had tracked down Les in Santa Fe, but Les had managed to pay the guy off, double what Di was paying him. "Poor guy looked so pitiful taking the money, but he says his mother has medical bills." The P.I. agreed to throw Di off Eliza's trail, to tell her that Vermont came up empty. But Di wasn't stupid. "I don't know what we've gotten ourselves into," Les had said. "Jesus. I'd just do anything for that kid."

It had taken Harriet a moment to realize that he meant Eliza. She didn't know where to begin. *Les* was the one who'd gotten them into this. And the protection he was now falling all over himself to offer someone else's daughter disgusted her. What protection had he offered Prudence in the last seven years?

And yet when she'd hung up the phone, she'd done nothing. She hadn't called Diane to confess. She'd told herself she was staying neutral, allowing the stars to align themselves on their own.

"Your mom *is* looking for you," Harriet told Eliza now.

Eliza closed her eyes. "She is?"

"Do you want to maybe give her a call?" Harriet asked.

Eliza curled into Harriet's arms again, and Harriet felt her shake her head. "No," Eliza whispered, and Harriet was surprised to feel a river of relief in her chest. Now, with Eliza's feverish head on her breast, she, too, felt the need to defend this cub from her own mama. It was the same proprietary impulse she exercised against the girl who'd given birth to Jude, to prove her maternal prowess, to make up for its derelict history. Diane Urbanski, the Jewish British widow ballerina, was no longer merely a romantic rival. She was another woman who was coming to collect.

Through May, as the first fists of bloodroot opened and the gauzy swans of fiddlehead raised their necks, Harriet and Eliza turned the garden, shook the rugs, walked together to the farmers' market to buy eggs and honey and cheese. Out in the greenhouse, Eliza watched Harriet blow two salad bowls, a set of wine goblets, and a bud vase. Out in the greenhouse, Eliza posed for a drawing, a full-length portrait of her naked pregnant profile, which Harriet let her keep.

Prudence spent more and more nights at her new friend Dena's house, leaving her room to Eliza. Had Prudence, the girl with whom Harriet had until recently shared a bed, shown jealousy or exasperation or the territoriality which Harriet herself had refined, Harriet would have known how to suffer this guilt. Instead Harriet was the one who felt jealous, of the mysterious people with whom Pru was now content to spend her time. There were new kids in Jude's life, too—boys showing up at the door with guitars, leaning their bikes against her house. Harriet let Eliza do her makeup. At the second-run theater, Harriet and Eliza saw *Moonstruck*.

Meanwhile, the music stabbed through the ceiling of the basement.

Harriet asked Eliza to translate the lyrics for her, but even she could make out only a handful of words. If Jude were to name his own children after the songs of his youth, they might be named Truth, Strength, or Justice. Purity, Brotherhood, Loyalty, Trust. The words filled Harriet with a measure of gratification—her son was singing the merits of purity!—but they also amused her, embarrassed her, and concerned her. What kind of teenage boys sang songs about purity? What had happened to songs about getting stoned? Getting laid? And if one had to sing songs about purity (she didn't mind songs about purity!), why did they have to be so hard on the ears? They were awfully *angry,* these songs. The classics of her own youth, about getting stoned and getting laid, were *strummed* on the guitar, they were hummed in the shower, there were harmonicas.

Les had attempted to take up the harmonica one summer, but it was a phase. He had other passions to cater to. When Harriet had first met him, when he was not much older than Jude was now, he had embraced drugs with the same unqualified exuberance with which their son now refused them. That, it turned out, had not been a phase. She hoped Jude's newfound sainthood was not a phase, either.

But how could it be anything else? Her son's life story was a series of phases: scooters, BMX, skateboards; metal, punk, hardcore. He had ADD, he grew out of a pair of shoes in six weeks, and the songs he now sang were an average of forty-five seconds long. He would be over it by the end of the summer.

Harriet watched the boys come and go. From the basement to the van, from Jude's room to the fridge. She listened for them on the stairs, on the fire escape, to the ring of the phone and the drone of their showers and the puerile wail of their guitars. She observed Jude's romance with straight edge as she might have observed his first love—warily, with a mother's pride, hoping that, in the end, his heart wouldn't break too hard.

THIRTEEN

The Champlain Recreation Center, like Jude's house, had over the years served Lintonburg in a number of faces. During the French and Indian War it was erected as a tavern, where the Green Mountain Boys were said to have raised their glasses and laid their heads. Burned down in the mid-nineteenth century, it was rebuilt to house the local headquarters of the Sons of Temperance. Now the brick building across the street from Ira Allen High School functioned as a voting poll, bingo hall, tutoring center, AA meeting room, and headquarters for the only Lamaze class within a fifty-mile radius. For years, the twin handrails along the front steps had been prime skating ground for Jude and Teddy, but they'd only been through the doors once.

Inside, there was not the scorched, masculine smell of armpit and feedback. The walls were not plastered with the syrupy film of dried sweat or the stickers and flyers of past performers; the bathroom stalls did not advertise Cro-Mags lyrics, anarchist doctrine, or the telephone numbers of girls who swallowed. Instead, across a scarred floor the waxy yellow of school buses and number two pencils, a pair of basketball hoops faced off. At the back of the room were a plywood platform painted barn red, a handful of old par can stage lights with the color burned out, and a sound system that was equipped to handle the karaoke nights, pageants, and poetry slams of the likes of Prudence Keffy-Horn. Jude and Johnny and Kram and Delph had moved a hundred folding metal chairs to either side of the stage, behind the piano, the volleyball net, and the chalkboard-on-wheels that said WELCOME TO SPAGHETTI DINNER FAMILY NIGHT! PLEASE FORM 2 LINES! The only chair that remained was stationed at the table inside the door, and Eliza sat in it, stuffing wrinkled bills into a cash box as fast as the youth of Lintonburg could hand them to her.

The flyer—

Live Music at the **REC CENTER!**

Jam Masters **PHROG**

and New York Hardcore from **ARMY OF ONE**

and **GREEN MOUNTAIN BOYS**

SATURDAY, JUNE 4, 8 P.M. $5

ALL AGES!

—had been lettered by Johnny, photocopied at the A&P, and posted on telephone poles citywide. When they'd pled their case for an alcohol-free venue to Barb Delaney, the gray-haired lesbian who ran the rec center, she'd licked the point of her pencil and said, "When do you want to start?" Johnny signed on as chaperon.

Delph, who used to supply the drummer of Phrog, called him up and asked him to top off their lineup. Now, all the kids who'd been trying for years to sneak into Jacque's to see them play, praying their fake IDs would get them past the door, walked in as though they owned the place. Some of the crowd had carpooled up from New York, guys who ran with Johnny's old band Army of One, which now sported a new lead guitarist. Johnny had convinced them to come up. In the dark of the gymnasium, it was hard to tell who was from New York, who was from Lintonburg, and who was from the periphery—Rutland, Montpelier, the far-flung farms of Linton County. There were hardcore kids in black jeans with chains drooping from their pockets and bandanas tied around the ankles of their boots, longhairs in layered Bajas, four or five skinheads in wife-beaters and suspenders, two black Rastas with dreads as fat as bananas, a punk with a lizard green Mohawk who was no older than twelve, and a pale-faced boy in a cape wearing what seemed to be vampire teeth. The girls could be counted on two hands. Two were fat, with silver hoops through their nostrils. One was making out with the vampire. Where did these people come from? And where were they last year when Jude was getting locker-slammed by Tory Ventura for sporting a devil lock? He'd had no idea how well he'd blend in his mask.

It was the Ronald Reagan mask he'd worn last Halloween with Teddy. He'd be onstage, but he'd be invisible. With Phrog playing tonight, Hippie might be there, too. And if Hippie was there, Jude hoped, Tory might be, too. Jude didn't want them to see him before he saw them. He wanted to have time for a sneak attack.

"Um, welcome," he said into the mike, shouldering his new guitar. The lights dimmed, and the crowd issued a lukewarm bellow. Jude squinted into the crowd. He didn't see Hippie or Tory. "Welcome to Spaghetti Dinner Family Night," he said.

Anyone in the audience that night would have seen the fortieth president of the United States, in camo pants and T-shirt, doing beautiful injury to his Les Paul. *Who the fuck are these guys?* shouted the kids in the crowd into their friends' ears, not just because the singer's face was concealed from view but because their sound wasn't bad, it was hard, it was wicked. *What the fuck is this?* they asked in the beat between songs, before the next one started up.

The fact was, even before the Green Mountain Boys' debut was over, Jude had forgotten it. The stage was a ship he was riding. His voice was a transmission from another planet. He was not on shrooms—*Get that shit,* he sang, *away from me!*—but he remembered the one time he'd been on this stage before, for a class play about the Green Mountain Boys in which he wore a tricornered hat Harriet had fashioned out of black felt. He and Teddy had sneaked a few shrooms before the call, and carousel horses had flitted in the aisles of the audience. He remembered only a single line from the play, spoken in a lisp by the kid who played Ethan Allen: "We will use violence and coercion, but we will take no lives!"

That was how the militia gave its name to the band. "They were vigilantes," Jude had recalled one afternoon in the basement. "Guerrilla citizens."

"Like Gorilla Biscuits?" said Kram, who was pawing through a pile of Harriet's nude drawings.

"Outlaws," Johnny clarified.

"It sounds like a bluegrass band," Delph worried.

Kram said, "My mom has a dinette set from Ethan Allen."

"It's not bad," said Johnny.

Jude had expected Johnny to head the band's lineup; it was the natural order of things. Johnny had led Army of One, and he sang, and he was the superior guitarist, and he was the oldest, and the straightest; he was Johnny. So Jude had been unprepared for Johnny to hand the mike over to him one afternoon while they practiced in the basement. "You try this one." It was as though Johnny were testing him, seeing what he could do. And before long it seemed right, Jude's voice the band's voice, Jude's basement, Jude's equipment, let's ask Jude. And even though Johnny was the band's spiritual taskmaster, the straight edge grandfather, he seemed to prefer the anonymity of second string. Teddy had been the same way, Jude thought. He was always willing to go along for the ride.

Teddy was not here tonight; he missed the rapturous woof of the crowd; the plea for an encore; the drunk, breathless step down from the stage. But here was his brother, finding Jude again in the humid press of the crowd, holding a plastic cup of water up to the lip of Jude's mask, easing his head back and helping him drink.

Toward the end of Phrog's set, Jude spotted Hippie. He was standing at the back of the gymnasium, performing a slow, swimmy dance that required closing the eyes. Jude felt his heartbeat slowly accelerate. He put a hand to his face to make sure the mask was still there, though he could smell its oily film, see the blurry flesh-colored sockets around his eyes. When Hippie headed for the door, Jude followed him outside and watched him cross the street, safely out of range of city property, to the chain-link fence in front of the high school. Hippie's bike was not in sight, but he was wearing his fag bag, as well as a suede jacket with tassels down the arms. Jude didn't want to get too close yet. He stood up against the building, watching the cluster of smokers gathered out front.

"Nice set, Mr. President," one of them called.

"Thanks," Jude called back. His voice sounded rubbery inside his mask.

"You guys going to have more shows here?"

"I don't know," Jude said. "I hope so."

Someone else joined him from the shadows, leaning an elbow on the wall. "Hey, man, can I get an autograph?"

Jude flinched.

"Fuck off, Rooster."

Rooster nodded toward the smokers. "What do you think those posers thought of your song 'Blowing Smoke'?"

"They're probably going to buy the seven-inch."

"Oh, yeah? When's it comin' out?"

"Soon as we record it."

Rooster smiled again. "Fuckin' Vermont." *Vahmont*. Jude had never heard so much New York in his state's name before. "Never thought I'd be playin' here."

Across the street, Hippie was joined by one of the fat girls, and she took out a cigarette for Hippie to light.

"Thanks for coming up, man."

"Thanks for lettin' us crash." Rooster shrugged. "I didn't think we'd see you again after Johnny left."

Jude said, "Your new singer sounds good, though."

"Yeah, but he can't tattoo worth a shit." In the wan light of the lamppost, Jude could see the dark contours of the tattoos on Rooster's arms, as thickly woven as Johnny's. He looked thinner than Jude remembered, his shoulders bony through his T-shirt. "So, where's the child bride?"

Normally Jude tried not to wonder what people must have thought of the whole arrangement: husband and wife and Jude, living under Jude's mom's roof. He tried not to think about what *he* thought about it. At first Eliza had included herself in the activities of the boys in the basement. She presented them with a tofu cheesecake she'd baked. She clapped encouragingly from her seat at the top of the stairs. But the louder and more crowded their practices became, the less she was around.

"We sent her home early," he said, even though she'd left on her own after the Green Mountain Boys had wrapped up, turning the cash box over to Johnny. "She needs her rest."

"'Course," Rooster said. Someone else exited the building; the noodley strains of Phrog swelled out into the night air, then hushed again when the door swung closed. The last of the day's light had been drained from the sky—it, too, was bruised tattoo blue—and now it was shot through with the faintest stars. At the bottom of the hill, the Adirondacks floated on the blade of the lake. "That picture is so pretty," Rooster said, "I just want to fuck it up."

It wasn't a cigarette Hippie was smoking, but a joint. Jude could smell it from across the street. Hippie's apartment had smelled like that same breed, and Jude remembered the night they'd bonded over that smell, Hippie lighting the bowl while Jude hit his bong, Hippie telling Jude what a bummer it was about Teddy. *I heard he choked on his own vomit, like Hendrix. That true?*

"That Hippie?" Rooster nodded his head at him.

"That's him," said Jude. "Johnny says to leave him alone."

Rooster shook his head. "Johnny's gettin' posi on me. He's just jealous you got a new guitar instead of payin' off some fuckin' dealer."

Jude looked from Rooster to Hippie and back again. He felt dangerously unhinged without Johnny at his side to hold him back. "You seen Delph and Kram?" he asked Rooster.

Rooster pulled at his bottom lip. It was what Johnny did when he was thinking. "I know some guys. Came up from D.C. You see the guy up front in the Champion sweatshirt?"

"How many?" Jude asked.

"They're good guys," said Rooster.

When he returned a minute later, nine guys were panting at his side. Their T-shirts were soaked, their hair spiky with sweat. Delph and Kram, plus the three other guys from Army of One. Two more, with Xs shaved in the back of their heads, Jude recognized from laser tag in New York. The other two were the guys from D.C.: the guy in the Champion sweatshirt and another, who was missing both front teeth. Alone, they were not formidable—most of them looked too young to drive—but together, they resembled a band photo: hostile and bored. "You guys know Jude?"

Jude whipped off his mask.

"Where is this pussy?" they wanted to know.

Then Jude was leading them across the empty street, their sneakers scuffing the pavement, toward the dark lawn of the high school. They were in the middle of the street when Hippie looked up and saw them. He seemed to be counting. Eleven. Eleven against one. Two if you counted the girl.

Then he recognized Jude. "Whoa," Hippie said, holding up his hands. A joint was still burning in one of them. "Look who it is. What are you, some kind of skinhead now?"

Jude stepped onto the sidewalk, smiling hugely. He couldn't help himself—his heart felt like a coil ready to spring. "Hi, Hippie," he said. Behind the chain-link fence, in front of the grand, stone edifice of the school, two flags—the Stars and Stripes, and the state of Vermont—flapped at the top of the flagpole. Behind Jude, the guys were spilling off the sidewalk and into the street, bouncing from sneaker to sneaker, waiting for his cue.

"You got some balls," said Rooster, "smokin' that shit out here."

"You selling that shit?" someone else wanted to know.

For them, it was all about jumping some small-fry drug dealer. They were just looking for confirmation—then the fun could start. But Jude wanted confirmation of something else. "Who helped you break into my mom's greenhouse, Hippie?"

Hippie stroked his beard. It was the kind of full, unkempt beard you see on old men, but twisted into two dreads, like a forked tongue. A look of surprise crossed his face, then recognition, then uncertainty. "Nobody helped Hippie do anything," he said, pushing his glasses up his nose. "Hippie didn't help anyone."

"Where's your friend Tory, then?" Delph asked.

"Hippie doesn't know what you're talking about, man." He nodded sternly at the girl, who scurried away. His narrow, greenish eyes were cloudy and cold. "Tory's not even in town. He's visiting colleges with his parents."

The idea of Tory involved in this well-behaved, adult-chaperoned venture—visiting colleges—let some of the air out of Jude's sails. "Look," he said, slamming his fist into his palm, "someone smashed up my mom's greenhouse, and if it wasn't you, you got your bodyguard to do it."

Hippie didn't deny that Tory was his bodyguard. But he seemed troubled by the association, his eyebrows knit under the frames of his glasses. He took an anxious toke. "Why would you think it was Hippie?" he asked. He released a series of smoke rings, like the tail of a thought bubble, and Jude could guess what was coming next. "Is it because you stole half a pound of super fruit from him?"

Jude didn't answer. They were standing on the sidewalk in the unlit space between two streetlights, and it was difficult to see in the dark. He stood with his arms crossed, returning Hippie's stare.

"I think you must have your facts wrong," said Rooster, stepping forward. "This kid's straight edge. Believes drugs of any kind are for the weak-willed. Doesn't touch the stuff." Rooster draped his arm around Jude's shoulder, and Jude felt the untapped force of all the guys behind him. Why deny it? What was Hippie going to do about it now?

Jude stepped forward, letting Rooster's arm drop. "No," he said. "It was me. I stole your shwag. You know what happened to it? My mom flushed it. *Wshhhh*. Gone. I'd do it again."

Hippie shook his head in disgust. His dreadlocks shuddered. He walked a few paces away, rested his hands on top of the fence, and bowed his head, his hair hanging over his face. Then he turned around and launched a brown wad of spit on the sidewalk. "I wouldn't go after your mom," he said. "I respect her talent, man. I told Tory to leave her out of it."

Hippie plugged his mouth with his joint, realizing what he'd said. Or maybe he'd let it slip on purpose; maybe he was giving up Tory to save himself. Either way, it was Tory who had broken into the greenhouse, maybe alone, maybe with some of his drunk friends, and demolished his mother's work.

Jude almost took a step back. They'd given Hippie a little scare. They'd wait for Tory to return to town and save their beating for him. Jude exchanged glances with Delph and Kram. They shrugged, waiting for his call. Across the street, from the rec center, a blast of applause erupted, drunken hoots. The audience wanted an encore.

Then Hippie said something else. "Brother, Hippie's been nothing but nice to you." He was shaking his head again, his hands on his hips. "When your little friend died, I gave you a good deal on that weed. Why would you rip me off?"

Jude's stomach sank to his bowels. It was what Tory had called Teddy, just before he'd pulled out his belt. Little friend. This feeling was followed not by anger or grief but by an excited relief; he'd been waiting for a reason to justify what he wanted to do.

"Call him my little friend again, Hippie."

Hippie stood there with his jaw clenched, joint burning defiantly between his lips. For a few seconds, no one said anything. No one cared to ask what friend they were talking about. They were there to fight, their X'd hands curled into fists, ready to swing.

"Hippie's heard things about you straight edge guys," said Hippie, nodding at all of them. "No sex, right? No sex with *girls*—too busy sucking each other's dicks."

They lurched and seethed behind Jude; he nudged them back. He wanted to be the one to throw the first punch. Who was this new Hippie? Why was he provoking them?

"Call him my little friend again, Hippie!"

Hippie ducked, pretending to put out his joint on the sidewalk.

He was leaning over, looking up, the leather tassels of his jacket swinging.

"Is that what you and your little friend used to do? Suck each other's dicks?"

How strange and pure this high—wanting to hurt someone, and knowing he could. There Jude was, standing above him. He swung his leg back and thrust his knee forward, clipping Hippie under the chin. Hippie sprawled backward against the chain-link fence.

They went as easy on him as eleven guys could—kicking him gingerly, roughing up his dreads. He kept squealing, "Peace, peace," and then he was just crying. They let Jude take the lead, clamping down Hippie's limbs while Jude pounded his shoulders, his stomach, his jaw. "Call him my little friend now, you hippie shit!" Jude's voice visited from far away. "You worthless hippie fuck!" Hippie didn't answer, but he was conscious; his glasses had fallen off, and his eyes, exposed, were blinking involuntarily. Straddling him, Jude leaned back and gaped up at the black sky, gulping air.

He shouldn't have let up. He should have known that Hippie wouldn't have goaded them if he hadn't expected backup. Here they came, charging across the street, led by the fat girl with the ring in her nose, the messenger. Not only six or seven hippies, but six or seven jocks, plus a dozen other hungry-faced boys in a number of uniforms. What were the teams? Who was winning? It didn't seem to matter. Someone opened the gate and the crowd emptied into the schoolyard, plunging headlong into the tall grass. The Phrog-heads, the jocks, the rest of the college stoners in bleached jeans and boat shoes who had nowhere else to go, met the straight edge kids running, and they all went tumbling down the hill. The skinheads found themselves on the straight edge team, and the little kid with the Mohawk—his hands stained the same green as his hair—was pummeling away on a jock. Jude couldn't account for Hippie—the guys holding him down had become otherwise engaged, and now Jude was the one on the ground. Some dude in a varsity jacket attacked him, and they rolled through the grass, Jude gripping the guy's jacket in his hands, the guy's stubble burning Jude's face. Jude took a punch in the hip, gave one in the chin, took one in the nose. Then, confused, turning, the guy leapt up and tackled a hippie. Jude stood, safe for the moment, his body a frozen column in the middle of the yard. Maybe the guy was just having fun. Roughhousing. Some people were in fact laughing. It looked like a hastily choreographed dance. *Rumble* was the word that came to mind. Like *West Side Story*. Never more so than when Johnny, appearing out of nowhere, pulled a switchblade on Hippie.

Jude saw the metal gleaming white under the single streetlight, but he couldn't hear what they were saying. Johnny, kneeling, held the knife low at his side. It was all Hippie needed to see. Putting his hands up, beard dark with blood, he backed away, limping swiftly across the lawn. His glasses were gone.

"You guys! Let's get out of here. These guys are crazy."

Heads rose; final punches were thrown. The whole thing had lasted no longer than five minutes, and within another five, most of the field was clear. Some members of the straight edge crew remained, catching their breath, hobbling to the swings.

Jude stood in the middle of the lawn, doubled over. He was enjoying the scene. He was watching the black eyeball of the sky, the dim lights of Linton Street. In a minute Johnny would come over and put a hole in his happiness, but now the flags were billowing in the breeze, and Jude knew as he knew the inside of those high school halls, where he and Teddy had been prey, that the Vermont flag was adorned with a shield, two pine boughs forming an *X*, and a crimson banner: "Freedom and Unity." He only wished that Teddy could be here, to witness with Jude the sweet taste of being on the winning team.

*

An hour later, ten of them were crowded in Jude's basement, spread out in sleeping bags. Several were wearing an article of Jude's clothing—sweatpants, a T-shirt, socks—to replace the torn or dirtied or bloodied clothes they'd arrived in. Several were in their underwear. Some held plastic bags of ice to a forehead, or jaw, or ribs; some sat with their chins tipped to the ceiling, toilet paper clogging their nostrils. Jude was one of them. In addition to the steady stream of blood, his nose issued a slimy black fluid, like oil. They assured him he was fine—it was the natural grime of a hardcore show.

Jude had already gotten permission from Harriet to put up Army of One for the night, but after they'd all come to his defense, he'd had no choice but to ask them to stay, too. Harriet liked very little about the idea. She'd come downstairs in her nightgown to find ten teenage boys standing in front of her open refrigerator, looking as if they'd been mauled by a pack of lions. "We were playing football," Jude explained. "Tackle," someone added. Jude took her into the living room and told her calmly, reasonably, that these guys were good guys, clean guys—like Johnny—that they just needed a place to sleep. Did she remember when she was young, when she hitchhiked and protested, remember Woodstock, when she lived in a tent with strangers? She was not accustomed to discouraging Jude from making friends—his new popularity, he could tell, relieved her—so after a round of questions and conditions, she let them stay. Everyone agreed, within Harriet's earshot, what a rad mom she was.

Besides! they said, crashing on some dude's floor was the whole point of being on the road. They sat Indian-style, lay on their stomachs, on the floor, on the old row of seats from the van, chugging Gatorade, staying awake through the Teen Idles' *Minor Disturbance,* through Minor Threat's self-titled, 7 Seconds' *United We Stand,* Agnostic Front's *United Blood.* The room was filled with the faint fumes of deodorant and the mothball aroma of sleeping bags.

Tomorrow, they said, they were going to see Bold at the Anthrax in Stamford, Connecticut, then back to school on Monday morning. "Want to come?" they asked, but Delph and Kram had to work, and Jude didn't have a ride home. They were used to that, weekends in their parents' crappy cars, driving to shows in Boston, Baltimore, Syracuse. They were all skinny from meals-on-the-go—most of them were vegan; it was hard to find health food in drive-thrus on I-95—and most of them bore the bruises and scars of their nights in the pit. One kid had broken his ankle jumping off a stage at a Verbal Assault show. The kid with the missing teeth had lost them in a fight at the Starlight Ballroom in Philly; the skinhead who'd removed them had given him fifty cents, like the tooth fairy—a quarter for each. They talked about the people they'd met on the road: the SHARPS, Skinheads Against Racial Prejudice—you had to look hard to see the *X*s through their swastikas; the fruitarians, who ate only food that grew on trees; the freegans, vegans who dove through Dumpsters for all their meals. Someone knew someone who tied bells to his shoelaces to warn insects on the ground that he was coming. Those posi guys could take a good thing too far.

Hippies, though—that was a new one.

"Dude," said one of them, "when Mr. Clean took out that knife, I was like, whoa."

It occurred to Jude that Johnny had been offering Hippie an out. What had passed between them in the schoolyard had been a quiet negotiation. *I don't want to use this, Hippie. Get out of here while you can.* Afterward Johnny continued to hold the knife at his side while he admonished Jude, not exactly brandishing it, but offering it as evidence. "Quit starting shit!" he'd said. "I'm tired of cleaning up after you."

"You know what he called Teddy?"

"I don't care, Jude."

"He called Teddy a fag."

"I don't *care* what he called him! You're the one who stole his weed. And you're riding your straight edge high horse?" He shook his head in disappointment. "A straight edge kid should be the one breaking bongs. You've got it all backwards."

Johnny had finally pocketed the knife, but he hadn't uttered a word as they'd all filed back into the building to load out their equipment. They'd left everything in the van, and Johnny had headed straight upstairs to Jude's room. Rooster had followed him to try to calm him down.

"Rooster feels bad," Jude said, "because he's the one who helped to start shit."

"Whatever," said one of the guys. "It's a hardcore show. What does Mr. Clean expect?"

"That's why he left his first band," said another. "He was pussying out."

"Doesn't he have a wife?" someone wondered. "What is he, eighteen?"

"Yeah, but she's pregnant," said someone else.

"That's not very edge."

"That's *totally* edge. What's he supposed to do, abandon her? He's committed."

"I don't know," Kevin said. "He goes around pledging a clean lifestyle, and it turns out he's knocked up some girl he just met?"

"Whatever, man, you were seeing that girl in Ohio."

"We were pen pals! She's in the scene!"

"She was until she graduated."

"True Till College, man."

Jude shot a look at Delph and Kram, reminding them to keep quiet. "Johnny really . . . cares about her," Jude said, even though he hadn't seen him acknowledge Eliza in days. "He's trying to help her."

"I'm sure he's helping himself to her upstairs right now," someone said.

"I wish he was down here, though. I want him to do *X*s on my hands."

"We could borrow his kit," said someone else.

"No way," said Jude. "He'd kill us."

"We can do our own," said Kram. He peeled up the sleeve of his T-shirt, showing off the poke-and-stick tattoo he'd given himself at age fourteen. KRAM. It was inscribed across his meaty shoulder, in haphazard pointillist fashion. In Jude's opinion, no one should take advice from a kid who did his own tattoo backward, but the guys lit up. "All you need is some India ink and a needle."

Jude stepped over the sleeping bags and went to Harriet's desk drawer. "Is this India ink?" he asked, holding up two black bottles. For once, he was glad to have an artist for a mother. In the sewing basket above the sink, he found a cloth tomato stabbed with needles.

Delph went first. No one was pussying out of this one. He offered Kram the back of his hand, eight other heads bent over them in a huddle. By the time Kram was done with one leg of the *X,* the rest of the room had begun their own, dipping the needles in the flame of one of Harriet's candles, then running them under hot water. Jude paired up with the kid with the missing teeth, tracing his Magic-Markered *X*s, blotting up the blood with a rag, then another when he'd soaked the first, so much blood that it was hard to see what he was doing. Then the kid did Jude's. Only the right hand—the left was too scarred from the fire at the temple. The tattoo hurt more than he'd thought it would. It took a long time. Toward the end, exhausted and numb, Jude fell in and out of sleep.

The single *X,* Jude saw when he woke the next morning, was dark and fat and a little crooked, and still crusty with ink. He sat up. Everyone was asleep, feet in faces, asses in armpits, mouths quivering a lullaby of snores. His head was heavy, and he felt as if he'd been pelted by several baseballs. He lay down again, but he couldn't fall asleep—he kept opening his eyes to look at his hand. As long as he had a hand, this *X* would be on it. *X* marks the spot. Jude was here.

Harriet and Prudence were at the kitchen counter, eating breakfast and sharing the *Free Press*. Arts & Culture for Harriet. Prudence was perusing a special insert on prom dresses, her face hanging three inches above the page.

"Oh, Christ. What happened to you?" Harriet looked from Jude's face to his hand.

"Mom! He has a tattoo!"

"That's not a tattoo," Harriet said, leaping up from her stool and grabbing his arm. "It's paint or something." She wagged his wrist. "My God, is that my India ink?"

"And you got beat up!" Prudence said, slamming down her spoon.

"Shut the fuck up, Pru."

Harriet put a palm to his forehead. "Look at your nose—it's purple."

"It was just a football game. It got a little crazy."

"One of the boys downstairs did this to you?" Jude shrugged away. "They're lucky I didn't see that bruise last night. Jude, Jesus, what am I supposed to say?"

"Say he's grounded."

"You had one good hand left," Harriet said sadly, studying the *X*. "And now you've ruined that one, too." She rubbed at some of the ink, hoping she might be wrong.

Upstairs, Eliza was in bed. She had been nestled here in her trundle since she'd come home the night before, dusk still settling at the window. She'd been here when she heard the boys arrive long after dark, the slamming of car doors, a set of footsteps, then another, passing by her door on the way upstairs. She was here when they left again this morning, the voices calling thank-yous and apologies and good-byes. "Are you okay?" Prudence whispered, coming back in to check on her, and Eliza had nodded and rolled over. Annabel Lee did not like her mother to sleep on her back. She did not like her mother to sleep at all.

"We'll wait until the baby's born," Johnny had told her. "You're pregnant with my brother's baby. Wouldn't it be disrespectful to his memory?"

When she'd asked him if she could wear his beads, he'd put a protective hand to his throat. Already the subway token he had given Teddy hung from her neck—what more did she want? "It's not a class ring, Eliza," he'd said.

She'd gotten out of bed only once, in the middle of the night, to empty the bladder that the baby liked to kick. She'd tiptoed up to Jude's room and stood outside the door, wondering if anyone was in there. But the room was quiet.

He'd be lying if he said he hadn't been counting the days until Rooster's visit. But then, he'd been lying about so much for so long now that he barely remembered what was real. That night, as he waited for Rooster's knock on Jude's bedroom door, he'd imagined the sick thrill of being with Rooster in the top bunk of Jude's bed— two boys at a sleepover, staying up late under the covers, and the relief of leaving the rest of the world downstairs. Rooster was what was real.

But when Johnny locked the door behind them and climbed the ladder to the top bunk, Rooster didn't follow. He sank into the bean bag chair in the corner. The desk lamp bled a thin, gray light.

"Baby, I'm sick."

Johnny sat with his legs dangling over the edge of the bed. He remembered the tree house he and Teddy had played in. He hadn't wanted to admit to his brother that he was scared of heights, but now he felt again that the ground was very far away.

"How sick?"

Rooster shrugged. His cheeks, once meaty, had caved in, as though he'd removed a pair of false teeth. Johnny had thought he'd been protesting his absence. Fasting out of stubbornness, or too heartbroken to eat. "Two hundred T cells. Whatever the fuck that means."

Johnny closed his eyes. He was sitting in the tree house in Delaware, and Teddy was below him, looking up into the branches, waiting for him to fall. He clung to the edge of the bed, hands shaking.

"Is that . . . still the virus? Or . . . ?"

Rooster pulled at his bottom lip. "The syndrome." He cleared his throat. "I got maybe a year."

The syndrome. Maybe a year.

"Maybe?"

"Maybe less. Maybe more. You can get a free test at a clinic. Results come back pretty quick."

And Johnny opened his eyes. The idea of needing a test—the possibility of being sick himself, something he had feared for so long—had not immediately occurred to him. For once in his life, he had not thought of himself first. And now the thought did not scare him. What scared him was being as far from Rooster as he was from Teddy.

"Come back with me," Rooster said. He didn't have much time. In the light from the desk lamp, Johnny could make out Rooster's blood-limned knuckles. He wondered how much of Rooster's blood had been spilled that night, if he knew how reckless it was to start a fight. He was a brutal son of a bitch. He would go down swinging.

But Johnny didn't go back with Rooster. He couldn't do it anymore—watch the people in his life drop like birds shot from a branch. Rooster slept on the bottom bunk, and in the morning he got into someone's car and went back to New York, where he delivered his uncle's sandwiches on his bike, fed the ducks in Central Park, and, for the first time, rode the elevator to the top of the Empire State Building and saw the city smoking all around him. When he got back to his apartment, Johnny was sitting on his bed, folding Rooster's laundry. It had taken him a little less than a week.

FOURTEEN

Johnny told Jude that Army of One's new singer had a bad case of mono, so he had to take the train down to New York to stay with Rooster and play a few dates with his old band. He wanted to show there were no hard feelings. This was fine by Jude. With Johnny gone, they could go after Tory Ventura without his interference. Tory couldn't stay out of town forever—graduation was coming up.

So Jude was left to lead the growing Vermont crew—the old metalhead friends of Kram and Delph who used to gather on Queen Bea's porch, the skaters Jude had seen smoking in front of the mall. There was Big Ben and Little Ben. There was the Korean kid, Matthew Stein, in the grade above Jude, who wore a caramel-colored hoodie summer or winter. There were two or three freshmen Jude had known in school, and twin brothers who trailed behind them on their matching BMX bikes, fingers cut off of their racing gloves.

They couldn't have been more than thirteen. They'd been found outside the middle school one day while skipping class, eyeing Les's old van as if waiting to be kidnapped. They climbed into the back, bikes and all.

They'd arrive at Jude's in clumps after school, sometimes greeting Harriet or Prudence at the door, clambering down the steps to the basement. They'd sit in the school chairs and listen to the Green Mountain Boys practice, thumb through records, mine the quarts of hummus Jude had his mother buy, pen the outline for a future tattoo with a Sharpie marker. The morning after the show at the rec center, Johnny had taken one look at Jude's tattoo and said, "That's awful DIY of you."

Everyone had a job. Jude strung the phone down the basement steps and made long-distance calls to remote time zones, booking hardcore bands to play at the rec center on their summer tours. Delph was talking to a guy he knew in New Jersey about how to start his own label. You just needed five hundred bucks (always five hundred bucks!) and you could send a demo off for pressing. Kram was printing T-shirts with the iron-on logo Johnny had designed, and Little Ben, who was on the newspaper staff at school, oversaw the zine. Someone was on the typewriter; someone was on pasteup on the floor; someone was on research and fact-checking; someone was on the phone, interviewing. Matthew inked the flyers for the next show, then headed to the A&P's Xerox machine with a sock full of quarters, then led a team to the streets to post them.

DIY was Jude's middle name.

There was no induction ceremony, no melding of spit and blood. Those who tattooed themselves did it with no pressure from Jude or anyone else. The only thing they had to give was their word—no drinking, no smoking, no drugs. Extra credit for no fucking or flesh eating.

"I heard going out with girls is okay, just no sex."

"I heard sex was okay, just not *promiscuous* sex."

"What about making out?" one of the twins asked.

"Look, you want to feel up girls," Jude said, "no one's stopping you. Just don't come hanging around here. You can't contribute when you're thinking about, like, whose skirt you're going to get your hand under in homeroom."

They stayed. They were scared of girls, anyway. Jude was handing them a get-out-of-sex-free card. I'm not ugly, I'm straight edge.

He was not so bold to think the same reasoning didn't apply to him; he was as horny as they were. But he enjoyed the challenge of self-restraint. He enjoyed the exercise of it. It was the one straight edge department in which he trumped Johnny, who'd been the guru of abstinence until he started sleeping with pregnant Eliza. It was also a game of stamina Jude played against himself. He would count the number of days he could go without jerking off, and each time he broke down (often after Eliza, the only girl he really saw, went bra-less under her pajamas, or leaned down to reach something in the crisper), his consolation would be a new personal record to break. Wet dreams, a lamentable side effect of his discipline, didn't count.

Bolstering this discipline were feelings of true nausea. If he had been intimidated by girls before he'd met Eliza, he was terrified of them now. The ease with which she had become impregnated—he had left them alone for an hour!—baffled him; it was as though, just by thinking about having sex with her, he'd willed her pregnant himself. Girls were incubators, they were ovens, they were uteruses. He could barely look at one without projecting a diagram of her reproductive organs over her clothes. He hated the associations that girls now engendered in him. He hated thinking about Harriet's fallopian tubes. He hated thinking about the insides of his birth mother, a teenager herself. A vagina was a thing he had squeezed bloodily out of before being given away.

Not that he hadn't daydreamed about being the father of Eliza's baby. If he'd been the one who'd found her upstairs at the party that night. In his more desperate moments, it seemed as though this future had been stolen from him. *He* was the one she had come to see; it had been *his* birthday. He'd all but claimed her. And if he were the father, she would not have to face having the baby of someone she'd never know.

This fantasy rarely lasted long. Dreaming about being the father was like dreaming that Teddy's baby didn't exist, and no one had more reverence than Jude for the DNA Eliza was carrying. Quickly he would revise the dream so that it was Johnny's place he took instead. It was Jude who had swooped in and married her, who was sharing hotel rooms with her, who would raise Teddy's baby with her. Why hadn't he thought of that himself?

Johnny chose a neighborhood he'd never set foot in before, in a borough as crumbling as his but anonymous. In the clinic-on-wheels, parked at the curb of a graffiti-faced church, he was Patient 9602. "For privacy," the nurse said. Apparently he wasn't the only one who didn't want his name recorded in some manila folder. He leaned his head back against the miniblinds while the nurse sunk the needle into his arm. He felt sorry for the woman, who spent her days searching for veins that had not already been destroyed. "It'll only hurt a little," she said.

At Rooster's place, Johnny took his kit and walked into the hall and dropped it down the trash chute. A moment later it crashed.

"What the fuck'd you do that for?"

"I'm done," Johnny said, coming back into the apartment and lying on his back across the bed. The eight-headed dragon would have seven heads.

"It wasn't your needles, John. But if it makes you feel better, if it makes you think I'm less of a scumbag, go ahead and think it."

Rooster was the only person Johnny had been with, but it had been five years since Rooster had started cruising Central Park: 1983. "Why the fuck you think they call me Rooster?" he'd liked to joke back then. "I'm the cock that rules the roost, that's why." He'd quit cruising when he went straight edge, before he met Johnny, but who knew how many men there had been before him?

Of course it wasn't Johnny's needles. But he couldn't ink another body. Not after this.

Rooster lay down beside him. What were they supposed to do now?

"The waitin' is the worst. Once you get the results, at least you know one way or the other." Of course, if the test was negative, Johnny would have to be retested in six months. He wouldn't be out of the woods. "We were careful," Rooster reminded him, and the past tense rang through the room.

The kids kept coming.

Jude smelled cigarettes on one guy's breath and sent him home; another guy went with him, saying "Fuck this shit" and walking fast. But the next afternoon, two more came to take their places, skinny, zitted-up kids with Bert and Ernie eyebrows who'd heard from someone who'd heard from someone else that they played killer music here; could they sit in? With Johnny gone, Delph and Kram were instantly the elders; no one knew that they were new recruits, too, that they were still imploring their mothers to leave the carne out of the chili. To show up the other kids, they gave up dairy and eggs, too, scowling at boxes of cookies and crackers that contained sodium caseinate, dry milk powder, whey. "Don't you know this shit shrinks your balls?" One by one, kids would sidle in and say, "Eaten nothing but plants for three days, man!" And they'd get noogies and ass-slaps from Jude and Delph and Kram, more approval than they'd gotten all year for their mediocre performances as students and athletes and sons, and they'd come in the next day as though they had no other place to be.

And Jude's contest of self-restraint went on. He gave up honey. He gave up Coke. Mouthwash. Processed sugar. His multivitamin, encased in gelatin. He went so many days without jerking off that he lost count. He worried that he might forget how to do it, as he might forget where Mario's secret coins were hidden in the Mushroom Kingdom, but he was committed, those were the breaks. Sometimes, when he thought about the genius ridiculous fun he used to have with Teddy, or when he'd accidentally listen to a really good Black Flag song about getting fucked up, or when he'd come across one of his old hiding places (he actually found a little shwag in the toe of a pair of leather sneakers he was throwing out—what he would have done for that a few months ago!), he'd get a whiff of the old Jude, who'd say, *What's next, man? A Megalife T-shirt?* But it didn't take long to shake him off. "By the restraint of his senses," said Johnny's *Laws of Manu,* "he becomes fit for immortality." He'd be lying if he said the Krishna stuff didn't weird him out a little, but he did feel immortal, he felt fabulous, indestructible, he was a straight edge god. Flushing the shwag, he felt a rush of righteous adrenaline in his veins. So maybe he was addicted to the game itself. What was wrong with that? It was like being addicted to wheatgrass, or jogging.

And he could *read.* He read antivivisection newsletters and liner notes and even a few pages of Johnny's Bhagavad Gita. On the back of the toilet was a stack of dog-eared, water-ruined zines, all of which Jude had read more than once. "Are you hooked on phonics, Judy?" asked Delph. It was still hard; he still struggled to align his letters; he still had to rest his eyes. But maybe he didn't have dyslexia; maybe he didn't even have FAS. Maybe he'd just been a burnout, and now his synapses were awakening after a long hibernation.

Meanwhile, the band practiced. Matthew filled in for Johnny on second guitar. On afternoons when Delph had to work, one of the twins played bass. By the middle of June, they had enough tracks for a seven-inch. They had at least twenty guys with their fists full of dollars, ready to buy it. *Army of Four,* they'd call it. An homage to Gang of Four and a nod to Army of One, but irresistible, said Jude, for a band named after one of the greatest military companies in history.

But they were broke.

"What are we waiting around for?" Kram said, working the bass pedal restlessly. Delph, too, wanted to get on the road, wanted to quit his job at the Record Room and haul ass out of Vermont. He was days away from graduation.

"We got to record the album before we can do a tour," Jude said. He wanted to do it right, to save enough to record at Don Fury's in New York, like Agnostic Front and Youth of Today. "Otherwise what are we going to sell at the shows?"

"We won't have money for the album until we can sell some merch. And we can't sell any merch till we go on the road."

"What about your old man, Jude?" Kram asked. "He's got dough."

But Jude didn't know where his dad was. In May, a child support check had been mailed from Las Vegas; a postcard had arrived a few weeks later, postmarked Tequila, Mexico, and written entirely in Spanish. The only word Jude recognized was *señorita*.

They could wait. They were booking more shows; they were gathering fans; they were picking up recruits off the street. They were out and about, in hiding no more. More than once, Jude had watched some hippie turn around in the street and change direction—duck down an alley, cut through a yard—when he saw their crew approaching, innocent as ice cream, out enjoying the spring day. That was the clout of the Green Mountain Boys. They were all the Green Mountain Boys now; the name had bled beyond the band to its crew of scouts, its brethren.

There had been a few situations. One midnight, they attempted to liberate a herd of cows from the confines of their pen on Dairy Road (the offspring of the cows they used to tip over in their sleep), but Delph's thigh was impaled on a barbed wire fence. No cows were freed. Delph had to get six stitches. Another time, Little Ben had called with news of a neighborhood barbecue, and they'd gone over with piss-filled water guns, fired them over the fence onto a sizzling rack of ribs. Cops were called by the neighbors, but Little Ben was the only one who got in trouble, a slap on the wrist, and the attention only made him more faithful to the cause. And another night, as they patrolled University Avenue with their baseball bats, a Jeep Cherokee full of drunk frat boys had lunged at them, and if Kram hadn't knocked out one of the headlights with his bat, they all could have been taken out at the knees. Since then, they'd tried to travel on skateboards, or to keep the van idling close by. More often than not, the Green Mountain Boys and their hodgepodge crew went unscathed, going out under cover of night, seeking out the small-town drunks and the stoners and doling out a temperate pounding, not threatening their lives but giving them something to remember in the morning.

Hippie had proved to be a problem no longer; word was that he now did business solely out of his apartment. Jude had heard stories about Boston crews following dealers into bathrooms, beating them up, flushing their drugs, and keeping their cash, but he didn't know any other dealers to harass, now that his father was gone and Delph was transformed.

But to Jude, Hippie's disappearing act was a promise. Sooner or later, his best customer would sniff them out. In the mall, on the street, Jude saw the fast-fingered mirage of Tory Ventura, snapping his belt from the loops of his Duck Heads. Jude's heart was a crowing bird, a rooster before a rain. In his mother's studio, where Tory had taken his bat to her work, where grains of glass still glittered on the floor like sand, he practiced taking a bat to the mattress that leaned against the wall. He swung until his arms ached.

*

If Teddy had been there, in the troposphere of Earth, in the spring of 1988, he'd have seen Lintonburg from above, hovering somewhere over the center of town, over the oblong bell tower of the cathedral, the streets a grid of budding green beneath him, bowing at the horizon with the gentle curvature of the globe. He'd see the uniformed figures on the baseball field, hear the snap of bats and the rustle of cleats on freshly shorn grass. At the high school, the final bell would be ringing, the kids gathering on the sidewalk, the golden buses slinking through the bus loop like the conjoined cars of a train set. Beneath a purple umbrella on Ash Street, Harriet would be minding her table, and Prudence would be drinking a wine cooler on Dena Jeffries's back porch. From Jude's basement, he'd hear the subterranean thump of the Bastards' old bass drum.

By night the town goes black and gold, the lake a riot of waves woken from months beneath the ice. Across Main Street, an army of boys marches eastward. They're hard to distinguish, clothed darkly against the dark streets. Ronald Reagan in a JUST SAY NO T-shirt, Kram also in green, an I L♥VERMONT shirt he found at the Salvation Army. A crowbar, a spring billy, pepper spray, a couple of baseball bats. A striped sock filled with three rolls of quarters—city weapons they wield with the workmanlike purpose of New Englanders. They won't use any of them but the BB gun, a relic Kram used to train on squirrels but now wouldn't point at any animal but a person, and now reverbs off the blue-jeaned buttock of some guy no one knows the name of. He's taking a leak behind the Dumpster of Wayne's Billiards, so drunk he doesn't seem to feel the impact, just falls over obligingly, heavy as a grandfather clock.

FIFTEEN

Eliza," Harriet said, "it's nearly one o'clock."

Eliza rolled over and looked up at the ceiling. She was in Prudence's bed, not the trundle, which Harriet had finally insisted on, for the baby's sake.

"I think the lettuce is ready to be picked. Should we make a salad for lunch?"

"I'm not hungry," Eliza said, and then cutting Harriet off, "the baby isn't hungry, either."

Harriet sat down on the edge of the mattress. She didn't have the energy to do this again, to assemble the mystical code of words that would get this child out of bed.

"What do you think he's doing down there?"

"Down where, honey?"

"Johnny, down in New York. It's been like two weeks."

"Should we call him?" Harriet suggested brightly.

"I did. There was no answer at Rooster's."

Harriet folded her hands in her lap. For years, before she herself became pregnant, she had hated the sight of pregnant women. She had imagined they were all members of the same smug sisterhood, waddling down the aisles of the supermarket, blissed out on their own estrogen. She had never known a pregnant woman who did not want to be pregnant. She wondered now if this is how Jude's mother had spent her nine months.

"Eliza, I think it's time we got you to a doctor. Sooner or later, your mother's going to come for you."

Eliza said nothing. She lay her arms across her eyes. The cat that had followed Harriet into the room hopped up onto the bed and nestled into Eliza's armpit, and Eliza reached blindly to pet its head. Harriet did not have a pamphlet. She had nothing to leave behind.

Wasn't there new medication? Johnny asked. Wasn't there treatment? But Rooster couldn't possibly afford it. Even if he could, Rooster wondered, would taking AZT weaken his straight edge credibility?

"True till death," he tried to joke, stroking the letters tattooed across Johnny's chest. Rooster's cheekbone, sharp as an arrowhead now, gouged Johnny's shoulder.

Johnny didn't laugh.

Rooster was right—it was the waiting. To distract himself, Johnny thought of the baby. Up, up, up, busy, busy, busy, that was the trick. The baby was already an angel, Teddy's golden-winged redemption, and now maybe it would be Johnny's, too. In three months, Johnny would be a father. His name would be on the birth certificate. John Martin McNicholas. No matter that it wasn't true or that one-third of the name was invented. All names at some point were invented. They would invent a name for the baby. The baby would be invented, too.

Johnny rolled over onto his elbow and said, "How do you find out the name of someone's father?"

"Someone?" Rooster said.

Johnny had been thinking lately about Ravi, where he was, who he was. He was the only other person, besides their worthless mother, who would be related to the baby. If Johnny was sick, Ravi would be the only one. Surely Ravi was alive. Why else would Queen Bea have bolted after Johnny clued her into Teddy's plans? What staggered Johnny was that he was the one who had scared her away, as though she believed Johnny could magically produce Teddy's father if he put his mind to it. The only useful information he remembered about Ravi was his first name and that at one point he'd lived in Miami.

But what if he *could* find him? Wouldn't Teddy want him to? If Queen Bea was so scared, maybe it would be easier than he thought.

"Vital Statistics?" said Rooster.

"Vital Statistics," said Johnny. Of course.

And the next morning Rooster and Johnny went to the Forty-second Street library and located the proper wing and the proper directory and endured the bespectacled librarians' stares at their shaved heads and tattoos—"Can we help you?" Rooster asked one—and found the proper phone number for the Dade County Department of Health, and provided the Social Security number for Edward Alvin Michaels, birth date 5/13/72. The next day, he mailed in a copy of the death certificate, and one week later, in Rooster's mailbox, there was Teddy's birth certificate, an even exchange. And there was the name.

Father: Ravi Milan.

They were just returning from the clinic, where Rooster had sat next to Johnny while he received another answer he'd been waiting for.

Negative.

Now Rooster gave him a tentative pat on the back. "See? Both good news."

But Johnny stood frozen in the lobby, the mailbox door swung open, Rooster's heavy keys hanging from the lock as though they might drop at any second.

*

"One of you must have seen him around. You go to school with him."

Jude's basement was crammed with the guys who'd stayed after practice. That's what they'd been doing: practicing. They were ready for something bigger than BB guns and cows.

"He's having a party after graduation," said Big Ben.

"Saturday?"

"Yeah."

Big Ben was going. They had to drag it out of him, but he had a girlfriend and he'd promised to take her. He hadn't wanted them to know about the girl.

Another party at Tory's house. He would be leaving Project Graduation early, where he had to make an appearance as Prom King. The party would be getting started around midnight.

"We can't take him on at his own party," Delph said. "He'll be surrounded by all his fellow pricks."

Jude rubbed his head. "So we'll have to do it before he gets there."

Everyone was in. Everyone hated the guy. He was the antithesis of straight edge—the kind of prick who was still so wasted on Monday morning that he was puking in the boys' room. He had two DUIs. He'd grabbed Matthew's sister's boobs. And he thought he could give *them* shit?

Big Ben and Delph and Kram would tell their parents they were at Project Graduation. Everyone else would say they were spending the night at Jude's, which they would be, eventually. Everyone except Little Ben, who was still grounded from the water gun incident. He'd have to hear about it in the morning.

"Okay, this is what happened."

"Tell him, fat boy. Start at the beginning."

"We're in the parking lot. Of course, right? When are we not in a parking lot?"

"Just tell him about the keg."

"You guys, shut up and let him tell me."

"Thank you. So there's no one around but us. We're looking for Tory's car. Big Ben's on the football field, with the walkie-talkie. He's eating goddamn elephant ears, he's throwing balls at the dunk tank. His lady blows chunks in the Bounce House."

"She wasn't drinking, Kram. She gets seasick."

"Everyone else is looking for the LeBaron. We're cruising around, can't find it. Just when we start to think he's not showing, here comes Salvatore, driving right past us, already drunk as shit, you can tell. Parks like a retard. And he and his girl go stumbling onto the field—you know that chick with the really blond hair? Bangs up to here? Missy something? So we go back to waiting. In the backseat sure enough there's a couple empty bottles of champagne. Drunk prick never learns, didn't even lock his door. Who the fuck drinks champagne in high school? But that's not all. We're sitting around taking turns rail sliding down the steps and for fun Delph jimmies the trunk and inside is this keg. It's full. And we're all like, score. Jude's on the walkie, he's like, 'We found the car, he's here,' and Big Ben's like, 'Yeah, I see him, he's here,' and then we start planning shit out. Jude parks the van next to his car, and then the two of us get in the backseat, in the LeBaron. Jude's behind the passenger seat and I'm behind the driver. In a little while, Big Ben's like, 'He's doing his thing.' That's when he rides in a convertible with the Prom Queen, like at homecoming. Around the field."

"Who was Prom Queen this year?"

"Who the fuck knows? Some chick."

"Karen St. John."

"So he's riding around the field. He's doing whatever. It seems like it's taking forever. Finally Ben's like, 'Heads up, he's coming out.' We get in position. We all pull on these ski masks, scary as hell. It's Delph, Matthew, and the twins in the van and me and Jude in the

LeBaron. There's this blanket that's got this grass and dirt all over it, and we cover ourselves up with it. We wait a shitload of time. But finally, here he comes, all drunk and loud, and he's laughing with his girl. He gets in the car and she gets in the car. We let them get settled, get a little smoochy, and then all at once we jump up and grab them from behind. They yell for their lives, like we're going to kill them. I've got my belt around Tory faster than shit. Not around his neck like with the wire in *Godfather*—just around his chest, to keep him in place. Jude's got his belt around the girl and his hand over her mouth, and thank God she's stopped screaming. He stays there shutting her up while the boys pile out of the van—Green Mountain Boys, fuck right—and help me shove Tory in there. We get the door closed and, Little Ben, we just go ape shit. Some of us are holding him down, some are just pummeling, kicking, whatever. We let the twins have some fun. They're in ski masks—what's Tory going to know? I got in a good lick across his shins. *Who's a pussy now? Who's a faggot now?* And he's dressed up like Prom King. He's got the furry red cape on, I'm not shitting, and Delph is going to town on him with his golden staff. Pussy used to give our boy shit—Teddy McNicholas? That prick thinks he can give our Teddy Bear a hard time? And I'll tell you what: it felt fucking good. We left him sprawled across the backseat of his car. His girl's not screaming anymore. We told her to drive the poor bastard home. No party for Salvatore. I found this tiara in the van. Isn't it nice? I think it makes me look glamorous."

"It's called a crown."

"Jeezum Crow, you guys."

"Tell him about the keg."

"Oh. We emptied it. Set it on a storm drain and just—*fzzzt*—pumped it right out. Then we put it back. That was Jude's idea. Add insult to injury. This morning, or this afternoon, or whenever Tory can walk again, he'll open up his trunk and take out his keg and it'll be light as a beach ball."

*

Prudence came home later that morning, storming into Jude's room. Jude didn't even know she'd been out. "Where have you been?" he asked her. "You look like shit." All the guys had gone home, off to graduation parties of their own, off to church with their families.

"I hate you," she said, throwing her backpack down on the floor. Jude was stretched out on the bottom bunk, reading *Schism*.

"Did you have a good time?" he asked, putting the zine down. "Getting wasted at some loser's house?"

"I hate you so much."

"What? What'd I do?"

"You know what you did!"

"What?"

"You put Tory Ventura in the hospital!"

Jude sat up. "Would you keep it down?" Harriet wasn't home, but the sound of his sister's voice made him want to clap a hand over her mouth. Maybe *in the hospital* was a manner of speaking. "Do you even know what you're saying?"

"I'm saying you and your convict friends beat up Tory. Missy Sherman told everyone. He's got a concussion, Jude! Do *you* know what that means?" Prudence put her hands on her hips. "It means you're in serious trouble."

"Fucker deserved it," Jude said, although his heart had begun a swift climb up into his throat. He stood up and started pacing. "I won't get in trouble if you don't tell Mom."

"*Mom?* Mom's the least of your worries. You know how long you go to juvie for aggravated battery?"

"It wasn't aggravated. I didn't lay a hand on him." It was true. He had met Tory's eyes only for an instant, while Kram and the others dragged him into the van. Jude had intended to be the one who led the ambush, had brought the baseball bat he'd swung so many times he'd worn it smooth. But when Tory lasered that look at him through the car window—a look of disbelief or supplication or fear—Jude stayed planted in the car.

"If you tell Mom, I'll tell her where you were all night."

"You know where I was all night? I was at Tory's house with everyone else, waiting around in the driveway for his party to start. Finally someone comes saying Missy took him to the hospital."

Jude rubbed his head again and again. Maybe the pussy wouldn't report it. Maybe he'd be too scared.

"Now no one wants anything to do with me. Everyone heard what you guys did and now I'm a pariah."

"Oh, come on. Those guys don't even know who I am, let alone that I'm your brother."

"They do *now*," she said and sank down on the bed beside him, starting to cry.

"Oh, stop it with the baby voice. We were wearing masks, Pru. How do they even know it was us?"

"She saw Dad's *van*, Jude. Everyone knows that's your van." Tarzan hopped into Prudence's lap, and she heaved several sobs into his furry neck.

"You shouldn't be at one of those lame parties anyway, Pru."

"You should be worrying about yourself. You're the one who's in trouble."

"I'm not in trouble," he said, nearly whispering. "I'm not in trouble, I'm not in trouble. He's all right, right? Tory? He's not going to die or anything?"

He'd put his hand on Prudence's arm, he realized, and now she yanked it away. They sat side by side on the bed, staring at nothing. His fingertips were warm where they'd touched the downy branch of her forearm, and suddenly he felt his hands clamped over Missy Sherman's mouth, trapping a scream inside her head. It had rattled like the call of a far-off bird. The belt he had slipped around her ribs wasn't his but Tory's, the braided belt that had lain coiled in his drawer since New Year's Eve, and it had taken little else to enclose her body in the cage of his arms and pin her against the seat—not a second, not a thought. They'd sat peacefully in the emptied car for what must have been three or four minutes, listening together to the muffled cries from the neighboring van, watching it rock. He could have done anything to her. When the guys dumped Tory into the backseat of the car, Jude released the belt into her lap, like a limp snake.

"I liked you better before," Prudence said. She was saying that a lot these days. "Before you went around beating people up. You were gentler," she said, "like Teddy."

Jude looked down at his hands. On the left one, across the inside of his knuckles, was a smear of pink. Lipstick.

He got out of there fast, jumped on his skateboard and headed downhill, gulping the painfully fresh air. He couldn't stay home and wait for a knock on his door. He'd be arrested. Or he'd be killed—Tory had friends. Either way, he was in over his head.

They'd go on tour. That was what they'd do. Di would catch up with them soon, anyway—they had no choice but to run. They'd get in the van and go find Johnny and they'd get out of here. Once again they'd get the fuck out of Vermont. He didn't realize how stupid it was to be seen out in the daylight until his board had carried him to Teddy's. Three rights and a left.

The house was for sale now, and Jude felt strangely remote, as if he'd never been here before. There was Teddy's window. There was the porch the band used to practice on. That was all. Not a flood of memories—a drought.

Slowly he made his way on hands and knees to the edge of the house and ducked under it. It was set up on cinder blocks, and Teddy and Jude used to hide out under here, smoking, drinking. Sometimes, when Queen Bea lost her keys, they'd crawl under here to push open the trapdoor that led to the kitchen. The crawl space was lower than he remembered—or he was bigger—and it was littered with unremarkable, half-buried treasures. Beer bottles, a child's plastic shovel, a bottle cap, which bit into his knee. A blank paper card, the size of a lottery ticket, bleached white. Under where the kitchen would be, he found the trapdoor, but when he tried to push it open, it wouldn't budge. He tried again, ramming it with his shoulder. Someone had nailed it shut.

How had he gotten so off course? It wasn't Tory Ventura he wanted to punish. Jude sat panting in the dirt. Tory wasn't the one who'd killed Teddy. He dug his fingers into the cool dirt. He clawed at it, the dirt coating his hands, rimming his fingernails, his tears coming in heaves, burning his face. He wiped a muddy track of snot across his cheek.

When Jude returned home, worn-out, filthy, there was no sign of anyone, but he was quiet anyway, treading softly up the stairs. He washed his hands and his face. Then he went to his sister's room and tapped on the door. No answer. Slowly he pushed it open.

What day was it? Sunday? Monday? The bed was unmade, sheets spilling in a spiral to the floor. And what was that smell? On the floor were a pair of jeans, a pair of shoes, a towel. It took Jude a moment to realize that the things were not his sister's, but Eliza's. Did he smell pot?

He rifled through Prudence's backpack hanging on the chair and the first few drawers of her dresser before he thought to check the fire escape. As he crossed the room, he thought of something Eliza had told him once. The second time she was kicked out of school, when she was caught with drugs in the pool, she had been alone. This had depressed Jude greatly. Before that, he had imagined that she'd been partying with friends, maybe skinny-dipping, maybe with a guy. Now he pictured her floating on her back in the Olympic-size pool, at sea.

He found her behind the curtain, on the other side of the open window, wearing a pair of acid-washed cutoffs, a polka-dot bikini top, her white-framed sunglasses, and her headphones. A sun-darkened line orbited the planet of her belly, plunging south from her navel. She was smoking a joint in the early summer sun, and on her face drifted an expression of overdue bliss.

SIXTEEN

ON THE EDGE

XXX FANZINE XXX
FALL 1988, 2.50$

Interview with Jude Green and Mr.
Clean of the Green Mountain Boys

ON THE EDGE: Your new seven inch [Army of
    Four] is totally hard. My favorite song
    is "Str8 or Die."

MR. CLEAN: Thanks man.

JUDE GREEN: We all worked on that one.

OTE: What are you guys up to now?

JG: We've been touring all up and down the
    coast this summer. We were in New York
    for a little bit, we played a matinee
    with Youth of Today and Uniform Choice

and Army of One at CB's, that was a
beautiful experience.

OTE: Your songs seem to promote a pretty
strict straight edge lifestyle. And I
heard about the fight at 9:30. Would you
say your intolerant of other hardcore
bands and fans that aren't straight?

MC: No were certainly not intolerant.
Were friends with some guys who are
straight and some who aren't. Were about
inclusion, not exclusion. Yes there have
been fights but there sort of typical.
The thing at CB's was just one of those
things where some guy kicks you in the
face and there was good-natured dancing
and Kram just gets sort of sensitive.
Well you've seen Kram, he's our drummer,
you don't want to mess with him.

OTE: Do you think the incident contributed
to the rumors about closing down the
hardcore matinees?

JG: That's not going to happen. Let's face it
the scene will never be without violence.
If some guy isn't respectful of us and
he's blowing smoke in our faces and
that's only happened two or three times,
yeah, there will be some shit going down.
Look at our song "Blowing Smoke." I mean
frankly you should know better than to
start shit with us.

OTE: When did you start going by Jude Green?

JG: That started I think at CB's, too, sort

of as a joke you know like Kevin Seconds
of 7 Seconds, but it stuck.

MC: Its not like I call him Jude Green or
anything.

OTE: And how'd you get your name, Mr. Clean?

MC: Yea, some guys started that when I
shaved my head. But I'm not really into
nicknames. The way I look at it is, the
atman in all of us is a pure force,
without ego.

OTE: Is that Krishna consciousness or
something?

JG: Yea, you know, like Ray Cappo's into.

MC: Krishna isn't a trend. He's the Supreme
Godhead, is the way I look at it, and my
music, at least, is an expression of his
love.

OTE: So all of you guys are into that?

JG: We're straight in every way. A hundred
percent vegan and we don't do drugs of
any kind. I don't feel they have any
place in my life, which I keep as pure as
possible. The body is a temple and all
that, but my temple is at the shows, with
the people, you know what I mean?

OTE: OK, Mr. Clean, I'm sure lots of people
have been wondering about this. What's it
like to be in the scene and be married?

MC: Oh, its wonderful. Its wonderful. To be
on the road and be able to share that
with someone you love . . . its just
amazing.

OTE: So your wife is straight too?

MC: Oh, yeah, yeah. We both lead a clean
      lifestyle. Especially seeing as she's
      expecting! [laughs]

OTE: So its true she's pregnant?

MC: Our family will be expanding in
      September.

OTE: What about you, Jude? What's your take on
      girls in the scene?

JG: I'd like to talk about the music, if
      that's OK. Were talking to X-Ample
      about doing a split seven inch. That's
      something cool.

OTE: That is cool. What about you, Mr. Clean?
      Will you be able to stay active in the
      band with a newborn baby?

MC: Oh, definately, definately. I can do both
      at once. I might not get much sleep, but
      I'll be at practice!

OTE: That's cool, brothers. I wish you all the
      luck in the world.

JG: Thanks, man.

OTE: True till death man.

JG: True till death.

MC: Hare Krishna. Thanks a lot.

photo courtesy of Ben Leblanc

Ben Leblanc
September 5, 1988
3rd per.

How I Spent My Summer Vacation
Have you ever driven up and down the eastern United States? Have
you ever been to cities such as New York City, Philadelphia, Washington, D.C. and Atlanta GA? Well I have. These are just some of
the many places I went this summer with a hardcore band called
the Green Mountain Boys who are from Lintonburg. They range in
age from 16 to 18 yrs. and follow the straight edge way of life. I take
pictures for their zine and they needed someone to help with their
equipment etc. which is how I got to be their roadie.

Not only did I get to see amazing sights such as the Empire State
Building, I also slept on people's floors, attended countless exciting
concerts and learned life lessons such as how to change a tire. Before
this I had never seen the ocean before and now I am proud to say
that I have been swimming in the Atlantic. I also skated down the
steps of the Lincoln Memorial which was amazing.

All in all I wouldn't trade my summer for anything. It was a
truely musical experience.

The high point came early. A day close enough to the Fourth of July,
birds circling low over Manhattan, Don Fury's studio on Spring
Street. In Delph's pocket were the five hundred dollars for which
he'd sold his car. The Green Mountain Boys were freshly show-
ered and freshly shaved, their clothes freshly laundered. They'd
stayed up late tuning their guitars. They'd eaten a hearty breakfast
at Angelica. Eliza was wearing her yellow summer dress, and a man
on the corner was selling enormous Technicolor fruit, and they all
stood on the sidewalk, waiting to be buzzed in. Jude was already in
the future, looking back at himself.

*

Back in Lintonburg, Jude had packed up the band with his father's gift for speed. It had taken under twenty-four hours to get the proper people in the proper vehicles; to fit their suitcases into the back of the van, Tetris-style; to fit the drum kit into the camper compartment; for Delph and Kram to quit their jobs, both without notice and without their final paychecks; for Matthew and Little Ben to beg permission from their parents to tag along; for everyone else's parents to say no; for Little Ben to get his deposit back on breakdancing camp; to transfer all rec center business to Big Ben; to bid good-bye to Harriet, who did not try very hard to stop them. When they left, they left in a caravan: Delph, Kram, and Matthew in the Kramaro; Eliza, Jude, and Little Ben—who was now, inadequately, just Ben—in the van.

Of course she didn't try to stop them. What could she do, short of putting the lock and chain back on his window, but watch from the door of the greenhouse as the cars pulled out of the alley, kicking up gravel and dust? Look at Eliza's mother. Look at what happened when you tried too hard to dictate your children's choices—they ended up running even farther from you.

With the kids gone, Harriet spent the afternoon busying herself in her studio. She still had work to do to replenish her inventory. She didn't know how much the marijuana Jude had stolen was worth, but surely her glass had been worth more. And surely the boys who had destroyed it were the ones Jude was running from again. Maybe, as she believed before, he'd be safer out of town. Only now, she had three children to worry about. She tried not to think about which cities they'd be driving through, whose floor they'd be sleeping on, but she was clumsy, distracted. Her hands shook; she cracked two tubes. She chatted too long with a ponytailed man who had come by yesterday. He hadn't bought anything then, but again she walked him through her gallery, all the pieces she displayed in fish tanks turned on their sides (the fish tanks, too, she'd had to replace). She shared a pack of American Spirits with the man, sitting in the plastic patio chairs that overlooked her garden. Normally, this was her least favorite part of her occupation—the exchange, the chummy small talk. That was Les's talent. He used to spend hours with his customers, shooting the shit while they smoked up the greenhouse; only when she called him in for dinner did he remember to collect any money. Her customers often seemed as puzzled as she was about what exactly the interaction required of them, whether the rituals that were in the job description of the drug peddler, the prostitute, the illegal arms dealer, even, in this state, the tattoo artist—those professions more clearly on the other side of the law—applied to the traffic of glassware. It had been many years—and a few drop-ins by the local police—since Harriet had inaugurated a bong with its new owner. Now she kept things simple. Rarely did she *talk* like this. She told the man with the gray ponytail about her work, her ex, the carload of kids who had just disappeared. It was almost dark when he kindly extinguished his third or fourth cigarette and left with his newspaper-wrapped bundle. Alone in the moon-shadowed alley, the folded bills in the breast pocket of her overalls, Harriet felt unclean, as though she *had* engaged in something illicit. Did he think she was hitting on him? (Was she?) Did he think she was some doped-out old tramp?

She returned to the studio, turned on the lights and the hood. Pru was staying at Dena's, and unless they'd broken down or been hit by a truck or killed by a hitchhiker, Jude and Eliza were safe in their van. They would be fine. They could take care of themselves. Leaning a knee on the rickety desk chair, she selected two glass tubes from the plastic pitcher at her workstation. She turned on the clock radio, tuned since the 1970s to Lintonburg's classic rock station. What had classic rock been called then? Just rock, she supposed. After hunting for a moment for her safety glasses, she found them hanging, along with her other glasses, on their separate chain, around her neck. She got her torch going, and she got her tubes spinning, and then, a miracle of molecules, it was one tube. Her hands were steady now. She fumed some silver onto the pipe and raked it. Nothing fancy, but it was a clean design. This is what she loved: the work. The evening hour, the smell of the propane, the industrious *whirr* of the hood. She lit a candle, then used the flame to light a cigarette. Paul Simon was on the radio. *Just drop off the key, Lee.* She turned it up. Maybe the pipe *did* look a little like a dildo. Maybe there *was* something unsavory about her line of work. The man with whom she'd apprenticed in Brattleboro at the age of seventeen (glassblowing had been only one of the skills he'd taught her) had later gone on to specialize in glass sex toys. Harriet had stuck nobly to her roots, though over the years, often while sitting in the principal's office at one of Jude's schools, she had questioned the nobility of pipes and bongs. Somewhere along the way, she had lost her fondness for pot; since Jude's hypothermia scare, she'd smoked it just once, missing him after the first time he'd left for New York, when she'd found a forgotten stash. But the fact was pipes and bongs were her livelihood. They bought cough syrup, field trips, socks. They had histories; they had temperaments; they were as knotted and regal and individual as trees. It still pained her, like some irrecoverable loss, to recall the grisly sight she'd encountered here those months ago, the glass bodies broken beyond recognition. She propped her cigarette in the ashtray and began to blow out the bulb, filling it tenderly with her breath. Nobody loved a vase the way they loved a bong.

Her lips were pressed to the tube like so, the bulb swelling like a soap bubble on the end of a child's wand, when she heard the door slam shut. Harriet turned her head, and her hands followed, and her left pinky, alert, trailed through the flame. The pipe bounced once on the edge of the table, not breaking, and then broke on the floor.

A man and a woman stood by the door. Harriet could see,

through her UV lenses, as she jogged to the sink and held her hand in the cold stream, that they were as startled as she was. But she felt her heart slow: for an instant, as she heard the crash of the glass, she had expected boys with baseball bats.

"I'm terribly sorry," said the woman, not coming closer. Her British accent had a cooling effect, like a salve. "We heard the music. We knocked." She turned to the man, who was wearing the sleek uniform of a chauffeur. "Could you wait in the car, Dwayne? We'll be a while."

"Do you take milk, or . . . ?"

"Lemon, if you have it."

In the crisper, Harriet found a quarter of something that resembled a lemon, its tissue eaten gray by mold. She served tea because she'd imagined serving tea, but a lemon had not figured into the picture. Harriet was a coffee drinker; she was one of those Vermonters with the liter-size mug, drowned with sugar and cream. Of course Diane Urbanski took lemon with her tea.

"I'm sorry," Harriet said, the tea spilling a little on the coffee table as she set the mugs down, "I don't." Would this be, in Di's mind, Harriet's first act of hostility? Or would she just read her as a bumpkin, the lemonless bumpkin ex?

Di waved her ringed fingers. Not to worry. Despite the fact that the couch was sculpted from a bathtub six inches off the ground, she appeared to have found a comfortable position. She was dressed for an interview: black pants and black heels and a white blouse winged open to reveal a sturdy rope of pearls. She was pretty, but not as pretty as Harriet had feared. Hers was the kind of makeup you could see from across a coffee table, dusting each of her perfect pores as pale as chalk.

"It was the ponytailed man, wasn't it," said Harriet, feeling foolish. "Gray hair? Glasses?" He'd been awfully friendly.

"Bob," Di confirmed, her eyes hard. "I would have been here earlier," she said, "if Bob hadn't taken so long to locate his backbone." He'd succeeded in convincing Di that there was no sign of any of the kids in Lintonburg, as Les had paid him handsomely to do, but after taking care of his mother's medical bills, he'd had second thoughts, sleepless nights. He couldn't, after all, keep a child from its mother.

"I know you wouldn't want to do that, either," Di went on, reaching for her mug.

Would Harriet want to keep a child from its mother? She studied her tea. An old friend of hers had once told fortunes by reading tea leaves. She'd had a little tea booth on Ash Street, a gypsy kerchief, gold hoops in her ears. Where was she now? Was Harriet the only grown-up stuck in the sixties, hawking her juvenile wares? Who was she fooling, playing this game of hide-and-seek with a woman she didn't know, pleading to be on the kids' team?

"She was here, yes," Harriet said into her mug. "But now she's gone. They just ran off, and that's the truth. They're on tour. They're on tour with the boys' band. I don't know how that happens, exactly." She was turning chatty again; she couldn't stop herself. "How can a bunch of boys just decide to start a band and go on tour? But that's the way they do it, I understand."

Di lowered and raised her tea bag. Lowered, raised. Harriet tried to decide whether she hated her. Did she resent her? Was she insulted by her? "I'd hate to resort to Les's level," said Di, looking truly repulsed. "But I'm willing to pay you whatever it takes."

Harriet, in the director's chair, cradled her tea in her hands. The liquid through the cup was hot, threatening to scald the bandaged finger she'd already burned. "Money?" she said stupidly.

"I won't press any charges," Di promised. Lowered, raised, plodding as a backhoe. "I'll forget she was ever here."

Harriet could not bring herself to feel sorry for Les, who had been duped out of his own bribe. But now this woman, too, thought she could buy her way into anything? What a match! Harriet put down her mug, rattling it against the table. "Do you think I'm holding the girl for ransom? Do you think I have her bound and gagged in the basement? Christ, I *wish* money could fix this." Yes, she hated her, she resented her, she was insulted by her, but she hated herself, too. "I let the kids stay here, and I probably shouldn't have, and I'm sorry. And I let them leave, and I even gave them a little money. Yes, I have a little money, too! But when I look back at these months, and I try to identify what I could have done differently, to keep my son from backing me into this corner, I honestly don't know what it is." She reached for her cigarettes and stabbed one in her mouth. "Do you think I don't want to know where my son is? Ever since your daughter rode that *goddamn* train into town, he has vanished. Do you know that? He might reappear every now and then, he might leave me his *cats* to look after"—she shoved the tiger-striped one off the arm of her chair—"but he's gone. He's gone, too."

On the top shelf of the homemade bookcase, white built-ins that stretched up to the ceiling, a wooden owl perched. It was a crudely carved statue, and Di had never liked it. Les had an identical one in his apartment in New York. The pair of birds must have divorced, too, and now Harriet and Les each kept one.

"How *is* Jude?" asked Di, attempting to recover some civility. She hadn't expected Harriet to be *angry*, angry at *her*. And she certainly hadn't expected to feel so shut down by Harriet's anger, to feel her own anger drain before it had the chance to surface. She hadn't expected tea. She'd expected pot, maybe. Over the years, she'd imagined getting stoned with Les's ex-wife, *bonding,* trading demeaning stories about Les's lack of ambition, the size of his anatomy, etc. But he was the last person she cared to talk about now. Les was an idiot. What else was there to say?

"I'm not sure," Harriet answered.

"I really *like* Jude," Di said pathetically. "He's a good kid." A series of expressions flickered across Harriet's face: surprise, possessiveness, pride.

"I like Eliza."

"She's a good kid, too."

"She is."

"How is she?" asked Di.

In a photo album in her apartment in New York, nine pictures chronicled Di's single pregnancy. In each picture, taken by Daniel, she held up an assortment of fingers: one for one month, two for two months. In the seven-month photo, she was posed in an arabesque, her leotard stretched tight over her expanding belly.

"I think she's scared," Harriet said.

"Of what?" Di demanded, her voice trembling. "Is she scared of *me*?"

Harriet put out her cigarette and lit another one, and when she offered the pack to Di, she was surprised that she accepted. "This may not be any of my business. But when you live in a house with four teenagers, you start to make observations." She had not expected to offer Di any counsel. "You probably know that we"—she waved her cigarette vaguely—"adopted Jude." *That* was when the problems began, Harriet thought. Not a few months ago, but on Jude's ninth birthday, the day her husband told their son he was adopted. She'd been so angry at Les, but she knew they shouldn't have waited so long to tell him. Even then, when Jude was a small child, she'd been so scared he wouldn't forgive her, that he'd love her less. And now look what had happened! It was keeping the secret from him that had turned him away from her. "She was just sixteen," said Harriet, "the girl who gave birth to Jude."

Di balanced her cigarette while she sipped her tea. The mug said DR. GERALD F. STEIN, D.D.S.: BRIGHTENING THE WORLD ONE SMILE AT A TIME. It was strange to be here and yet strangely familiar; she felt as uncomfortable here as she had in Les's apartment. The house even *smelled* a little like Les. It smelled lived-in, the air dense with dust motes and cigarette smoke and the gas from the stove. The cushions of the couch were slightly damp, as though they were sweating.

"I would hate to think," Harriet went on, "that she had been forced to give him up. That I had stolen him from his rightful mother."

Di smiled around her cigarette. She couldn't help it. She brushed a tuft of cat hair from her pants. "What on earth is a 'rightful mother'?" Were *they* rightful mothers? In Di's mind, there was no such thing. No parent ever acted in her child's "best interest"; no parent was a hero. A parent wrote her child's story every day; the story was what the parent left behind. Teenage pregnancy had not been in Di's script for Eliza. Di had the power to revise this scene; she could excuse Eliza from her own bleak future. She didn't want her daughter to be trapped in telling someone else's story before she'd had the chance to tell her own.

"I guess I have no idea," Harriet admitted. She blew two tunnels of smoke from her nostrils. All these abandoned children, she was thinking. Jude, and poor Teddy, and she guessed Johnny and Eliza, too, and Prudence—lost, inscrutable Pru. All left by one parent or both, in one way or another.

Yet here they were, Di mused (snatching up the thought like a cigarette): Les's two exes, trying to recover them, and now it was *they*—the mothers—who had been deserted by their children.

How odd! thought Harriet, that Les was the least they had in common. It was their children's desertion that mattered to them, that left them alone. Jude and Eliza and Johnny had devoted themselves, fiercely and exclusively, to one another, but Harriet and Di weren't capable of forging an alliance together, despite what they shared. The only people they'd ever felt that kind of loyalty toward—perhaps this was the mistake they both had made—were their children.

Well, that was what loyalty did, didn't it? It corroded. It collapsed on itself. Harriet thought of the songs Jude sang. About Loyalty. About Purity, Brotherhood, Trust.

Originally a cheery two-tone—the bottom half white, the top robin's
egg blue—the Dodge A100 van was first owned by a Canadian cannabis farmer, who had converted it into a camper by the time he sold
it to Lester Keffy in 1970. Back then, with its split windshield, its
bug-eye headlights, its overall grooviness, you could almost pretend
it was a Volkswagen bus, which was the effect Les had been going
for. Later, to mask the pockmarks of rust, Les painted the van lavender, baptizing it the Purple People Eater. Over the years, the ele-
ments had worn away the paint; behind the greasy prints of muted
purple, streaks of rusty white and blue shone through.

Intent on renovation, back in Lintonburg, Jude had administered his own streaky coat of paint, this time with the nearly empty
can of green Les had once used on the greenhouse, and to Jude's
satisfaction, the camper van now looked more like an army tank
than a hippie bus. He'd taken down the flower-print curtains, and
over the rust-eaten IMPEACH NIXON—HE "BUGS" ME, he'd affixed a
newly pressed bumper sticker: GREEN MOUNTAIN BOYS.

Inside the shining armor, however, the contents of the van were
familiarly rank. The one row of seats that remained was seamed with
duct tape; in other places, the corn dog stuffing spilled forth. The
carpet was clumped and flaked with ancient contaminants—gum,
potting soil, pot—and had over the years loosened itself from the
floor, so that the edge of its layers—the mud-gray crust; the spongy,
marbled mantle; the black, gelatinous core—now curled into a crisp
tongue, and upon entry via the side door, was something to trip
over. The headliner had also become unglued, so that sitting in the
backseat was like sitting in a drooping tent. Jude had tried to thumb-
tack it back into place, but the tacks stuck fecklessly; every now and

then one fell like the first startling drop of rain. Between the low-slung ceiling and the equipment piled high in the back half of the van, rearview visibility relied mostly on faith.

For the first time since Jude had transported the householders to Vermont, the three of them were alone in the van. Now they were leaving New York again, and he was in the backseat, sharing it with Eliza's oversized suitcase. Johnny was at the wheel, and on the other side of the blusterous engine, sitting above the front axle, was Eliza, sunning her bare feet on the dash. The Kramaro, crammed with the rest of the crew, darted ahead of them; Delph hung his middle finger victoriously out the passenger window. It was ten o'clock in the morning, and it was summer, and these were the best years of their lives, and they were crossing the George Washington Bridge, the Hudson a spangled blue ribbon laced through it. On the boom box that served as car stereo was the new album by Side By Side, with whom they had just performed; behind Jude were one thousand copies of their own seven-inch record, which had just been pressed in Haworth, New Jersey, and released on Green Mountain Recordings, the label Delph had produced out of thin air.

On the front jacket was the logo Johnny had sketched—two pine boughs forming an *X*. In light of the band's name, Jude had requested bayonets instead, preferably dripping with blood, but he'd acquiesced, and the logo now decorated their bass drum, their T-shirt, their sweatshirt, and their bumper sticker. On the reverse side of the album was a photo taken by Ben, the four of them posed in the band shell at Tompkins, where Mayor Koch was trying to enforce the 1:00 A.M. curfew. Wasn't going to happen. *Curfew?* said the look on the faces in the picture. *Fucking curfew?* Ben and Matthew and Delph had never been to the city before; Kram had once visited a Long Island aunt who'd said, "Manhattan? You got a death wish?" During the week that they'd crashed at Rooster's place, Eliza and Jude and Johnny had done their best to show them around. They spent an entire day skating Washington Square Park, waited three hours for the ferry to the Statue of Liberty, which Delph insisted on seeing. Went to shows at Wetlands, the Ritz, the Pyramid. Ran into guys. So many guys. On any given afternoon twenty of them could be found hanging out at Some Records on the Lower East Side, selling demos and T-shirts, posting flyers for the next show. It was there they ran into two guys from the show in Vermont; their poke-and-stick Xs had healed thick and dark. Then they all found their way back to Rooster's, whose apartment was as packed and disheveled as Tent City. Delph slept in a chair, and Ben slept in the bathroom, curled around the toilet like a cashew. And though they imagined once or twice that they saw Di walking out of a building, or thought they heard her calling their names, they never did. The city sheltered them.

Harriet had reported, when they'd called collect, that Di had come and gone. "I think she might have said something about heading for Chicago."

"Chicago?"

"She might be looking for Eliza there."

"Why there?"

"She might have been . . . thrown off."

Jude's mouth dropped open. "Mom, did you tell Eliza's mom we're in Chicago, because if so, thank you."

As for Tory Ventura, Big Ben had learned through his girlfriend that Tory, who had three broken ribs, a few missing teeth, a shattered kneecap, and a concussion, had decided not to press charges. "He must be scared shitless," Kram had said, but Tory Ventura hadn't left Kram in the snow with a mouth full of piss. Jude knew Tory wanted to keep this off the record so he could come after Jude himself.

It gave Jude a sense of satisfaction, that his instincts to run had been right. But now, after this weeklong high, this breathless bodega-food binge, they were rocketing out of New York, light-years away from Vermont. They were reunited, and they had made another narrow escape, and not only from Tory and Di. They were safe also from the secrets they had kept from one another, and the secret they had all kept together. Johnny was a model husband. Eliza was a model wife. Jude was a model friend, his Converse straddling the engine between them. "What about Joan?" he asked. "For Joan Jett."

They were discussing girls' names for the baby, rock-and-roll alternatives to the southern, dour Annabel Lee. Theirs would be a punk rock baby.

Over the clamor of the engine, Johnny said, "Jett isn't her real last name. It's Larkin."

"I don't care what her last name is. I'm not naming my baby Joan."

"I've always liked La Toya," Johnny said.

"Belinda," Jude offered.

"She's not punk enough anymore."

"You know Joan Jett ran away at fifteen?" Johnny, who was cupping a bag of sugared peanuts in his lap, tossed a handful into his mouth and passed them to Eliza. "Her mother was sleeping with her boyfriend. That's when she formed the Runaways."

"Like us?" Eliza wondered, adjusting her sunglasses. They liked to conceive of their situation in terms they were familiar with. Punk bands, musicals, young adult novels. Jude and Johnny were the Greasers fleeing the Socs, and Eliza was Cherry Valance, the girl from the right side of the tracks. They were the Runaways, betrayed by their parents, only they'd stitched their way into and out of so many states it was hard to keep track of which one they were running from.

"She's also vegan," Johnny said. "And she produced the Germs' album."

"Wait, what was Belinda Carlisle's name in the Germs?"

"Dottie Danger."

"Dottie Danger! That's good."

"And Lorna Doom. Lorna Doom played bass."

"Or what about Exene," said Jude, "from X?"

"Ooh, that sounds very edge," Johnny said. "A straight edge baby."

Would their baby be a straight edge baby? Jude caught a glance from Eliza in the rearview. Would their baby, Exene McNicholas, toking on her mother's THC-rich umbilical cord, be received into the straight edge order? They'd made a pact, Eliza and Jude: he wouldn't tell Johnny if she quit; she'd quit if he didn't tell Johnny. What had she been thinking? Did she have a shred of self-discipline? Did she believe for a second she was mommy mate-rial? These were the accusations Eliza had spewed, not Jude, as she paced Prudence's bedroom, holding her hair in her hands. Jude had listened quietly as she bawled herself out, and when she was done, there was little he could add. Then she'd answered herself with explanations: she'd just been so *lonely,* so *hopeless,* it was so *hard* for her to get out of bed, did he know what she meant? She'd never really been into pot—maybe it was Les pushing it on her all these years—but now she could see its allure, its sedative weight, it sent her on a vacation from herself. Of course she had thought about Annabel. But that was why she had done it—so she wouldn't have to think about Annabel. It had been weeks since she'd seen her husband, months since she'd seen her mother, even *Jude* didn't pay attention to her anymore.

That *even* had plunked on his heart, heavy as a nickel. As though *Jude* were the one she'd thought was a given. What else could he do but cover for her? And watch her like a hawk? There had been only one other time, she told him. All in all, she hadn't even smoked a whole joint. Would that kill anyone? Harriet had smoked pot, Jude reasoned, and Prudence was alive. Prudence did not have three ears, or her liver on the outside of her body. The baby would be okay.

What made him furious—was this irrational?—was that she'd gotten the pot from Pru. Eliza had found it in her backpack. In a lipstick case. Prudence.

And what was silly was that it had been unnecessary. She had been mourning her lampoon of a teen marriage, and then the moment she returned to New York to reclaim her husband, it was as though all her fears had been made up. Another, more paranoid, more self-destructive and hormonal Eliza had invented them. And *this* Eliza, the Eliza she truly was, was being greeted by her groom with a kiss, a brotherly kiss but an earnest one, and she was enjoying the scrape of his stubble on her cheek, and the patting of her belly, as though it were a cocker spaniel he was meeting for the first time. "What are you doing here? You got so big!" They were standing on the stoop in front of Rooster's building on Avenue B, everyone embracing, the boys calling one another uncouth nicknames. It was as though Johnny had just been away on a business trip. He *had* just been away on a business trip!

Johnny had been making Rooster dinner when the caravan had arrived in New York. A mashed banana and peanut butter, sprinkled with Grape-Nuts. It was Roo's favorite, innocent as baby food. This they had planned to eat on the Murphy bed out of Roo's grandmother's Depression glass bowls while they watched *The Wonder Years* on the rabbit-eared TV. For a while there, in the sanctuary of Rooster's studio, they had been the householders, one husband taking care of the other.

Then the buzzer had buzzed. "Don't come up," he'd said. "I'll come down"—as startled and ashamed as if he'd been caught midfuck. Downstairs, his friends' bright, eager cars were double-parked at the curb. There was his pregnant, radiant wife, carrying his dead brother's child, and who gave a shit that the guys had gotten into a little trouble with Tory Ventura while Johnny was gone. The prospect of returning to these simple, juvenile crusades, of breaking out of the contaminated apartment for the open road, was suddenly too sweet to resist.

And on the road, Johnny could track down Ravi. A man in a house in Miami—it was a treasure hunt he could win, a tangible destination in the intangible summer that lay before him. His brother's father—didn't he owe it to Teddy to find him?

He'd broken it down for Rooster over breakfast at a diner on Second Avenue, where they could be alone.

"Teddy's dad could be helpful with the baby," Johnny said. He didn't say, *He could have money*.

"So take me with you," Rooster said. "I never been to Florida." A road trip; palm trees; Army of One and the Green Mountain Boys, reunited for a summer tour. Johnny could play with both bands. This time he really would need to fill in for Army's new singer, who was doing a study-abroad summer semester in "fucking Paraguay."

But Johnny was tired of doing double duty. He was tired of waiting for the other shoe to drop. In a year, maybe less, maybe more, Rooster would be dead. And Teddy's baby would be alive.

"You got to understand," Johnny had said, mashing his toast under his fist, "you're not the only person who needs looking after."

Rooster skated his thumb over the bread crumbs on the table. His own toast was untouched. He didn't have much of an appetite these days. "I'm not sayin' you need to look after me," he said quietly. "I'm sayin' you need to look after you." He squinted at Johnny, his eyes as black and wet as a lamb's. The skin beneath them was shadowed with gray.

But Johnny had paid the bill and said good-bye and climbed into Jude's van, and now he was steering it over the bridge, heading for the New Jersey Turnpike and points south. Their van. Their baby. Their punk rock child.

"I still like Annabel," said Eliza. She passed the peanuts to

Jude. Later, each of them would remember these sun-dappled minutes in the van, the last stretch of peace they'd have together before pulling into the dense, slippery traffic of the highway. Not far past the bridge, the cars slowed for the toll. The lanes separated, rivers into rivers, and along the booths ahead, the green and red lights blinked a distant message. In the lane to the left, two cars up, the Kramaro was idling. It was the music that caught their attention—No for an Answer. Out of the open window, Delph's arm was dangling a cigarette.

Johnny saw it, and Eliza saw it, and Jude saw it. Never mind that dangling cigarettes were the least of their own transgressions. They were past that now. They were going to do better, for their baby.

Johnny pressed his palm to the horn.

SEVENTEEN

When they got to the motel outside Philly, Jude said, "You might as well tell us everything," and they did. Delph and Kram were both smoking again. Delph had quit for a while, he had, but it was the road, he said, being in a car. It was like drinking a beer; it just went with smoking. At which point Kram cleared his throat. He'd had a few beers with the boys. The boys? Well, Delph. And Matthew. They'd gone to a girlie bar near Times Square. Kram and Delph had introduced Matthew to his first beer and his first naked girl. They were in New York, man. When else were they going to live it up?

Little Ben remained pure, perhaps only because he was so radically underage.

Also, Kram had eaten three Whoppers and the beef-flavored fries.

No meat for the rest of them, but come on, some Doritos every now and then? A little bit of mayo?

"We've met these straight edge guys," Kram said, draped across one of the double beds. They'd gotten two rooms adjoined by a bathroom, four beds for seven people. It struck Jude that Kram was a man with nothing to lose. No college. No plans. He wore the same reckless, hungry look he'd seen on Tory Ventura on New Year's Eve. "They have girlfriends. They're not all vegan."

Delph said, "They're not even all vegetarian."

"That's good," Jude said. "Good for them. Let's all lower our standards because everyone else is fucked up."

Johnny tossed his bag on the floor and said, "Go easy, Jude. You can't force a man to do what he doesn't want to do."

Go easy? How had Johnny gone so soft? Now he was the peace-maker, the Zen master. As long as he had his hands on that baby, he didn't care about anything else.

"I'm still into the whole lifestyle thing," Kram said, picking a scab on his arm. "I mean, it's cool, I totally respect it."

"We're trying," Delph said.

"Well, try harder," said Jude.

At the show that night, at the Starlight Ballroom, Jude sang with unusual vigor, barking orders between songs. "Hoods up, mother-fuckers!" and "Let's fuck this place up with some positive aggres-sion!" The kids roared. At the end, he threw down his Les Paul, barked "True till death!" and catapulted off the stage, running in the air until he fell into a forest of raised arms. The rest of the band unplugged their equipment and loaded out in silence, and it was only when they returned to the motel that Jude had the feeling it was a silence built not against one another but against him, that in a matter of hours, when he wasn't looking, the scrimmage lines had shifted. Johnny and Eliza said good night, shuffled into the marital chamber, and closed the door. Jude was left with the weak-willed pussies in the second room. Delph and Kram claimed one bed, Mat-thew and Ben the other. Jude spread out one of the sleeping bags on the floor. He attempted some tired banter about homos—he'd rather sleep on the floor!—but they were already asleep, or pretending to be.

Next door, Johnny spent half an hour sorting needlessly through his duffel bag, brushing his teeth, doing push-ups, until Eliza did him the favor of asking him to sleep in the other bed. "Would you mind?" she said.

It was true, now that she was so big, that she slept more soundly on her own. Back in New York, she'd shared Rooster's Murphy bed with Johnny—there was no room to spread out—and as exhilarating as it had been to curl up beside her husband (not quite touching, but close enough to feel his warmth), and to sleep at the head of seven underdressed boys (as though she were the queen bee of their little honeycomb, and Johnny her lucky mate), that week had been hard. She'd tossed and turned, and Annabel had tossed and turned, and the boys had snored, and every time she had to hold in a fart was an acute and tedious battle of will, and every time she had to get up to pee, she had to step over bodies, and squeeze past Rooster's bike, and his drums stacked to the ceiling, and then wake up poor Ben, who had to wait outside the door until she was done. It was during these wakeful hours that she considered calling up an old friend. Would Nadia be home this summer? What would Nadia say if Eliza showed up seven months pregnant at her door?

But the real reason she asked to sleep alone was to put Johnny out of his misery. She was not certain why he was so reluctant to share a bed with her. First his excuse was that they weren't married; then it was because of Harriet; then it was because of Teddy. Was that really it, because he wanted to honor Teddy? As though Eliza had been the great love of Teddy's life?

Maybe he wasn't as experienced as he'd claimed to be. Maybe he was just nervous; maybe he really was a virgin, like his brother had been. He was so monastic, so chivalrous, almost squeamish in his chastity—it made sense. Straight edge was a convenient front for the sex-scared: reject it before it can reject you. Or maybe, Eliza sometimes thought, he was just gay. He'd always been careful to say it was *girls* he avoided, not sex per se. "Sounds a little queer to me," Les had always said about straight edge. And all the clichés applied: he was a neat freak, he dressed with pride, he was a *nice guy*. He owned a teapot, for God's sake. Not just a kettle, but a clay teapot he'd bought at the flea market, with matching teacups. Sometimes, in fact, she *wished* Johnny was gay. Then at least she wouldn't be at fault.

But no, Johnny was not a virgin, and he was not gay. His distaste for Eliza was more distinct. She hoped that the distinction lay in the fact of her gestation—a condition that would be cured in a matter of weeks. Didn't men refuse to have sex with their pregnant wives all the time? That she could understand. In fact, the thought of actual intercourse—she felt so *big,* so *unfresh*—made her a little nauseated.

Whatever the nature of Johnny's relief, the look on his face when she made the suggestion was so abjectly grateful that she felt a little choke in her throat. Couldn't he at least pretend to be disappointed? He kissed her on the forehead and climbed into his own bed, and pretty soon he was snoring softly. For a few minutes she was happy to be sleeping alone. He snored sweetly, and this infuriated her more than the Harley-Davidson snores of the boys next door—deep, rowdy, phlegmy snores, like Les's, that constituted a white noise she could sleep to. Listening to the teakettle whistle of Johnny's nostrils required the same maddening alertness as counting Annabel's hiccups.

At least now she knew where he was. Their last few weeks in Vermont—this was the irrational, crazed, desperate Eliza—she had been convinced that what was keeping him in New York was a girl.

She'd imagined him sleeping over at this girl's place. Showering with her, eating breakfast with her. He was going to stay in New York, or he was going to run away with this girl. He had disappeared. He had left Eliza with a fucking kid to raise.

But there was no other girl. There was no *other woman*. The preposterousness of this phrase was proof in itself. Here was her husband, a few feet away.

Still, the oily residue of this worry coated her stomach. She rolled onto her back. Just sleep. Sleep!

Eliza swung her legs over the side of the bed. She struggled to stand up, and the mattress emitted a rusty groan. Johnny stirred, smacking his lips, then resumed his snoring. In the dark, Eliza waddled over to the army duffel on the floor, squatted, and slowly, slowly, unzipped it. Johnny continued to snore. She sank her hands into the contents of the bag. His sketch pad, and something heavy, like a glass vase. What she mostly felt were Johnny's clothes, still slightly muggy from the hot car. She had the queasy feeling she was wrist-deep in the guts of a warm-blooded, barely dead animal. She didn't know what she was looking for.

The door between the boys' room and the bathroom creaked open. Eliza snatched her hands out of the bag. After a moment, she heard another knob turning, and she remembered suddenly the goose bumpy thrill of being in another bathroom, with Teddy, listening to someone try the handle on the other side. Then the door between the bathroom and her room opened, too. She remained crouched on the floor, hoping the darkness would hide her.

"Eliza?"

It was Jude's whisper.

She stood up and waited for him to pad closer. Gropingly, they found each other in the dark. She whacked him, as quietly as possible, on the shoulder. Then she took his hand and led him outside.

*

"What the hell are you doing?"

"What the hell are *you* doing?"

The view from their door, glimpsed in the dim light of a moth-swarmed bulb, was of the parking lot. The Kramaro and the van were surrounded by five or six vehicles in only slightly superior condition. Beyond the parking lot and a stand of trees, I-95 rushed by.

"I couldn't sleep," Eliza said. "Okay?"

"Me neither. I heard something. I wanted to check the van." At Jude's side was a large black gun, which he was doing his best to hide.

"Jesus! Where did you get that?"

He had no place to put it, no pockets. He was wearing a T-shirt and a pair of boxers. "It's my dad's. It's no big deal."

"That's McQueen?"

"Yeah. He gave it to me."

"Jesus, Jude. What do you think you're going to do with that thing?"

Jude shrugged. "We're in Philadelphia. It's got like the highest murder rate in the country."

"So you're going to shoot the guy breaking into the van."

"Not necessarily."

"Are you sure you weren't just spying on me?"

"*Spying* on you. No. I was maybe *checking* on you. I heard someone moving around. I wanted to make sure you were okay."

"You mean you wanted to make sure I wasn't getting high. Jesus, Jude!" She smacked his arm again. "You have the ears of a fucking Indian!"

Eliza was aware that this was not the proper designation. Teddy was Indian. *Gandhi, not Geronimo.* Her child would be a "fucking Indian." She pictured her daughter's face. Her black, almond-shaped eyes, her endless eyelashes. Powdery, cardamom-colored skin. (How Eliza missed the smell of Neena's cooking!) Eliza knew her daughter would be beautiful, and perfectly formed; she would have her ears pierced early, the way the babies in Spanish Harlem did. This was a familiar vision. It kept Eliza company when she lay awake at night; it had limitless backdrops and Easter-hued outfits; it was not unlike the happy fantasies of any expectant mother.

But it scared her, too. It scared her that her child would look like a stranger. She slid down the wall and lowered the bulk of her ass to the ground.

"Eliza? You okay?"

"I'm okay. I'm just really tired."

"You want something? Something to drink?"

"Yeah, a scotch."

Jude sat down beside her. He placed the gun on the sidewalk between them and leaned against the wall. It was a balmy night, breezy enough to scatter the skirt of Eliza's nightgown. Jude's blue paisley boxers made her think of sperm.

"You know what fetal alcohol syndrome is?" he asked her.

"Don't lecture me, Jude. I was kidding."

"I had it. I mean, I have it, I guess." He was staring into the parking lot.

"Jesus, Jude."

"I mean, I might have it."

Eliza had given some thought to what happened to babies when their mothers did drugs, but she hadn't considered that one day the babies would grow up to be teenagers.

"I'm sorry. I didn't know."

"I guess I'm supposed to go to the doctor to find out for sure."

"Maybe you don't have it, then."

"Come on. Look at my face."

"What?"

Jude looked at her. He had these swimming-pool-blue eyes, even bluer than Johnny's, with these sleepy, heavy lids. He had these out-rageous freckles and a little boy's ski-jump nose and the reddest hair she'd ever seen, just a trace of it, such a tragedy that he'd cut off all that perfectly wild red hair.

"It's a nice face," she said.

Nice. It was so much more than nice, but she couldn't think of a better word. You didn't call a boy beautiful, not a boy who was your husband's best friend, not a boy who didn't like girls and who went around picking fights and who you really did think was beautiful.

"Does it bother you," she asked him, "that you don't look like your parents?"

Jude folded his hands in his lap, then cupped his elbows with them, then dropped them to his sides. His thighs were long and pale and unfreckled, and the hair on them was a different red, ginger.

"Have you *seen* how bald my dad is?"

"Well, that they don't look like *you,* then."

"Sure." He shrugged. "It would be easier if they had my dashing good looks."

The hair on her own legs, several days unshaved—she found it impossible to shave in the shower at seven months pregnant, not to mention while sharing a bathroom with six boys—was bristly and black. She pulled her nightgown over them as far as it would reach.

"Seriously, though. Did you ever think about looking for them? Your birth parents?"

Jude shook his head quickly. "Not really."

"Really?"

"If they wanted to find me, they could."

"Maybe they think you don't want to be found."

"Well, maybe I don't." He thought for a while. "I guess I don't have high hopes for them wanting to be part of my life, seeing as the ones who adopted me don't."

"Oh, come on. Harriet and Les love you. They're just as screwed up as any other parents."

Jude was staring out at the parking lot again. He said, "You know who I'd like to find instead?"

"Who?"

"Teddy's parents. Teddy's mom and dad. I don't even know if she knows he's dead. And Teddy didn't even know if his dad was dead. He never even met him."

"What would you do if you found them?"

Jude rubbed his head. "I don't know. I guess I'd just decide if they were good people or not. So I'd know."

"Well, maybe the parents who gave you up were good people, but they had to give you up anyway."

"Eliza." Jude swung his gaze over to her. "You're not giving up that baby."

"I know," she said. "I'm not." She wasn't lying. But she'd be lying if she said she didn't think about it every day.

"Look," he said, "you're going to be fine. The baby will be fine. Look at Johnny and Teddy—they're brothers, and they don't look anything alike. Look at Matthew—he's Korean, and his parents are Jewish. What's it matter who the kid looks like?"

He was making an admirable case, but Eliza could see him struggling. They had learned only days ago, over twenty-cent tacos at San Loco, that Matthew was adopted. He'd reported this fact with perfect indifference, Tabasco sauce dripping down his chin, the same way he reported that he had two sisters, that he was from Ontario, and that his father was an orthodontist. In fact, he'd administered Jude's braces, and Jude hadn't even known they'd been the same Stein. Eliza had watched Jude watch Matthew. Was it possible, Jude must have been thinking, not to care?

"But what am I supposed to say," she went on, "when people ask about her father? What am I supposed to tell *her* when she asks?"

There would be no pretending that Johnny, blond and blue-eyed, was Annabel's dad. The idea seemed suddenly absurd: why

would they even want to? Why not tell the truth? Why had they
allowed the facts of her pregnancy to become so thickly veiled in
secrecy? Fathers died all the time. They died before their children
were born, or when they were babies. Fathers died in wars and accidents; fathers died of the flu while sailing across the Arctic; of aneu-
rysms while sitting in their offices, on conference calls to L.A. Why
then would Eliza allow her child to be born into shame, a particular
condition the three of them, it seemed to her now, had conspired to
invent?

She was jogging her charms again. Locket, star, keys, the engage-
ment ring she had taken off when her hands began to swell, Teddy's
lucky subway token. This last she pressed between her fingers, feeling the warmth of her skin through the perfect void in the center.
Something to remember him by. She knew nearly nothing about
Teddy. This was what was shameful. Should she tell her daughter
that?

Jude was saying something sweet and useless, about telling the
truth, about love. His knees were pulled close to his chest so that
Eliza could see the sculpted underside of his thigh. She had nearly
exhausted herself with thinking. She could fall asleep right here, on
the sidewalk, with the moths sweeping over their heads, listening
to the dips and swells of Jude's voice. Her head lolled back against
the wall. She wasn't sleeping but enjoying a half-awake dream about
sitting next to a boy, and talking.

Through the white-hot month of July, the Green Mountain Boys
became well acquainted with I-95. The black-hole beltway of Washington, D.C., the Richmond cathedral so close to the highway you
could lean from your car and almost touch the stained glass window.
In Vermont, they'd grown up without billboards, but on 95 they
were as regular as cows—South of the Border, Yeehaw Junction,
Café Risqué, JR. "From Brassieres to Chandeliers!" The grand,

gray cities were one and the same, a cordillera of skyscrapers and bridges and no-shoulder construction lanes, an industrial plant hanging over the plain of a rust-colored bay. The air was sweaty and sweet, thick as saltwater taffy.

The venues themselves, and the places they slept, also took on a resemblance. They played two churches, a VFW Hall, the Knights of Columbus, a roller rink, a few clubs. In Atlanta, while Jesse Jackson and JFK Jr. slept at the Omni, where the Democratic National Convention was taking place across town, they stayed at the Super 8, which they learned had been dubbed the Eight-Ball Inn, for the coke outfit that ran out of a block of rooms. When they could, they stayed with friends, guys from other crews they met on the road. Once, they slept in someone's dorm room; once, they camped out in a couple of tents in someone's parents' backyard. In return, the band offered free T-shirts, or copies of their record. Several nights, they slept in their cars—in cranked-back seats, in the musty roof compartment of the van. They parked under the extraterrestrial lights of rest stops, Jude's gun tucked into the waistband of his shorts.

The money they made at shows—five- or six-dollar covers split among five or six bands of five or six guys each—barely covered gas. It would not pay for college or a Lamborghini Countach. It might cover a bean burrito. If you wanted to talk to your mom, you called collect.

The bathroom routine. Seven sets of teeth to brush, and Jude's retainers to clean when he remembered, and Eliza's contacts to remove from and return to their pink plastic bed. There were the politics of showers and bowel movements, of pubic hair left on the soap. Who had slept on the floor last time, and who got the sleeping bag with the broken zipper, and who had blown his load while sleeping next to whom. The hours in the car—the burn of a sun-baked pillow on your ear, the clammy perspiration of a paper cup of soda, the arguments over directions, the arguments over who got to drive, who had to drive, who had driven from Rocky Mount to Fayetteville, the gas station bathrooms, the gas station pay phones to call some guy who set up shows in Gainesville, Florida, to make sure he could fit you in. Then piling out of the car. The anxious hours before a show, the twilight rush of finding a Laundromat, finding something to eat, meeting the other bands, we played there, love your record, of giving an interview for some kid's zine, of loading in their equipment, of skating some cobblestoned corner they didn't know. The sound check, the merch table, the kids milling about out front, comparing new tattoos, Delph selling the *X* stamp he'd had made for fifty cents a hand. Then the dimmed lights. The roar, as inevitable as gravity.

Then the blackout hour. It was a sensation Jude could only imagine was like sex. If the hours beforehand were like the anticipation of a date—not *Will I get a blow job?* but *Will there be a fight?*—the show was sex itself. It was carnal, it was communal, it was religious. It was Harriet and Les's orgy. Yes, there would be a fight. Yes, someone would misinterpret dancing for fighting, or fighting for dancing. Some jock would push some skinhead too hard, and someone would get a boot in the face. Yes, someone would grab the microphone, tongue it, and then hand it back. Mucuses would abound. Someone would dive into the crowd, and his balls would accidentally get fondled. In the morning, they would be purified. The shows purified them. Yes, it would be a night to remember.

It was in D.C.—no, Baltimore—where Jude, bleary-eyed, in the middle of the night, stumbled into the bathroom of a kid Johnny knew, above a noodle shop. They'd had dim sum after their show, and that duck sauce wasn't sitting right. The apartment was packed tight with people. When Jude found his way to the bathroom, the door was unlocked and the light was off, and when he turned it on, four guys were crammed elbow to elbow in a ring-around-the-rosy with their pants around their knees, jerking one another off. Their eyes had been closed, and what haunted Jude later was the dreamy look on their faces, just before he blinded them with the light. They scrambled to get their pants up—"What the fuck, man?"—except one of them, who put his hands on his hips and narrowed his eyes at Jude. "You in or out, Green?"

He was out.

He turned off the light and closed the door. He lay down on top of his sleeping bag and stayed there until the sun came up, his stomach cramping into knots, and he didn't say a word about what he saw, not to Eliza or Johnny or Delph or Kram, who'd put the phrase *circle jerk* in his head in the first place. He pictured Tory Ventura in the locker room with the rest of the football team, the same retarded look on his face. There were black smudges of paint under their eyes, they were wearing cleats, the white knickers around their knees were grass stained. This is who they were running from?

On they went, to the next city, and the next. Were they any good, the Green Mountain Boys? They were fast. They were new; they were becoming familiar with their own talents. They were the band penciled in at the bottom of the flyer, the last-minute guys who rounded out the bill. They were the guys from Vermont who played New York hardcore. They were sort of Krishna-core, they were sort of radical, they were sort of backwoods, like some lumberjack crazy with an ax, all those songs about brothers and brotherhood, you had the warrior and you had the guru, you had the whole package, they were hard and they were straight and they were fast. Wicked. Even after so many nights on the road, they seemed a little amazed that they were here. They were amazed, and they were grateful, and they soaked their shirts. Those who followed them from town to town witnessed a slight but perceptible maturity of sound, a compression. They responded to one another; they began to breathe together. The singer went, "One, two, three, go!" And the band did.

EIGHTEEN

For fifteen years, every letter that Ravi Milan received was from his son. If the address was handwritten, or the sender's name unfamiliar, or if the letter was forwarded from the post office, Ravi maintained a hope, until the seal was broken, that the contents of the envelope would lead him to Edward. The letter he'd retrieved from the mailbox that June evening, postmarked New York, New York, had been no different, but he had never imagined that the news, when he finally received it, would be of his son's death.

This letter had been followed rapidly by two others, to which Ravi had made his swift, somber, and increasingly concise replies. Then came a short period of silence. By the time he heard from Johnny again, by phone, he had been able, for some hours of the day, to put Edward out of his mind. He had a new wife to distract him, and her two lunatic Pomeranians, and the hibiscus hedge they

were putting in, and, at the office, countless cases involving other
people's doomed families, including the divorce of a couple who,
after spending months torturing Ravi's answering machine with
details of the other's affairs, cocaine binges, and shopping sprees,
decided that they wanted to remarry. He had all but forgotten that,
in his last letter to the boy, in his grief-stricken desire to keep his son
in his life, he'd written, "If you ever find yourself in Miami, I hope
you'll call."

He recognized Johnny—no longer a boy, but a full-grown man—
as soon as he entered the restaurant. Ravi was unfashionably early
and was already nearing the bottom of his first Manhattan. Should
he have invited him over to the house instead? He'd worried that
his decision to forgo a tie was too casual—with his navy blazer, he'd
chosen his gold anchor cuff links—but Johnny was wearing jeans
and a white T-shirt, like an American film actor from the fifties. He
was also wearing earrings and an eye-catching assortment of tattoos,
but there was no doubt in Ravi's mind: he was the little boy he had
loved for a short time, and had sheltered in his home, before Bonnie
Michaels had run off with him and with their son.

"I thought even vegetarians ate fish these days," Ravi said once
they had dispensed with their hellos and their orders. He'd chosen
a seafood place on the bay, with tanks of lobsters and rafters cob-
webbed with fishing nets.

"Not this one," Johnny said, but his smile was meant to reassure.
Ravi could tell already he was a good kid. Tattoos or no, Bonnie or
no, he'd done well for himself.

"So, tell me about this rock band," Ravi said, as though Johnny
were his stepson, and they were meeting for their weekly meal
together. They had a lifetime to catch up on, but the conversation
had settled on the present. Neither one of them seemed anxious to
overturn the facts of Edward's life and death, which had already
been exhumed, examined, and buried again during their brief

exchange of letters. Johnny had written that Edward—Johnny called him Teddy, an infantile name—had died of a drug overdose. This just after Bonnie—who now called herself Beatrice McNicholas—had left the town they were living in, Lintonburg, Vermont, which had followed six or seven other hamlets of similar camouflage. And this just after Johnny, in response to Edward's questions about his father, had threatened to help find him, sending Bonnie running again. The fact that his son had wanted to know him was a sour comfort, like the taste of a red wine turned to vinegar.

In a manila envelope, Ravi had sent Johnny the mementos, carefully copied on the office machine, that had lived in a shoe box for so many years. *HOUSEKEEPER SNATCHES SON?* from the local section of the *Herald,* the question mark that had embittered Ravi more than any epithet; police reports detailing the search for the missing child Edward Michaels; and a photo of the four of them at the beach—Bonnie and Ravi in plastic beach chairs, the baby in her lap, towheaded Johnny in a diaper in the sand, their eye sockets blackened spectrally by the sun. These were the days before the faces on the milk carton, but Ravi would have tried that if he could. He had driven all over the country. (His wife, Arpita, had learned about the United States in a boarding school in Connecticut. Ravi had learned about it by searching for his son.) He had offered a reward. He had hired the best lawyers he could afford on a gardener's salary. When that hadn't worked, he'd become one himself. Fifteen years later, he had not found his son, but he had made a decent living furnishing divorces to disgraced American wives.

Ravi did not fail to appreciate the irony: Bonnie had left him because she was disgraced. She had never been his wife, but the day she'd discovered his dalliance with the woman who worked behind the front desk, she and the boys were gone. He'd expected her to be back in a day or two, once she'd cooled off. Bonnie had been a drinker. (He hadn't been then, but he was now.) She had a temper.

They'd go dancing in South Beach—it was the seventies, they were young—and he'd dance too close to another woman, and she'd take the boys and stay with a friend, and come back in the morning, hungover and forgiving. But this time she'd also taken Ravi's prized family possession, his grandfather's marble statue of Lord Krishna, no taller than a bottle of wine, with a flute raised to his lips. The heirloom had made its journey across the ocean with Ravi, and no doubt Bonnie had hocked it at some pawnshop off the highway for a few hundred bucks. With it, she had the means to move into a place of her own, and after stealing from him, she knew he wouldn't take her back.

And now there was this irony, too: that after fighting so spitefully for Edward, the coward had abandoned him. He wondered if Bonnie, who had callously killed off Ravi long ago, knew their son was dead, and hoped she did, and hoped she blamed herself.

Ravi sucked on the ice from his vanished Manhattan. Johnny was talking about his band. Their letters had been written so hotly, as though the two men were young lovers discovering each other. Now they sat in the air-conditioned calm. What was the word? Anticlimactic. There was little that connected them, besides their grim fascination with their roles in Edward's story. "It's just a thing for the summer," Johnny said. "In the fall, I've got other things to focus on."

"Are you going to college?" Ravi signaled the waitress for another Manhattan.

Johnny was drinking water. He was too young to drink alcohol, but the waitress had offered him wine, and he'd declined. The tattoo circling his elbow was Sanskrit, and he was wearing one of those beaded necklaces the Hare Krishnas wore. Did the boy's fascination, Ravi wondered, extend into the realm of his brother's heritage? The thought appealed to Ravi's pride, and also insulted it. Was the boy disappointed that Ravi hadn't chosen an Indian restaurant? That he was not dressed in a kurta and turban?

"Well, no," Johnny went on. "I've sort of got news. I should have told you already, but I wanted to tell you in person."

This meant that he'd wanted to size him up, Ravi deduced. He was a cautious kid, not quick to trust. That was the result of being raised by Bonnie. Johnny whipped his napkin into his lap and said, "Ravi, you're going to be a grandfather."

Ravi smoothed his mustache, pressing it down with his thumb and forefinger, a habit he did not like, but now could not help. Yes, he had once loved this boy, but he was not his father! The kid had written something about searching for his own father, Marshall, who had not surprisingly turned out to be a con. Bonnie had never had anything good to say about the man, but later, Ravi had wondered if she had demonized Marshall, too, if he was out there searching for Johnny the way Ravi was searching for Edward. Okay, so the guy really was a deadbeat, and Ravi felt sorry for the kid. But what did he want from him? Did he want him to be a substitute, now that he was starting a family of his own? Ravi was no substitute for his father, and Johnny was no substitute for his son. Was it money the kid wanted?

"Congratulations," he managed to say as he arranged an inane smile on his face. "You're going to be a father. And not long ago you were just a boy yourself."

"I'm going to raise the baby," said Johnny. "But Teddy is the father."

Ravi ceased stroking his mustache. Johnny was wearing an inane smile as well.

"Edward?"

Johnny nodded. "Edward."

The waitress brought his drink and served their food, and it cooled in front of them. A sixteen-year-old girl was going to have his dead son's child, and Johnny had married her in order to raise the baby. The baby was due in September. Very soon! Johnny spoke of levirate marriage, and *The Laws of Manu,* but Ravi wanted to know the details. Where were they going to live? When could he meet the wife? When could he meet the child? Ravi's heart was beating so fast that he was sweating. He stood up, took off his jacket, and hung it on the back of the chair. He wanted to call Arpita. Arpita was at the Epcot Center with her sister and her nieces. Remember the talk they'd had, after they'd found out about Edward, about no one carrying on the family name? (At forty, Arpita said her dogs would be her only babies.) Well, Ravi's son, who had been a baby when he'd last seen him, was going to have a baby! Was it possible to call the Epcot Center? Had she left the number for their hotel?

"Well," said Johnny, "we'd like to go back to New York."

Ravi returned to his seat. "So far away?"

"We were staying with a friend in Vermont for a while, but we've been forced to relocate again. My wife's mother—she's not too hot on the idea."

"Hot," Ravi said.

"She wants us to give the baby up. She thinks I'm the father." Johnny stabbed a tomato, then, reconsidering, withdrew his fork. "Everyone does, actually. We thought she'd be more likely to support our decision if she saw that we were serious about each other, that we wanted to be good parents."

Ravi didn't understand. "But why not tell her it is Edward's? Teddy's? It is a wonderful thing."

"She's going to find out soon enough. But first, we want to make sure we're . . . protected."

Of course. It was legal advice he wanted.

"You are married, my boy, yes?"

Johnny nodded.

"Good. You are a smart boy. Now, did she give consent? Your wife's mother?"

"No, but it was in New Jersey. You don't need it there if the girl is pregnant."

"Then she has no legal recourse, none whatsoever. It does not matter who the father is."

Johnny relaxed visibly.

"Unless," Ravi said, "she sues for custody."

"Sues for custody? *She* doesn't want the kid. She wants us to give it up for adoption."

Ravi smiled sadly. "Not your mother-in-law, my boy. Your wife."

Johnny was tugging on his lower lip. On the inside, beneath his youthful gums, was a tattoo Ravi could not quite read. Why on earth would anyone put a tattoo there? "Why would she want to do that?"

He was still a boy, unschooled in the depravity of the fairer sex. Ravi would die for Arpita, but he had a prenup. When he got home, he would pray to Shiva that his grandchild would be a boy.

"Against women," said Ravi, "we cannot protect ourselves enough."

"How much did he give you?" Rooster wanted to know.

"A lot," Johnny said. "At first I said no, but he said it would be an insult."

"You wouldn't wanna insult the man."

"He said it's for the baby."

"It'll be a well-diapered kid."

Johnny was calling from the pay phone in the McDonald's parking lot in Vero Beach, Florida, where the band was letting off steam in the Ronald McDonald playground, pelting one another with the plastic balls in the ball pit.

He had told himself he wouldn't call Rooster, not yet. But the excitement of meeting Ravi had sent him to the phone. He needed to share it with someone.

"How are you feeling?"

"If I tell you I feel like shit, will you come back to New York?"

"You know I can't. They think I'm talking to some guy in Cleveland."

"Why Cleveland?"

The recording interrupted to request another quarter, and Johnny complied.

"We're supposed to do a show there."

"Well, cancel Cleveland and come back to New York. Ain't nothin' you want to see in Cleveland, baby."

Johnny closed his eyes and imagined the month that lay before him, empty, endless. He didn't know if he could spend thirty-one more days in the Kramaro, listening to Kram and Delph complain about Jude, or in the van, listening to Jude complain about Kram and Delph, or worst of all, listening to Eliza's silence. He certainly couldn't tell them that he'd met Teddy's father (he'd told them he was going to the local Krishna temple). He couldn't tell them that Teddy's father had warned him to keep an eye on Eliza at all times, or that Johnny had already been doing just that.

Through the door of their Philadelphia motel room, while they thought he was sleeping, Johnny had listened to Eliza accuse Jude of accusing her of being on drugs. It had not exactly been a revelation, but Johnny had to fight the urge to jump out of bed. He'd let his guard down. He'd been distracted by Rooster. The next morning, he found his duffel bag open on the floor, and since then, when going through her suitcase and her makeup bag and her backpack, he made sure to zip them back up. He never found any drugs, but this morning he did find a drawing, folded in quarters and tucked inside her pregnancy book. It was a nude drawing of Eliza, and in the corner was Harriet's signature, and it was so beautiful—the drawing, the girl—that he nearly confessed everything. It seemed such a waste, this pregnant body no one would ever see. He hated himself for squandering her, for using her as he was.

Now, on a bench under a palm tree, Eliza was watching the ball pit through her white-framed sunglasses.

Rooster said, "We'll say you guys have a show to play back here. Actually, you do."

"We do?"

"At the Pyramid. When I hang up the phone, I'm gonna set it up."

"What if they don't have space?"

"Johnny, Jesus, they always have space. If they don't, someone else will. We'll play at fuckin' Tompkins. Do you know how crazy it is here this summer? The Missin' Foundation don't book fuckin' shows. They're just showin' up on the street. There's a show every night, and our fuckin' singer is in fuckin' *Paraguay,* and I'm here slam dancin' with myself, waitin' to croak. Where else you want to be but New York?"

Johnny pictured Rooster up there without him, throwing himself into the pit, looking for someone to spill his blood. "You're not starting shit with anyone, are you? You know you can't be getting into fights."

"Who's gonna stop me?" Rooster asked. "You?"

Jude waded out of the ball pit and sat down on the bench next to Eliza. Eliza raised a hand to shield her eyes against the sun. Johnny couldn't hear what they were saying.

"I can't do both, Roo. I can't take care of you and the baby, too."

Now Delph and Kram were drowning Ben in the ball pit. "Quit it, fag!" Their shoes lay in a pile at the edge of the chain-link fence, like the shoes in the hallway of the Krishna temple. Johnny missed the Krishna temple. He missed the smell of the subway, and Blind Jack, and his cats, whom Prudence had promised to take care of. He didn't want to be on the run anymore. He wasn't like his mother. He wanted things to be the way they used to be, before his mother disappeared and Teddy died and Eliza got pregnant, before Rooster got sick. He wanted to need no one.

But he'd done what he'd come to do. He'd met Teddy's dad. He'd cased him out. *Call if you need anything else,* Ravi had said at the bank as he'd handed over the envelope of cash.

"Just come until the baby," Rooster said gently. "When will you be able to come, after the baby?"

Again, the operator demanded twenty-five cents.

"Baby, when will you be able to see me, after the baby?"

"We need to go back to New York," Johnny told them.

"Why?" Jude asked. "What's wrong?"

"We have a show at the Pyramid."

"What about Cleveland?"

"Cleveland canceled. And you"—he pointed to Eliza—"haven't seen a doctor in three months. And we need to find a place to live."

"They just *canceled*?" Delph said.

"So the tour's just *over*," Kram said.

Eliza said, "I thought we don't need a doctor."

"You want me to deliver this kid in the van?" he said, forcing a smile, and even a little laugh.

"What about Di?" Jude asked. "What if we run into her? What if the doctor has to like, report to her?"

"I got it under control, Jude. I talked to a lawyer. He says we're safe. Di can't make us do anything we don't want to do."

"You talked to a *lawyer*?" Eliza said. "When?"

"While you guys were eating your Happy Meals. Let's go."

The first thing Jude wanted to do when they were back in New York was eat a bean burrito at San Loco, but Eliza wanted to go by her apartment. Not inside. She just wanted to stand on the street and look up at it. "That way I won't run into her. It's like, lightning doesn't strike the same place twice. Or like being in the eye of the hurricane—we're safe there."

"Be careful," Johnny warned them before they left Rooster's, after they unloaded all their stuff at his place.

"Aye-aye," Eliza said, dragging Jude out the door.

"I don't like the way he talks to you," Jude said finally as they boarded the uptown 1 train at Times Square. It was the middle of the day on the last Saturday in July, and about 150 degrees in the train car.

"You mean like he's my dad?"

"I don't like the way he treats you, either." The car wasn't full, but they took seats side by side. "I don't like the way he thinks he calls all the shots."

"Now you're talking about the band."

"Yeah! We make all these plans together, and then he just cuts the tour short, just like that? Without even talking about it?"

In truth, Jude didn't mind being back in New York. He was tired of the packing and unpacking, of not knowing where he'd sleep from night to night. Johnny thrived on that—he could sleep anywhere, he'd grown up in motels—but maybe Jude was a homebody after all.

"You'd tell me, right," Eliza asked, "if Johnny was seeing someone else?"

Jude looked at her sideways. She was wearing the Yankees shirt Les had tie-dyed for her, and the cutoff shorts she rolled down at the waist. His own shirt was like a second skin, and Eliza's knee and elbow were glancing moistly off of his.

"Who would he be seeing?"

"I don't know. Don't you think it's strange that he keeps coming up with an excuse to come back to New York? That all of a sudden he wants me to see a doctor and find us a place to live?"

"Johnny can't be seeing anyone. He didn't even see anyone before he was married. Not since he's been straight edge, at least."

"Okay," Eliza said. "Okay." She was fanning herself frantically with a newspaper she'd picked up.

"That was always his thing." Jude reached for a sheet of the newspaper on the seat and crunched it into a baseball. "No one's allowed to go anywhere near girls, and then you come along, and the rules suddenly change." He hurled the ball at a window. It fell dully, then tumbleweeded a few feet down the aisle. He'd been carrying around this silent little orb of injustice, and when he'd finally discharged it, it sounded like an accusation. Maybe it was.

Eliza stopped fanning. She said, "The rules haven't changed that much. He still hasn't come anywhere near girls. At least this one."

Jude gave her a long look. The lights flickered above as they bounced along.

"We haven't consummated. Okay?"

Slowly the train came to a halt. Eliza's weight bore into him, then caromed off. A few yards away, a guy in sunglasses and a leather jacket—leather in July—looked up at them, or at least Jude thought he did, as though he, too, were surprised by this news.

She hadn't slept with Johnny. How was it possible to be so weightlessly happy when she, the bearer of this heart-lifting news, looked so miserable? She did not look relieved to have shared this truth with Jude. She looked at him as though he were responsible for her misery. As though he should have had his eyes open. He should have known.

"You haven't?" was all Jude could say.

"And I find it insulting," she said, "that you assumed we did."

"Eliza, you're married to him."

"So you think I'd just marry anyone? I'm some helpless girl who needs a guy to take care of her?" The guy in the leather stood to exit the train, and then, apparently changing his mind, sat back down. "You think I'm some indiscriminating slut?"

"*No,* Eliza." Jude unsealed his body from hers. "You're the one who married him. Why did you, then?"

"You didn't have to come with me, Jude. I mean, thanks, but you know, I don't need a babysitter."

"Fine. I won't babysit you anymore. Sorry for being a friend."

The next stop was Seventy-second Street, and he walked out of the car. On the street, he was greeted by the invigorating freedom of being in a new place, a corner he'd never stood on before. This, along with an irrational empowerment—she hadn't slept with Johnny!—and his anger at her—why had she attacked him like that?—propelled him down the blistering sidewalk. He didn't know where he was going. He remembered, now that he thought about it, that both beds in their motel room were sometimes unmade. Jude had assumed that they'd been having such ambitious and nomadic sex that they'd simply traveled from bed to bed. He was walking south, the waves of humidity carrying the smell of taxi exhaust and hose-sprayed sidewalk. And also curiosity—*why* hadn't they slept together? Who hadn't slept with whom?

He turned around and began to run. How could he just leave her like that? With the leather pervert eyeing her on the train? What if Di did see her? What if she wasn't going home at all, but going somewhere to get a fix? He ran all the way to Riverside, then north, but when he got there, she was not standing in front of her building. He stood under the awning next door, catching his breath.

She stopped in the median at Broadway and Ninety-first. Neena was standing at the fruit stand across the street, inspecting an apple. Plastic grocery bags were looped over her arm, and nestled inside an Indian print sling, a baby clung to her stomach. Eliza decided that she would wait here on the curb for Neena to see her. She would let her decide. But she didn't look up. Would she even recognize her, another pregnant girl on a street corner in New York? Eliza flew across the street, in front of a bike messenger and a honking bus, and stood panting before her. She slipped her sunglasses back on her head. "Hi, Neena."

The honking had stirred the baby, who fussed in its sleep. Neena took in the whole enlarged shape of Eliza. "It's you. Goodness, you nearly run me over."

"I saw you across the street. It must be a big shock to see me."

"Your mother been very worried. Very angry with me for letting you go." Neena, weighed down by the bags and the baby, did not offer a hug. "Where you been?"

It sent a strangely warm current over her skin, her mother's familiar worry, her housekeeper's familiar iciness. "Vermont, Florida. Everywhere. Who's this?" Eliza nodded at the baby, who was wiggling in its sling. The baby had the same crimson dot on its forehead as Neena, and tiny gold studs in its earlobes.

"Grandchild," said Neena. "My son's."

"It's a girl?"

"A baby girl. Bala."

"Bala." Eliza reached, tentatively at first, and then as though she did it all the time, to stroke the baby's head. It had as much hair as a full-grown man, and it was as silky and warm as the spun sugar Neena used to make. Her little eyes were closed, and she looked as though she were fighting a difficult battle in her dreams. Eliza had never, ever touched a baby.

Suddenly Neena unleashed the largest smile Eliza had ever seen on her face. "She making relief," she said, bouncing the baby a little with her hips.

Eliza withdrew her hand.

"When your baby will be born?" Neena asked. Her smile vanished as quickly as it had come.

"September."

"September when?"

"I'm not sure," Eliza said.

Neena made a dismissive, horsey sound. "Your mother will be glad you home. I tell her when she calls."

"No, I don't want her to know," Eliza said. "Where is she? She's not home?"

"She looking for *you*. In Chicago. She call at my son's house to check if you call. I helping with the baby."

"She's still in Chicago? You're not staying at my mom's?"

"I just there to cook in the big oven and water the bonsais."

Now Eliza could see that Neena's blouse was wet, where the baby had clamped its mouth on one of her breasts. It was hungry. Eliza lifted the keys from the chain between her own breasts.

"No one's staying there at all?" she asked.

NINETEEN

After weeks of sleeping in the van and in motels and on Rooster's floor, moving into the air-conditioned sanctum of Di's apartment felt like a luxurious crime, as though they were breaking into some movie star's mansion and were waiting for the police to arrive. It was the size of Tower Records, and had things like a Macintosh computer, a laser-disc player, and a bidet, which Delph and Kram used immediately, reporting the details of their experiences. Delph and Kram took the two single beds in the guest room, and Matthew and Ben took over the living room. Johnny stopped by long enough to drop off his stuff in Neena's quarters, where he had his own TV and mini-fridge and telephone line. He said, "I'll stay at Rooster's if someone else wants it," and Eliza said, in front of everyone, "I'm sure you would," and then Johnny left to meet Rooster at Tompkins to pro-test the curfew. Evidently the householders no longer cared about keeping up the appearance of sharing a bed. Jude took Di's room, because no one else wanted to share with him, either, and because no one else wanted the responsibility of staying in the master suite. In the top drawer of Di's dresser, beneath a layer of silky underwear in metallic hues, was what Jude determined to be a vibrator, which he tested against his wrist, then returned to its drawer. All of these items, along with the thought of his father having sex with Di here, creeped Jude out; nevertheless he was glad for a room of his own. He peeled back the sheets on the king-size waterbed and slept soundly on the cool, silver surface.

At home in her own bed at last, Eliza watched an old tape of *Santa Barbara,* paged through her Greek textbook (she'd forgotten nearly every word), and ate the banana pudding Neena had left for them. She felt strangely safe here. It was the last place her mother would think to look for her. And if she did: so be it. She was tired of running.

But she still couldn't sleep. The down mattress pad she had always loved was too soft for her now. Twice she got up to tell Matthew and Ben to turn down the video game they were playing on the computer. Twice she got up to pee. After the second time, she stopped at her mother's door and knocked on it. Jude answered in another pair of sperm boxers, these red. This time he was shirtless.

"Sorry about before," she said, sinking into the pool of her mother's bed. "I'm not mad at you. I'm mad at Johnny."

"I tried to find you, but you weren't standing outside like you said." His voice was hoarse with sleep. "I didn't know where you went."

"You came after me?"

"I was worried."

"Neena had this little baby, her granddaughter. She was *this big.*" She cradled an invisible baby in her arms. She wanted to say that she looked like Teddy, but this wasn't precisely true. She closed her eyes and tried to conjure his face, but his features swam out of her reach. "I can't remember what Teddy looked like," she said quietly.

Jude's eyes were closed, too, his face raised to the ceiling. "He was handsome," he said. But Eliza could tell that he was seeing something more behind his eyelids, contours sharper than he could describe, or cared to.

She lay down across the sheets, which smelled like the lavender soap Neena laundered them in, and she told Jude that she used to sleep in this bed after her dad died, to keep her mother company. Eliza wanted to sleep in it again, but Jude didn't lie down beside her. When the baby kicked, he didn't want to feel it. Eventually she said good night and walked back down the hall to her own room.

That week, they came and went.

Eliza and Jude window-shopped at the baby boutiques on the Upper West Side, where a crib shaped like a sailboat cost a thousand dollars. Delph and Kram played pickup with some guys in Central Park, and Matthew and Ben went to work selling merch at Some Records. They reunited only for an occasional meal, and the show at the Pyramid, which Rooster did book. Delph and Kram left early to go to some club in Brooklyn some girls had invited them to. Di's dining room table, polished as a pond and the size of a shuffleboard court, was quickly buried by maps and guides, ticket stubs, subway tokens, backpacks, cassettes, Gatorade bottles, granola bars, a jingle jangle of spare keys.

Johnny and Rooster went to the Love Feast at the Krishna Temple on Sunday night. On Monday they skated their friend's half-pipe until Rooster got too tired. On Tuesday they swam at Coney Island, deep in the ocean where no one could see their limbs tangled underwater. On Wednesday they watched another friend paint a train car in Harlem, a city of skyscrapers and lights and highways as intricate as any eight-headed dragon, then watched the police paint over it. They were starting to crack down now. Even in the month Johnny had been gone, the police had begun to multiply all over the city, lifting their rodent heads out of the manholes. You could hardly suck a token anymore.

On Thursday they walked to the West Village, where gay men strolled hand in hand, walking good-looking dogs, licking ice cream cones, wearing shirts or maybe not. Johnny felt that he knew his city, that New York belonged to him, but sometimes he skated into a neighborhood that felt like a foreign country. The gray calm of the Upper East Side, the flamboyant calm of the West Village—he was not certain he was comfortable with either of their customs. On Christopher Street—barely a mile away from Tompkins Square Park, the AIDS center of the city—it seemed possible to forget about spermicide and sterilized needles. Up in their clean, spacious bedrooms, surely men were dying here, too, but on the street it was like Candy Land for fags, all these gorgeous, healthy men snuggling up to their soul mates. Experimentally, Johnny let Rooster lean him up against someone else's building and kiss him in front of the world, and in Rooster's mouth Johnny tasted each flavor he'd eaten himself, painfully intensified. For a sun-blinding moment he was not Patient 9602. Then they walked back to Rooster's.

Alphabet City, the Bowery, the Lower East Side, Loisaida— these were the places where Johnny belonged. In Alphabet City, there were shadows to hide in. Here you didn't advertise being gay or straight or rich or poor; you just tried not to get your ass kicked. You just tried to get by. This attitude had been evident the past Saturday night, when the neighborhood of blacks, Puerto Ricans, Eastern Europeans, Italians, Jews, Yippies, skinheads, bohemians, anarchists, artists, musicians, squatters, gutter punks, junkies, and drunks gathered in Tompkins to unite with the homeless against the extravagant monolith of the Christadora House, the sky-high rents of the East Village, against the army of Mayor Koch. Keep Tompkins homeless! This was what Johnny loved about his home: its home-lessness. Everyone was displaced, everyone was half-vagrant. *$1500 Rent* said the Missing Foundation's graffiti, and the neighborhood said fuck that. The Missing Foundation were there on Saturday night, and Blind Jack and Froggy and Jones, kids on bongos, mara-cas, conch shells. Someone threw a bottle against a police van, and Jerry the Peddler got arrested, and the rest of the park's residents were scattered about the Lower East Side, or who knew where.

As for Blind Jack's friend Vinnie, he was dead of AIDS—he'd died in the park while Johnny was on the road, Rooster told him. "Jack tried to wake him up one morning, and he wouldn't budge. Just lay himself down on the ground with a newspaper spread over his face, like he knew it was time." Johnny would have expected Rooster to deliver this news with spite, to use it to turn the knife of guilt in Johnny's gut, but he looked too frail to fight. And who else was there to blame, besides the city itself?

Johnny's beloved slum was under attack, and already the neigh-borhood was planning a rematch for next weekend. Now these mutineers of the Lower East Side, the miscellaneous fuck-ups who'd had no one to prey on but one another, had come together to rage against something else. The curfew. They were as pure and as primal as teenagers revolting against their parents.

On Friday morning, Johnny knocked on Eliza's bedroom door to tell her they had plans. He had made an appointment to see an apartment, and then another to see a doctor. He was wearing his linen jacket and a thin black tie.

"I was going to feed the ducks with Jude," she said.

"Well, you'll have to feed the ducks another time."

In the bathroom, she brushed her teeth, put in her contacts, and put on her makeup. Usually Johnny's plotting worried her, but she was more relieved than suspicious. She had a picture in her mind of the apartment—it was one of the pictures that she called on to put her to sleep. It would be necessarily small, but it had an eat-in kitchen with a window box of geraniums like Harriet's, and an exposed brick wall, which she would paint white. Everything in the baby's room would be white, too (not pink)—the crib, the single teddy bear, the rocking chair she would take from her bedroom at home. She dressed methodically, trying on several items from her own closet before moving on to her mother's. She settled on a long madras dress and a pair of penny loafers a size too small for her swollen feet. Over one of her shoulder pads, she hung the leather strap of a purse.

"Jeezum," said Kram, who was standing in the kitchen, eating breakfast. His hand was stuffed into a box of cereal as if into a mitten. "Where are *you* guys going?"

In the subway station, rather than jumping over the turnstile, Johnny deposited a token for her, and then another for himself. She didn't mind that, on the train, instead of talking to her as Jude would, he read a discarded copy of the *Post*. They appeared as ordinary as any other young couple on the subway—the husband looking sternly at his newspaper, the pregnant wife beside him peering into her compact. One of the ads at the top of the subway car was for a women's hospital. In it, a woman with her eyes closed held a newborn to her shoulder. The mother looked wise and serene, as though she'd been injected with some celestial barbiturate. Eliza wondered if Johnny had chosen a doctor from this hospital and hoped he had.

By the time they got out at Astor and climbed the stairs to the street, Eliza was exhausted. On the walk east across St. Mark's, she had to stop to rest in the shade. They passed a police car parked on the street, and on the next block, two more. At Avenue A, police vans and trucks blocked the entrance to Tompkins. Beyond them, a herd of cops milled inside the otherwise empty park.

"Where are all the homeless people?" Eliza asked.

"Where do you think? They kicked them out."

They continued walking across Seventh Street now, past the other people who'd stopped to see what was going on. Some of them were trying to get the cops' attention; two men hanging over the fence were chanting, "Pigs out of the park!"

"You guys going to be here tomorrow night?" Johnny asked them.

"You know it, Mr. Clean."

"What's going on tomorrow night?" Eliza asked, her shoes pinching her feet.

"We're demonstrating. I want you to steer clear."

"What are you demonstrating against?"

She stopped to catch her breath, and after a few steps Johnny turned around. "Eliza, this park is home to a lot of people. They just got kicked out of it."

"But they're not supposed to be there."

Johnny spit out a laugh. He looked at the park and shook his head. "Where are they supposed to be?"

They said nothing else as they finished their walk. Twice, Eliza slowed in front of one of the more attractive buildings on the street, one with scrollwork or arched windows, hoping this was it. The building they finally stopped at was between C and D, around the corner from Johnny's old place. The plywood in the two first-floor windows gave the building a sleepy expression. Across one of its closed eyelids, red letters spelled HOME SWEET HOME. Johnny did not smile at this as he nudged a toppled bicycle out of their way with his shoe. They climbed all five flights of stairs.

"You weren't kidding," said the landlord who buzzed them in. "This girl's got one in the oven."

For the first few minutes in the apartment, Eliza's imagination worked hard to transform it into an acceptable place to live. It was an airy, tall-ceilinged space, probably a factory converted at some point into a loft. The walls were indeed brick, and the graffiti could be painted. The broken windows could be replaced. She tried to picture herself with a broom, and Johnny with a hammer, the two of them building a home here. In the kitchen, the cabinet doors and drawers had been removed, and Eliza found their blackened remains in the middle of the charred floor, beside a bare mattress and a single spoon.

Johnny came up behind her and put a hand on her waist. "A little scummy, you think?" he said into her ear. His voice, and the way he leaned close, were conspiratorial, creating for a moment a private space between their bodies. She gave him a thin smile, relieved somewhat, her heart quickening at the same time.

"You ain't going to find lower rent in Alphabet City," said the landlord, hitching up his pants.

Johnny asked, "You got electricity in this place? Hot water?"

"Hell you think?" said the landlord. "My brother let the place go off the grid, but now that I been taking over, this place is certified."

"Richie go back to Rikers, or what?"

"I don't know where he is, tell the truth."

Johnny said he was sorry to hear that.

"You're the kind of kid I want to get in here, Mr. Clean. We need to clean this neighborhood up."

"I don't know about that," Johnny said. "I kind of like it the way it is. What's the rent again?"

Eliza stood still while her husband negotiated, unable to articulate her state of disgust, betrayal, and now boredom. Was he really agreeing to take this place? They were talking about a deposit, keys. "I'll meet you downstairs," she said and walked down the five flights without stopping.

Outside she sat down on the steps. In the bright daylight, Eliza could see a spiderweb strung across the bent spokes of the bicycle, and a tortoiseshell spider tightroping across it. She was studying it so raptly that she didn't see the woman running down the street until she was quite close. It was a homeless woman she recognized from Les's neighborhood, red-haired, emaciated, and naked. She ran in a shuffling sort of way, as if her ankles were shackled, and on her face was a look of not fear or desperation but the benign concentration of any New York jogger. Not until she passed, revealing her profile, was it clear that she was pregnant.

"There's no lease," Johnny told her as they walked to their next appointment. "We could just stay there month to month, until we find a better place."

"I don't know why we can't just stay at Les's."

"Because we're not taking any more handouts from Jude's parents, that's why."

Eliza said nothing. Her feet were killing her.

"I didn't sign anything. If you want, we can look some more." She thought he said this with some resentment. She stopped on the corner of East Sixth, removed one shoe, then the other, and handed them both to Johnny. The sidewalk was hot, but it was a miracle on her feet. If she was going to live in that apartment, what did it matter if she walked barefoot through Alphabet City?

"Where's the doctor's office?" Eliza asked, following him around a corner. She wanted to be in a clean, cool exam room, in a paper gown, the reassuring hands of a doctor on her belly.

"It's close. Bleecker and Mott."

"It's a real doctor, right? Not some guy you know?"

They slowed as they neared Johnny's old apartment. Eliza barely recognized it. The building was covered with scaffolding, and a pair of trucks was parked at the curb. From inside came the sound of hammers, a saw; two men in hard hats hauled a bundle of two-by-fours into the third-floor window. Johnny watched them with what looked like regret.

"Your old place was better than that dump," she said. She couldn't help herself.

Johnny kept walking, and Eliza followed. "Maybe I can see about getting it back. Now that it's going to be a luxury condo, it might be good enough for you."

"Luxury condo? I doubt it."

"What do you want, Eliza? The Christadora? You want a doorman?"

"I don't want a doorman. I just don't want a crack house."

"Just because some squatters lived there doesn't mean it was a crack house."

Eliza's bare feet slapped the sidewalk. "Do you know how hypocritical you are? You call yourself straight edge, you call yourself *Mr. Clean,* and you're friends with a bunch of junkies and drunks? Who live in that *filth*?"

"So I should turn my back on them? We should just throw them out of the neighborhood like trash?"

"Don't blame me. I didn't make up the fucking curfew. I just don't want my kid playing in a sandbox full of human turds."

They were walking briskly, not looking at each other. "You worried you're going to catch the cooties, Eliza?"

"It's called AIDS, Johnny."

What were they even talking about? Eliza had only a vague sense, picked up from slivers of the news, from dinner parties with her mother's friends, that AIDS was seething in the lower quadrants of her city—the gay neighborhoods, the junkie neighborhoods, those unshaved regions of New York's anatomy that she didn't quite care to inspect. She couldn't help that it didn't concern her, and she was not prepared for the intensity of loathing on Johnny's face. He walked on, even more briskly now, swinging her shoes.

"Do you even know anyone with AIDS, Eliza?"

"No." It hadn't occurred to her that this was something to be ashamed of. Or that Johnny himself might know people with AIDS. "What, you want a medal for every friend with AIDS?"

Now Johnny stopped in the middle of the street. First Street and First Avenue. She'd never been on this corner before. It felt like the nerve center of the city. The muscle in Johnny's jaw hardened, and his hands tightened around her shoes. For a moment, she expected him to hit her with one of them. She almost welcomed it.

"You're a stupid girl," he said quietly, looking her in the eye. "You don't know one goddamn thing." Then he turned and crossed to the sidewalk. Eliza trotted after him.

"I don't need this shit!" she said, catching up. "I don't need your help."

"Fine, Eliza. I have other things to worry about. If you don't need my help, go home and call your mom."

"Maybe I will." Why not? He was the one who said her mother couldn't force her to give up the baby.

"Wonderful. Enjoy your trust fund. I hope you sleep tight in your eight-million thread count, Egyptian cotton—"

"I haven't *slept* since I was fifteen."

"What does—"

"If you haven't noticed, I'm pregnant! I can't sleep." She stopped walking, exhausted. "I just *lie* there." Her voice was small. She grabbed two fistfuls of sweaty hair. She wanted to pull it out at the root. "I just lie there, *thinking* . . ."

"Put your shoes on."

"I *can't*," she moaned. "My feet are the size of—"

"Put your shoes on, Eliza." He dropped her loafers on the sidewalk. "We're here."

She looked up at the yellow brick building in front of them. The small sign that hung beside the entrance said PLANNED PARENTHOOD MARGARET SANGER CENTER.

"This is it?"

Still barefoot, she padded over to the door and peeked in. The glass was cool on her hands. Inside were the same front desk, the same metal detector.

Your handbag, miss.

It seemed like a long time ago. On the way to the clinic in New Jersey, she had been sick in the bathroom on the train. What was growing inside her had made her sick. Or what she was about to do had made her sick. If she had handed over her bag, if she had walked through the metal detector.

"Don't tell me you're too good for Planned Parenthood."

"I'm not going in. Not here." She spoke quietly, and Johnny matched his voice to hers.

"Eliza, I know you've been doing drugs, and I don't want to know how much, or what kind. You'll be lucky if that baby doesn't have brain damage. You are going inside."

They were standing very close. Eliza could see the beads of sweat above his lip. Then the door to the clinic opened, and they stepped out of the way. Johnny hurried to hold it while a girl stepped out. She was alone, not visibly pregnant. Johnny and Eliza watched as she walked to the curb, put on a set of headphones, and lit a cigarette. Perhaps she was waiting for a ride.

To Johnny, Eliza said, "I was going to get an abortion. I could have."

This did not seem to surprise him. But saying it aloud brought the nausea rushing back. Her body was boiling hot, but her arms were trembling with goose bumps. Johnny was still holding open the door, and the air-conditioning rushed out at them.

"Do you know why I didn't?"

He let the door fall closed. His face was drawn. He already knew, but he didn't want to hear her say it.

"The same reason you married me. Because your brother's dead."

"Eliza—"

"If he was alive, I wouldn't be stuck with this baby, and you wouldn't be stuck with me."

She turned and walked to the curb, where the other girl was waiting. A taxi passed by, and Eliza raised her arm, but it kept driving.

"Eliza, where are you going?"

Another taxi approached, and this one slowed for her.

"Take your shoes!" Johnny rushed over and held out the loafers, one forefinger hooked inside each heel. She didn't want them. She didn't want anything from him.

"Give them to one of your friends," she said, and got into the car.

Johnny walked south.

He dropped the shoes in a trash can and kept walking until the island ended and the water opened before him. It was blindingly white. Far across it, the ferry floated on its surface, life jacket orange. Now he wished he'd kept the shoes so he could throw them into the water. He wanted to throw something into the water, but he had nothing to throw.

All he had in his pocket were a few copied keys and his wallet, heavy with Ravi's cash. He had waited outside the bank in Miami while Ravi had withdrawn the money from the teller. He had not spent a dollar, and he had told no one but Rooster about it. Watching the ferry sail away, untethered and bright, Johnny couldn't help thinking that it could buy him and Rooster two tickets out of New York, out of his marriage. Maybe it could buy Rooster some time, a dose or two of meds.

Johnny felt the spirits of the city howling for his attention—not the dead but the waiting to die and the waiting to be born. Yama, the god of the dead, was the one who decided which souls would be sent to the heavenly realm and which would be cast into new bodies on earth. Johnny had appealed to him to bring Teddy back, but he wondered now if reincarnation really was a curse, if his brother would be better off in the afterlife, floating as free as the ferry on the water. He wondered if the baby would be better off with someone else's past lives instead.

Across the water was the graveyard skyline of Staten Island. Were they still over there, his father and his uncle, living in the same cell, sharing a bunk bed, like brothers were supposed to? Eating breakfast together, playing poker, saying good night? If Johnny saw them on the street, he wasn't sure he could tell them apart, but he wasn't sure it mattered. They were one and the same. Max and Marshall. His father's betrayal was his uncle's. His uncle had abandoned him as his father had, left him out in the cold. Johnny would never do that to Teddy's baby. He would never do that.

But maybe there was a way to leave a baby without leaving it in the cold. He imagined, for the first time, Eliza handing the baby to someone else, someone who could care for it. As Harriet must have cared for Jude, rocking and bathing and feeding him as though he were her own.

"Who was that?" Jude asked his mother.

"Who?"

"That voice. Some guy's voice."

"I didn't hear it."

Di's cordless phone was known to play tricks on the ear, to abduct the voices of other callers, but he was sure he'd heard a man say something to his mother, and then his mother, putting her hand over the receiver, say something to him. It was late, close to eleven. Past his mother's bedtime.

"You're in one piece? You're not calling from the ER?"

"I'm at Eliza's. We're staying here."

Harriet paused. "Is her mother there with you?"

"No. That's why I'm calling. Now *we* can't find *her*."

Jude was lying on Di's waterbed. From the living room, he could hear the moaning saxophone of the Playboy Channel.

He'd been sitting out there yesterday, watching TV, when Eliza had walked in the door. Although he'd been waiting for her for some time, he had not expected her home so soon, and he had not expected her to return alone. "I want my mother," she'd said. She had not been wearing shoes.

"She wants her mom to come home," Jude explained.

Harriet said, "Well, I think that's wise."

"But Di's not answering her car phone. We need to find her. Is she still in Chicago?"

Jude could hear the muffled voice again, then his mother's sigh.

"I knew that was a bad idea, throwing her off. And a lot of good it did—now you want her to know where you are. Do you have a pen?"

The front door of the apartment slammed shut. Jude hung his head into the hallway long enough to see Johnny storm into Neena's room. Then that door slammed, too.

"Uh-oh," Jude said.

"What's going on, Jude?"

"I think Johnny and Eliza got in a fight. I think he just came back for his stuff. He didn't sleep here last night. I don't know."

"You're too young for this," said Harriet. "You're all too young."

"Mom, how easy is it to get a divorce?"

For months the sharp little word had been residing quietly in his head. Yesterday it had loosened, like a kernel of food from his retainer, and now it was out of his mouth, free.

"Oh, don't tell me."

"I don't know. Maybe they'll make up."

"She needs her mother," said Harriet. "This is ridiculous. We should be arrested. *I* should—"

"Hey, baby."

The words were as clear as if they had been spoken at Jude's side.

"What?" he said.

"What?" said Harriet.

"Everything but my toothbrush. Did I leave it there?"

"Hold on," Jude whispered to his mother, although it was clear that the voice hadn't heard them, and she hadn't heard it. It was not the same voice he had heard before. It was Johnny's. It was one side of a conversation, transmitted from Neena's phone line.

"I'll be home soon," said Johnny.

"Come home, Jude," said his mother. "For Christ's sake, just come home."

TWENTY

ey, baby.

After Jude hung up the phone, he lay down on the bed again. Down the hall, a door opened. The TV cut off. "Will you guys help me carry this shit?"

He had never heard Johnny call anyone that. Not his wife. Not as a joke. *Baby* was not *dude* or *man* or *fag*. He'd said it with an adult affection, a degree of intimacy that made a fist of Jude's balls.

He said the words aloud. "Hey, baby."

And he felt Teddy's hot breath on his face. Teddy blowing a gust of pot smoke into his mouth.

On the phone, no voice had answered Johnny. The empty space rang in Jude's ears. Then the front door, again opening, then closing, silenced it.

Sitting up, he looked at the number he'd scribbled on the back of a flyer. Di's hotel room in Chicago. How had his mother managed to get that?

Jude put the paper in his pocket and walked down the hall. Everyone was gone. He knocked on Eliza's door. He didn't expect her to open it, but she did.

"I thought you were Johnny."

Jude's balls loosened. On the TV behind her, *Santa Barbara* was on pause. Julia was embracing Mason, but over his shoulder, her face had an unsettled look. Eliza had taught Jude all the characters' names.

"He just left. I think everyone went to the protest."

Leaving the door open, she turned, walked to the unmade bed, and lurched backward onto it. She laid her wrists over her eyes. The lower half of her body hung over the edge, her knees dropping gently apart, her nightgown draping a shadow between her thighs. His body went rigid. He closed the door behind him.

He deserved her, and Johnny didn't. This had been his belief all along, but he had lived with his discontentment uneasily; he'd felt unentitled to it. Now his desire flamed up in him, fully formed, righteous; he held a ticket; he had the burden of proof . . .

"You know how your phone does that weird thing with the voices?"

Eliza lifted one of her wrists from her eyes.

"I just heard Johnny talking to someone. He was on Neena's line. He called the person 'baby.'"

Slowly, she sat up. His heart was pounding with anticipation, but the look of dread on her face brought it under control.

"Who was he talking to?"

He sat down beside her. He tried to remember what he'd heard. Johnny was moving back out. He was probably staying with Rooster. He was always staying with Rooster. Unless he was lying about that, too. There could be someone else. But Jude didn't think there was.

When his father had told him that he was adopted, the revelation was both terrible and gratifying—a piece of news that restored order to his universe, an answer to a question he hadn't thought to ask. *Of course*. He knew with that certainty that the person Johnny had been talking to was Rooster.

But he would give the truth back if he could. At sixteen, he still wished he could shake his father's words out of his ear.

"I don't know," he said. "I couldn't hear her."

Who was he protecting, Eliza or Johnny? She was looking at her bare feet, which dangled off the bed, not touching the carpet. Sometime when Jude hadn't been looking, her henna tattoos had faded and then disappeared. He looked at his own feet, in a pair of white tube socks with a hole in the right toe.

"You wanted me to tell you, right?"

She looked at him sharply. Then she leaned across the space between them and kissed him on the mouth.

At first, they remained perfectly still, their lips joined in patient purpose, like the ends of two cigarettes, one igniting the other. She tasted like Yoo-hoo. It took him some time—ten seconds, a minute?—to realize that his eyes were open, intent on the fact of each of her eyelashes. Closing them, he sank into a deep dark. His mouth was open, too. Mouth-to-mouth. How long had she wanted to do this? Their tongues were unmoving, the breath through their noses shallow and rough. For the first time, the hard-on in his lap seemed appropriate. He was unembarrassed of it, grateful for it. His friend was gay, and Jude—here was the evidence—was not. Of this he was ecstatically sure. Casually, as though he happened to feel like it at the moment, he slipped his tongue over the ridge of her bottom teeth and into the cocoa sweet galaxy of her mouth. Her tongue curled over his, a sprouting vine, a wave. He felt electrified. He felt as though something amazing and rare were happening to him, like becoming famous. His tongue grazed the gap between her two front teeth. It found a favorite molar, it toured her scalloped gums. Was it vegan to kiss her like this, to want to eat her mouth? Was it straight edge to want to be inside her?

Without unfastening their mouths, they eased back onto the bed. They did this with the care and determination of two people setting a heavy tray on a table. They lay on their sides, each of their heads on her pillow. The spongy interior of her cheek, the canal under her tongue. Thank God he'd removed his retainers this morning! His erection was lodged between her hip and her belly and the bed. He was dangerously close to bursting. Touching her was a bad idea, it was asking for trouble, but here was his left hand, his burned, ruined hand, now rising from the ashes, now slinking without his permission from her wrist up the length of her forearm, pausing at her elbow, circling the reed of her bare bicep, as though testing her, determining if she were fat enough to eat, and then, satisfied (their kiss still unbroken), making a sly dash for second base, fitting itself under the soft globe of her breast.

He didn't explode. She didn't say no. Once there, his hand knew what to do, making a slow meal of it, taking its time. It was surprisingly full, unlike anything his hand had felt before, and she did not seem to be wearing a bra. No, she certainly was not wearing a bra. Nothing separated his hand and her breast but the thin cotton of a white nightgown. He could feel the ridge of her nipple, goose-bumped, warm, and now wet. Her nipple was wet. Was that something that happened to girls? Was that good? For a moment he was relieved, that she had burst before he had, that the glow radiating inside him had held its ground, while hers, irrepressible, had spilled forth. It wasn't until she withdrew from their kiss that he realized this was not a normal fluid of carnal excitement. It was something new, a substance neither of them had encountered for many, many years, and it was filling his palm. Breast milk.

He whisked away his hand. Rolling away from her, he wiped it on the thigh of his jeans. "Sorry!" both of them gasped.

Eliza struggled to sit up, clutching her leaky breast. "Oh, God," she said just as Jude said, "What the hell?" Spreading outward from her right nipple was a yolky yellow stain.

"This has never happened before!" She looked at Jude. Her expression passed from worry to amazement to humiliation, then back to worry again. Then her jaw dropped comically, and her face attempted a bitter, grown-up wit. "Oh my God, I guess they *work!*"

"They definitely work," Jude said. He was still wiping his hand on his jeans. Eliza closed her mouth, straightening it into a firm line.

"I didn't mean to," she said.

"It's okay," he said, but he sat up, too. His erection had faded. She folded her arms over her chest, closing her eyes. He wanted to put his hand on her shoulder, but he was afraid to touch her again.

"I guess you won't be doing that again," she said.

He dropped his eyes to the bed. The sheets and blankets were pink—rose pink and a meaty pink, like the inside of a mouth. A newborn baby. This had been the bed the three of them had been sitting on when she'd told them she was pregnant. This was the nightgown she'd been wearing.

When he looked up, her eyes, still closed, were leaking now.

"Eliza," he said, but he didn't move. He was frozen by the feeling that they were not alone. Teddy was there in the room with them. So was Johnny. Most of all, the baby was there with them, under her nightgown, not to be forgotten, even for an hour. This was what happened when you lay down beside a girl.

Eliza swung her legs over the side of the bed. She struggled to reach the Keds on the carpet and to fit them on her feet. He felt that he should help her, but didn't.

"Don't worry about it," she said. "I'm used to it. Johnny didn't want to touch me, either." She stood up and wiped her mouth with the back of her wrist.

"Eliza," Jude managed, "that's not it."

"Don't tell me. If I weren't pregnant, right?"

Crossing the room to the closet, she whipped off her nightgown, turning the back of her nearly naked body to Jude. Again, he looked away.

"You and Johnny are exactly the same. I thought you weren't, but you are. I know you both want it to be a boy. The only reason you've stuck around this long is because you expect me to have a little Teddy for you to play with."

"That's not true!" Jude sprung up from the bed. "I liked you, even before I knew about the baby."

"Well, you don't have to anymore. You're off the hook, because I'm giving it up."

She yanked her yellow dress off a hanger, pulled it over her head, and turned around.

"Eliza, you don't mean that."

"I do mean it. It's not some spur-of-the-moment decision. I've thought about it, and I've decided, and it's my decision, not anyone else's. Do you want to know why?" She put her hands on her widened hips. "Because it's my baby. Not yours. Not Johnny's."

From her closet, she took out a cardigan and buttoned it over her dress.

"Where are you going?"

"To find Johnny. I'm going to tell him."

"No, you're not," he said. Then, "I'm going with you," and when he followed her, she didn't protest.

The taxi could only get them as far as Third Avenue. St. Mark's Place was choked with people, people spilling out of bars, people hanging off of balconies. An ambulance screamed toward the park, parting the sea of bodies, nudging cars to the curb. On the sidewalk, two cops on horseback galloped past.

"Hey, Eliza! Jude! Welcome to Mardi Gras!"

On Les's fire escape, Davis and a friend were leaning over the railing, smoking cigarettes and watching the show.

"Hey, Davis!" Jude called. "What the hell's going on?"

"The pigs are back, man. Be careful out there."

Jude tried to cover Eliza's body as they made their way down the street, steering her with one arm, shielding her with the other. In the cab, she'd listened to her headphones. The space between them was incalculable. If he hadn't stopped kissing her. If he hadn't pulled away. It all seemed like hours ago. Now, as he ushered her along, the faintly sour heat of her body brought back their kiss with violent clarity. On his lips, her saliva had dried to a delicate crust.

"This is stupid," he said. "Can't this wait until tomorrow?"

"I'm fine," Eliza said, pushing her way through the crowd just as a couple of punks sprinted by, jostling her elbow.

"Watch it!" Jude shouted after them. To Eliza he said, "This is why we don't let you in the pit."

"What?"

He leaned close to her ear. "This is why we don't let you in the pit!"

Tonight the pit was Tompkins Square Park. The same dark, festive atmosphere hovered over it, the feeling that you might get kicked in the nuts at any time, that it would be a night to remember. Who would show up, what were the teams. He should have turned her around and forced her back into a cab, but he didn't.

Why should he protect her anymore? If she was giving up the baby, what did it matter? A loud pop, an M-80, sounded in the distance. They both jumped. "That was a firecracker," Eliza asked, "right?"

The crowd thickened. Arms windmilled, shoes flew. Some people were running toward them and other people were running past them, toward the park. Near First Avenue, a stalled fire engine blasted its horn. In front of it, a wall of people was blocking its passage. "Hell, no! We won't go!" they were shouting, and a bottle flew through the dark and broke against the side of the truck, and then another, shattering a headlight. The truck kept honking, but no one in it was moving.

The crowd surged. From behind Jude and Eliza, a team of horses came galloping toward the truck. The mounted cops were wielding nightsticks. Leaning out of their saddles, they brought their clubs down on the crowd. A polo match. Two cops thrashed their clubs against a passing bike, the handlebars, the tires, the guy's legs. He fell off onto his side.

Jude and Eliza kept moving. "This is over a park?" she yelled in his ear, tripping behind him. "Slow down! My feet hurt!" He yanked her roughly by the hand. The smell of gasoline, a tattoo of firecrackers, a broken bottle under Jude's foot. A cone of light from a video camera, and then a crash as it met a nightstick. "Fascists!" someone yelled. Beside them, a girl on a boy's shoulders fell headfirst into the crowd. Men poured out of a bar carrying bottles of foaming beer. It splashed all over them, all over everyone. Somewhere someone was on a megaphone, but the voice was just a voice, without words. It was drowned out by something powerful and bright. They moved forward as if into a wind, shoulders together, heads down. They *were* moving into a wind. Trash scuffed against their ankles. Eliza's dress whipped against her knees. Jude lifted his face. High above Avenue A, over the entrance to the park, a police helicopter hung from the black sky, its propeller churning up a dust storm in the street below. Its searchlight sifted through the crowd with a super-human glow. An alien invasion, a hurricane. It found a soaring bottle, a horse rearing up on its hind legs.

"We're never going to find him," Jude shouted to Eliza.

"Fine!" Her hair was lifting off her shoulders. "Go home!"

Under the drone of the helicopter there was the weak beat of bongos. A drum line was wending its way through the mob. "Die, yuppie scum!" their voices were chanting, just loud enough to hear.

One of them, a woman with two long braids, struck Jude's hand as she thumped past him.

"*You* die!" he called after them. "*You* go home, you hippie shits!"

"I think I hear him!" Eliza yelled. "On the megaphone."

Jude listened. From across the street through the park, a voice was speaking with a placid urgency, like the voice of God at the Krishna temple.

"Where did he get a megaphone?" Eliza wondered.

Of course Johnny was on a megaphone. What the fuck was he defending? The junkies? The dealers? He'd been handing out fruit to the homeless, playing priest to Tent City, while all the time he'd been butt-fucking Rooster. How many times had he claimed to be going to the park, or the temple, or to do a tattoo, when he'd been going to Rooster's place?

There was no way into the park. They shoved south, squinting into the flying debris, their hands slippery with sweat. "Pregnant lady here," Jude said. "Watch the fuck out." There were all the times he'd gone to Johnny's place in the middle of the night and he wasn't there. There were all those weeks, after they were in Vermont, he'd been in New York, playing with his old band.

He spit on the ground, kept moving. The dust and dirt needled his skin.

After their first show, when everyone was crashing in the basement, Johnny and Rooster were alone in Jude's room. In his bunk bed.

"WHOSE PARK? OUR PARK. WHOSE PARK? OUR PARK."

"I see him! You see him?"

Eliza pointed. Facing a brigade of thirty or forty cops, two rows of demonstrators were sitting across Seventh Street like kindergartners at story time. Some were playing drums, maracas. There was Delph, and Kram, Matthew, Ben, Rooster. Johnny sat in front, leading the chant, wearing the white robe he was married in.

"WHOSE PARK? OUR PARK."

It was a voice meant to hypnotize. *Trust me, you're getting sleepy.*

It worked. Jude stood still in the middle of the street, under the spell of Johnny's voice. He was suddenly very tired of moving.

Eliza's hand slipped from his. Without looking back, she darted ahead, the space between them stretching wide, and wider, uncrossable. He watched the black broom of her head bob through the crowd. He lost sight of her, then found her, then lost her again. The dust storm lashed around him.

Slowly, Johnny's voice came to a stop. Eliza dropped to his side. Across the crowded street, Jude watched their mouths moving. What were they saying? The things that people said. Fuck you, I hate you, it's over. Whatever they were talking about, they weren't talking about Teddy.

Jude floated through the crowd. Watch it, watch out. Eliza was handling her necklace. She was handing something to Johnny. It glinted dully under the streetlamp. It was her ring. Jude moved toward its light until he reached them.

"Johnny, get up."

Johnny looked up at him. His face was in shadow, but Jude could see on it an older brother's irritation. He was tired of Jude playing at his feet.

Beside him, Rooster put a hand on Johnny's shoulder. "This is a fuckin' sit-in, kid," Rooster said.

"I'm not talking to you, Rooster."

"Jude, go home," Johnny said. "This doesn't concern you."

They were all looking at him. They were all wrong. Nothing had concerned him more.

He was thinking of Hippie and Tory as he kicked Johnny in the gut, Hippie crumpling against the fence, Tory's screams rocking the van, and now Johnny slumping over into Rooster's lap as Rooster pulled Jude's other leg from under him, toppling him to the ground. Jude lifted Johnny by the back of the neck and landed two punches dead in the center of his face before they all fell on top of him—Rooster, Delph, Kram. There must have been more, but he couldn't see. He felt the tread of rubber on his body, knuckles. The sirens howled. The M-80s popped. The fists rained down on him, cleansing him. He didn't fight back. And yet they were the ones crying out. The pummeling slowed. The mass lifted. The cops were clubbing them off of him.

Then, through the megaphone, Johnny's voice. "She's pregnant!"

The helicopter swept its spotlight over them. It found a shield, a helmet, a club; Jude, struggling to sit up; Rooster on his hands and knees; and Johnny flying to Eliza, who lay on her side, her hand to her head, spilling blood on the street. Her eyes were open, and she was looking at Jude. Then the light swept away.

TWENTY-ONE

When Eliza opened her eyes, she saw their faces from left to right. Even in her state of disorientation, her brain processed the people sitting at her bedside in its trained latitudinal sequence. Jude, with a black eye, in a hospital gown. Beside him, with a suntan, Les. On the other side of the bed, holding a paper cup of tea stained with her fuchsia lipstick, her mother.

"Is the baby okay?"

Les tossed his crossword onto Eliza's blanketed legs. "The patient speaks."

Eliza's voice was groggy, her limbs heavy. An IV was taped to the back of her hand, a plastic clip attached to her finger. And there was something strapped to her belly, a belt. She let her eyelids flutter closed. She remembered all the commotion in the park, a fight, screaming for the boys to get off of Jude. She didn't remember anything after that. When she opened her eyes, Jude averted his. She remembered kissing him in her bed.

"Right as rain, darling." Di picked up Eliza's hand and stamped her knuckles with her lipstick. "The heart rate was up for a while, but now it's stable. They gave you something to sleep."

Yes, she had slept. She'd slept better than she had in months.

"In fact, you've been asleep for seven years," Les said. "This is actually your fourth child."

"Les, what are you doing here?"

"You were hit in the head last night, darling," said her mother. "By a police officer. You have a concussion."

"You were concussed," Les added, miming the swing of the night-stick.

Jude said, "You passed out in the ambulance."

"Ambulance?"

"Tell her," Jude said.

"Tell me what?"

"Tell you nothing. She's awake now, gentlemen. You can go."

"I think she's going to find out," Les said.

Jude rubbed his scalp. "They shaved your head."

"Just part of it, darling, for the stitches."

Eliza lifted her hand to her head. It was wrapped in a bandage.

"Thank you very much, Jude, you can take your father to the waiting room now."

Jude and Les rose to their feet. Les said, "You look great, sweet-heart."

"Honestly, it's not much," said her mother after they left the room. "It's just a patch over your ear. You remember Randall, the one who did the stage makeup before Angie. His lover is a wigmaker. He's got this fabulous shop in SoHo with nothing but beautiful wigs made from human hair. We'll find you something beautiful."

Eliza traced the bandage. Her head didn't hurt; she couldn't feel a thing.

"We won't waste our time worrying about hair. Hair grows back. You're safe, and the baby's safe. We should be glad all we have to worry about is a little hair."

"I don't care about my hair, Mom."

It had been more than three months since she'd seen her mother. Her makeup was carefully applied, her hair pulled back tightly in its braid. The only thing that was different was the faint glaze of dark hair above her lip, dusty with powder. She'd waxed her mustache for years. Without Les to kiss good night—or without Eliza—she'd stopped.

"I moved back home," Eliza said. "We were trying to reach you."

"I know, my darling. I know everything."

Eliza scooted up in the bed. "Jude told you? You didn't give him a hard time, did you?"

"I certainly did."

Di was pleased to fill in the details. She knew, after weeks of false leads, that they had been in Vermont. She knew, after a weeks-long wild-goose chase to Chicago, where Jude had called her at her hotel, that they had not been in Chicago. She knew a bad private investigator. She didn't know who was a bigger piece of work: Les or his ex-wife. She knew that, apart from her first trip to the ER and her present one, Eliza had not seen a doctor. She knew about the six weeks of cocaine and the marijuana and now the doctor and nurse did, too. She knew about Johnny's indiscretion. She knew what had happened in the park, and if Eliza thought she wasn't going to bring the fattest lawsuit the City of New York had ever seen, she'd better think again.

She took a long sip of tea.

She knew that Eliza had decided to give up the baby. Was that right?

Eliza, petting the tape on the back of her hand, nodded.

Her mother petted the back of Eliza's hand, too. She thought that was a wise and brave choice. She knew that Eliza had missed her and that Eliza knew she'd missed her, too. She knew that Eliza was sorry and that Eliza knew she was sorry, too.

The nurse came in then. "Someone's awake!" She padded around in her sneakers, checking monitors, the IV. They wanted to keep her here one more night, she said, to make sure her brain didn't swell. While the nurse adjusted the strap on her belly, Eliza looked at the ceiling, staring at the white lights until tears burned in her eyes. The nurse held up the banner of paper spilling out of one of the machines. "You see these dips and peaks?" she asked, tracing them with her finger. Eliza squinted at the graph. "This is your baby's heartbeat. It's following a nice pattern now."

Eliza cleared her throat. "The drugs I did—did they hurt the baby?"

The nurse hung her clipboard at the end of Eliza's bed. Di gazed into her tea. "There's no way to know yet, honey. You quit the hard stuff in the first trimester—that's what counts."

After the nurse left the room, Di took up Eliza's hand and began gently, absently pushing back each of her cuticles. Always file your nails in one direction, so they don't tear. If you tap your nails on a table, they'll grow faster. Eliza closed her eyes. Maybe it was the sleeping pill. She felt light, as though she were floating in her hospital bed on a slow-moving river.

"Mom? I don't think you quite know everything."

Her mother stopped massaging.

Eliza said, "Johnny's not the father."

Her mother sat up straight in her chair, spilling her tea in her lap.

"I knew it. I knew that kid was acting." Les punched the button with the side of his fist, and a can of Coke clunked down through the vending machine. "It's nothing to be ashamed of, champ.

Why cover it up?" He extracted the can, opened it, and took a long sip.

"It's not me," Jude said. "Why do you always think it's me?"

"No? Come on. I've heard the way you talk about her. You're telling me you two haven't . . . ?"

"We haven't, we haven't." Did everyone think they had? Why was Jude the last one to assume the two of them were a possibility?

Les leaned against the vending machine. They were in an alcove of the waiting room. No one could hear them. "Who's the daddy, then?"

Jude told him.

Les chewed over the name, sliding it around on his tongue, trying to recall who Teddy was exactly, how he might fit in. "Teddy. Yes. That makes sense, now that you mention it. When she went to visit you, right?" He shook his head: what a shame.

"We thought if we said Johnny was the father, Di would let her keep the baby. They could raise it together." The opposite now seemed just as likely. Would Di have insisted Eliza give up a dead boy's baby?

"You know, Lady Di was pregnant more than once. She had some . . . procedures." Les slurped his Coke, his eyes distant. "One of them was Daniel's. Her husband. It was before they were married. They were young, they weren't ready." He was speaking with some bitterness, but Jude didn't think it was the abortion he was bitter about. "I know she regretted it, after he died. Wanted a son. I bet she wished she could bring her husband back to life."

They strolled into the waiting room and took two seats in front of the TV. The news. Jerry Falwell endorsing Vice President Bush. "Dipshits," Les muttered, crossing his legs, ankle to knee. He'd arrived on the red-eye from San Francisco that morning, after Harriet had called him, worried about Jude. Eliza's hospitalization was a surprise, and Les was happy to take advantage of the coincidence. Concerned parent, times two. Jude was inclined to resent him for this posture, as he had the last time they were stuck in a hospital waiting room together. But his dad *had* flown across the country. He'd come to his rescue again.

But who did Jude need rescuing from? Not himself this time. He was not on drugs. Not Tory or Hippie, who were hundreds of miles away. Not the cops who had bruised a few of his ribs but had saved the bulk of their bruising for Eliza. Not Di anymore. Eliza had made her decision, and he doubted there was anything anyone could do to change it. Jude saw himself now for what he was: inessential. He was the tissue that bound the essential members together—Teddy, Johnny, Eliza, those who were joined by blood or by sex. Jude was joined to no one by neither. He was beyond rescue.

Now the news was showing footage of Tompkins. The cops had yielded around six this morning, leaving the park to the remaining protestors. Dozens arrested, dozens injured. A skirmish, a melee. In the daylight, the park looked no more ruined than usual; for the first time Jude could remember, people were pushing brooms through the street. Jude knew he was supposed to be angry at the pigs, but Jude was the one who'd started the fight. Jude was the one who'd put Eliza in the hospital. But if Johnny had been a good husband, they wouldn't have been in the park in the first place. If Johnny had been a good husband, Eliza wouldn't be giving up the baby.

They'd allowed only one person in the ambulance with her, and Johnny had pulled the family card. Jude had run through the dark streets to Beth Israel—just let her be okay, just let the baby be okay, and he'd give her up, he'd give up the baby—only distantly aware of the ache in his ribs. The nurse had insisted on getting him cleaned up and into a bed. When she applied some antiseptic to his busted lip—"This'll sting a second, baby"—he did a poor job of hiding the erection under his gown. He lay in the bed, behind a curtain in the hallway, for an hour and a half, tasting the iodine and Eliza's mouth, before someone would tell him she was okay. He said he was her stepbrother.

Jude twisted the hospital bracelet around his wrist. He was barefoot, nothing on his body but his boxers and the gown.

"Dad, you know any fags?"

The waiting room was full, but his voice was low, one of many. A baby was wailing.

"Don't call them that, champ. Say *fairies* or *queers*."

"Do you—"

"Look, champ, if you're trying to tell me you bat for the other team—"

"*No,* Dad."

"I'd accept you. Your mother would accept you. You're a good kid, despite the hell you've put us through this year, but look, I deserve it. Maybe if I'd been there to provide some masculine influence—"

"Dad, I'm not a queer!" He lowered his voice to a whisper. "I like girls."

"You sure?"

"I like Eliza. She's a girl."

"So you *have*—"

"We haven't—done anything. We made out. Yesterday. That's it."

"Jude Keffy-Horn, you little shit."

"Is that weird? Since you used to go out with her mom and all?"

Les rocked his head back and forth, thinking. "It's a little weird."

Jude's heart lumbered forward. It was exhilarating, saying it out loud. "I don't know if she likes me, though. I mean, I think she's pissed at me."

"Why is she pissed at you?"

He replayed the scene in his head. Kissing her had been like playing a song, or eating a meal at one of the nice restaurants Di had taken him to. The kiss had steps, phases—a bridge, a chorus, an appetizer, something to cleanse the palate. It had a shape, a momentum—and then it had stopped. Jude had stopped it.

"I liked it. It was great and everything." He left out the part about the breast milk. "I guess I just got a little weirded out. I'm supposed to be straight edge."

"True."

"And she's pregnant. With Teddy's kid."

His father placed his soda on the table beside them. "It's a little weird," he said, not unkindly. "But soon she won't be pregnant."

Jude leaned forward, his elbows on his knees, and sank his forehead in his hands. Away from Eliza, in the noise of the waiting room, her pregnancy now seemed a small matter to overcome, a curable condition. It would be as if the baby—and Teddy—had never been born. It was the worst possible outcome. They had let Teddy down. They had held this miracle in their hands, nurtured it, fought for it, and then, together, they'd dropped it.

He felt it fall: a baby over a ledge. He felt it fall many, many stories, never landing, just diving through thin air.

But what then to do with this immense relief, this joy rolling out like a carpet before him, the surprise gift of their youth returned to their hands?

He wondered if his own birth mother, unburdened by him, went on to live her life and kiss boys.

"Will they let you outside in that getup?" Les stood up, stretched, and crushed his soda can. "I need a smoke."

First Avenue was sleepy with Sunday-evening traffic. A school of taxis swam together from light to light. Cigarette butts littered the sidewalk around Jude's bare feet, and the air was warm with restaurant grease and petrol, the uriney stink of trash. Still, it felt good to be outside. The air wasn't as pure as Vermont air, but it was just as rich, just as distinctively laced. He inhaled.

"You know what I think, St. Jude?" Les lit his cigarette. "I think it's time we were roommates again. I've missed New York. Now that Lady Di isn't a crazy woman anymore, I'm going to talk to Davis about getting my old place back. What do you say?"

"I don't know," Jude said. "I guess I'd have to think about it."

"Don't worry about your mother," Les said. "Now that she's got a man friend, she's not so alone. Isn't this groovy, all this love in the air? Your mom found someone, you found someone. Now I just have to—"

"A man friend? Wait, who did she find?"

"She didn't tell you?" Les exhaled out of the corner of his mouth. "She's got a man friend. A P.I., of all things."

"A P.I.?" Jude could only picture Tom Selleck.

"Di hired some New York investigator to track you guys down. He found me first. I tried to keep him off your trail, but eventually he caught up with your mom. By that time, though, you guys were on the move again. He kept visiting your mom to buy pipes and fell for her. Ended up helping her scatter some bread crumbs to Chicago to keep Di busy."

Jude's head was spinning. "Wait. You and Mom both tried to keep us from Di?"

"And now he wants to move to Vermont, live the country life. Romantic, huh?"

"Mom has a man friend? Who's a private investigator?"

So he hadn't imagined the voice in the background. His mom hadn't dated anyone since his dad.

"Any asshole can be a P.I." Les told Jude about his friend's brother who took a class at John Jay, had some business cards printed up, and now charged top dollar to take pictures of husbands fucking around on their wives. Les tapped his cigarette at his side. The bitterness edged his voice again. "But she deserves to be happy. She's a special lady, your mom."

"What about Di?"

Les shook his head. The suntan on his face gave him a ragged, inflamed look. His fingers released his cigarette; it dropped to the ground. "I'm done with pining for old flames. She wouldn't take me back, anyway."

Which old flames his father was referring to he didn't know. Surely there were many in the vast bank of his past, before his mother, during, after. Husbands fucked around on their wives, and private investigators took pictures of them. People fucked, fucked up; they married, had babies, divorced. His father was as guilty as any of them, and for years Jude had despised him for it. Now, watching his tattered Birkenstock stamp out the cigarette on the sidewalk, it occurred to Jude that his father, for reasons of his own, might be as heartbroken as he was.

"You know, your mom used to get pretty upset about abortion." Jude wondered if he was thinking about Di again, or about Ingrid Donahoe, the woman who had aborted his child to save her marriage. "It wasn't fashionable, in the *Roe v. Wade* days, for a modern gal like your mom to oppose abortion. But, you know, she wanted a baby more than anything." He shrugged, as though he was still not sure this was a wise idea. "Anyway," he said, turning to go inside, "Teddy's kid is going to make some mother very happy."

His father pressed his hand lightly to Jude's spine, where the hospital gown opened to his bare back. Then, the glass doors sliding open before them, he followed his son to the entrance.

They stayed at the apartment on St. Mark's, Davis in the loft, Jude and Les sharing the futon. Davis made breakfast for dinner—grits and Kentucky scramble and buttermilk biscuits. Jude had toast. He called his mother. He'd be coming home soon. Late into the night, Les told stories of his travels, cannabis by cannabis—Mauwie Wauwie, Swiss Miss, Holland's Hope.

Uptown, Eliza and her mother watched *Santa Barbara*. Eliza

napped on the divan. For dinner Neena made them saag paneer and fresh chapati bread, Eliza's favorite, and they ate on the balcony, watching the joggers in Riverside Park, their sweatbands glowing like distant planets in the settling dark. The boys were gone. On the dining room table, under a ring of spare keys, Kram and Delph had left a note—*Thank you for your hospitality*—and eight dollar bills to cover the bottle of wine they'd made use of, a 1981 port. The only things left were Jude's.

The following morning, Di paid a visit to her lawyer, a colleague of her late husband's, to discuss a lawsuit against the City of New York and an annulment, on the grounds of nonconsummation, of her daughter's marriage to John McNicholas. Neena went to the grocery to restock the kitchen. Eliza stayed home. She painted her toenails. She called Nadia and talked to Nadia's father. Nadia was at her mom's place in the Catskills. She had a new horse: Rome. Did Eliza want the number?

No, thank you, she didn't.

She was playing one-handed scales on the piano, a Yoo-hoo in her other hand, when there was a knock at the door. Jude stood on the other side of it, wearing one of Les's Hawaiian shirts. His eye socket had faded from a deep purple to a jaundiced brown. His lip was cut, too.

"I still have my key, but I didn't want to bust in. I just want to pick up my stuff."

She held the door open, and he stepped inside. Hitching up his shorts—those were Les's, too—he looked around the apartment as though he hadn't been there before.

"What were you playing? It sounded pretty good."

"Nothing. Just scales."

Jude looked across the room for a place to sit, then shoved his hands in his pockets and leaned his shoulder against the wall.

"Anyone home?"

Eliza shook her head.

"How you feeling? I like your head wrap thing."

"Thank you. Neena gave it to me." She reached up and touched the top of her head, stroking the silk scarf. "They gave me a list of things I could take for pain, but I don't want to take anything." She put her hands in her lap. "What about you?"

Jude shrugged dismissively. "You got it worse than I did. I wish it was my head that got split open."

Eliza took a sip of her Yoo-hoo. Then she slipped off her scarf. "You can make it up to me." She found the end of the bandage and unwound it, undressing her head, and released the ribbon of white gauze. Across her left temple, nine stitches held together a naked patch of scalp. "Do you have your clippers?"

He shaved her head in the living room, Eliza sitting on the piano bench, Neena's purple scarf now wrapped around her shoulders. He circled her body, the clippers humming, her dark hair feathering to the floor. She didn't open her eyes until the sound stopped. In her mother's bathroom, her back turned to the sink, she angled Di's hand mirror in front of her face.

"Now you're really punk rock."

"We're twins," Eliza said, putting down the mirror on the sink. She swept the scarf from her shoulders and dropped it over his head.

"Do I look punk rock?"

Eliza said, "You look like Little Red Riding Hood."

"I wanted to ask you something," he said, taking off the scarf. Scattered across the marble vanity were the various toiletries he'd left behind. Noxzema, shaving cream. Like the skeletons of some spiny-backed mollusc, his retainers.

"You're not going to ask me to marry you, are you?"

"Do you want me to?" Jude asked. The scarf around his shoulders looked like the shawl Johnny had worn on their wedding day, the shawl she had tied to her own.

"Not anymore," she said. "Sometimes I wished we were the ones who were married, though."

"You did?"

"It's stupid."

Jude tried to hide his smile by playing with his lip. "Well, sometimes I wished the same thing."

She was rubbing her shaved head, and now she took another look at it in the mirror. "What were you going to ask, then?" she asked his reflection.

"If you're sure," he said, rubbing his own head reflexively. "About the baby."

"I'm sure," she said. Her other hand was on her belly, and, reflexively, she began to rub it, too. He copied her. They rubbed their bellies and their heads.

"Is it pat your belly, rub your head?" he asked.

"No, it's rub your belly, pat your head."

They attempted this for a minute, watching each other in the mirror. He kept messing up and patting his belly. "It's not that hard!" Eliza said, laughing. He gave up and reached for the handful of charms hanging from her neck. He fingered the subway token. Teddy used to hold it up to his glasses and peer through the hole at Jude.

"What's in this locket, anyway?"

Gently, she took it back from him. "It's a secret."

Empty-handed now, he dropped his hands to her belly. She closed her eyes. He held his hand over her T-shirt and he rubbed. It was a Green Mountain Boys T-shirt, extra large. Clockwise, he polished her belly. He leaned in to kiss her and closed his own eyes, and no one but the mirror was there to witness their image, their profiles locked at belly and mouth.

They remained in this position until, at the distant door of the apartment, there was another knock.

"Maybe Neena forgot her key," she said.

It was Johnny. Linen jacket, tie. The bridge of his nose was bruised, and beneath his left eye was a jagged cord of skin, not yet a scar. Beside him, smaller than Johnny, also in jacket and tie, was an Indian man with a briefcase.

"Oh my God," Johnny said to Eliza. "Did they do that at the hospital?"

"Jude did it."

"She had hair before," Johnny said to the man. To Eliza, he said, "The doorman let me up. But I thought I should knock."

"Thoughtful," said Eliza. Over her shoulder, Johnny caught Jude's eye, then abruptly dropped it. He was not here to return any punches, Jude saw. He had some more formal method of retaliation in mind.

"He might as well hear this, too. Can I come in?"

The visitors did not sit down. Jude stood by the piano, arms crossed, the foliage of Eliza's hair scattered at his feet.

"Who's this?" Eliza asked, nodding to the man with the briefcase. Whoever he was, Jude was grateful for his presence, for the excuse not to get into another confrontation with Johnny. He wore a precise mustache, a pair of metal-framed glasses, and too much of an expensive cologne. Where had Jude seen him before? The temple? He recognized some feature, the narrow span of his shoulders, the controlled way he moved his body, as though he hoped he would appear not to be moving at all.

"This is Ravi Milan," said Johnny. "He's a lawyer. He's Teddy's dad."

Eliza and Jude didn't move from where they stood. Ravi did not extend his hand but nodded politely at each of them. "I have great respect for the life you're carrying," he said to Eliza.

"That's his friend Jude," said Johnny.

"That's not his dad," Jude said. "Teddy's dad's dead." But the eyes, the small, fragile hands . . .

"I'm sure you have many questions," said Ravi. "I'm happy to answer them—"

"But we have business first," Johnny finished.

Ravi stepped over to the piano bench, set down his briefcase, and opened it. Out of it he produced a handful of printed pages, bound with a black plastic clip, which he handed to Eliza. Over her shoulder, Jude squinted to read the letters: PETITION FOR ADOPTION.

"What is this?" she asked Johnny. "You put on a tie and you think you can adopt my kid?"

"That's not what it says," said Johnny.

"Did he tell you we didn't sleep together?" Eliza asked Ravi. "That we're husband and wife, but he's been sleeping with someone else? Should you tell the judge that? Did he tell you he doesn't have a job, an apartment, a fucking *phone*—"

"Miss, if you'll read the form—"

"This is what you've wanted the whole time. Why didn't you just say so from the beginning!"

Ravi, looking over her shoulder while remaining as far from her as possible, pointed to the typewritten entries on the bottom of the first page:

```
PETITIONER(S): Ravi and Arpita Milan.
RELATIONSHIP TO ADOPTEE: Grandfather,
stepgrandmother.
```

Ravi said, "My wife and I would like to adopt your child."

Neither Jude nor Eliza heard much after that. Intermediary parties, open adoptions, hearings, consents. Eliza was screaming, a blue vein pulsing under her stitches. Amidst her protests, Neena arrived from the grocery and spilled a plastic bag of canned spinach across the floor. Ravi bent to help pick up the cans. First uncertainly, then like old friends, he and Neena chattered on in a language that no one else understood.

TWENTY-TWO

Jude took the 1 train to the 7 to the 6, piecing together Manhattan. At home, Les was on the futon, snipping dried leaves into the bucket between his knees. He packed some fresh bud into the bowl of his newest bong, Raquelle. "You look like you could use some of this," he said.

Jude imagined the smoke rising up to fill his lungs. The sweet taste of ashes.

"No, thanks," he said. He went to the bathroom. He took off his father's clothes. He turned on the cold water in the shower and stepped inside. The man with the briefcase was still there in his head, Teddy's ghost come back to haunt him.

At eight o'clock the next morning, the phone in Ravi's hotel room rang. He rinsed the shaving cream from his face, patted it dry, and, in his bathrobe, crossed the room to the TV to turn down the morning news. On the fourth ring, he picked up the phone. It was the young man he'd met the day before, the friend of his son's. Had Ravi had breakfast yet?

They met downstairs at the café in front of the Union Square Inn, at one of the two tables on the sidewalk. Ravi ordered a poppy seed muffin and coffee. The boy ordered a bagel and juice. Flies darted around them in the heat, over their plastic silverware, the emptied pats of butter and jam. Ravi told him what he knew—about Bonnie, his search for Teddy (he was getting used to calling him that), the letter from Johnny. From his briefcase, he withdrew the manila envelope containing the newspaper clipping, the case reports, the photo of the four of them at the beach. The boy looked them over.

"You do believe me?" Ravi asked.

Under the table, the boy rolled his skateboard back and forth.

"So she wanted him for herself," he said.

Ravi swallowed a hard lump of his breakfast. He did not take pleasure in revealing the truth about Bonnie, but this boy, like Johnny, had to know. "She took him to spite me. It was a rash decision, a heated one, but one that she was stubborn enough to live with. Teddy was a"—Ravi fluttered his hands, searching for a word—"I'm sorry to put it this way, but he was. . . ."

"A pawn?"

Ravi winced. "An instrument. An asset. She knew he was valuable to me." He emptied a packet of Sweet'n Low into his coffee, even though it was already too sweet. "I've seen it with my clients again and again. More than money, more than homes and cars and boats, parents use children to settle their scores. Of course, we had very little money, and we weren't married. Our child was all that was of use to her."

Jude thought of his parents, conspiring to keep Eliza and Johnny and himself away from Di, the elaborate and inconsequential game of checkers the adults were playing. "But that doesn't mean she didn't love Teddy," he insisted. "All that time she'd been hiding him, and then she just left him behind?"

Ravi told him about Teddy's wish to find his father, about Johnny's call to his mother on Christmas, his attempt to help his brother. "If they had found me," he explained, "I could still have pressed charges. I could have sent her to prison for the abduction of a child. So she abandoned Teddy to save herself."

That word—*abandoned*—it was a spiky little briar patch. Jude tried not to think of his own birth mother, but he was caught. It was better, wasn't it, to be abandoned as a baby, before you could be blamed, or blame yourself? "But why didn't she take him with her?" Jude asked.

Ravi smacked his lips lightly, as though he were trying to rid his mouth of a bitter taste. "I imagine that, as her hate for me lost its edge, she ceased to care so fiercely."

Jude squinted into the sun. Ravi was speaking abstractly, but Jude caught the compact weight of his implication, like a shot put in his lap. "To care about Teddy, you mean."

Ravi waved his hands, as though to soften that idea. "Perhaps she meant to come back for him, to send him some explanation." Jude knew the benefit of the doubt Ravi was extending was for Teddy's sake, not his mother's. "But, of course, she never got the chance."

From the pocket of his shorts, the boy took out a Velcro wallet, patched with stickers, and from the wallet he took out a photo. He handed it to Ravi. In it, a group of American teenagers smiled widely, toasting the camera with their red plastic cups. Jude leaned across the table and pointed. "That's Teddy." At the edge of the picture was a boy, eyes closed, mouth open.

"It's not a very good picture, but it's all I've got on me."

Ravi stared at the photograph, his mouth also hanging open. Edward. What was he trying to say, his son, what word was he trying to speak to him?

"Johnny hasn't shown me any pictures," was all he could say.

Jude put his wallet away. "You can keep it. My sister's got another one at home. They put it in the yearbook."

Ravi thanked him, tucking the picture away in his briefcase.

"Tell me something," he said. "Your friend wants to give up the child. Why doesn't she want to give it to me?"

Jude downed the last of his orange juice. He was glad that Teddy's dad hadn't abandoned him, that at least one of his parents was decent. But what might have been a happy reunion with his friend's father had been poisoned by Johnny. When Di had come home, shortly after Neena, she had ordered Johnny and Ravi out of the apartment, and Jude had gathered his things and left, too.

"Because," Jude said, "she doesn't want Johnny to be able to see the baby. He's just been using her so he can hold on to Teddy."

"But why shouldn't he see the baby? Eliza can see the baby, too. Doesn't a child belong with its family?"

Ravi's clipped sentences, his backward, belated desperation to control his grandchild's future, reminded Jude of Di. It occurred to him that they would make a fine couple. Ravi and Di, filing their paperwork, placing long-distance phone calls to private investigators while they swirled wine in their glasses. It was impossible to imagine this man with the slovenly Queen Bea, who would have made a more appropriate mate for Les. How did anyone end up with anyone?

"I didn't get to raise my son," Ravi said. "This is my second chance." He presented his credentials. A house with a pool in Coconut Grove, a position at the second largest law firm in Miami, a loving wife who would be a loving mother. He started to take out his own wallet, to show Jude pictures of his own, but Jude didn't want to see them. He didn't want to know what the woman who would hold Teddy's baby looked like. All his life, he thought he wanted to know the face of the woman who had given birth to him, but a single picture, a name—it would be too much. It was the not knowing that protected him, the blank page that allowed him to believe she might be anyone, or might not exist at all. He could have been raised by wolves. He could be the son of God or a test tube miracle or for all he knew he could have fallen to Earth with the snow from the sky.

We welcome with love our gift from above.

The waitress came by to clear their paper plates and to refill Ravi's coffee. When he was little, Harriet hadn't told Jude about his adoption—Les had gotten to him first. Even now, she rarely mentioned it, the glass elephant she'd built to fill their house. She, too, preferred to be blind to it, to pretend Jude had sprung from her alone. He wondered now if his birth mother felt the same way, if anonymity was a gift to her, too.

"Look," Jude said. "All this time you've known Teddy was with his mom, right?"

"That's right."

"You pictured them together, you saw her making him lunch and dropping him off at school. First grade, second grade. All that time, you couldn't sleep at night, right? Wondering if he was okay, if she was treating him right."

"That's right," said Ravi.

"I think Eliza doesn't want to wonder the same thing about her kid."

Maybe he was wrong. Maybe Eliza just wanted to stick it to Johnny.

"So she'd rather give the child to a stranger?" Ravi looked exhausted.

"A stranger would want the baby because they want a baby," Jude said. "Not because they wish Teddy was alive."

Ravi took a final swill of his oversweetened coffee. He shook his head, but he didn't dispute this. It was true that he hadn't been in the market for a child. Arpita had taken some convincing. But he hadn't been in the market for a wife, either. *Surprises happen,* he'd told her. *Wonderful surprises, Arpita.* Not long after their meeting at the restaurant, Johnny had called with the proposal that had already been forming over the Milans' dining room table. "Ravi, how big is your house?" And that was it. Ravi could not say no.

He leaned forward and tapped his briefcase. "This is a shame, quite a shame. It would be easier for all parties if she would cooperate. We wouldn't have to sue for custody. We could avoid the court battle, the battery of tests. We would be acting in the best interest of the child."

The boy stopped rolling his skateboard. "What kind of tests?"

"A DNA test, a drug test. Johnny tells me the girl has been abusing drugs. If we must, we will request that the judge order a test to determine if she is fit. Fit to decide her child's fate." The waitress returned with their bill, and Ravi placed a credit card on the table. "I have witnessed my share of unfit mothers," he said. "I know one when I see one."

Rooster answered the door with a towel around his waist. He'd had a good thirty seconds between the buzzer and the knock to throw on some clothes, but he stood there at the door bare-chested, barefoot, the black curls on his tattooed chest matted and wet. He was a hairy motherfucker, and he'd lost even more weight. He looked like a drowned black cat.

"Where's Johnny?"

"Why? You gonna finish kickin' his ass?" Rooster did not sound threatened, but the Band-Aid on his forehead, covering his own wound from the riot, made it difficult for Jude to take him seriously.

"I know he's staying here. I know he sleeps in that bed with you, okay?"

Rooster thrust Jude into the apartment and closed the door. It seemed bigger, though not big, with the Murphy bed hidden away. Johnny's army duffel was in the corner, next to his tattoo case and his guitar. "Jesus, you got a loud mouth, kid." Rooster was half-laughing. "Tell everyone for all I care, but Johnny won't be very happy with you." He swaggered into the bathroom. With the door open, he sprayed a shot of deodorant into each armpit.

"I'm not happy with him, either." Jude dropped his skateboard against the door. "Where is he?"

Rooster said, "Went out to buy some rubbers," examining his teeth in the mirror. *Rubbas.* "Regular and Magnum. I won't tell you who gets which."

"Oh, Jeezum, don't make me throw up."

"You axed me."

Jude stood with his arms crossed in the middle of the room. He didn't want to sit. Every surface he imagined Johnny and Rooster fucking on. He had been mostly successful in fighting off these images, but now, in this apartment, they were not to be escaped. It wasn't long ago that he'd learned how gay men actually had sex; Teddy's mother, laughing at them, had used the word *heinie.* Now he saw Rooster bending Johnny over the bathroom sink, the kitchen counter, the milk crate on his delivery bike. Johnny fucking his hairy back, this man named Rooster who said "axed," this bald, punk, homo Tony Danza. Rooster crying out, *Ay, oh, oh, ay!*

"Did you come over here to tell Johnny he's a fag? 'Cause it ain't news to him, not no more."

"I need to talk to him about Eliza. His wife."

"Soon to be ex." Rooster came out of the bathroom. "His lawyer guy's workin' on a divorce as we speak. The Krishnas don't look kindly at divorce, but it don't look like he's got a choice."

"Yeah, well, Johnny needs to tell his lawyer guy to back the fuck off Eliza. She's not giving him her baby."

Rooster shrugged. "The guy wants to adopt the kid. Ain't nothin' Johnny can do about it now."

"He can back him the fuck off. If they even think about making her take a drug test"—Jude was stabbing a finger in the air—"they will be fucking sorry. He's put her through enough shit already."

"Man, don't axe me, but if the girl's been doin' drugs, what she needs to take is a drug test."

Jude stepped up to Rooster and stabbed his finger into his pec. "You know why she was doing drugs? *Two* fucking joints? Because Johnny was here in this shithole, fucking *you*. She's *sixteen* and she was alone and she was scared, and Johnny didn't give one shit about her. He's been using her all along, as a cover for what he's been doing with you. Mr. Clean? What a fucking joke! And if he doesn't back the fuck off her baby, I swear to God, I will *tell* her who he's been fucking. I'll tell everyone."

"Calm down, kid."

"You want all your friends knowing about you guys?"

"You think a bunch a straight edge kids are gonna care? We're all fags anyways. It's a fuckin' front. So shut your fuckin' homophobic mouth for a second and listen to yourself." Rooster tossed Jude's hand off him. "*You* sound like the fuckin' jealous wife." From the bag of laundry, Rooster plucked out a T-shirt and pulled it over his head. Youth of Today. "You sure you ain't the one that's jealous?"

Rooster let the wet towel drop to the floor. Jude looked away, but not before he saw the bottom half of Rooster's uncircumcised dick, fat and limp, hanging below the hem of his T-shirt.

This was who Johnny had come home to? This was his type? Had he known all the time he liked guys, had he gazed across rooms at them, at Jude?

So he was jealous. But not because he wanted Johnny to gaze across a room at him. He was jealous of that code word he'd uttered to Rooster—"baby." He was jealous of them in the way he was jealous of Eliza and Teddy, the coupling so dear they, too, had kept it private. He was jealous of everyone who knew how they wanted to be loved.

Finally Rooster pulled on a pair of what looked like Johnny's camouflage shorts. "He'd rather marry a girl he doesn't love than admit that he's with you," Jude told him. "You think he gives a shit about you? All he cares about is Teddy's fucking baby. He's obsessed with Teddy's fucking baby!"

Rooster sat down on a stool and leaned an elbow on the counter. He looked tired and suddenly old, the floppy bandage on his forehead doing a poor job of keeping him together. "That makes two a youse." He pointed two fingers at Jude. "You guys gotta get over that kid. Look at you, look how pissed off you are. How long's he been dead, six months?"

"Don't fucking say that, Rooster."

"It's a shame and all, but Jesus. You know how many kids have OD'd in this town? It fuckin' happens. Why the fuck you think I'm straight edge?"

"Fuck you, Rooster! You didn't know him."

"Neither did Johnny! He barely even knew the kid. He hadn't seen him in like two years!"

The small flower of satisfaction this comment brought forth swiftly wilted. Jude paced across the room, kicked the minifridge, and squatted on the floor, his head in his hands. It was true: Johnny barely knew Teddy. He barely knew Jude, either. They had both wanted to be the one who knew Teddy best, they had both been Teddy for each other, and now the make-believe had come to an end.

When Rooster spoke again, his voice was softer. "Green," he said. It was the voice he used to talk to Johnny on the phone, to call him "baby." He looked for a moment as though he wanted to tell Jude something. It was the distant look he had outside the rec center in Lintonburg as they admired the view together, the mountains, the lake. And then it passed.

Rooster nodded across the small room to Johnny's bag on the floor. "The guy's been carryin' around his kid brother's ashes in a duffel bag. That's creepy, man. I've been tryin' for months to get him to leave you and Eliza and that baby alone."

Jude stood up. "He's got Teddy's ashes in there?"

Rooster nodded. "In a fuckin' flour jar, man."

Jude took three sweeping steps over to the bag and unzipped it. Rooster didn't stop him. Jude rifled through piles of clothes, a freezer bag of cassettes, and then his hand struck something solid. He hauled it out. A clear glass canister, like all of Queen Bea's kitchen canisters, with the orange rubber lid. Embossed in cursive in the glass was the word *Flour,* but inside were the pebbled remains of Teddy, his bones and skin and teeth, bits of stone and shell in sand.

"Take it," Rooster said.

"I'm going to," Jude said, cradling the ashes awkwardly in his arms. They weighed perhaps as much as a newborn baby, and he looked down at them with the same terror and awe with which a new father might look at his child, holding it for the first time.

"Look, don't worry," Rooster said. "I don't think John's gonna interfere in your business no more."

"What does that mean?"

"I got a feelin' he's gonna have other priorities soon." Rooster's voice was grave. He touched the Band-Aid on his forehead, pressing it into place. "He ain't gonna have a choice." Jude didn't know what Rooster was talking about, but he felt a small spring of sympathy for him. Did he have no mother to tend to his wounds?

He stood up, propping the ashes on his hip. Then he put his skateboard under his other arm and left the apartment. He did not see Johnny on the stairs or in the street. He didn't see Johnny again, not that day, not ever.

*

"You're leaving?" Eliza asked.

Jude's own duffel was packed, slumped at his feet on the kitchen floor. He wound the phone cord around his hand.

"Something just came up," he said. "I just have to do something back home." His father was on the futon, pretending not to listen. Jude couldn't say what he wanted to say. "Don't worry—I don't think Teddy's dad is going to go through with the adoption."

"Why not?"

"I talked to him."

"I don't get it," she said. She sounded baffled, but resigned to, even fond of, her bafflement. She seemed to have learned that it was the prevailing wilderness in which she would have to exist. "When am I going to see you again?"

Jude unwound the phone cord, then wound it again. Through his bag, he could feel the weight of the glass canister against his ankle.

"You want to come with me?"

"Back to Vermont?"

"Just for a few days. Tell your mom I'll get you home safe. Way before the baby's born."

Eliza sighed. Sixteen, and she had the sigh of a forty-year-old woman.

"I know you're tired," Jude said. "Just one more trip."

When he hung up, his dad came into the kitchen. Jude took McQueen's case out of his bag and handed it to his father, trading him for a wad of cash.

"If you change your mind, the loft is yours. Davis is going to be out by September one."

Jude put the cash in his pocket. "I'd have to learn to get used to living off drug money."

"A straight edge kid like you—that's a moral conundrum."

For some reason, Jude's conscience, ready to fire, sent up an image of Hippie. The next generation of Lintonburg pot seller. The picture was of Hippie hobbling off the high school lawn, his glasses lost, as blind as Teddy, and Jude decided that, if for no other reason than to clear his karma, he would finally return to Hippie the money in his pocket.

Les hauled Jude's bag up from the floor. "I'll walk you to the van," he said.

TWENTY-THREE

The van was parked in the alley in the morning. When Harriet saw it through the window above the kitchen sink, she dashed in her robe and moccasins up the stairs, past the bathroom, where Prudence was singing in the shower, past Prudence's open door, where the great mass of a bald Eliza was passed out across the trundle bed like Rousseau's sleeping gypsy, up to the third floor. Jude didn't stir when she pushed the door open, or when she sat on the edge of the bottom bunk. It was when she touched the cut on his lip that he bolted awake. He sat up and looked at her, at the bedroom around him, at the lemony light drifting through the curtains, then lay back down.

"Fuck," he said. "I was dreaming I was driving."

Had his voice deepened, or was it just hoarse with sleep? "You guys must have gotten in late. You want to tell me where that cut on your lip came from?"

"Born with it."

"What about that black eye?"

"Doesn't matter anymore. Bridge over troubled water."

Harriet fought the urge to touch the bruise under his eye. "Water under the bridge, you mean?"

"Whatever. I don't know your hippie songs." He yawned. "Hey, Dad said my name isn't from that hippie song. He said it's from the saint."

"He did, did he."

"It's not?"

She reached for his hands, weighing them in hers. "I guess it's both. But really we gave you the name because of what it means." His burn was twisted with scar tissue, healed to a muscley pink, and on the other hand, the *X* had healed, too. "When they brought you to me, ten days old, I couldn't believe you were finally mine. I was so grateful. You were like a little bundle that had just fallen from the heavens. And I thought, *Jude*. In Hebrew, it means 'Praise.' Or 'Thanks.'"

Harriet gave his hands a squeeze, and Jude, his blue eyes swimming back—or ahead—to some memory or dream she might never know about, squeezed back.

He had come home, and he would leave and come home and leave and come home again, with new scars and tattoos, but now he let her hold on to his two fragile arms, the limbs that might have been broken had he been home last Saturday evening, when five boys had knocked on the front door. Most were thick-necked football players in their jerseys. One was the dark-eyed boy who had knocked on her door with Hippie several months ago—though Hippie wasn't here now—before the incident in her greenhouse. His knee was clamped into a brace, and he was fondling the handle of a wooden cane. Harriet did not care to know the details of the neighborhood wars that had sent Jude running. But perhaps it was this injury, she dared to wonder, that had prevented this gang from making their counterattack in a timelier manner.

"Is Jude home?" he'd asked, like any of the boys, in recent days, who'd come over to raid her fridge.

But this time Harriet had not moved aside. The hairs on the back of her neck had gone cool. And then Bob had come downstairs, the gun he never wore holstered now across his shoulders and under his armpit in one of those equestrian contraptions that made him look like a soap opera police chief. Maybe it was the moment she'd fallen in love, when he'd leaned silently, smilingly against the doorframe and slipped his arm around her waist. "No, he's not," she told the boys.

"Where is everyone?" Jude asked now, withdrawing his hands from hers. "I heard about your . . . man friend."

"Bob," she said, trying not to smile. "Bob's on a job this morning."

"What's with Bob? Why didn't you tell me?"

"Bob's cool," said Prudence, who was leaning in the doorway in a towel. "He plays the pan flute, and he can say the Gettysburg Address backwards."

Jude sat up. "Why would anyone want to say it frontwards?"

Bob came over for dinner. Bob made seven-spice couscous with the green beans and tomatoes from Harriet's garden. He'd picked up the recipe in Casablanca, where he'd tracked a woman who'd married some rich guy and then emptied his accounts. He'd tracked a guy who'd stolen a helicopter, tenants who'd jumped rent, and an underground cockfighting league, run in a number of Bronx basements. He was done with that wretched place called New York. Two weekends after setting foot in Vermont, he'd moved his sick mother out of their condo and up to a cabin on the lake. And he started every other sentence with the word *happily*. "Happily, I was able to track down the no-good crook." "Happily, they had a whole batch of fresh mint." But he called Jude's mom "honey" and she called him "honey" back. At one point, he took off her glasses, buffed them on his apron, and slipped them back on her face.

Jude and Prudence did the dishes. Jude washed, Prudence dried. Eliza lay on the couch, her wet bikini still dampening her dress from her swim in the lake that afternoon. "I just want to be *weightless,*" she'd said. Now Bob was doing hypnotherapy on her, showing her how to put herself to sleep. Prudence told Jude that Tory Ventura and Missy Sherman had broken up, that he was off crutches, and that he'd gotten a football scholarship to Duke. He'd be leaving town within a matter of days. Jude tried to conceal his relief.

"Did you miss me?" he asked his sister. One of the cats— Tarzan—mashed his face into Jude's shin.

"Yeah, it was really lonely not having someone trying to run my life all the time."

"Are you still smoking?" Jude handed her a plate.

"Just crack. And just when I'm drinking."

"Clearly you need my male influence."

"I've got Bob," Prudence said.

"What's Bob going to do? Hypnotize you?"

"Mom said it really works. He's got her down to like half a pack a day."

Jude submerged his hands in the suds. Maybe his mom would be okay without him. She had Bob now.

"Pru, what if I stayed in New York?"

"With Dad?"

"Want to come with?" He lifted his hands out of the water, scrubbing another plate. He rinsed it and handed it over. "Give him a chance. Let him spend lots of money on you trying to buy back your love."

"Are you taking the cats?"

"I think the cats are staying put."

Prudence polished the plate with the tattered dishrag. Jude held another dripping plate while she placed it on the rack. "Maybe I'd visit," she said.

"You could take the train," said Jude.

After Bob had gone home and Harriet and Prudence had gone to bed, Jude unlocked the greenhouse with the key his mother kept in the fake rock in her garden. This was the darkened scene Tory had entered when he'd broken in, and Jude felt his ghost, still fresh, as well as Les's. Along with the sear of Harriet's burnt glass, the place smelled faintly of his pot. The old sleeping bag, in which Jude had received the news of his adoption, happened to be sitting in the lap of the rocking chair from which Les had delivered it. Jude lifted it—army green, hugged by a bungee cord—and sank his chin into its center.

"Can people see in here?" Eliza asked, pointing up to the painted glass ceiling.

"Just the lights," Jude said, but he didn't want his mother to see even that. He locked the door. With his flashlight, he found the melted stump of a candle and lit it.

Eliza walked over to one of the fish tanks that housed Harriet's glass. She took out a bong and pretended to hit it. "Mmm," she said, blowing out a mouthful of imaginary smoke.

"Funny," said Jude.

He slid the old mattress leaning against the wall onto the floor, then uncoiled the sleeping bag, unzipped it, and spread it open across their bed. He felt dizzy, as though he were made of a gas. He pulled his shirt over his head, tossed it in the rocking chair, and lay down. Eliza followed him, coming down knee by knee, then hand by hand. They lay on their backs, side by side.

"We're like old people," Jude said.

"I feel all googly from that hypnosis stuff."

"Googly?"

"Like, relaxed."

He reached for her hand and fit it in his. The candle puddled a yellow light across the floor, over their legs. He couldn't see anything beyond the painted glass ceiling, but he could imagine the stars coming out on the other side, bright as they were only here, millions of miles from any city.

"Is she going to hate me?" she asked.

They stared up at the underbelly of the roof, dark as a womb.

"Who?"

"Annabel."

Jude closed his eyes. He thought of all the people who had done this before him, lain beside another body, seeking its warmth, like the two figures in the diagram his mother had drawn for him years ago. Queen Bea and Ravi, Harriet and Les, Johnny and Rooster. His unnamed mother and unnamed father in some unnamed room. Eliza and Teddy. If this was the crime they'd committed, it wasn't the worst thing in the world. This was forgivable.

"No," he said, opening his eyes. "She's just going to miss you."

There were no eyes upon them. They were alone. He leaned on an elbow, close enough to kiss her, and then he did. He put his hand on the nape of her naked head. She did the same. Outside, the crickets pulsed.

"Is this why you brought me back to Vermont?" she asked. "So you could take advantage of me in the bong house?"

"It was my master plan."

They kissed again. His fingers tangled in the bow of her bikini top. His hands were shaking. He leaned closer. His weight pressed over hers. Her dress was soggy with sweat. Or lake water. Or maybe something else. He didn't care.

"Hold on," she said.

"What?"

"My back."

She struggled to sit up. He sat up with her. She was frozen for a few seconds, her legs straight in front of her.

"You okay?"

"I'm not supposed to lie flat. It puts pressure on a vein or something." She took a deep breath, then let it out. Her face was in shadow. "Did you think your first time was going to be with a pregnant bald girl?"

"What?" he said, smiling, embarrassed, not knowing what to say. "It's good."

"It's good," she agreed.

They kissed sitting up for a while, and then she pressed his shoulders back down to the floor, and then, slowly, ploddingly, she straddled him, tucking her knees against his ribs. Now she was inside the ring of the candle's light. In one motion she peeled off her damp dress and in two more she untied the strings at her back.

"You're gorgeous," he said. Her belly was a white moon floating on the lake. Between her breasts, her necklace flashed.

In the morning, they started in the garden, scattering handfuls like seeds. Then three rights and a left to Teddy's. They crawled under the house, tossed a handful there, too, into the dirt and sparse grass, over the softened shards of green bottles stubbled with sand. Under the football stadium, down Ash Street, across the high school lawn, they shook out Teddy's ashes from the plastic bags in their pockets, a trail of bread crumbs like a map of Lintonburg. The lake glittered on the mirrors of Eliza's sunglasses. From the stone wall that edged the park, Jude could see down into the tops of the trees on the shore, into their knotted brains, the variegated greens of their leaves. He couldn't help but think of the woolly thatch of hair between Eliza's legs, but for the last twelve hours, there wasn't much that didn't

remind him of sex. The knobs on his dresser drawers were twist-
able nipples. The emergency brake, over which he'd leaned to kiss
her, a giant erect dick. The soda straw squeaking in and out of the
X poked in the plastic lid of the cup passed between them, her spit
mingling with his, the molecules of their bodies clinging invisibly to
one another: sex.

There was one more place to go. On the ferry to Plattsburgh, the
upper deck was filled with families and couples, summer campers in
red T-shirts, fathers with cameras strung around their necks, mothers holding on to their children's elbows as they leaned over the railing, hoping to steal a sight of Champ. The water and the sky and the
mountains were so blue they were almost transparent, a holograph
transmitted from space. It was a nearly windless day.

When they had pulled away from the dock, when the trees on the
shore were no longer individual trees, they found the quietest corner of the boat, and Jude took the last plastic bag from his pocket. It
was a little smaller than the plastic bag of pot he'd stolen, which his
mother had flushed, leaving its heartbreaking dust behind. When
Jude emptied the ashes over the railing, they didn't scatter in the
breeze, or splash. Somewhere between the boat and the surface of
the lake, they simply disappeared, soundlessly, swallowed by the air.

In an hour they reached New York, and the passengers filed out
of the ferry and onto the dock, heading for the Ethan Allen Home-
stead or Port Kent. Eliza and Jude remained on the upper deck,
their twin scalps gleaming in the sun, holding hands because they
didn't know what else to do. They weren't going to the other side,
Jude told the woman who approached them, concerned, as if they
were small children. They were just taking a ride.

TWENTY-FOUR

The eastern perimeter of Central Park, from the waiting room window, was dappled orange and gold and apple red, the first insinuations of fall. It did not remind Jude of sex. There was plenty of that here on the maternity ward, where Jude had witnessed (in the cries of pain from Eliza's next-door neighbor, a cart of metal instruments wheeled down the hall, the pink-skinned newborns behind the nursery glass) the inevitable end of the reproductive act. On the other side of Mount Sinai a glass pavilion was being erected, eleven stories high and a block wide, which according to one of the construction signs was meant to contribute to the patients' sense of buoyancy and recuperation.

It was a coincidence that the baby would be born in the same hospital as Jude, but not a big one: it was, after all, one of the biggest hospitals in New York. There were three floors of nurseries, and he visited all of them, looking through the window at the empty incubators, where he'd spent the first hours of his life. They were waiting for the next baby, maybe Eliza's. Beside Jude, Di tapped her fingers on the glass and made grotesque faces at the babies, as if she were going to gobble them up or kidnap them on the spot. They paid her no attention. She'd been more relaxed since the annulment had come through and the Milans had dropped the adoption suit. In a single envelope, Ravi had returned the annulment forms with Johnny's signature and wrote that he had decided, with his wife, to adopt a child from India. Whether he had had a change of heart on his own or with Johnny's help, Jude could only guess. In another envelope, postmarked San Francisco, Eliza found a series of large, crisp bills, and a note, in Johnny's elegant script, that read simply "For the baby."

September, going on October. Jude was wearing the new Converse he bought with his dad's back-to-school money. East Side Community High School, where he was actually reading *The Outsiders* in English II and had a D in biology for refusing to dissect a pig fetus. He went to an assembly on AIDS, skated the basketball court after school. Two of the guys had devil locks. There was a girl with a Black Flag T-shirt who sat next to him in world history, but he told her he had a girlfriend. He told her she was in Europe. When she got back, she'd be going to Emily Dickinson on the Upper West Side—that part was true. For lunch he went to San Loco with one of the guys from Army of One, who was a senior there, and it was from him that Jude learned Johnny and Rooster had taken a Greyhound to California to start a band and see what the scene was like out there.

It was early evening when the baby finally arrived. Eliza wanted Jude and her mother in the room. Even when the baby was out of her—not a girl but a boy, although this, too, Jude wouldn't ever have the heart to tell her (dark-haired and terrified, testicles swollen as big as a peach)—she kept her eyes closed tight. She knew how easy it is to fall in love.

He wouldn't tell her, either, about visiting the baby in the nursery, hours old and sleeping, Eliza's blood still smudged on his skin. In a rocking chair, Jude accepted the bundle from the nurse, and despite himself, the first thing he did was hunt for evidence of the baby's genes, the science project—blue and yellow make green—at which no one in the history of the world has ever failed to be amazed.

But the baby looked like no one, not his mother, not his father. If it weren't for the bracelet cuffed around his inconceivably tiny wrist, he could have been mistaken for any other baby in the room, plucked up by any parent who walked by. For a moment, that possibility seemed within the natural order of things, and before it ended, Jude handed the boy back to the nurse.

The last show is technically on Sunday, with Patti Smith headlining, but for hardcore fans the night to say goodbye to CBGB is the last night the Bad Brains play, with Underdog and the Stimulators. It's their third night in a row at CB's, and you can tell. H.R. is singing with his hands in his pockets. He's fifty fucking years old; he can sing with his hands in his pockets if he wants. Jude does his own hands-in-pockets sort of dance, though the kids are trying to stir up trouble in the pit. He's still a skinhead, but only to hide his male pattern baldness.

The place seems no older than it ever did, still stuck together with gum and sweat. Security is there to make sure you don't take a piece of history home with you, but there are a dozen cell phones raised like lighters, catching the video footage to be uploaded to the world in the morning. Just the kind of forced ceremony that Jude had expected, but he's a dad now—it doesn't take much for him to get emo.

Earlier, they walked the neighborhood, Jude's wife carrying their daughter in her sling. *Stomp* is playing at the Orpheum on Second Avenue. The rehab center next to Les's place has been converted into luxury condos, a St. Mark's Market, a Chipotle, and the CBGB OMFUG shop. A few doors down are Andy's Chee-pees St. Mark's and Search and Destroy, where the punk rock kids are paying fifty bucks for vintage Misfits T-shirts. Dressing like a punk doesn't get your ass kicked anymore. The biggest miracle of all: children are playing in Tompkins Square Park. Nannies, jungle gyms. The band shell has been taken down, and there's a dog run now. On the walk back to Les's, they counted the tattoo and piercing parlors on his block. Eight. They joked about stopping to get the baby's ears pierced—Jude's wife has always wanted a baby girl with pierced ears—but they kept walking. They didn't want to be late for the show. Les is babysitting tonight. It's the first time he's met his granddaughter, but he's not the first to nickname her Red.

In Jude's wife's locket? A picture of Red, a picture of Jude.

Not a bad thing, for your daughter to be able to play in a park. But Jude's glad Johnny isn't here to see what's happened to the neighborhood. Johnny would have something to say about the $19,000 rent that shut down CB's. Johnny would start a riot. Part of Jude expects to see him here, sacrificing himself to the pit. Jude would know him if he saw him, just as well as he'd know Teddy. He misses them both in the same way, as though they are both gone to the same world.

"Do you see him?" his wife asks.

But it's the kids' show tonight. There are ten thousand Johnnys and ten thousand Judes, throwing themselves against one another to see what they can start.

"No," he says. He doesn't tell her who else he's looking for, the boy who is eighteen now, older than Teddy ever was. The ink black hair, the eyelashes like the bristles of a paintbrush, the look like he's

got a secret up his sleeve. How old will Jude be when he stops looking for that boy in the crowd, at the supermarket, in the airport,
wondering which gate he's flying out of?

The show comes to an end. Feedback, applause, that ringing in
the ears when voices rush in to fill the void. They linger outside for
only a few minutes, waiting to see if something else will happen.
Then they start on foot for St. Mark's. The baby is asleep, waiting
for them, and they have a flight to catch in the morning.

ACKNOWLEDGMENTS

I am enormously grateful to the following people and places for their help in writing this book.

For their information: Julie Babcock; Marty Babcock; Seth Duppstadt; Maria Greco; Esther Palmer; Richard Bailey of Club 242 Main, Bald Bill and Rob Dix of Yankee Tattoo, and Tom Toner of Good Times Gallery, all of Burlington, Vermont; Art Eisenberg of the DNA Laboratory, University of North Texas; Paul DeRienzo, "The History of the Tompkins Square Park Police Riot"; Noah Haglund, "Fire Sacrifice: A Hare Krishna Wedding"; *Inside Straight Edge,* a National Geographic documentary; Ed Rosenthal, *Marijuana Grower's Handbook;* and especially the following authors and editors: Michael Azerrad, *Our Band Could Be Your Life;* Steven Blush, *American Hardcore: A Tribal History;* Ross Haenfler, *Straight Edge: Hardcore Punk, Clean-Living Youth, and Social Change;* Beth Lahickey, *All Ages: Reflections on*

Straight Edge; and Cris Wrenn, Alex Brown, and John Porcelly, *Schism.*

For their insight: Ann Beattie, John Casey, Lan Samantha Chang, Robert Cohen, Deborah Eisenberg, Kathryn Kramer, Alice McDermott, Tom Paine, Francine Prose, and Helen Schulman, whose voices still ring in my ears, and especially Christopher Tilghman, who told me to keep going; all of my workshop friends at the University of Virginia, who made scrupulous comments on hundreds of pages; my brilliant and bighearted late-draft readers: Mary Beth Keane, Anna Solomon, Ursula Villarreal-Moura, Gina Welch, and Callie Wright; Adelaide Wainwright and Abigail Holstein, assistants extraordinaire; Jim Rutman, my dream agent and the smartest person I know, who gave me a second chance; Lee Boudreaux, whose unmatched enthusiasm and painstaking edits did as much for my manuscript in eight weeks as I'd done for it in eight years; and all the other talented people at Ecco who helped bring this book into the world.

For their support: the Poe/Faulkner Fellowship at the University of Virginia, the Bread Loaf Writers' Conference, the Virginia Center for the Creative Arts, *The Virginia Quarterly Review, Poets & Writers,* my superb students and colleagues at James Madison University and Ithaca College, and all my friends and family, including Sandra Squadrilli and Ted Lech (the original saints of St. Mark's Place), Sam, Keri, and Cameron. Thank you especially to my brother Peter Henderson, whose birth led me to ask questions; to my uncle Peter Babcock, whose death led me to ask more; and to my eternally generous parents, Ann and Bill, who told me I could do anything.

Nicolas, you can do anything, but don't ever do any of the stupid things in this book.

Finally, for his information, insight, support, and much more: Aaron Squadrilli, whose story made this one possible.